THE HERE AND NOW

A NOVEL

ROBERT COHEN

SCRIBNER PAPERBACK FICTION
PUBLISHED BY SIMON & SCHUSTER

SCRIBNER PAPERBACK FICTION
Simon & Schuster Inc.
Rockefeller Center
1230 Avenue of the Americas
New York, NY 10020

First Scribner Paperback Fiction edition 1997

SCRIBNER PAPERBACK FICTION and design are trademarks
of Simon & Schuster Inc.

DESIGNED BY ERICH HOBBING

Manufactured in the United States of America

1   3   5   7   9   10   8   6   4   2

The Library of Congress has cataloged the Scribner edition as follows:
Cohen, Robert, 1957– .
The here and now : Robert Cohen.
p.   cm.
I. Title.
PS3553.O4273H47   1996
813'.54—dc20   95-22009
CIP

ISBN 0-684-81561-3
0-684-83141-4 (Pbk)

For Claudia

ACKNOWLEDGMENTS

I would like to thank the Lila Wallace-Reader's Digest Foundation for their generous support.

For their patience and attention I would also like to thank Mona Simpson, Denise Shannon, Jane Rosenman, and especially, Ted Solotaroff.

The falling is for the sake of the rising.

HASIDIC PROVERB

CONTENTS

THE HERE AND NOW

IN FLIGHT

I met Magda high above the earth. It was a triangular excursion—New York to Houston, via Chicago—and we were on the second leg, an hour out of O'Hare and rumbling south. I sat brooding by the window in a cone of light. Magda was two seats away on the aisle: thin, long-nosed, eyes like teardrops, skin so milky it bordered on translucent and threatened, if one looked closely enough, to reveal every hidden capillary in her face. Only I was not looking closely, not just then. The sun, glancing off the wing, was in my eyes, and I was preoccupied by affairs left half-completed behind me, and so nothing, not even the hazy spectacle of the heartland below us, scarred and pulsing in the midsummer heat, quite had the power to touch me.

I was flying to Houston to attend the wedding of my friend and former roommate Warren Pinsky, who was about to be married for the third time. Regarding that optimist, more later. For reasons of economy I had chosen a discount flight from Kennedy that morning which required a stopover in Chicago, adding several hours to the trip. There was no movie. To divert me I had only the *Times*, an article I was editing, and my own reflection, pensive and sleepy, framed in the sun-shot window. It hardly seemed enough, so I threw in a couple of vodkas for good measure.

What is travel but a kind of expensive drug? Over Cleveland I closed my eyes and, surrendering to the cold liquor and the dull roar of the engines, fell asleep. In my dream I sailed through a field of pure energy. New York was only a couple of words, a short, clunky phrase in another language. I'd given it up. I'd given up my job, my apartment, my car, given up Donna, given up everyone and everything I knew, and without these tethers to hold me I began to drift and glide and inflate like a balloon, ascending to a point so high and giddy with light it seemed to belong to another, better world.

However, it didn't last. After a while I woke up, which in my present state was more a kind of falling down. A stewardess came by with coffee. I took a cup and drank it slowly, gazing out the window and thinking, as people will in flight, rather pleasantly of nothing. A young Hasidic couple had moved into the adjoining seats and were whispering quietly to themselves, ignoring me altogether. Fine. Outside our winged shadow wafted over the endless cornfields, trailing the plane at a distance of a hundred or so yards like some obstinate but well-intentioned younger sibling, and I busied myself watching it for as long as the coffee could be made to last. Then I picked up the article I'd been editing, and went to work.

The article had to do with fusion—not one of my specialties. Ronnie Oldham, a colleague of mine, would have been a better choice for the material; but then Ronnie, as he occasionally saw fit to remind me, would have been a better choice for almost all the work I did. "It's because you lack grounding," he'd told me once. "Intellectually speaking, you're sort of a vagrant."

It was true: I had moved around a great deal at the magazine. Not that I was alone in this. The magazine was a popular general-interest weekly of moderate if conventional ambitions—a middlebrow almanac of the culture—and with so much ground to be covered at such frequent intervals it was company policy to retain a core group of floating sub-editors, all-purpose text doctors who shifted from department to department, filling in where needed. There were usually about half a dozen of us, though turnover was high. It was a little like flying standby; not everyone could handle the strain. Eventually, after a few years, one would either luck into a niche that felt suitable or else one would quit. For a variety of reasons I had to this point done neither. Though I intended to change that, if I could.

But all that would have to wait until I returned from Houston.

I worked on the article to the best of my ability, but there were multiple distractions. Children were crying. Stewardesses rustled by, pushing their wobbly carts. The engines made a fine high noise of exhaust. Soon my eyes fell closed again, and I drifted that way for a while, until in time I became aware of a conversation taking place close by, a rapid whispering in another language, one so like the language in my dream I felt I must be dreaming this too. Perhaps I was. There are those who claim we are all conspirators in a dream with no beginning or end, and are not the authors of this dream but merely the medium for it, the vessels through which consciousness travels. I don't know; I am only an amateur in these matters. But as we flew south the tenor of the conversation intensified. There was a male voice, loud and decisive, and a female one: low, edgy, slightly nasal, the diphthongs colored petulantly by Brooklyn.

Finally the female gave a bitter sigh and said something that sounded like "*Die, new?*"

For a moment I was sure that someone really had died, so intense was the accompanying silence. When I opened my eyes I discovered the Hasidic couple looking anxiously in my direction, as if the corpse under discussion were me.

"Ah," said the man, "you're with us, now?"

"See?" whispered his companion. "I told you. We woke him up."

"Ridiculous." The man turned to me sternly. "We woke you up?"

"No, no. I'm fine."

It took me many years of heavy losses at poker to realize

what the Hasidic couple now learned right away: that I do not have a poker face. It was clear that they had woken me up, and that moreover, in line with some obscure protocol governing long airplane flights, their having done so now committed us to a conversation.

"Forgive us if we did." The man shifted in his seat to direct upon me a look of unapologetic intensity. "We didn't mean to bother anybody."

I gave him a look right back. He was no older than I was, though he seemed so at first because he was wearing a suit and a hat, both black, and because of his beard, which ran all the way down his unshaven neck and was thick and curly and red like his hair, and because of a jauntily prominent potbelly that was not quite hidden by the folds of his jacket. At the same time he had a boyish face. His cheeks were rounded and pink, as if swollen by a wad of chewing gum; his eyes, lit by a mote of sunlight, shone a bright Caribbean green. My presence beside him appeared to engage his curiosity. He sized me up from head to toe, as though I were a mystery that required a great deal of assessment. I suppose, looking back, I was sizing him up the same way.

Meanwhile over his shoulder, his wife—by then I'd spotted the gold band on her finger—was staring too. She looked as if she had been born into this world to stare. Her eyes were enormous, set so far back in their cavities that they appeared to be even darker and more expectant than they were, and possibly because she knew this she averted them quickly when they met my own. Whether this was shyness or pride, I couldn't tell, but it touched me. She wore a long gray skirt and a faded yellow sweater that might have been gay a few decades ago. Her hair, too, sculpted into high shiny brown waves, seemed to belong to another time, or perhaps another woman; because it did not go with her clothes and seemed out of proportion to her face, it made her difficult to fix. I judged her to be in her mid-twenties, and worried. When she bent to sip at her ginger ale, her cheeks looked hollowed-out, deprived; the bones flared like wings. Beneath the pallor her blood seemed animated by restless, circular energies. She finished the drink and touched one finger to an ice cube, experimentally.

"You're a Jew?"

The question had come from the husband, though I was aware of the wife listening for the answer as well. It was not so much a question, really, as a statement of preliminary fact.

"Sorry?"

"Why are you apologizing? You haven't done anything wrong. I just asked, are you a Jew?"

"Half," I said. "I'm half-Jewish."

"What are we, mathematicians? You're a Jew or you're not."

"My father was a Jew."

"And your mother?"

I gave a weak smile. "Not."

"Ah." He took it in slowly, as if he'd never heard of such a thing before, and when the information had been digested I could see it had dampened his metabolism somehow. He ran a finger along his lip, smoothing the erratic line of his moustache, and looked out the window at the white spun sugar of the passing clouds, thinking it over.

As it happens, my father was born in Hungary, and in the genetic combat that formed me it is his coloring, features, and hair that have won out. These roughly correspond to those of an archetypal Jew. Also, I might add, to an archetypal Italian, Greek, Georgian, Lebanese, or Serb. Over the years I have been taken for all of these fine peoples. Apparently, between my looks and my temperament I am something like type-O blood: almost anyone who wants to can lay claim to me.

Now the man turned to his wife and whispered something rapidly in their private language. She whispered back. It sounded a little like German, but it wasn't German. Probably it was Yiddish. Wasn't that what Hasids spoke? All I knew of Hasids was that they were the old pious Jews you saw on television, or in sentimental plays on Broadway, or in those Vishniac photographs of Poland before the war; or even now, in certain badly frayed side pockets of the City, in Brooklyn, the Lower East Side, the Diamond District. You glimpsed them out of car windows, walking head down on narrow streets, incurious and remote in their medieval black coats, perpetually in a hurry, as if the modern world were one huge malign obstacle course and History itself was on their heels.

Well, I thought, so what? Let them live how they want. As someone whose consciousness took shape around 1970—a time more friendly to dreams, especially collective ones, than the present—I still had one foot in the door of the alternative life myself. I still read the *Nation*, still boycotted grapes, still wondered if Johnson killed Kennedy. I did these things reflexively and without cynicism. It seemed to me that culture worked best when it was messy and contentious, democratic to a fault. All those freakish and subversive groups out there— the righteous, the fervent, the nutty, the inspired—had their roles to play in the national drama, vestiges of a particularity that another America (the one we'd once thought was arriving) would have cherished as its true mandate, instead of doing what the real America (the one we'd underestimated) had always done best: that is, hosing down the differences, boiling them out in the terrible tank.

As for religion: I had no use for it myself, of course, but no doubt it had its consolations for others. Just so long as they left me alone.

"The nose," I explained with a smile, "I get from my father."

The smile was not returned. He leaned closer. "Nothing else? A *bris*?"

"You mean am I circumcised? Yes."

"Where?"

"Oh," I said, "the usual place, I think."

He frowned. "I meant, in the hospital or at shul?"

"Hospital, I think."

"Bar mitzvah?"

"No."

"No? And what else?"

"Plenty," I said. "Plenty of other things too."

My voice gets sharp when I'm cornered and this may have registered on him. Backpedaling for the moment, he offered up an autobiographical detail of his own. "Aaron Brenner," he said, and gave me his round right hand.

I took it. "Sam," I said. "Sam Karnish."

"Tell me, you live in Houston, Shmuel?"

I didn't like what he'd done to my name, but for the moment I chose to ignore it. "Just a visit," I said. "A friend's wedding."

"Ah." I watched him hesitate—for a moment he too seemed shy—before asking, "This friend is Jewish?"

"It so happens, yes."

The obviousness of his pleasure at this answer irritated me too. I sneaked a peek at his wife—her eyes were closed, hands folded across her lap, the fingers pink and puffy at the tips. A nail-biter.

Aaron Brenner then informed me, in a confidential whisper, that they were flying to Houston for a medical procedure. "Marvelous facilities they have down there," he said.

"Yes, I know. My friend who's getting married, he's at the Med Center."

"You see?"

"See what?"

He waved his wrist impatiently. "Your friend, what is he, a specialist?"

"Radiologist."

He frowned.

"He's a wonderful guy," I added obscurely, in Warren's defense.

But the man's thoughts were already racing ahead. "Tell me, Shmuel," he said, "you're a gambling man?"

I blinked at him in surprise.

"I saw you making notes," he explained. He pointed to the

sports page, upon which I had indeed been making notes. The horses were a new interest of mine, a new source of speculation, a new money problem I'd fallen into in hopes of solving my old money problems. I'm afraid that's how it was with me. Horses, lottery tickets, games of chance, wish-and-a-prayer—despite the odds I remained perpetually on the lookout for quick and neat solutions. "You have horses running at Belmont?"

"Not today," I said.

"Just as well. Saratoga, you know, starts in a couple of weeks. Better to wait. Marvelous track. The very finest."

"I'm afraid I don't know much about it. I've only gotten into it recently. Just dabbling a little."

"Ah," he said. "A dabbler."

"I mean it interests me, of course, the whole subculture . . ."

"Yes, of course," he agreed. "The *sub*culture."

"I take it you play yourself?"

He swiveled his head to see if his wife was still listening. "A little," he said softly. "Now and then. I'm working on a system."

"That must make it more interesting."

"It's essential. Otherwise you're just wasting money. Throwing it away."

"You're probably right," I said, thinking of all the money I'd thrown away these past months, unsystematically.

"Actually this is the second one I'm working on now. The first system was easier. With the first," he explained, "I was just starting out, reading everything I could get my hands on. This by itself took about a year."

"A *year*?"

"Sure. I had a job, you know. And there was a lot to study. Not that it was hard. I mean, the *Zohar*, that's hard; but this? This was only paying attention. So then what I did was, I started going to the OTB office on my way home from work— not to bet, just to listen to people talk. As a Hasid, you know, you're practically invisible; most people assume you don't even speak English. So I got to hear a lot. Enough to know the whole sport's fixed."

"It is?"

"Sure. It's the only logical explanation. If those little facts they give you in the racing form meant anything, it would be only a matter of science to clean up. Any fool with a computer could do it. No," he asserted, "it's fixed. I saw that early on. So what I did was, I threw out the horses completely. Instead I concentrated on the jockeys. This is their livelihood, you know; they're just little men with big reputations to keep up. To do this, they have to win a certain amount of races. So I'd watch for losing streaks, and then bet heavily on the other end."

"And? How did you do?"

"Not bad. Better than even. Maybe a little better than better."

"That's great," I said. I was starting to get a little tired of him and his systems.

"It was and it wasn't," he went on. "Because even if I was right about it being fixed, I realized it was more fun to play as if it wasn't. Sometimes maybe it's better not to be so smart, and just go along with the game. So I moved into system number two. This is the one I'm still working on."

"Well," I said. "Good luck."

He gave me a penetrating look. "I'm boring you?"

"No, not at all."

But he grew quiet. Fiddling with some fringes that were sticking out the bottom of his jacket, he gazed at the back of the seat before him and mused to himself along whatever lines Hasidic people muse to themselves in idle moments. Left alone, I unfolded my newspaper and looked over the little blockish charts from Belmont. I should have done some research beforehand, I thought, as he did. I should have put some work in, approached it like a professional. How could I expect to walk into such a chancy world without preparation?

Some minutes later, my neighbor touched me lightly on the arm. "Tell me, Shmuel, you want to maybe *daven*?"

"No thanks."

"Don't say no just because you don't know how. I'd be delighted to teach you. Here," and he dove beneath the seat to grab his carry-on bag, "I've got an extra tallis."

It was around this point in the afternoon, with this loud cheerful stranger doubled over beside me, rummaging through his bag and murmuring something of a proselytizing nature I couldn't make out, that at last I began to grow embarrassed. Craning my neck, I glanced around at the other passengers. Were they listening? Did they think I was a Hasid too? In the narrow seat I felt strapped in, vulnerable, exposed to every one of the world's noisy and belligerent pedagogies. When would it end?

But no one was watching. No one except Aaron Brenner's skinny, taciturn, and, on second glance, rather lovely young wife. She saw me all right. For one brief, complicated moment, our eyes met across her husband's broad back, and something flickered between us. I did not know what; I didn't think she did either. But the corners of her mouth shuddered, as if whatever it was had confirmed her worst suspicions.

Now I waited for her to put a hand on her husband's arm, to warn him away from me. But she didn't. Without a word, she rose from her seat and went off down the aisle toward the bathroom, tottering on her plain flat shoes. For someone so short—she was only about five two—it was surprising how wobbly she was. She seemed to have no center of gravity.

Now Aaron Brenner straightened up, brandishing a black book with Hebrew letters on the cover.

"Here," he said, and deposited it in my lap. Then he drew forth a pouch of blue felt, out of which he pulled, like a magician, a tangle of black stringy leather. "Here. I'll show you how to do it."

"Do what?"

"*Tefillin*," he said. "You know *tefillin*, yes? At least you must half-know?"

"Listen," I said. "No offense, but I'd rather not."

"No? How come?"

"I'd just rather not."

"I'd rather not, I'd rather not. You remind me of that man, what's his name. In that story."

"Bartleby?"

"Right. Sure."

"You're familiar with Melville?"

"What am I, a dope? Of course I'm familiar. Once I had plans to be a writer myself. As a younger man, you know?"

I knew. Like many of my colleagues at the magazine, I too had dreamed of a literary life. In my twenties I burned to make a large statement, a grand new synthesis. But meanwhile what had I actually *done?* At this point, most of the things that defined me were negatives: I no longer smoked, I was no longer married, I no longer owed the IRS for back taxes. These, I thought bitterly, were my accomplishments.

"Sure," he said, "Melville, Twain. Henry James. At college I was lonely, I spent all my time at bookstores, so I thought maybe . . . why not? Writers, the life they lead, staying up late, reading in bad light, worrying over words and phrasings— writers get bad eyes and headaches, while the rest of the world goes to nightclubs. All writers, in this sense, are Jewish."

"And all readers?"

He smiled. "Them too."

"That sounds like a wonderfully inclusive religion."

"You bet your life. Wonderful and inclusive. You're what, thirty-two, thirty-three?"

"Almost thirty-six."

"You look younger. I'm thirty-eight myself. Magda's twenty-four. Six days a week she watches television. I talk books with her it's like talking to a chair. You're married?"

"Not just now."

"Too bad. An unmarried life is incomplete. Don't you find this to be so?"

"Yes," I said. "But I found it to be so when I was married, too."

Frowning, he waved his hand, as if I had just filled the air between us with smoke.

"Your wife when you were," he said. "She read or watch television?"

"She went to movies. I suppose you could say she was Unitarian in that respect."

He did not so much as smile. "And the children," he said, "they're with her now?"

"We didn't have children."

"Oh?" He leaned forward. "And why not?"

The question was a simple one, and for a moment I was certain I had within me a simple answer. But I didn't. What kind did I have? Running them through my head, I grew depressed, and signaled the stewardess for another of those little bottles of vodka.

"What about you?" I asked, cracking the metal band.

"What about what?"

"Your children. Where are they now?"

He scratched his beard vigorously and shifted in his seat, as if preparing for a long, complicated story. But in fact he said nothing. His eyes sought out the prayer book on his lap, and seemed to find evidence there of some distant abstraction. A minute or so passed in this manner, him studying the prayer book and me studying my drink. Then he lifted his head again. "Listen, Shmuel, Mister Half and Half, you want to pray with me? I don't want to press you."

"I think I'll pass."

"Knowing," he said, "is not thinking."

"I know," I said. "I know I'll pass."

"Okay fine." He nodded, not altogether unhappily, and rose, squeezing past the empty seat where his wife had been. Only then did he appear to realize that she was gone.

For a moment he looked around the cabin calmly, even loftily, as if his interest in it was merely an architectural one, having to do with the tangents and vectors of steel that held it together. Then he went back to his business. He reached into his blue felt pouch and pulled out a frilly shawl that must once have been white but had now faded to the color of very old teeth. He lifted the fringes to his mouth and kissed them soundlessly. Then, in one swift motion, he draped the whole thing over his head and shoulders and proceeded out into the aisle.

Now that he was in full view, he began to provoke some commentary. Kids pointed and giggled. Their parents whispered admonitions and shifted nervously in their seats. One stewardess made a face and then, recovering, just as quickly erased it. I waited for someone to yell out with the news: a man was praying in the aisle of the plane! The sight was both funny and ominous and at the same time only a kind of benign afterthought to our flight through space.

"Hey," someone said none too softly behind me. "Where's he think he's going, Israel?"

Just then I felt an odd pressure in my head, as if the plane had suddenly dipped, or risen. It occurred to me that I would stand and defend my seatmate. I would announce to the entire plane that this man in the funny black clothes had gone to college, had played the horses at Saratoga, had read books by Herman Melville and Mark Twain, had a fetching young wife with whom he presumably enjoyed sex at night, and that he was in any case only thirty-eight years old. But what was the use? The way he looked just then, framed by the merciless geometry of the aisles—head bent under the prayer shawl, rocking back and forth, murmuring rapidly over his black book—Aaron Brenner could as well have been a hundred and eight, a thousand and eight. And I found it hard to conceive of a world in which such a man was not, and would not always be, very much alone.

And yet, thinking back on it now, I could not say with any confidence who was alone and who wasn't. Or whether anyone else on the plane was as discomfited by the sight of him as I was.

Finally his wife came tilting back up the aisle. Her cheeks were flushed, as if she'd been running, or drinking, or screaming. She slid around her praying husband without a word.

Once she had settled in her seat, she did not look in his direction, or in mine, or in any other direction for that matter. She closed her eyes and kept them closed until we landed in Houston.

THE FLOW

Though we'd been friends for close to twenty years now, I was not looking forward to Warren Pinsky's wedding. Oh, I loved him, of course, in that hopeful and evasive male way, a by-product of passionate youth that lingers on into middle age no matter how little there is to talk about. Or how much. Which it was with Warren I could no longer say. But having dutifully attended his first wedding, and his second, as well as the various engagement and bachelor and follow-up parties that accompanied them, I was getting at this point a little partied out.

Then too, these milestone events cast a kind of absolute light upon one's own life, a raw and brilliant glare, rather like an X-ray, that pinpoints every dark spot or flaw, every shadowed fissure.

There were several of these to contend with. My career for example was stuck in neutral, and no matter how hard I worked the gears I could not seem to pull myself out. In June I'd taken two weeks off to polish up some articles I had been playing around with for much too long, and which I intended to submit to the magazine on speculation. They were what we liked to call "think pieces"—book and film reviews, an analysis of Middle East diplomacy, and a where-are-they-now on the baseball heroes of my youth. I'd rewritten them half a dozen times, and then rewritten them again, and when I was finished I read them over coldly and found to my surprise that they were actually pretty good—though not as good, of course, as the work I *would* do, once I really got untracked.

Or so I intended to tell Ray Spurlock, our managing editor, when we met to discuss my future.

It was axiomatic at the magazine that Ray Spurlock was a likable fellow. Warm, avuncular, good-looking, he was the sort of executive who inspired almost as much affection as he did admiration, and almost as much admiration as he did fear. His eyes were pale gray, almost blue; his face, like old upholstery, full of merry brooking cracks. Despite his enormous salary he dressed like a harried untenured professor, favoring tweeds and bad ties, shapeless shoes with fuzzy surfaces. But there was nothing fuzzy about his mind. Ray Spurlock's mind was one of those vigorous, lucid, multichambered, and zippily efficient organs that appear in the species as if by divine will and are promptly commissioned to run things. It was impossible to work at the magazine and not have the man's high clear voice in your head, glossing your own, inciting you to excellence. Certainly I did. Which was why, when he called me into his office one morning and bade me sit on his sleek leather sofa, all the saliva seemed to disappear at once from the inside of my mouth. "Let me be direct," he said crisply. "I can't run any of this stuff."

I digested the news slowly, if at all.

"It's not that they don't show talent. If talent was the issue, there'd be no question. But talent is not the issue. Talent is never the issue."

I waited for him to tell me what the issue was.

"The issue is focus. The issue is structure. The issue is viewpoint, perspective. Now," he said, peering at me dispassionately over his bifocals, "allow me to give you a synonym for these pieces here. Bullshit. Bullshit is the word that suggests itself."

"Ray," I said, "come on. I worked on those for months."

"Did you? I'm sorry to hear that." He considered the page in his hand, filled with red arrows and crisscrossing lines, all the busy calligraphy of failure. "What you've got here, bucko, is a grab bag of halfheartedness. The political stuff is flaccid. The reviews are clever but indecisive. The baseball piece is sheer nostalgia. Not," he said, "that there aren't some nice things. I'll admit you write with facility. I laughed several times. I was impressed by your vocabulary and the quality of your insights. In fact for what it's worth, I think you're one of the most promising stylists we've had around here in a long time."

"Thanks."

"But none of that matters in the slightest, of course."

I cleared my throat. "Maybe it would help," I said, "if you explained what you mean by perspective."

"That's for you to figure out."

"I had a feeling you were going to say that."

Spurlock stretched and yawned. "Wake up, my friend," he said. "The world's well stocked with wise guys who pick things apart. What it needs is someone to show how they fit together."

"How what fits together?"

He smiled sadly, not hearing me. There were big leafy plants on either side of his desk. Through the foliage, Ray Spurlock blinked drowsily, a jungle king. His life, I reminded myself, was not quite so easy or efficient as it looked. On the wall above his head were framed portraits of his wife and three daughters; the youngest was said to be in an institution of some kind for cerebral palsy. Or was it the oldest? ". . . occurs to me," he was saying, "that maybe politics is just not your thing."

"Then what is?"

"You tell me."

I did not answer right away. Outside the sweeping window, the sunlight was in motion, dancing off the glass and steel, the vaulting arches, the spiraling aspirations of midtown. "I want to stop floating around," I said. "Stop subbing, stop editing other people's text. I want to dig in and do some stuff of my own."

"Great," he said at once. "Go ahead."

"You'll let me?"

"Of course. Talk to Ronnie. See if you can come up with some assignments to work on after hours. I'll be happy to look at anything you produce."

I fidgeted. "I was hoping to move out of Science, Ray. I heard there was an opening for a book critic. Or maybe something in the front of the book."

"Sorry, bucko. I'd like to accommodate you but my hands are tied." He leaned forward intently, gray eyes narrowing. "You may have noticed a certain unease lately on the upper floors. Closed doors, whispered discussions. People looking worried in the elevators."

"Aren't there always?"

"Yes and no," he said. "I'll just say that at present I don't foresee any repositioning among the staff. Let me clarify that: any *upward* repositioning. Take my meaning?"

"So it's true about the layoffs."

"I can't confirm or deny."

"And the young Brits who've been spotted in the cafeteria?"

"I can't say anything about that," he said. "By the way, Arlen Ashby was looking for you this morning."

"What did he want?"

"I haven't the foggiest." Spurlock sneaked a look at his watch. "Listen, I'm sorry these pieces didn't work out. But hang in there. Talk to Ronnie. Science is an advantageous place to be these days, you'll see. I just got a terrific piece from one of our stringers out in L.A. Did you know that even as we speak, thousands of kids are out there forming New Age communes in cyberspace?"

"No."

"This is the sort of material you could be tackling, you know. Cutting edge. The brand new. Who reads books anymore anyway? Seriously. Who has time?"

I had time, of course. I had plenty of time. But it seemed unserious, even unprofessional to admit this to Ray Spurlock;

it would only confirm how wayward and precarious was my standing in the zeitgeist. "It's just not my area," I said by way of final appeal.

"Areas." Spurlock frowned, straightening his tie. "Who's to say? My area, I believe, is where I am now. It may not be true but it's useful to me to act as if it were. What I'd like to suggest to you, bucko, is that your area is where *you* are now. Follow?"

"I'm trying," I said.

"Well, we'll discuss all this sometime over lunch. But now you'll have to excuse me, I've got a meeting."

Afterward, I went down to my office to complete the day's work. My concentration was poor. From my desk I could hear ringing phones, muttered curses, the hollow percussion of keys tapping on a keyboard. Words were being processed. That was what happened to words these days. And what was happening to me?

As the hours passed, the bad news of the morning gnawed its way through my head, and my back, a reliable barometer in these matters, began to stiffen. Finally I went and stretched out on the burgundy carpet. There I lay staring up into the gridded ceiling, listening to the dull and vengeful roar of the city going about its business. It was not a posture that encouraged one to feel particularly good about oneself. But it gave me time to think for a while, to digest what Ray Spurlock had said about my work lacking a viewpoint. Perhaps he was right. Certainly the view from the floor was a limited one. I would have liked to discuss the matter with Donna, my girlfriend, who had if anything a surplus of viewpoints. But Donna and I had separated.

This was nothing new. Ours was that kind of closeness: involuted, messy, full of abrasion and division. And yet each new separation, when it came, managed to disorient us completely. Each new separation had a rich, idiosyncratic life of its own, bore its own unique freight of melancholy and emptiness. Each new separation seemed a little harder than the last one to shake off.

*   *   *

All of which was on my mind as I filed in for Warren's wedding.

The event took place on Sunday morning, early enough that the fifty or so guests looked odd and diffident in their good clothes, vaguely surprised to find themselves here instead of their own kitchen tables, working their way through coffee and newspapers. The ceremony was brief. The tanned young rabbi who conducted it was not so much lacking in feeling as hurried and decorous in its expression, as if his thoughts too were elsewhere, say on an open tennis court that lay shimmering under the blaze of sunlight, awaiting his return.

Afterward, the reception—held in one of the windowless banquet rooms of the Medical Center Hilton (an internists' convention occupied the main ballroom)—seemed almost to proceed by rote. The musical entertainment was provided by the Bob Smith Band, a trio of white men in white jackets. Warren, of course, was unavailable. His parents, whom I'd once known fairly well, were no longer alive, and his brothers were occupied with relatives and children. Left to my own resources, I chatted a bit with the other guests, drank some wine, nibbled some hors d'oeuvres, tapped my feet mindlessly to the music. Then, just as I was beginning to feel overwhelmed by my own superfluity, the bride appeared.

Her name was Debbie Solomon and she was twenty-four years old, and perhaps that tells the story right there. One year of medical school under her belt and already, Warren had said over the phone, a budding star. Indeed her voice, which I'd heard in the background, was sharp and clear, the voice of a woman who has emerged from a limited set of trials with all her cleverness and ambitions intact. I may as well admit I found it heartbreaking to listen to. Where did these Debbie Solomons come from? And why were there none left for me?

"Hi," she said. "You made it." Glowing and purposeful in her white dress, she offered me her cheek. Her skin was cool and smooth and splendidly perfumed, and I was so happy to be engaged in this way, to be making such an intimate connection with this poised and budding young star, that I held my lips to it for perhaps an extra second or two. "Oh, that's so nice," she breathed in my ear, and by now I was half ready to marry her myself. Then she patted me on the shoulder and pulled away. "Thank you for coming. It means so much to us."

It was clear she had no idea who I was.

Before I could enlighten her, a cousin from Philly swooped in on taffeta wings to bear her away. This left me out on the rim of the dance floor looking for a place to put my hands as the band went into a rendition of "These Foolish Things" so muted and vague it might have been playing underwater.

Left alone, then, I did what any normal person with a stiff back and no one to dance with would do in the situation: I drank.

I do not hold liquor very well in the best of circumstances. It has to do with my metabolism, which I inherited from my mother, who is slightly anemic, and which inclines me toward sluggishness, especially in the afternoon. There was an open bar at the Pinsky wedding, overseen by an unfriendly young man named Steve. Steve did not appear to much like the catering business. With his stiff white shirt, his thin black tie, and his aristocratic expression of controlled distaste, he seemed to have an unnerving effect on everyone who approached him, and so along with the heat and the tepid music he may have been responsible for the general drift of the party, as the afternoon waned, toward lethargy and confusion. Or was it just me? I found that the more I saw of Steve the more difficulty I had thinking straight in his presence. Thus not only did I wind up consuming a good deal of alcohol, but I also veered recklessly from one kind to another, which is how in a little over three hours I came to consume a bourbon, a Bloody Mary, a glass of red wine, a glass of white wine, a Tequila Sunrise, a vodka and tonic, and two imported beers, to say nothing of the glass of champagne we were all given when it came time to toast the happy couple. By which point I was nearly insensate.

It didn't help matters that *I* was the one selected to give the toast. As the best man—as in fact the only one of Warren's old friends to have made the trip down from New York—I should have realized it would be up to me. But I hadn't. So when the band fell quiet, and the ensuing silence was broken by that frenetic clinking of butter-knife-on-water-glass that signals a toast, I went ahead and looked around for the absent toaster like everyone else. Where was he, anyway? Why didn't he go ahead and get *up* there already?

Then someone was touching me on the shoulder, and someone else was calling my name, and someone else was urging me to stand. A chorus of whispers went around. I could see, over at the head table, Debbie Solomon, the woman I loved, blushing expectantly. Beside her my friend Warren Pinsky was beaming and nodding, eyes lazy with emotion, already moved, it seemed, by whatever it was I was about to say.

I cleared my throat a few times, stalling. What had I said at Warren's first wedding? At his second? I could no longer remember.

"Warren and I," I began, "were roommates at college. Roomies. The guy was wonderful to live with. Kind, considerate, generous with time and money. Always had something going. Some new poet he'd read, some new friend he'd met, some new obsession he was obsessing over . . ."

Someone out there chuckled uncertainly.

"Remember Zen, Warren? All things flow, you used to say, from the same source. Of course, this was before the Gurdjieff phase, the Maharaji phase, the Freud phase, the Trotsky phase. Or was it after? It was hard to keep up. We were a little in awe of the guy, I admit. Such a Renaissance man. If he ever found the right channel, he was capable of greatness. That's what we used to say. And us too of course. Us too . . ."

I could hear Steve at the bar, plinking ice cubes into a glass.

"But where was I? Oh yes, Zen. A marvelous discipline. As I stand here, I'm reminded of the words of the great master Suzuki, who, when asked to define the concept of Satori, replied: 'It's just like real life, only two inches off the ground.' Which, if you think about it, is a nice description of marriage too. Just like life but a little higher. A little higher and a little lighter . . ."

This drew a smattering of sentimental applause.

"My own marriage, of course, now rests several inches *below* the ground, as it were. But that's another story. Or is it? Because past hopes, they have a kind of half-life, don't they? Ticking away, giving off heat. . . .

"Take Warren and me. We were going to be artists. Going to make brilliant books and films that would address the American condition. Because we were sure, you know, there was one. Because America was capable of greatness too. This was the whole problem. Like Milton's Satan—the burden of potential, soured dreams, etc. . . ."

There was some minor rustling, some scraping of chairs. I realized that I was sweating, heavily.

"But enough about the past. One of the endearing things about Warren is that he doesn't dwell on such things. Warren lives in the present, in what the mental health professions call the here and now. Which is why we're here today. Because maybe the world doesn't need any more brilliant films, after all. Maybe what the world needs, I mean really needs, is more weddings. What do you think, Debbie? I mean, as a member of the younger generation, what's your viewpoint? Do all things flow from the same source? And what's all this about cyberspace, anyway? Where *is* it? Is it important to know? Because, if I can speak personally for a moment, I find it hard to grant reality to something I can't see. Which brings us back to marriage, I suppose. So let's raise our glasses, ladies and gentlemen. Let's drink a toast to marriage, and to the happy couple, and to . . . to . . ."

I paused; to what? I couldn't think of a thing to add. It occurred to me, however, that I had already added a great deal, perhaps even too much, and that if I wanted to I could just stop right here and sit down. So I did.

There followed a charitable interlude of applause, after which everyone fell silent and busied themselves trying to comprehend, if not forget, just what it was I had said. Somewhere in there the band started to play. The guests began to move around again, dancing and talking as they had before, though their voices for some reason were louder to me now. At the head table, Warren was staring off into space, his mouth pursed in thought. Beside him his bride had leaned back in her chair in order to chat with her mother. Nobody seemed to be paying me or my odd speech the slightest attention. Nonetheless, I went off to the bathroom to hide for a while.

In the bathroom I ran into Howard Solomon, the bride's younger brother. We had met the night before at Warren's earnest but uneventful bachelor party—six men who didn't know each other sitting in the courtyard of a Mexican restaurant, under a leering moon, trying to get drunk on watered-down margaritas. Only Howard Solomon had managed it. It appeared he hadn't come down yet, either. His tuxedo jacket was off, he'd loosened the top two buttons of his shirt, and as I entered the bathroom I heard whinnies, wah-wahs, and various percussive noises coming from the back of his throat as he stood watching himself play air guitar in the mirror above the sink. "Hey, man," he said, noticing me at last. "Awesome toast."

"Thanks."

"Really. It was like this guy I saw on cable once who spoke in tongues."

"Thanks."

"Hey, are you okay? 'Cause you look kind of pale."

"I'm fine," I said. "I've just had a little too much to drink."

"Tell me about it. I'm like totally blitzed." Howard was nineteen and, he'd informed me the night before, "between commitments." Short and broad-shouldered, with whorling acne scars on his cheeks and brown hair pulled back into a frizzy ponytail, he had round, cartoonlike biceps that could only have come from the gym. Perhaps because of the effort they had cost him he seemed just then a little tired. His eyes were narrow and listless, and his head kept nodding up and down as if he were listening to a piece of desultory inner music. I could smell the beer on his breath. "That was fun last night," he said.

"Yeah."

"Warren's cool. I like having him in the family. It makes, like, the whole thing bigger."

"What thing?"

"Shit, I don't know." He giggled nervously. "*Everything*."

On that note he turned on the cold water and doused his face. Outside I could hear cats prowling in the dumpsters, their back-and-forth choreography of desire and avoidance. Howard, dripping, studied me carefully in the mirror as I searched my pockets for a comb. All I came up with, however, was some change, a book of matches, and a business card: *Aaron Brenner, CPA, Brooklyn, New York.* On the back he'd scribbled his hotel number for the five days they'd be in Houston. "Call," he'd said as we deplaned. "Come by for a meal. We could both use the company."

What did he mean, both? I thought of his wife, her youth and containment. Did she want company too? What did it matter? The card might have been a souvenir from some distant expedition, a piece of foreign currency I had no use for. I slipped it back into my pocket, where it rested amid the lint and the pennies and the tiny scraps of receipts, the standard detritus that accumulated there, and resumed my search for the wayward comb.

Around this point Warren himself walked in. "Hey, guys," he said coolly, and headed for the urinals.

"Hey," Howard said. "What's up, bro?"

"Not much. You know, just the wedding and all."

"Cool."

"Listen, Warren," I said, addressing myself intently to his back. "I'm sorry I went on like that. I don't know what came over me."

"Bah," he called blithely over his shoulder. "Forget it."

"No, really. It was way out of line. As soon as I get out of here, I'm going to go apologize to Debbie."

"You were fine, Sammy. Really."

"I was?"

"Sure. You lost me a few times there, I think. But I actually found the whole thing kind of moving."

"And Debbie?"

"Debbie?" Warren shrugged. "She thought it was a little on the gloomy side. Maybe even a tiny bit insulting. But then she doesn't know you."

At which point Howard Solomon, who had been sleepily observing our exchange, cleared his throat. "So listen," he said, "you guys feel like a walk?"

"A walk?" Warren laughed. "Where?"

"I don't know. I mean, let's just, like, *walk*, y'know? Go with the flow. Whatever."

Warren, nodding, glanced in my direction hopefully. Inside this radiologist slouched a latent guru, waiting to be born. And inside the rest of us, perhaps he was there too, a chubby little man in the lotus position, speaking calmly of what we are helpless to control. Was that the whole trick, to shut off the distractions and listen, to stand in the middle of the aisle at forty thousand feet, surrounded by clamor and derision, and pray? "Yeah," he said. "Why not?"

"Warren," I said, "this is your *wedding*. That's why not."

He frowned. "Oh, just a couple minutes, Sammy. What do you say? Fresh air. A bit of the old flow."

Suddenly the day—the whole summer—had caught up with me in full. "Fuck the flow," I said.

"Fuck the flow?" Howard Solomon giggled. "Righteous."

"I've had the flow up to here. I'm flowed out."

"Now, now." Warren laid one doctorly hand on my shoulder. "This is a party, don't forget. Let's keep it positive. A walk might not be a bad thing. Clear our heads. We'll pretend we're on some profoundly beautiful beach with our pants rolled up, talking over the big questions."

40

It's no easy thing, walking amid the low, formless riot of strip malls and condo complexes that comprise the city of Houston, to pretend you're on a beautiful beach, but so what? All things being equal, a moving body will move forever—that is Galileo's law of inertia, a law to which all things adhere. So the three of us filed out of the bathroom and down the hallway and out into the parking lot. In truth it was nice to be outside. The sullen whoosh of the traffic did sound like an ocean of sorts, and the Gulf breeze smelled sweet. Howard Solomon walked along in front, his uselessly muscled arms swinging at his sides, charting a path for us through the maze of developments. He was kicking rocks with his high-tops and humming a tune I didn't recognize. He did both with unexpected feeling and skill.

"Copland," said Warren. "*Appalachian Spring.*"

"You know, I may be nuts," I said, "but I sort of like that kid."

"He's a savant of sorts, Debbie says. SATs that go through the roof. Also he's my brother-in-law now. How's that for strange?"

"No stranger than anything else."

Warren looked over his shoulder for something in the distance, but couldn't seem to find it. "Third time's a charm. That's what they say."

"Who?"

"How should I know? The other guys who've gotten married three times, probably."

"They must know what they're talking about then."

"I'm just a silly jerk, aren't I, Sam? Tell me the truth."

"Are these the big questions? Is that what we're doing now?"

But Warren didn't seem to hear me. "The depressing fact is," he went on, "I still believe in it. I still believe in marriage."

"Does Debbie believe in marriage?"

"What's not to believe in? She's twenty-four, for Christ's sake. She believes in everything."

"So it's a match. That's not depressing."

"It's not?" he said, brightening a little.

"Of course not. It's the best thing that could happen to you."

Warren smiled. "Ah, Sammy. You should come visit more often, you know. It does you good to see me, I can tell."

"You're probably right," I said.

At which point we turned around and began walking back to the hotel, Howard now trailing a few steps behind. So far this had been, I thought, easily the most precarious of Warren's weddings. But it seemed to me that the line between believing in nothing and believing in everything was a precarious one too, so precarious it might not even exist, and so it was fitting that I be walking beside him at this moment. Warren seemed to think so too. He kept draping his long arm across my shoulder, telling me how good it was to see me. "So how're things at the magazine?" he asked. "Still plugging away?"

"Actually, I'm trying to write now."

"Good for you. Any luck?"

"Not much."

"Good for you," he said again, apparently distracted. "By the way, did I tell you I'm quitting therapy?"

"No."

"According to Debbie, this whole insight thing is passé. A macho romantic concept, she says. The heroic individual out on the margins, struggling with his demons. She says the focus is on systems now."

"Systems?"

"Sure. They drag the whole family in, watch how they interrelate, the dynamics. A new approach. Much faster. More scientific."

By now we were back at the hotel. Altogether, we had been gone less than ten minutes. When we arrived at the glass door of the lobby, Warren paused, patting his bald spot in a way that implied deep concentration, and watching him do this—he'd been doing it, it seemed to me, since before he *had* a bald spot—I felt a brief squeeze of the heart. A new approach, I told myself, might be a very good thing for us all.

Then we pushed open the door and reentered the wedding.

"Hey, where you going?" Warren called after me. "It's still early. You haven't even told me about Donna yet."

"I have to go."

I found my suit jacket where I'd left it and began to make my way toward the front exit. It was still only midafternoon and I would have some time to kill upstairs or at the airport, but that was all right. I could use a nap anyway. My insides were swollen from liquor. Also, as happens to me in large events of this kind, even those wherein I do not make a spectacle of myself, I was left with a small residue of shame. Who has not had the feeling, coming home from these affairs, that they have said all the wrong things, made all the wrong moves, flailed their way badly through a noisy, fitful sleep?

On the threshold of the lobby I was jostled by a man in a black suit who had poked his head in to hear the music, and for a moment I was thrown off-balance.

"So," he said. "Mister Half and Half."

I recognized him, but dimly, as someone I had met once a long time ago, perhaps in another life.

"This is the wedding?" He gestured over my shoulder at the proceedings behind me. "The one you talked about?"

It was the man from the plane. The Hasid. Odd how he had flitted across my mind just a few minutes before, and now here he was. As if that little twitch of the synapses was all it took to summon him.

"Aaron," he said, clasping my hand between his own. "Aaron Brenner. Remember?"

"But . . . what are you doing here?"

"Why not? This is my hotel." He pulled his room key out of his pocket and dangled it in front of him impatiently, as if to say, Here, now you believe?

"So," he said, "how are you?"

"Good, good. And you?"

"How should I be?" He leveled upon me a piercing stare, as if I'd arrived late for an appointment the two of us had made some time ago. "For us, you know, this question isn't simple. When you ask how are you, what you're really asking is, what is the present state of your religious life."

"Oh. Sorry."

"Don't be. Mine is very good. And yours?"

"Mine? Mine's fine. Out of this world."

In response to this enthusiasm the Hasid gave a mild and reflexive little shrug. I remembered from our conversation on the plane that he and his wife had come down to Houston for a medical procedure. "And your wife," I asked, "she's feeling better?"

He shrugged again, and stood on tiptoe to peer over my shoulder. Then, like a character in a joke, he answered another of my questions with another of his own. "This wedding, you said it's Jewish?"

"That's right."

"But," he complained, "nobody's *dancing.*"

Together we turned to look over the parquet rectangle in the center of the room, upon which three couples in their six-ties—the same three couples who had been dancing all after-noon—were gliding and stepping rather niftily to the music. No one joined them. On the sax, Bob Smith treated himself to an extended solo. The drummer put down his sticks and lit up a cigarette, squinting through the smoke, bemused. Perhaps he was not the regular drummer but a replacement, pressed into service at the last minute. In any case the gig was almost over; soon everyone would be getting back to more serious pursuits.

I cleared my throat. "Not a very lively crowd, I guess."

"And you, Shmuel?" Aaron turned and eyed me specula-tively. "You're more lively than they are, down deep?"

"Maybe I am," I said. "It's hard to say. Frankly I'm a little drunk at the moment."

"Of course you are. Why not? A wedding is supposed to be a celebration. You know the midrash about Queen Jezebel?"

I shook my head. The only Jezebel that came to mind was from a Bette Davis movie, and I didn't even know what a midrash *was*. But right then I was reluctant to go into all the things he knew that I didn't. He was pedantic enough as it was. Besides, some of the wedding guests had begun to stare.

"A wicked lady," he said, "who came to a bad end. But the dogs would not eat the soles of her feet. Because bad as she was, when she was alive she always danced at weddings."

"Listen," I said, pointing to my watch, "I'm afraid I really have to get going now. I have a plane this afternoon."

"What time?"

"Five." I pushed the time up an hour to convey a greater sense of urgency. In other words, I lied.

"I'll drive you," he said.

"Don't be silly. I'll take a cab."

"I'll drive you. It'll be my pleasure."

"Look, that's really nice of you, but there's absolutely no reason—"

"Nonsense. The car's rented and sitting there, why should you pay for a taxi? Besides, I've already been to shul today, plus the museum; I have nothing left to do. It would be a favor to *me*."

"No, really. I can't. You have your wife—"

"My wife is upstairs, bored out of her mind. She'd love an excuse to see the city. Do her good."

By this point I had no idea for whom this favor was actually intended, and why. But if he was so eager to drive me, why resist? After the lie I'd just told and the toast I'd just given, I was anxious to please, to do some good for someone, even if that someone turned out only to be myself. "Okay," I said. "I'd be grateful."

"Good."

"Let me get my bag and I'll meet you down here in ten minutes."

"Take your time. You might want a shower first." He refrained from adding what must have been obvious: that I looked like I could use one. "We'll go whenever you say."

Upstairs I did take a shower, a very long and hot one. When I emerged, the bathroom was cloudy with steam but my head at last was clear. I knew the toast had been mishandled. But one nice thing about Warren Pinsky was that he did not hold grudges, and as for his new wife, perhaps I could still redeem myself with a couple of phone calls, or a thoughtful and expensive gift. Besides, this world of theirs down here, it wasn't mine, I was only a weekend tourist, passing through; already I was looking past it, as people do on Sunday afternoons, to that other world, the one that awaits our return.

When I came down Aaron had vanished. He was neither in the lobby nor in the gift shop nor anywhere along the bright, mirror-lined corridor. As I stood there, sandwiched by reflections, it began to seem as plausible as not that he had never really been there in the first place. After all, I'd had a lot to drink. For that matter, I'd had a lot to drink on the plane, too; perhaps he hadn't really been *there* either. Perhaps he was only a figure in a dream, some phantom born of disorientation and fatigue. A shadow. And his wife? A mere shadow of a shadow. And me? I wondered. What would that make me?

Eventually I found Aaron Brenner not in some back alley of the imagination but pretty close to where I'd left him, in the Gulf Coast Room of the Medical Center Hilton. Only he was no longer hanging back on the periphery as he had before, peeking in from the doorway and making judgments. Apparently he'd decided to do something about the dancing after all. He'd decided to lead it.

When I walked in he was at the hub of two concentric and revolving wheels, the first of which was exclusively male and the second exclusively female. The men were performing what I recognized from other Jewish weddings to be a *hora*. I could see at a glance, however, that this was not your standard-issue *hora*, your five-minutes-of-perfunctory-*hava nagila*-shmaltz-for-the-grandparents. This was instead some sort of primitive Eastern step-dance, some big athletic cousin of a *hora* that was a good deal wilder and more arduous, a good deal louder. Among other acrobatics, it appeared to require a certain quotient of whirling, foot-stomping, shoulder-gripping, partner-swinging, and general hollering, with periodic interludes devoted to strenuous squatting leg-kicks in the Russian style.

With all the commotion it took me a minute to spot Warren Pinsky in the inner circle, waving a handkerchief and whirling about. He was torqued up pretty high. His jacket was off—huge half-moons of perspiration were spreading across his back—and his cheeks and forehead were flaming red. Let me just say that I had seen the man dance before, and it wasn't pretty. At parties, he'd flail through a series of elaborate Motown hand gestures intended to distract you from his feet, which did not so much move as clump back and forth dispiritedly for a while, a couple of balls-and-chains. The charm of this effect Warren, I think, radically misperceived. But if you liked him, as his former wives and I did, you forgave him for it.

Now, however, at the center of the dance floor (*the center of his life*, I found myself thinking) he seemed transformed. Sweaty and intent, he stomped shoulder to shoulder with Aaron Brenner, matching him kick for kick, grunt for grunt, whirl for whirl, bellowing out keening ululating cries at regular intervals—no longer a neurotic radiologist from Long Island but some woolly and prodigious desert animal in high rutting gear.

The outer circle, all female, were clapping boisterously. At the front tables the older generation nodded along in a swoon of memory and blood sugar. Catering assistants peered in from the kitchen. They seemed amused in a nonchalant way. But then catering assistants have seen it all, I expect.

Meanwhile Bob Smith and the band, game but overmatched, tried to keep the beat.

It was not quite the same wedding I had left half an hour before. I'll admit that I took this somewhat personally, and was not above blaming it on the chubby man in the black suit, who was supposed to be driving me to the airport at the moment, not leading an impromptu conga line. I waited until there was a break in the action—another several minutes—and then insinuated myself onto the dance floor.

"Sam!"

Warren greeted me like a long-lost friend, which picked me up a little. Everything was forgiven. He staggered dizzily for a moment, then leaned over to catch his breath.

"I see you've met my friend Aaron," I said.

"What, him?" Warren jerked a thumb to indicate the man in black, who was now wiping his face with a handkerchief. "Wild man," he huffed. "Where'd you find him, anyway?"

"He found me."

"What?"

I waved my arm, too tired to explain. "Forget it."

"Well," he said, "whatever. I'm glad he showed up, though. Things were pretty dull. I was almost getting nostalgic for that bizarre toast you gave."

"It looked like fun," I said. "The dancing."

"It was. Hey, who's that? Must be his wife."

And there she was. At the center of the dance floor, amid all those stout Texans, she looked, in her scarf, her ankle-length plaid skirt and long-sleeved blouse, even smaller and even younger than she had on the plane. Her hair too was different somehow, more curly and full, perhaps a shade darker; it tilted her proportions a bit, rearranged her field of gravity. Feeling at this point a little tilted and rearranged myself, I watched her closely and with some sympathy, a vague sense of shared estrangement. In profile one could make out through the layers of her clothing the swell and slope of her breasts. No doubt there was more to her than I had perceived at first. But it was an effort to see the woman through the clothes; they kept her at a remove.

Anyway, she seemed vexed about something. She was standing there not quite looking at her husband as she spoke to him, and in response he was offering his usual mild shrug and not quite looking at her. Married people, I thought.

"Her name's Magda." I have no idea why, other than the fact that I suddenly remembered it, I chose to share this information with Warren.

"Kinda cute," he said.

"Yeah, well, she's married."

"So what? So am I." Which did not exactly fill me with confidence that this would be the last of Warren's weddings. The groom might have been a little worried on that score himself; abruptly, as if remembering something, he craned his neck to scan the crowd. "Excuse me, Sammy. Got to talk to the people. You'll call me, right?"

"I'll call you," I said, and watched him thread his way across the room.

Now that the excitement was over the band had gone back into its Valium trance for a Lou Rawls medley, and several couples—more than before—were beginning to fox-trot. It seemed to me that aside from Magda Brenner, I was the sole occupant of the room who had not as yet taken part in the dancing.

Finally Aaron glanced up and saw me. He pointed to his watch. Time?

I nodded.

He said something to his wife. Immediately she turned in my direction, seeking me out, her eyes steely and narrow.

Hey, I thought, *I didn't ask for this.*

And then he appeared at my side. "We'll go now," he said. "Magda," and he jerked his head to indicate the woman trudging head down, as if through heavy snow, a couple of steps behind him, "has decided to come with us after all."

"Oh, great," I said. And then, over his shoulder, "Hello."

I'd aimed the word in her direction but somehow it must have glanced off or missed the target because it failed to register on her features, dissolving instead into the particulate noise of the room at large. Aaron urged me toward the exit. His wife followed, face averted, as if from an unwholesome smell. I mumbled that this wasn't necessary, I could still take a cab, I didn't want to inconvenience anyone. By now we were in the lobby. Aaron waited impatiently for me to finish, then said, "You stay here. I'll get the car."

The lobby's carpet was as smooth and rich and luminous as that great Houston export, Astroturf, and I gave it a thorough examination as we stood there waiting for Aaron to return. When I glanced up, Magda, who'd been staring out the plate-glass window, now sought refuge in the carpet too. Her breathing was shallow, audible. Either she had a deviated septum or else I made her nervous. I was beginning to make *me* nervous. This wasn't my idea, I wanted to say. Then I checked myself. Then I went ahead and said it anyway.

"What?" She gazed at me blankly. Her eyes were very dark. They seemed to swallow all the available light.

"Your giving me a ride," I said. "It was your husband's idea. I was happy to take a cab."

She nodded, then resumed her meticulous study of the carpet.

"Are you feeling okay?" I asked.

At this, she lifted her head again and gave me another blank look. Perhaps, I thought, English wasn't her language. Perhaps she only spoke Hebrew, or Yiddish, or Polish. Clearly she did not speak Karnish.

"Your husband, back on the plane, said something about medical treatment. I hope it's all gone . . . smoothly."

Now she inclined her head so that she was looking at me sideways—it appeared to be her posture of concentration. For a moment she said nothing, seeming to replay my words in her head. Then she smiled. Her smile was, like most of her expressions, rather complicated: girlish, inward, hesitant, perhaps even a little cruel, and though I did not know whether I was the object of it or merely a witness, I was so relieved to have finally elicited a response from her that I didn't care.

"But it's not for me," she said.

Before I could inquire any further, a shiny blue Ford pulled up in the circular driveway. The horn beeped merrily twice.

"There he is," she sighed.

She appeared to hesitate for a second.

"I don't understand."

"For him," she said. "For him."

She shook her head in a peremptory way, as if closing off a long press conference that had been devoted to this subject, then proceeded through the revolving door. I followed. Like most revolving doors, this one was sluggish and awkward to use, and there was a moment, inevitably, where we briefly stopped moving forward and our motion was arrested. It was only a fraction of a second, but it felt as if we were stuck there for years, unable to push free.

Soon enough we were out, however, and headed toward the blue car.

We drove down the endless freeway. Magda sat quietly in back, looking out her window, and I sat just as quietly up front, looking out mine. It occurred to me that I had seen almost nothing of Texas over the weekend. Perhaps there was no Texas left to be seen, only the flatness of the land, the immensity of the sky, and thousands of big shiny trucks with bumper stickers about Jesus. The sun elbowed in through the windshield. Thanks to the air conditioning, which Aaron Brenner had going full blast, even the chevron of light felt cool. Aaron's driving, on the other hand, was almost fanatically tense. The whole twenty miles he sat hunched over the wheel, pulling at the curls of his red beard with one hand and oversteering with the other, all the while discoursing on a number of subjects—kosher cooking, Brooklyn politics, current trends in Talmudic scholarship—which did not in any way concern me. I asked him several questions, though, to be polite, and because he was an intelligent man and it did not harm me to listen. Besides, he was giving me a ride to the airport, saving me thirty-odd dollars. In addition, he was suffering from some mysterious illness he would not admit to. And finally, as if that weren't enough, there was the matter of certain carnal fantasies I was beginning to entertain about his wife. These were good reasons, I thought, for feeding him questions and listening to the answers. However baffling or esoteric the things he said, they were easier to reckon with than this other question-and-answer session that had switched on inside me.

The last thing he said to me, at the airport, was, "I want you to come for Shabbos next week, after we get back."

I smiled. I knew, of course, that I would never see these people again. Even to consider meeting in New York returned us to where we'd been on the plane: an unlikely and burdensome flirtation with the exotic, like a sidewalk conversation with a wino. But bringing a wino home with you—or going home with *him*—was another matter. And in the end what would I have to show for it? A story to tell my friends. A bit of cheap cultural imperialism. A bad idea.

I sneaked a glance at the backseat. There was Magda, clutching her arms to her sides, looking out the window. Her nostrils were so tiny I wondered that she got any air through them.

The engine was humming, bad idea, bad idea.

"You'll call?"

"Sure," I said.

"Promise?"

I smiled. I could not remember the last time I'd been asked to deliver on a promise. But I went ahead and swore I would come, when I knew for a fact that I wouldn't. I had already disappointed several people that day; why not disappoint this one too?

"Good," said Aaron Brenner. "I look forward."

He gave me their home address in Crown Heights, writing it on the back of one of the little CPA cards he seemed to carry everywhere. I put it in my pocket, next to the card he'd given me two days before. Then I grabbed my garment bag and stepped out onto the hot macadam. Closing the car door behind me, I sensed that in my absence Magda would not move, as most of us would, from the backseat to the front.

Indeed, when I looked over my shoulder, I saw that she hadn't. Her head, framed in the sloping back window, looked tiny and delicate as a doll's. Her husband was addressing a remark to her in the rearview mirror. Whether she answered him or not I was unable from my vantage point to tell. Finally he gunned the engine and pulled away.

The terminal was cold, and smelled of popcorn and cigarettes. People were streaming around me, clutching possessions, making transitions, filling the air with small talk of departure and return. Flight announcements echoed through the vast interior spaces. I listened hard for mine.

On the way to the gate I had to dodge a posse of Hare Krishnas. With their shaved heads and tangerine glow they strode across the gleaming floor, chanting their strange music over and over, unaware, or perhaps merely unconcerned, that the words were getting lost in the ambient noise.

CHAPTER 3

I Am in No Way Defensive About My Marriage

Back in New York, I immersed myself in routine. I caught up on work. I puttered around the apartment. I read books, listened to public radio, saw the necessary movies. I had friends of intelligence and feeling whom I drank with in downtown bars, sharing complicated stories, swapping advice. Afterward, thundering back uptown on the subway, it seemed possible to believe that my life was not going so badly after all. True, there were cavities, major ones, perhaps even alarming ones. But I also had a good deal more freedom than most people. And freedom was great. Freedom was a precious resource. Freedom was something to be savored.

I was feeling so free and so great that I went out to Macy*s, spent a hundred and thirty dollars on a cappuccino machine, and mailed it off to Warren and Debbie in Houston, hoping to atone for my performance at the wedding. This was now the third extravagant wedding gift I'd bought for Warren, I realized, and he was not yet forty. Meanwhile he still owed me for my first.

About my marriage I will make full disclosure, being in no way defensive on the subject. Melinda Marks was her name. We were together six years, approximately four of which we were married, approximately two of which we were miserable. We'd met at a party of some kind at NYU. Warren, who had dragged me there—who was, in those days, *always* dragging me to parties—introduced us with his usual stoned aplomb. "Please," he'd implored her, "take this guy under your wing. He's deserving but ineffectual. Look at those big sad eyes. A bad case of all dressed up and no place to go."

Melinda, affecting no interest, frowned. She seemed tired. A scholarship kid, she carried a heavy load of course work all week and then spent Friday and Saturday nights waiting tables at Chumleys, where she was ogled, abused, ignored, and stiffed by her own classmates. Under the circumstances she had no time for sudsy or ironic banter. Even her fine blonde hair, dangling onto her forehead, was an annoyance. She brushed it back with the flat of her hand; when that didn't work, she tucked it severely behind one ear. If that hadn't worked I believe she would have gone ahead and cut it off. Slim-hipped in jeans and a tee-shirt, too busy for makeup, she looked as if she had already that semester taken on one project too many. "Okay," she said flatly. "Let's dance."

"What?"

"C'mon, Sammy," Warren said, "get with the program." He seized Melinda's hand, then seized mine, then folded the two into a ball, laying his own on top in careless benediction. "Step up and greet your fate."

And so she was. If I had been lacking for poise and purpose in my life, Melinda appeared to have these things in surplus. In her little efficiency on Sullivan Street she baked her own bread, cut her own hair, sewed her own fashions. From her ears dangled bright green alligator earrings she'd made out of wires, beads, and findings; for a time these became coveted items around the theater department, where she majored, and where it was generally agreed that one day she might just hit as an actress. Melinda herself was dubious. She thought she was unpretty, head too big, eyes too small, and voice too deep for ingenue roles—better-suited to weary mothers, suicidal best friends, tough small-town girls who got away. The near-broken, the down-but-coping, the Sonyas, the second-act Irinas: these were the parts she embraced, the molds she poured herself into, fluid and smoldering.

In the end, we too were a kind of theater piece. I remember the view from Melinda's window in the afternoon light—the shadowy jumble of the Village tenements, their coats of soot zippered with fire escapes, and, farther south, the glittering glass and frenzied tilt of Wall Street—was like some thrilling stage flat which we had ourselves constructed from the scattered materials of the streets, as if no part of the city, not even its worst, most disposable junk, stood outside the playhouse of our emotion. Not that it was all magic and sighs. At first there were the usual problems: the sex was bad, our friends didn't mix, and we had a few minor skirmishes over territory. But we hung in there. And soon we began to notice how alert we had become to the texture of things: how rich our food tasted, how much light poured through the windows in the morning and how satiny and weightless was the dark of the evening, and how implicated we were in each other's lives all of a sudden, how easy to be together and how hard to be separate, two and not one.

I was twenty-one years old and had not been successful in love before and so was not prepared for its effects. It was like some high mode of transport, one of those predawn taxi rides when the road unfurls like a ribbon, the steam puffs merrily out of the sewer grates, and all the lights are green. It seemed to extend my reach. I had more viscera, more nerve endings; more things touched me but did not hurt. Other people, that odd and profligate species, came into better focus. Out on the streets, feeling easy and fingered by grace, I'd smile at every stranger, dispense a handful of change to every homeless person, every panhandler, every raging soul with a petition. I could afford to do these things because I had Melinda. Because I was part of a couple now, dashing through the canyons of SoHo with the other couples, that extravagant club to which I'd miraculously gained entry, my pockets were deep and full of treasure.

And then, as happens with miracles, it began in time to seem a little less than miraculous, merely a pleasurable turn in reality's road, something that could have been predicted with the proper map, something I'd earned and would go on earning, inevitably.

Then one day school was out. As a gesture of our seriousness we moved uptown, to a tiny one-bedroom apartment on West Ninety-fourth Street. The kitchen looked into an airshaft, the neighbors were out of Roman Polanski, the hallway smelled of aged and incinerating matter, but the rent was two hundred dollars a month. Besides we would not be there long. It was only a transitional home, a holding action until we could gather our resources for something better. A temporary arrangement.

In the autumn we were married at City Hall. I was on jury duty so I was in the neighborhood anyway, and Melinda ran out on a lunch shift, pretending to be sick. Or was she pretending? I felt a little queasy myself.

So did Warren, who'd come in from Brooklyn to witness what he had wrought. With him he brought his soon-to-be-first wife, Petra, a very tall and reticent Swiss girl who studied with Martha Graham. Warren was starting film school at Columbia. This was before Petra developed problems with the bones in her feet and Warren developed problems with his adviser, his peers, his program, and, he claimed, the cinematic medium itself—problems which would eventually lead to Petra's return to Europe and Warren's interest in radiology. But that was later. On the day of our wedding the two of them were just beginning to spread their wings, and so were we. After the ceremony we had lunch at a noodle joint in Chinatown, playing wheel-of-chance with the lazy Susan and making rather too glib a production of reading our fortunes. That took care of the honeymoon. Then I paid the bill and returned to the courthouse for the afternoon testimony, Warren and Petra went back to Brooklyn, and Melinda was left to ride back uptown on the subway—alone, worrying the area of her finger which for reasons of economy and bohemianism we'd disdained to cover with a ring—to the temporary transitional home in which, a dozen years later, I still resided.

And yet, for all its apparent wrongheadedness, our marriage, I maintain, was a hopeful, deliberate, even *innocent* act. We were not going to content ourselves with the easy things—the shacking up, the drifting, the extended adolescence. No, we were beyond that. Melinda was going to be a great Chekhovian actress and I was going to be a great, well, *something*, and meanwhile we'd be married, because marriage would put us on a higher plane of intentionality than our peers, because marriage was what serious people like us did to assert to the world—or at least to our parents, or to ourselves—that we were more capable and mature than we looked, and thus deserving of good treatment.

The world, however, is a moody place, with assertions of its own. It let us have our way for a while and we enjoyed a couple of good years before one day it seemed to change its mind about us altogether. And then, as that great Chekhovian, Chekhov himself, might have said, then came the hard part.

This was at the beginning of the Reagan era, a period of retrenchment for us all. I had dropped out of graduate school for the second time and was embarked on a series of demeaning part-time jobs, trying to pay off some small portion of my student loans. Melinda, ever practical, had put acting aside and was auditing classes in the Russian department at Columbia, trying to decide whether to enroll. We were also trying to arrive at a consensus on such matters as where to live, whether and when to have a baby, and who should come home at five o'clock to feed the cat. None of these decisions came easily to us. We'd take long contentious strolls down in Riverside Park, arguing so viciously as to startle the pigeons into flight. Our lives were too confining. Our apartment was too confining. Manhattan itself was too confining. Meanwhile this rustle of wings. The Hudson just sat there, a big gray field strewn with refuse, some of it ours.

Then Melinda got pregnant.

It seemed an especially long walk we took that afternoon, though it was in fact no different than usual, down to the Boat Basin and back. Neither of us spoke. The wind messed with our clothes, our faces, our heads, reminding us that nothing was inviolate, nothing stayed still. We paused for a while to look at the boats. In the autumnal gloom, leaning against the railing, leaves falling over us like so much ash, we watched those tapered fussed-over vessels bobbing with the tide like so many intrepid bath toys, playthings in some silly, effervescent dream. My chest was tight. In truth I felt very close to Melinda at that moment. My love for her was a knot in my throat; I could hardly breathe around it, waiting for her to say yes. Yes. There were a thousand sound and practical reasons to say no, of course, but I wanted a yes. Yes and we would have the kid. Yes would turn the key, yes would open the door. We had never even known the door was there, but it was, we could see it now, we'd been waiting for it, readying ourselves for it: This moment, this space between worlds, this gray area that was ours to define. This choice . . .

But I was wrong. I must have been wrong. Because Melinda just stood there, jaw locked up tight, still-flat belly pressed against the railing, about to be late for yet another four-to-midnight shift, clutching the neck of the shapeless Mao jacket she'd bought on Orchard Street the previous winter and dearly loved, even though it didn't fit, had never fit, and, I understood in that moment, never would fit for as long as I knew her. "*Oh shit*," she groaned finally, arms half-drowned in the sleeves, "*this can't be how it's supposed to feel.*" And me behind her, unsure where to put my hands, thinking, *it can't be, it is, it can't be, it is* . . .

That night Melinda came home later than usual and put on a tee-shirt before climbing gingerly into bed, where she fell asleep, or pretended to, right away. Not that it mattered. It was already over by then. Even before we got to the clinic, even before we sat down in that room with the mauve carpet and the cheery Muzak, the black girls with their sad-eyed mothers, the Italian girls with their heavy makeup, the Irish girls with their complicated freckles, their no-neck boyfriends fanning sleepily through *Sports Illustrated*—it was already over. Melinda's jaw was clenched; I could hear her molars grinding away as I turned over my credit card—just another retail transaction—watched them run it harshly through the brace, and tear off my receipt. Then we sat and waited to be called. Melinda stared straight ahead. With great delicacy and concentration I picked some lint off my sock. After a few minutes, one of the Irish girls began crying noisily into a tissue. "I wish she'd shut up," Melinda whispered fiercely. "Can't you make her shut up?" But it seemed I could not do that, either.

At first we tried to salvage the marriage in the method of our culture, by going into counseling and by shopping for real estate. The therapy did not work, or perhaps it worked too well: our insight on the subject of all we held against each other grew at such speed that by the time our first mortgage application was rejected we had broken up for good.

Melinda moved to Boston. Somehow in the division of materials she came away with most of the furniture and all of the righteous indignation. I was allotted the apartment, the stereo, the debts, and the therapist.

I saw him once a week for the next four years. His name was David Wolff. A big soft-bellied guy with bushy hair and formidable eyebrows. David's manner was low key, informal to the point of rudeness. He'd answer the phone when it rang. He'd complain about his kids. He'd pop an allergy pill, contemplate his date book, glance out the window, fiddle with his watch. To visit David was to be reminded that the world was a rich and clamorous place in which one's individual neuroses played only the smallest of parts. He did not favor intensity or long Freudian silences. He had never finished his Ph.D. He had written no books; indeed, from the evidence of his office, he had *read* no books. I doubted if he had even chosen the African masks and Impressionist reproductions that hung on the walls at predictable intervals, as if ordered as a starter kit from some do-it-yourself office catalog. Seeing it for the first time, I'd felt sorry for David, almost as sorry as I'd felt for myself. The city was full of shrinks and this was the best I could do? A lousy MSW?

But David was not the lousy one, of course. I was. I was in terrible shape: lonely, underemployed, full of unfocused rage. During my years with Melinda I had managed to develop a good deal of faith in myself, but now it was gone. Now there was nothing. Only the wreckage to be sorted through, the postmortems, the blame.

Which David was all too happy to affix. What did I expect? he wanted to know. Everything at once? Middle age at twenty-five? "These kind of delusions are typical of personality disorder," he said. "There are narcissists who boast and narcissists who apologize. You're the second kind. You apologize when someone steps on *your* foot."

"Maybe so. But isn't that better than the other?"

"What's better?" he asked. "What's worse? Both are destructive; both completely overvalue their role in things. But yours is the kind that gets less done."

Indeed, my progress through space had ground to a halt. My concentration was in tatters, my libido a joke, and I seemed to succumb to every stray cold germ that crossed my path. It was as if my body was looking for excuses to shut down, clam up, burrow in. Only in David's office would I let go. Wednesday mornings I'd cross the park, around the reservoir and its fenced-in, sparkling clarity, its circling joggers and traveling fowl, and then out into the immaculate grid of the East Side. David would usher me in warmly. We'd sit facing each other, two youngish men in leather armchairs, discussing serious matters. In baggy corduroys and oversized sweater, he'd sip meditatively on his coffee mug and nod along with a pained expression when I went on too long for his taste. "Well," he said once, "in a race to nausea it's best to be brief."

He was a fount of such expressions. If my insurance would

have covered it I'd have gone to see him every day, just for his company. Then too, it was in David's office that I first met Donna Frye.

She was sitting on the couch in the reception area, leafing through a magazine and sipping a cup of take-out coffee, her kinky black hair like some disorderly protractor framing the angles of her face. When she looked up I thought I saw reproach in her eyes—I'd startled her in the middle of something. Then I saw that she'd been crying. Not over me, of course, not yet; not even, as it turned out, over *her*, but over the final chapters of *Anna Karenina*.

Donna Frye's parents had divorced late in life, and perhaps as a result she was rather tender on the subject of love's duration. She herself had never married, though she'd lived with a man for several years and had a daughter with him, Alice—a bright, funny, willful child who in deference to all the shit she'd had to deal with had been spoiled a bit more than was good for her. I spoiled her too, once I came on the scene. Why not? Her father lived with someone else now and she had me and her mother to contend with.

A great sage once wrote that if we marry we shall regret it, and if we fail to marry we shall regret it. I would like to report that in my brief time on this planet, I have tested this proposition from both sides, and it is sound.

The week after I returned from Houston, Donna had her apartment painted. This was not in itself unusual. Donna had her apartment painted about once a year, in part because she was a woman of restless and capricious tastes, and in part because her super, a Dominican gentleman named Carlos, was infatuated with her. The poor man had suffered from my visits over the years. Emerging from the elevator in the morning, sleepy, baggily outfitted, I could see the effort it must have cost him not to stave my soft head in with a wrench. Even in his spattered overalls Carlos cut an imposing figure: tall, white-haired, exuberant, Cesar Romero with a potbelly. I often teased Donna, and she often teased me, to the effect that Carlos would make a better catch. Carlos would take her dancing, which I didn't. Carlos would buy her flowers, which I didn't. Carlos would fly her and Alice to the islands every winter, which I didn't. Above all, Carlos would paint her apartment once a year, which I didn't, as was being evidenced yet again the week I returned from Houston.

Donna called to tell me this. We had had an ugly scene a few weeks back and not spoken to each other since. Nor were we, her tone coolly implied, speaking now. But she wanted to inform me that she and Alice would be staying at her sister's apartment on Seventy-ninth Street for a few days, should I wish to contact her for any reason.

"Okay," I said. "Thanks for letting me know."

There was a pause, a little space that allowed us each to run a cost-benefit analysis on the prospect of a conversation.

"So how are you?" I asked. "What have you been doing?"

"Me? Oh, wonderful, marvelous, extravagant things."

"Like what?"

"Well, let's see. There's work. Doctors' appointments. Baby-sitters. Meetings with the co-op board. An occasional glass of cold wine in front of the television. And you?"

"I went to Houston."

"Oh, right. The wedding. You and that creepy friend of yours, what's his name—"

"Warren."

"Right. Warren. *Warren.*"

"What's this about doctors?" I asked. "Is Alice sick?"

"Alice? You must be kidding. Alice is never sick. Alice is indestructible. Alice is the mother of us all."

"You sound a little tired," I said.

"Yes," she said. "Poor me."

Neither of us said anything for a moment.

Finally I cleared my throat. "Listen, I have an idea. If the kid's so indestructible, why not leave her with your sister and come over?"

"Right now?" Donna took a breath. "I don't think so, Sam."

"Why not?"

"It's late. I'm in my bathrobe. Also, I'm pretty sure I don't want to."

There is, however, a peculiar charisma to destructive or imperiled relationships beside which the rest of life can seem—particularly in the dark hours—pale, fey, even super-fluous, and so perhaps this explains how it came to pass that Donna stayed not at her sister's place that night but at mine, where she did not really want to, and where together we proceeded to collaborate in some of the most vigorous and decisive lovemaking in our history. The word took on a peculiar reality for me that week: Lovemaking. Love-makers. With all of our problems, it had become for both of us by this point a kind of strenuous, hopeful, literal exercise: we were really trying to *make* it.

"Oh boy," she sighed afterward, toying with the hair on my chest. "Here we go again."

"Yes."

"Of course this is all a terrible mistake, isn't it?"

"Possibly so."

Donna was silent for a moment.

"I mean," I said, "no, of course this is not a terrible mistake."

She nodded encouragingly. "Keep going. Tell me something. I don't care how silly or trivial. Just talk."

"I'm thinking of quitting my job," I said.

"I take it back," she groaned. "I do care."

I laughed. What a game character. If only I'd had a sister like Donna, I thought, my life might have turned out completely different. But perhaps it was not too late. Because after a few more nights like this, lying in bed under a ceiling striped by moonlight, sweat cooling on my skin, entangled by taut brown limbs that were not my own, listening to a steady intake of breath that was not my own, feeling the percussive rumble of a heart that was not my own, what had the week before seemed clear to me—our unsuitability as a couple—was no longer clear at all. Nothing was. Donna's weight on my chest as she slept was a comfort; or was it a burden? The casual discarded pile of her underclothes on the floor: a mess, or the softest, most aromatic of pillows? The tangents of moonlight on the ceiling above us: a ladder to fulfillment, or the bars of a cell? We should do ourselves a favor and get married, I thought. And then a moment later: we should do ourselves a favor and break up for good.

What did it matter? Marriage was itself only a temporary solution. I thought of my own, and those of my friends, like Warren Pinsky, who, I now remembered, was in Hawaii at the moment on his honeymoon. Was he staring at the ceiling too?

In the silence I could hear people moving around in the other apartments. The divinity student in 9F humming in the shower. Mrs. Pearl from 9H yelling at her cat. The attorney in 9J playing his Willie Dixon tapes before bed. The building was full of such people. Lone wolves, shut-ins, dropouts: a halfway house for black sheep. Just then the refrigerator compressor kicked on. Donna didn't stir. A scent of apricots rose from her scalp. *I don't know her*, I thought. Her very closeness, even the quiet regularity of her breathing, was somehow a reminder of this. I did not know her, I had not known Melinda, I could not know other people. What was it that shielded their reality from me? Donna had come over on Wednesday ominously hinting, lest I get the wrong idea, of new men in her life. Then we'd proceeded to bed, where both of us had apparently gotten the same wrong idea at the same time. And now in a few hours the sun would come up, and it would be Friday, and in her apartment Carlos would be putting the last touches on the molding, and still the subject of our future had not been broached. Why? Was Donna as uncertain as I was about wrong ideas and right ones?

Then I noticed something on the floor. A slip of paper that must have fallen out of her pants. I ignored it for a while. Then a paranoid idea began to take shape. I had of course assumed Donna was lying when she spoke of new men in her life, that this was only one of the trivial guiles lovers employ to give each other pain. But suppose I was wrong. Suppose the slip of paper was a note from her new lover, some kinky endearment or imperative. Suppose it was an offer of marriage.

Gently I slipped out from under her and went to retrieve the piece of paper. Then I tiptoed down the hallway. I felt wired, alert, a burglar in my own apartment. The quality of the paper stock was high, and this too disturbed me; it conveyed an aura of substantiality. My own notes were written on flimsy pink pads I stole from the office. Was she dating a banker?

I went into the bathroom and locked the door behind me before I switched on the overhead light.

The note was not a note, it turned out, but a business card. *Aaron Brenner CPA, Brooklyn, New York*. And on the back: *718-555-8890. Come!*

The next morning I propped the card against a stapler, consulting it at intervals as I proofed some text. According to the calendar, I had agreed to come to Brooklyn for dinner that same evening. Not that I had any intention of going, of course. For all I knew this Brenner fellow spent half his life running around the world dispensing business cards to strangers and inviting them to his home. Even if by some fluke I *did* go, how did I know he'd remember he invited me?

But I wasn't going, so it didn't matter. Instead I would work at the office all day, then go down and have dinner with Donna and Alice at their Chelsea apartment—to celebrate the fresh coat of paint on the walls and to facilitate, a bit later, the Big Talk About the Future we'd been avoiding all week to such terrific sexual effect.

The office was quiet. Though this was not unusual for a Friday in midsummer, it disturbed me a little. There was a thickness in the air, a feeling of suspended breath, shoes ready to drop. The elevators opened and closed mysteriously. The watercooler made odd hollow gurgling sounds. I wondered if I was missing something. Around ten, Ronnie Oldham emerged from his cubicle but, untypically for him, did not stop to poke his head into mine. Was he avoiding me? We had not seen much of each other since my two weeks off in June. Perhaps he was simply busy. Or perhaps he and Ray Spurlock were up to something, conspiring together, dividing my fate between them.

The office, like most offices, fed on this sort of psychic confusion. Every memo, every fragment of chitchat, every closed door or extinguished light could be read at least two ways. Even my hiring had been a protracted, curvilinear, and ultimately inscrutable affair, involving three different interviews and a strenuous series of tests and evaluations. Finally, after several weeks, I was ushered into the office of courtly, silver-haired Arlen Ashby. Arlen's shades, I remember, were drawn. Having had no small amount of gin at lunch that day—I could smell it on his breath—he had taken on the mannered suavity and gentleness of spirit that one finds in a certain kind of alcoholic in the late afternoon. Perhaps this was why my résumé had such a pleasing effect upon him. It may have helped that Arlen too, as he informed me at once, hailed from upstate. Or perhaps it was my two aborted master's degrees, or my brief stints as an entry-level functionary in advertising, publishing, and bartending (his eyes lit up at this last one) that intrigued him. Whatever it was, something about me that day seemed to appeal to the man, and inspired him to overlook my middling scores on the editing tests and give me a job.

I was sent to work at the copy desk for a "trial period." After one month I was transferred to the Movies desk to replace Guy Somers, who was on leave that season writing screenplays in Los Angeles. When he returned, speaking wistfully of development deals gone sour, I was moved to Sports. There I subbed for an amiable psychotic named Howard Herman, who was ostensibly at home working on a mystery novel but was in fact under treatment at Creedmore. Following this I spent eighteen months in Business filling in for Janet Sharpe, our gifted young reactionary, who'd left to write speeches for the lieutenant governor's office. Then one spring afternoon Al Pasko, a senior editor, resolved his midlife crisis by sailing off to Bimini with a twenty-three-year-old congressional aide, and in the subsequent scramble I was moved to Political Affairs.

Finally, after years of sitting at other people's desks while they were off pursuing their glamorous pursuits, I landed in the back of the book again, in a quiet corner on the thirty-first floor, among the coterie of brilliant grinds who put together the Science page. And it was there, improbably, I'd found a sort of home. The thick-glasses crew, for all their brittle intensities, were believers in a cause—the values and protocols of Science—and like most believers there was a sweeping wholeheartedness in their approach to things, a capacity for discipline and engagement that was itself a kind of devotion. They worked impossible hours. For fun they ran marathons, learned Chinese, played chess with their computers, went to the Galápagos. The planet, they seemed to think, was awesome but not infinite in its complexities. The borders between the known and the unknown could be perceived. With the right methodology, perhaps they could even be transgressed. The one thing they could not be was ignored.

Slowly I began to adjust to their ways, tune into the strange hard frequencies of the scientific mind. My father had been a chemist and so perhaps I was not quite so foreign to such matters as I imagined. Pecking at my keyboard, I discovered an order that was like a musical presence behind the waves of info-static, a high keening song that had been playing in another language, it seemed, all along. Across my desk came pieces on strange attractors, soil enhancement, genetic engineering, and many other odd, engaging topics I knew nothing about. How could I? I'd been a generalist, a liberal artist: eager for synthesis, starved for coherence. These limitations in fact gave me a weird value. Colleagues poked their heads into my cubicle to run ideas past me or solicit advice. My opinions were taken seriously even as they were condescended to for being underinformed. I was a kind of resident Everyman, our on-site stand-in for The Reader—that fickle, unimaginative creature who flipped through our pages while on the toilet.

"You're a convert waiting to happen," Ronnie Oldham told me once over lunch. "A piece of fly paper for every stray idea."

Perhaps he was right. The office was located near Radio City on Sixth Avenue—an area in which such things as soil and its enhancement seemed as distant and dreamlike as the Arctic—and I remember times when I'd emerge from the lobby at the end of the day and crane my neck to find my own alcove window hanging there on the thirty-first floor, a yellow moth stuck in the illuminated web that was midtown, and I would feel, amid the flapping pigeons and the swirling paper and the violet disorderly rush of the evening, a kind of vertigo that bordered on happiness.

However, it didn't last. After a few months the novelty turned to routine, my interest began to flag, my work grew spotty. Soon I found myself devoting more and more attention to the particulate grid of the ceiling, where I sought answers to the question of where I was headed next, and when. And what, in a general sense, I was *waiting* for.

The phone rang at my desk. "Just calling to confirm," Donna said brightly.

"Seven o'clock, right?"

"Try to come early if you can. It's Friday. She's always bouncing off the walls by six."

"I'll come at six-thirty."

"Good. Oh, and I forgot, it's her half-birthday tomorrow, so bring a cake."

"Half-birthday?"

"I know it sounds stupid. It's one of those mother's things you find yourself doing sometimes. Just bring a cake, okay?"

"Chocolate?"

"Naturally. Wait, hold on—" She put the phone down. I could hear her chewing out her secretary, whom she adored, some mix-up about the day's appointments. She worked as an aide to the Bronx borough president and so mix-ups and appointments were her life. "Last night," Donna said in a low voice when she came back on the line.

"What about it?"

"I was magnificent, wasn't I?"

"Yes."

"Tell me."

"You were magnificent."

"I wanted to hear you say it."

"And me?" I asked.

"Oh, you . . ." her voice had turned mournful.

"What's the matter? You sounded so brisk and happy a second ago."

"It's just that I remembered something I have to do today."

I waited for her to elaborate upon the point, but she fell silent.

"Listen, I have to go. I'll see you in a few hours. We'll have a nice party. We'll talk."

"Sam?"

She hesitated. I could picture her behind her desk up in the Bronx borough hall—a dark, green-eyed, big-haired woman in a paisley sundress, doodling in the margins of a legal pad. "I heard you, you know. Padding around last night."

"My back was stiff," I said.

"Mmm."

"I could really feel it last night."

"Really," she said.

"Yes. Down at the base of my spine. Like something was going on, something was about to happen. Ever get that feeling?"

"What?"

"I said, do you ever get that feeling?"

"I used to," she said, and clicked off.

*   *   *

Around four-thirty I knocked off and, feeling restless and deprived of light, decided to walk the whole way home.

It was a warm summer day. The air was sulphurous and heavy in midtown, but as I headed north and west there was a mild breeze. I went down into Riverside Park and took the footpath along the Hudson. Small pools of oil floated on the water; in them hapless rainbows struggled to life. Docks listed and creaked, gulls wheeled overhead. There were salt traces in the breeze, a kind of brackish ripeness as sweet as it was sour, and as I neared the docks that led to the Boat Basin I thought, as I often did, of that chilly afternoon with Melinda eight years before. Eight years. And yet here I still was.

But I was not alone. The weather had drawn all of us out—joggers, tennis players, old people, roller skaters, martial artists. Catholic girls skipped home in plaid skirts and kneesocks, chanting silly rhymes. Emerald flies circled the benches. Dogs strained at their leashes, sniffing the ground, chasing phantoms. At Eighty-third Street, a group of teenage boys were hanging out in their hockey shirts and backward-facing baseball caps, smoking cigarettes and talking shop. There was a quality of martial aggression in the way they occupied the path that told me they were not going to move out of my way. I would have to walk around them.

They watched me pass without comment. Then a couple of the larger boys, as if in afterthought, yelled a few taunts in my direction, and another one—tall, thin, and ravaged by acne—called me a name. I was aware of being afraid, but not very much. I could see that they were only restless and bored, wired with hormones they were unable to channel—as I had been at their age—and would soon lose interest if I kept walking. Which they did. They grunted a few more insults and then fell back to their desultory huddle, leaving me to finish my walk alone.

On the phone machine there was a hang-up. It might have been someone from the office. Or it might have been my mother, a creature of habit, who called regularly on Fridays at four o'clock, in response to which I had become a creature of habit myself and regularly arranged to be out at that hour. It was terrible of me but not, I think, uniquely so. Or it might have been Donna, who disdained leaving messages, calling to confirm our dinner, or cancel it. It might have been anyone. New York was full of blinking lights, crossed signals, missed connections. It might have been anyone at all.

An hour later I was shaved and dressed and rushing down Broadway. It was after seven. The sun was an enormous flame just dipping to extinguish itself in the river. I had fallen asleep after my shower and was now running late. In my haste I nearly stumbled against an elderly man in a fedora and rain-coat who was ahead of me on the sidewalk. He walked very slowly, round-shouldered, feeling his way over the cracks with tiny steps.

I recognized him from my building: he lived on the fourth floor. He had a Polish accent and about a dozen cats and his wife, who had always been very kind to me in the elevator, had died in the middle of the night a few years before. I waved as I brushed past but he did not appear to notice. I suppose that after a lifetime of noticing things the elderly must grow tired of it and begin to hoard their concentration, reserve it for the essentials, the fight against time and infirmity. Under one arm, I observed, he carried a blue felt pouch with gold Hebrew lettering on the side. That Hasid, Aaron Brenner, had had one like it on the plane. For his *tefillin*. A kind of ornate Jewish blood pressure device, from the look of it. How odd they were, these rituals of devotion!

It was only standing on the platform a few minutes later—breathing the dank, fetid air of the station with a hundred other people awaiting the downtown train—that I remembered those kids in the park. Their communal presence, jocular and bored. The arrogant way they'd shouldered me off the path. The name they'd called me . . .

Hebe.

A dumb little word. The whole ride downtown it echoed clumsily in my head, a belt buckle banging in an empty dryer. It was like the first time someone called me *Mister Karnish*. My instinct was to duck, certain it was aimed not at me but over my head, at the shadow of my father. Wasn't he the Mister? Wasn't he the Hebe?

As we squealed and swayed through the underground tunnels, I watched my reflection flicker, pale and yellow, in the train's black windows. Just a word, a dumb little word. For a while I played around with it in a fussy, clinical sort of way, as if it were a small bomb to be defused. I tried to dissect it into parts, harmless lexical fragments, bits of mere sound. But this proved difficult to execute. Not everything lent itself to such treatment. Not everything, it seemed, was as divisible into pieces as I was.

CHAPTER 4

SUMMER OF LOVE

We all get tired of living in the past. But apparently the past never tires of living in us.

There were times that summer when, encountering my own reflection, I would recognize the face of someone else, some not-quite-me whose features roughly corresponded to my own. In recent days I had begun to spot this person more and more around the city, in windows and mirrors and a thousand walking dreams. Each time it gave me a peculiar feeling of light-headedness—as if life was carrying me toward something, or death was carrying something toward me, or we were both in motion all the time, orbiting each other like moons.

I did not attend my father's funeral. But I'll come back to that in a minute. A little background first.

I grew up in Rochester, New York. It is a nice enough city on a modest scale: gray, windswept, lake-oriented, middle class. Because of its proximity to Canada a certain geographical suspension obtains that is endemic to border regions, a betweenness. It is in the weather, in the air, in the audio and visual signals that ebb and flow across the lake, and like any other form of radiation it seeps into the body in funny ways, leaves hot traces in the mind. This may account for the area's enduring appeal for radical and religious movements—the Mormons, the suffragettes—and for one of those arcane bits of local history one learns about in grade school: The Great Disappointment of 1844.

In October of that year, the members of an obscure adventist sect, the Millerites, flocked to Rochester to witness the Revelation. It had been prophesied that the Revelation would occur on a particular day—a Wednesday, I think—and would be audible from a particular hillside a mile west of town. So the Millerites settled in to wait. Around sunset, the first waves of confusion set in. The next day saw some spirited debate; the next, some petty violence. Finally, after a week or so, the cold winds blew down from the north, and the heavy weather fell, and only then did the Millerites return to their homes, leaving that gloomy burg on the lake to soldier on, no more or less godless than before. And that was The Great Disappointment.

Of course, even if He *had* shown up, it would scarcely have mattered to a family like mine. Ours was a secular life. We had a house in a good area of town, an A-frame, smallish but built to last. My mother had gone with the realtor to pick it out, and my mother—a tall, brisk, convivial blonde, with a bouffant modeled on Jackie Kennedy's—had a shrewd eye for what was solid in this world and what was not. An only child, her father dead in a car crash, a mother who from some chemical imbalance in her head heard voices and suffered visions throughout her long life, she'd learned early on to nurture herself and take counsel where she could find it. From a high school history teacher she'd caught the socialist bug, spent long lonely evenings in her bedroom reading about the Spanish Civil War and listening to the Weavers. In college she volunteered for Henry Wallace and Adlai Stevenson and, almost as a matter of course, began to date a succession of Jewish men. One she met on a crosstown bus: a dark, underfed, rather cynical young man with an evasive European accent. He worked as a junior chemist at Kodak, he said, though his ambition was to become a doctor. Together they went to foreign movies, jazz clubs; they smoked cigarettes and talked about the Bomb. They eloped.

I was born three years later. The pregnancy was uneventful.

In the sixth month, running a hand over my mother's belly, her mother solemnly declared me twins. No one paid her any attention, of course. No one even remembered what she'd said later, when the problem developed. A twist of the umbilical cord, a tiny, all but invisible tie-up in the dark reaches of the birth canal; nobody's fault, just one of those quirky random events that tear the veil off the quotidian world and expose it in all its perilousness. The result was that I was born healthy but my brother, my twin, who followed me out a half-minute later, was stillborn.

I suppose there's no getting over such things, not really. But if the death of my brother broke my mother's spirit, when she healed she healed stronger, the way bones do, they say. She joined the Y, grew muscular from swimming. In the little free time she had off from school—she'd gone back for a master's in social work—she read to the blind, doled out food to the hungry, drove cancer patients to their doctors' appointments. Her weekly calendar sat by the kitchen telephone, dense with hieroglyphics. I came to resent the sight of it. A few unmarked pages, a couple of weeks of doing nothing; would that have been so awful? But she had always been a doer, my mother, and Loss had only turned up the heat and made her impatient, high-minded, and confrontational as well. By the time I was eight she had acquired a minor reputation around town as a pain in the neck. A *professional* pain in the neck—chair of two or three service organizations, the loudest civil rights advocate in the county, and an officer of the Democratic Party, itself an impoverished local minority that needed befriending.

Because she often had meetings downtown that ran late, I'd be called upon to cook—or more accurately, to heat up the casseroles my mother had cooked and frozen over the weekend. This, then, was my political apprenticeship, my contribution to the good fight. This was how I could please her. I could not march in Washington or Selma, I could not raise funds for Eugene McCarthy, but I could heat the oven and cut up the grapefruit and be sitting there at the kitchen table, watching the afternoon shadows envelop the backyard, when my father walked in at six-fifteen.

My father.

My father was a self-effacing man. Ask him to pose for a picture, he'd duck his head. Throw him a birthday party, he'd come down with a cold. Tall and angular, with a sharp-cut nose and sleepy brown eyes, he operated on some high bleak ironic frequency that most people never heard, as if he were forever retelling some joke at his own expense. It was hard to know how seriously to take him. Even his affections were opaque. Toward me they took delicate, reticent forms, soft pats with his hands and little bird-pecks with his lips. I was his only child, his only survivor; he did not toss me in the air, turn me upside down, tickle me until I peed in my pants. He did not let go. He appeared to keep part of his energies in reserve, as if concealing his impatience for me to grow up already so we could speak of more interesting matters than toys and comics and baseball and the addition of simple fractions. Like many adults, he often seemed frustrated for no reason. He rarely drank or hit or raised his voice, and yet I was aware of his temper the way one is sometimes aware of a lake or a valley: by the cumulative mass of everything that surrounds it.

The fact is I felt sorry for the man. He did not take much pleasure in other people's company. He'd accompany me to Little League games and on a good day he'd chat with the other fathers for an entire minute before opening the newspaper. With my mother he went to barbecues and cocktail parties and pretended to enjoy himself as she dominated the room with her bright efficient smile, her intelligence, her will. But the paper went with him. It went with him to the swimming club too, where he'd sit smoking on a lawn chair, shirtless, his lean chest scrubby and dark, wearing the same long pants, black socks, and brown hat he wore to work. Occasionally he'd lift his head from the crossword, gazing down wryly into the pool (my mother a steady presence along the margin, patiently stroking out her laps) as if the very clarity of the water was a source of humor to him. He never went in. He never so much as put on a *bathing suit*. But every time the lifeguards blew their whistles, he'd jump, and his face would turn white. Every time.

If from my mother I learned to honor resilience and present-mindedness, my father, then, without intending to, taught me a kind of dreamy and reflexive *other*-mindedness. There were four chairs at our dinner table—they came in a set from Sears—and at times I'd catch him addressing himself to the empty one, to some invisible auditor who joined us regularly for coffee. After dinner my mother would talk on the phone, and he'd go out to the yard, chain-smoking, looking over the herb garden and the woodpile and his other domestic undertakings, as if only in this thin band of twilight—with the roar of distant mowers and the insects chuttering in the trees around him—could he ever believe in their reality. Or perhaps it was just the reverse, and it was their unreality he sought, their transparency. Who knows? He was one of those men who seems forever to be conducting private symphonies in his head, but the score he kept to himself.

Of course he was Jewish and my mother wasn't but this was not a deep subject for any of us. He never went to synagogue, or referred to Jewish or Zionist issues, or affiliated himself in any way except for the incidental fact that many of his friends from work were also Jewish. But so were many of my mother's friends from work. For that matter, many were not. Some distinctions are so vague they are not worth harping upon. Each year we were invited to two or three seders for Passover; sometimes we went and sometimes we didn't. We never hosted one ourselves, though my mother—an agnostic Presbyterian, from a long line of agnostic Presbyterians—would have been willing to, I think, if only to show off what a good cook she was, and to underscore that while she did not put any store in religion, neither was there anything in it to fear. It simply was not important enough.

So I was not half-Jewish and half-something else, but half-Jewish and half-nothing. In short, an American kid.

If anything, this pleased my father. He wished me to be as normal, as uncomplicated, as possible. His own accent was an affliction to him. He mumbled, he cleared his throat; had there been a pill to make accents disappear, he'd have taken it. That no such pill existed was unfair. But then unfairness was a condition of life, was it not? His older sister Rose had been the best violinist in their school while he could barely get the thing to squeak. Was that fair? As a result of this unfairness she had gone to the institute in Budapest, where she chose to remain when the rest of the family left for New York in 1937. Fourteen years old the last time he saw her, curly red hair and a plump, heart-shaped face that had already begun to attract attention from the boys—and yet it was he who got out and Rose who did not, he who went to college and Rose who did not, he who got married with a house and a job and a child and Rose who did not did not did not did not.

All of which may or may not have been on his mind that January morning, when, hauling out the trash cans—this was about two years before he died—he discovered a swastika on the garage door. We knew at once where it came from. It was the work of those merry folks in the John Birch Society, a popular group in those days whom my mother had taken as her mission to antagonize. Painted a deep red, the swastika would not wash off. "Good," she crowed, delighted. "Leave it. Let them all see." But my father didn't leave it. He went out into the cold to paint it over, a process that required several coats. I sat there eating pancakes and reading the sports section, waiting for him to finish. There was some sort of Indian Guide powwow that day and I needed him to accompany me, which would undoubtedly be a trial for us both. So I was in no hurry. Occasionally, I'd lift my head to see him out there, hunched over in his beret and black gloves, his face narrow and gaunt, his expression remote—not so very different, to be honest, than had he been shoveling the driveway. But the thing would not go away. Later that night I saw him out there again, a dark silhouette against the snow. And above him the moon, riddled and pocked and half-drenched in shadow.

Like most of our friends in Rochester, we used to take our summer vacations down at the Finger Lakes. For three weeks my parents would rent a cottage on the southern shore of Canandaigua Lake, near Bristol Springs. I do not know why we never tried the northern shore, where the bass were said to be larger and more fickle, or for that matter why we never tried one of the other scenic lakes—Hemlock, or Conesus, or little Honeoye—nearby. Perhaps we did. But in my memory it is always the same place, always Canandaigua Lake, and that musty little cottage with the sagging davenport, the eternally blocked, unusable fireplace, and the screened-in porch where my father sat and smoked and listened to the radio, and retreated, if such a thing was possible, even farther inside himself. And always the same summer, 1967, when the biopsy results came back from the lab, informing us of the stomach cancer that would kill him the following March.

Not that I had any idea at the time, of course. Marriages are conspiratorial by nature. To be a child—an only child—is to be locked in a cell of incomprehension. And that was how the cottage functioned that summer, like a Chinese box, with sliding doors and hidden vaults. So I went about my business, fishing and canoeing with my summer friends in my inviolate summer bubble, and my mother buried herself in files she'd brought from the office, and my father grilled fish and sweet corn for supper, then passed the remainder of the evenings in an Adirondack chair on the porch, sipping hot tea out of a glass and observing the action of the wind on the lake as if in that rippling collage of shadow and light he could read his fate. Gnats orbited his dark head like electrons. Perhaps, had I been paying attention, I might have seen that his face had already begun to show the first losses of weight and color— was he hearing those lifeguards' whistles?—and that my mother's had begun to yellow and sag as well, from too little sleep. I might have seen that. And while I was at it, I might also have discerned, through the washy night-static of the radio, that across the globe in Asia boys not much older than I were getting killed in great numbers, and other boys not much older than I—and girls too—were streaming into a park on the far side of the continent, trailing music and laughter. For among other things, that was the Summer of Love.

Oh, I don't blame myself. I don't. You learn what you can and at your own pace; there's no use poking around the ashes, years later, with guilt's long stick. My father lived and his sister didn't. I lived and my brother didn't. My mother lived and my father didn't. Can these things be explained to anyone's satisfaction? Does it matter, does it affect the outcome, whether we understand them or not?

Though born with my mother's blonde hair and rosy coloring, over the years I have darkened in any number of ways, so that I now resemble my father more and more—the long face, the brown eyes with their intimations of melancholy and abstraction, the prominent nose. And yet I prefer to think of myself as my mother's child. She was the one who, for all her lost causes, her high idealism, chose the earthly way. She was the one who bore down on life with clarity and reason, who refused to give in to the lassitude and sentimentality of grief. It was her wish, for example, that I stay home the day of the funeral. "I have to go but you don't," she said. "What good does it do? You're morbid enough as it is."

She was right, of course. What good would it do? So I didn't go. I played it smart. I made a bid for solidity: I walled up my father inside the here and now. But how smart is smart? How solid is solid? Because sometimes when the noise of the world recedes and I am left with only the noise of myself, I believe I can hear him, or my brother, or someone, shuffling around in there, each step ponderous and slow as a heartbeat, looking for a way out.

THE MASTER
OF THE TURNING

Somehow I missed my stop.

It might have been the clatter and roll of the subway. Or perhaps I was off wandering some labyrinth of memory and not paying attention. Anyway I missed it. I missed it by a lot. In fact, by the time I recovered my wits, we had left Manhattan altogether and were rocketing along the bottom of the East River, headed toward Brooklyn.

At this point it was seven-thirty, which did not bode well for Donna's little party. Given the precarious condition of our relationship at the moment, it might even have been construed as sabotage. Construed by Donna, I mean. Trapped in that hot, airless car, pressed on all sides by countless tons of water, I knew myself to be innocent of wrongdoing. Anyway, the solution was simple: I'd call her from the next stop and explain what had happened. It was the kind of thing we'd laugh about later in bed. Later, in bed, we'd really have a great time, I thought, laughing.

With the best of intentions, then, I got off at the next stop, Clark Street. It was now seven-forty. The platform was deserted. A stench of summer urine rose from the littered tracks. I discovered a pay phone on one of the support columns, stuck in a quarter, and dialed Donna's number. Busy.

I called back. Busy. Called back. Busy.

Quarter to eight.

Relax, I thought, it's a test of some sort, a reckoning of will and desire. I called back. Busy. Called back. Busy.

I walked the length of the platform. The concrete was strewn with pages from the morning tabloids, gray and muddy, tracked by countless heels. I read the headlines as best I could, then turned and walked back to the phone.

Busy. Called back. Busy. Called back. Busy.

Five minutes to eight. I took the receiver of the phone and weighed it in my palm. It felt comfortable there, a solid instrument, smooth and shapely, dense with mechanical logic. I bashed it as hard as I could against the pillar.

It really was a solid instrument: everything was left undamaged but the side of my hand.

The man in the token booth now glanced up from his *Post* to bestow upon me a look of doleful and infinite patience. Was he sovereign over this empire of departure and return, or merely a fellow prisoner? In any case, the condition of neither the phone nor my hand worried him in the slightest. He yawned and went back to his reading.

I decided to call Donna's machine at work. She wouldn't be there but perhaps she would think to check in for messages. The truth was I preferred to speak to her machine, to which I'd confessed on similar occasions in the past, and which could be counted on to maintain a cool neutrality no matter the offense. These phone machines were a wonderful invention. I called mine all the time, just to see if someone had called in the past few hours, since the last time I'd checked in, just to see if I might be *missing* something. That private code—my own little piece of the mathematical dream—was access, or so it seemed, to the whole vast realm of the Possible. The soft squeal of the tape rewinding was like an animal sound; it quickened my blood to hear it.

The phone on the platform however, in retribution for my assault, had eaten my quarter. I fished in my jeans for change but found only a nickel and some pennies and, crumpled into a tiny ball, another of Aaron Brenner's business cards. How many had he given me? Every place I turned I seemed to find one.

Had I really promised the man I'd come for dinner? For the life of me I couldn't remember who I had promised what.

And I had forgotten the cake as well.

Eight o'clock. Suddenly I was starving. Eight o'clock on Friday night in the greatest city in the world, and my presence on that deserted platform seemed only to confirm how flimsy and troubled a charade was my adulthood. How long had I been underground, anyway? It felt like years.

I fingered the card in my damaged hand. A bad idea. A weird, awkward, indulgent thing to do.

On the other hand, so was arriving at Donna's two hours late. Alice's bedtime, I recalled, was eight-thirty. So I would get there just in time to have her furious mother all to myself.

There I was, stranded on the middle island of the platform. My hand hurt. My back was stiff. Out beyond the tiled walls, in the network of tunnels that ran like arteries and ventricles from the station's subterranean heart, came the rumble of an advancing train. Good: I'd let it decide the matter for me. If it was headed inbound, I'd ride it home. Outbound and I'd ride it to Crown Heights.

It was inbound. I let it go.

I'd just come from inbound, hadn't I? I knew all about inbound. Inbound was furious static, an empty apartment, a locked roof. I let it go. That hour of a Friday night, the train was full. Bound for Manhattan, its lurid pleasures, its secular marvels. I let it go. People were staring at me through the windows. What was I doing? Why wasn't I moving? I let it go.

Now that I was feeling so choosy I chose to let the next one go after that.

Finally an outbound train arrived, headed for Coney Island. This time I got on. It was one of the older trains and the air conditioning wasn't working. The car had that stale, too-bright look cars get when they are practically deserted: that end-of-the-line unhealthiness. It lurched forward, stopped, lurched forward again. The subway map provided by the MTA was covered with graffiti, but I looked it over anyway, trying to count, through the Day-Glo scrawl of competing logos, the number of stops to Crown Heights. It turned out that Brooklyn was a big city unto itself; there were a great many stops to cover. Well, it figured, didn't it? Either direction I traveled, at that point, I was bound to be in for a very long ride.

Having lived in New York for some years now, I had in the course of things made excursions to all sorts of marginal neighborhoods, but until that Friday evening I had never been to Crown Heights. Marginal was not the word for it. Even to approach the general vicinity of marginal would have required ten or so years of gentrification. The wide boulevard of Eastern Parkway, which ran through the center of Crown Heights, separating the Hasidic enclave from its black neighbors, was cratered and torn. Down the median strip ran a shadowy no man's land, strewn with chunks of pavement and rusty abandoned vehicles and blue police sawhorses that were either left over from a recent fracas or put up in anticipation of one to come. Broken glass glittered in constellations under the anticrime lights. In it a warning could be read, a reminder to New York of what people in Belfast and Beirut already knew: that separation is hard, ugly work. Just how hard and ugly I'd never know, not from one evening. And one evening, believe me, was all I intended to spend here.

Across the median a group of young black men were standing in front of a liquor store, smoking quietly, looking me over. Perhaps they weren't poor and perhaps they weren't drunk; it didn't matter. The questions were the same. What was I doing here with my big white face and my big brown wallet? To whom did I belong? But these were my questions, not theirs. They, after all, knew. It's really very simple, the binary operation of urban life. I was on this side and they were on that.

But being on my side had put me, for the moment, pretty much alone. In coming to Crown Heights I had been expecting something out of Chagall: children streaming from the synagogue, men in fur hats dancing beneath a crescent moon. But the moon was swathed in clouds, and no one was dancing, or even walking, upon the crumbly tilted sidewalk, save for two weary women in hospital fatigues, toting their grocery bags home in the prosaic half-light. The shops along Kingston Avenue were closed. I passed a bookstore, a Caribbean grocery, a laundromat, Yaffa's Academy of Wigs; across the street was a pizzeria, a newsstand, and a maternity boutique. In the darkened windows flyers were posted, offering tours in Israel, weekends in the Catskills and Poconos ("Dance to the Yossi Soibelman Orchestra"), puppet shows, lecture series, and theatrical productions ("Yeshivah Mesores Avos of Hungary Proudly Presents an Evening of Song, Dance, and Drama at Yeshiva of Flatbush High School").

Spanning the two sidewalks, a huge white banner snapping in the breeze: "Moshiach Is Coming! Be a Part of It!"

A part of what? I wandered in the muggy darkness from block to block, checking each sign hopefully against the address on Aaron Brenner's card. It dawned on me after a while that, strictly speaking, I was already lost. But I didn't panic. My intuition told me to be patient, that despite all appearances the course I was taking would prove in time to be the right one. That I was being guided.

After a couple of blocks I happened onto President Street, which in its width and prosperity was like a suburb unto itself. There were maples and dogwoods, and spacious lawns, and big houses with fancy trim and station wagons and children's toys strewn around the driveways. Pots clanged purposefully in the kitchens. Voices called through open windows. All of President Street seemed to be inviting me to dinner. But then I checked the address on the card, and I saw the Brenners did not live on President Street. They lived on Utica Avenue. So I kept walking. On the next block the houses drew closer together again, three-story brownstones and modest brick singles, ringed by fences, the lawns smaller and less fertile, the cars older, sagging with rust. Utica was the block after that. And it was there, at the eastern end of the shadowed street, that I found the house I was looking for.

When I knocked nobody answered. I was not a believer in heaven but I had a personal vision of hell: it was myself bashing phones against pillars and knocking hopelessly on closed doors throughout eternity. I rose on tiptoes, straining to see through the diamond-shaped window at the top of the door. And there they were.

It was in truth like something out of a movie or dream. The Brenners were sitting on high chairs around a huge oval table, swathed in white cloth and bedecked with an enormous silver candelabra and many heavy platters of food. Aaron, Magda, another Hasidic couple—I judged them to be in their late twenties, but it was hard to tell in those clothes—and two small, pallid boys with long brown curling sidelocks. The chandelier was on low. Candlelight flickered over the remains of the meal, conferring its ephemeral intimacies, its painterly shadows.

Aaron, as usual, was talking. Instead of a suit jacket he wore a shiny black robe over his white shirt; a plush blue skullcap sat high upon his hair like a crown. Food was on his plate, but he ignored it. His round cheeks were flushed from some obscure agitation. Perhaps it was pedagogic in nature, for he had a book open on his lap, and he punctuated his speech by jabbing one page with his index finger repeatedly, as if the words were so many nails to be socked into place. As he talked and poked, his eyes in their wanderings flicked by me but did not stop. He hadn't noticed me. No one had as yet, which meant I could slip away if I wanted to. This knowledge relaxed me somewhat.

The others at the table appeared to take Aaron's belligerence in stride. Doubtless this was not the first time they had been invited to dinner only to have to sit through a lecture. At the far end sat Magda. In the glow of the candles she looked like a bride. She was wearing a white dress that hung loosely on her shoulders, as though it had originally been tailored for a more ample woman, and it drew one's attention both to her rotten posture and to the steep curve of her neck, which protruded like the stem of a proud but delicate flower. At the moment she was gazing not at her husband but at the clouded glass of the window behind him, which was open the merest crack. Her expression was wistful.

The boys, slumped in their chairs, looked bored. They too wore velvet skullcaps. Their sidelocks dangled at their ears, framing their long, narrow faces. From time to time they would play with the curls, absently twisting them around their fingers, corkscrew style, until they were reprimanded for this behavior by the other woman at the table, who was no doubt their mother. She could have been Magda's mother too—or sister, aunt, or cousin. In any case, it was she who spotted me first.

She didn't say anything, didn't let on, merely sat there pretending to listen to Aaron and sneaking looks at me occasionally from time to time through the wispy smoke of the candles. If my presence worried or surprised her, she refused to show it. Perhaps she was accustomed to strangers peeping in through the window as she ate dinner.

Now that I'd been seen, however, there was no sense in remaining outside any longer. The door was unlocked. In fact it wasn't even fully closed. I took a breath, pushed it open, and stepped inside.

"Hi," I said in a loud voice. "Sorry I'm so late."

Embarrassed, I spread my arms in an ironic flourish, *Here I am.*

"So," said Aaron Brenner, unsmiling. He did not seem particularly surprised to see me either. But he looked rather satisfied, as if a small wager had just been resolved in his favor and we were now going to split the profits between us. "You had trouble finding the place?"

"Not really. Maybe a little."

"Good."

And with that he seemed to forget all about me again, turning back to the table and taking up the point he'd been discussing. I waited for him to finish. Peering out from the foyer, I thought to myself: these are religious people in the middle of their Sabbath, talking about the Torah or something of that nature, and I am not going to enter at this point without a specific invitation. Meanwhile, to pass the time, I examined the apartment. Most of the furnishings were dull, utilitarian: the sturdy plaid sofa, the colorless rugs, the modest stereo, the low end tables inscribed with faded rings. There were books, shelves and shelves of them, but they were spine-worn and without jackets. There was no television. Nor were there any plants, with the exception of one spindly cactus on the windowsill from which bloomed, improbably, a pale blue flower. The place lacked any sense of luxury or design, of two tastes conjoined in dialogue, and perhaps that was why it made me so uneasy; it reminded me of my own apartment after my marriage broke up—barren, uncoupled. The sole concession to aesthetics was an Ansel Adams print on one wall. The golden West: cool crystalline moonrise, El Capitan in shadow. It might have belonged to anyone. As might the pile of newspapers by the front door, and the iron bars over the front windows, and the snaking line of white powder along the floorboards, which I recognized at once to be boric acid, for the roaches.

Well, I may not have known anything about Judaism, but late-century New York interior life was something I knew well. Dinner parties in stuffy apartments, fighting off the roaches and the clutter, trying not to think about what was going on out there in the streets, the transactions being struck, the fortunes rising and falling, the lights burning all night in those twin towers, mirrored in the black harbor. While here you were, huddled inside, bars across the windows.

I was reasonably certain I could handle myself under these conditions. Despite the fact that their hair, clothing, and language were out of some eighteenth-century *shtetl*, the Brenners and their friends, I thought, were modern city people, no doubt more like me than not. There was nothing to worry about. But then why did I have the impression that everyone at the table had forgotten who I was and was now patiently waiting for me to leave?

Finally Aaron Brenner looked up from the huge leg of chicken he was now devouring, and blinked at me in surprise. "*Nu?*"

This tiny syllable seemed wonderfully efficient for expressing impatience, befuddlement, and annoyance, all at once.

"You're coming in, or not?"

"It's just that I wasn't sure you still remembered—"

"Remembered? Remembered what?"

I shrugged. "Who I was."

"This is a problem for you," Aaron said, "being remembered?"

He grabbed me by the wrist, led me—pushed me—into the empty chair to his right, and watched testily as I wriggled out of my sport jacket and settled in. His gaze had that CPA intensity again, auditing me, noting everything from the color of my socks to the tilt of my ears, recording each detail with a kind of puzzled sadness, as if my features were the inventory for some small business that was failing to cover its expenses. "Okay now?"

"Fine."

"Comfortable?"

"Sure."

"Good," he said. "Because there's a saying: the moment you enter my house it becomes your house. You become the master. So you see, it's really not for me to ask you to sit down. Quite the contrary."

"Oh. I see."

"He sees."

Now that we had established how well I saw, Aaron went ahead with the introductions. The other couple at the table were Magda's sister Hava and her husband Zev. Hava was five years older than Magda and somewhat less severe in her looks. The arc of her nose was less steep; her bosom was more matronly, belly a perfect mound. Her cheeks, lit by the candles, were rounded, rosy and moist, two sun-ripe nectarines that would not remain firm much longer. Zev, on the other hand, had a lanky frame with a long neck, no shoulders to speak of, and a ragged blondish beard. He was friendly but dull. The feints and volleys of social discourse seemed lost on Zev; as the others talked he sat there doggedly silent, occasionally snorting agreement or giving off quick gratuitous nods and smiles that were like little palsied tremors of intentionality. And yet for all his nervous tics he was apparently that rare thing, a happy man. His tie was fine silk, his teeth were bright and straight. His eyes glittered with energies that the rest of him seemed aware of but powerless to articulate.

"Hava and Zev live in the neighborhood," Aaron explained. "Two streets over."

"That must be nice," I said. And then, because his expression remained utterly blank, I added, "To have family so close, I mean."

He gave me a candid look. "You have siblings you're close to?"

"No."

"Then you're all on your own?"

"I suppose so."

One of the boys tittered and said something in another language, at which everyone at the table laughed. Everyone but Aaron.

"Moishe here says that doesn't sound so bad to him. But then he doesn't know, does he? It isn't so wonderful, let me tell you. The younger the spirit, the more it needs company. On the other hand it's true that one has fewer constraints when one's alone."

I nodded uncertainly and glanced across the table to see how this other hand sat with his wife. But she was lost in her plate.

"Moishe and Arye," Zev put in, "they're very close. They

THE HERE AND NOW

help each other with their studies. Wonderful scholars. Isn't that right, boys?"

The boys nodded in tandem, then looked to their mother for their next cue.

"And more to come," she said.

I did not quite comprehend this remark at first. But then I put together the pride and authority in her voice and the burgeoning swell of her stomach, which she rubbed periodically like a genie's lamp, and I realized that another wonderful scholar was on the way.

As if to encourage or reward all this fecundity, the sideboard had been laid out with a staggering amount of food. Huge platters of chicken and meat, potatoes, salad, noodles. Two long braided challahs, torn to pieces. Several bottles of kosher wine; assorted whiskeys and liqueurs. Everyone but Aaron seemed to have finished some time ago, but the food was still out and their plates were still on the table, greasy with congealing fat, strewn with bones. Two hours late, by this point, for whichever dinner I'd been heading for, I was starving. Beneath my clothes I felt transparent. No density, no substantiality, only the hard magnetic pole of my appetite. How would I ever fill myself up?

I thought briefly of Donna, sitting alone at her kitchen table, breathing paint fumes. Why wasn't she here? Why wasn't I there? Why weren't we both somewhere else?

"Here," Aaron said, handing me a skullcap. "Put this on."

"Why?"

"Why not?"

The skullcap, made of very thin material, felt light and snug on the back of my head. Having never worn one before, I was afraid that it would slip off if I moved, so I tried to move as little as possible.

"Eat, eat," Aaron said.

I ate. My host, sucking meditatively on a wishbone, observed me closely. He wasn't the only one. The two little boys were staring at me with a kind of awed but impersonal deference. Perhaps it had been explained to them that I was a member of a rare species known to be harmless if given a wide berth during meals. Their parents were staring too of course. I seemed to be the center of attention for everyone. Everyone but Magda. She stared not at me but at her plate, where a piece of chicken breast lay almost intact, the yellow skin having been removed in a long, delicate operation and draped neatly over her potatoes. She'd hardly tasted them either.

When I had finished most of what was on my plate, Aaron seized the bottle of Chivas Regal that had been waiting all this time at his elbow, and poured what in any bar in America would have been considered a triple scotch, straight-up. "Now have a drink," he said.

As I had already shown my willingness to dress and eat on command, there seemed no good reason not to go ahead and drink too. But this was my first hard liquor since the Pinsky wedding—the Pinsky *debacle*, I reminded myself—so I tried to take it slow. I approached the scotch with mild, tactful sips, looking over the painting on the opposite wall. As paintings go, it was very bad: an amateurish, garishly executed portrait of an old Hasid with piercing blue eyes and a formidable white beard, the kind of item one might see priced for two dollars at some rundown Catskills flea market. And yet I recalled seeing the same face an hour before, in the window of a bookstore on Kingston Avenue, and in a number of the other windows on that street as well.

The man in the painting appeared to recognize me too. All the while I ate he seemed to be following the movements of my mouth and fork and finding them somehow wanting. "Who's that?"

"You don't know?" Zev asked, thunderstruck.

"I'm afraid not."

The boys tittered again into their fists. Their moods had improved considerably since I'd walked in the door. I was proving to be a real riot out here in Brooklyn.

"A very great man," Zev told me. "You've heard of the Rebbe?"

"I'm afraid not."

Why did I keep saying that? What in the world was there to be afraid of?

"You must get to know him soon. An extraordinary man, the Rebbe. A descendant of the *Besht* himself."

At this point I was not going to admit, of course, that I was afraid I'd never heard of this *Besht* fellow either. "I take it he's some kind of religious leader for you, is that right?"

They all seemed to be waiting for Aaron to answer. After all, he was responsible for the presence of this ignoramus at the table, it was his job to do the remedial work. But my question, or my proximity, or something else altogether, had begun to agitate Aaron Brenner. He finished his drink and poured another. He did not appear to hold his liquor any better than I did. The pink in his cheeks had deepened to red, and his eyes had lost some of their acuteness and were beginning to swim in their sockets. My question dangled in the air, unaddressed.

Aaron, my education abandoned, began, after a moment's pause, to hum a little melody under his breath. I've done that sometimes, lost track of myself as some latent song unfolded within me, and so I waited tolerantly for him to realize he was doing it and stop. But he didn't. The humming grew louder and louder. No one so much as raised an eyebrow. They merely nodded along, enjoying the show. In truth Aaron carried the tune quite well. But I was unaccustomed to giving myself over that way, and had to force myself to listen.

At a certain point, finally, he stopped. Then he started again. This time not humming but singing. He closed his eyes and began to slap out a rhythm on the table with his hand, gathering the melody into syllables, yai-dai-dai, yai-dai-dai. What did it mean? The song, as if in accordance with its own laws, grew louder and louder as it went on, turning over upon itself like waves, mournful and yet paradoxically joyous—a sort of happy dirge. Sweat popped out on Aaron's brow; a vein pulsed feverishly in his neck. By now he was pounding the table hard, real blows that made the silverware jump. And still he kept singing, yai-dai-dai, yai-dai-dai. Soon Zev had joined in—his voice a soft, pleasant tenor—and so had the boys, and so, I discovered, however unwillingly or unconsciously or inaudibly, had I.

Afterward Aaron kept his eyes closed, savoring the silence. Perhaps he was hearing a song there, too, carrying in the breeze from other houses, other worlds.

"That was very nice," I said after a while.

Aaron shrugged. "I come from a musical background. My father in his spare time sang in the opera. As an extra, of course."

"Can I ask one question?"

"Ask," he said.

"How come the women don't sing?" Neither, I noticed, had once opened her mouth.

"Who says we don't?" said Hava sharply. "You hear what's in my head?"

"Take it easy," Aaron said. "He asked a fair question."

"And I gave a fair answer."

"There are fairer ones, however. Why snap his head off?"

I sneaked a look at Magda. Apparently something very important was going on at the edge of her fork.

"You see, Shmuel," Aaron resumed, in the tone a very wise man might employ with a very simple child, "the fact is, women's voices are arousing to men. Don't you find this to be so?"

"Sure, the good ones. Is that wrong?"

"And when you're aroused," he went on, "what happens to your concentration? Out the window. This also is why we separate the genders in shul. Also why our women cover their hair, knees, and shoulders. Why they wear thick stockings, not thin ones. When we pray, we want to immerse ourselves in prayer, not distract ourselves with sex."

I spoke up then for distracted people everywhere. "What's so bad about sex?"

Hava tsked, rose from her chair, and disappeared down the hallway. Aaron watched her go without regret.

"You don't understand," he said. "You keep saying bad and wrong, like you have us mixed up with Puritans. This couldn't be farther from the truth. Sex, we can agree, is a wonderful activity. But not the only activity, yes? Just one wonderful thing among many.

"And you'll find, by the way, that our women don't mind receiving different treatment under the laws. They see it for what it is: a compliment."

"Oh? How's that?"

"Women stand closer to God. We men, look at us. So much hard work, so much study and prayer, and for what? Only to become the way women are by nature—pious, creative, intuitive. Spiritual."

His voice climbed somewhat on this last word, making of it a question. He was looking down the table at his wife. But he seemed to have no better luck with that shy, proud, involuted character than I'd had. The object of our attention sighed distractedly, pushed back her chair, and stood; after which, with no evident piety, creativity, or spirituality, she began to carry the remaining plates into the bright yellow kitchen. As a housewife, she appeared to be rather clumsy—trying too hard, or perhaps not hard enough—and so it took her a long time to clear the dishes. I had an opportunity to study her in the interim. Tonight her hair was wavy and sandy-brown; in its shallow folds the candlelight swayed. I could see the blades of her shoulders poking through her white dress, like the stunted wings of a bony, grounded angel. She had an expressive back. This was fortunate, because the front of her was not expressive at all. She had not so much as looked at me since I'd poked my head in the door. Then again she had not looked at her husband, either.

I was getting out of my chair to help her clear the table when I was arrested by Aaron's firm round hand.

"Sit," he said. "You're our guest."

Well then, why didn't he get up and help her? Why didn't anyone? She looked tired enough as it was.

"You asked before about the Rebbe. You know, there are those in our community who believe that he is himself the Moshiach—that everything we want is that close."

"What do you think?"

He smiled sadly. "There's a saying: Before the gates of Rome sits a leprous beggar who waits. This," he said, "is the Messiah."

I waited for him to continue, but apparently that was the whole saying.

"You follow?"

"No."

I wasn't turning out to be very good at this. But what did I know from Roman lepers and messiahs? I had all I could handle with day-to-day life on Ninety-fourth Street.

"It's very simple. The question is, what does he wait for, this messiah? That's the question." Having stated things with such concision, he leaned back, stroked his curly beard, and watched my expression avidly. I can't imagine he saw much there to reward him.

Before I could venture an answer, the two sisters reappeared, bearing desserts. Poppy-seed and lemon cakes, wrapped candies, a conical Jell-O mold of some sort, and still they kept coming. No wonder Magda seemed so worn out; look at all the cooking she'd had to do. A new stiffness had set into her neck and shoulders when she was out of the room, but I did not know who among us was the cause of it. Jaw clenched, she set a pot of coffee down with sufficient force that it spilled onto the tablecloth. The coffee itself looked weak. There was no milk for it, but I remembered some Jewish injunction against mixing dairy and meats, so didn't ask for any. Instead I contented myself with one of those terrible nondairy creamers they give you on planes. Wrestling with the top, I was reminded dismally of the trip to Houston, the one responsible for my presence here at this table with these strangers, and all by itself that homely plastic thimble of noncream about did me in. The randomness of things! When would they ever cohere?

But I was still wearing the smile I'd entered with, that tentative, earnest, willing-to-be-engaged smile I brought to all formal occasions, and I willed myself to keep it up now. "Okay," I said, "I give up. What does he wait for?"

Hava clucked her tongue. Apparently she knew the answer already, and was not above gloating over it.

"Not what. Who."

"Okay. Who?"

"He waits for you," Aaron said simply.

"For me."

"That's right. He waits for you."

"Listen," I said, "I really am sorry for coming so late. I know it was rude."

Aaron sighed into his glass. "You still don't understand, do you? The point—"

"Let him eat," Magda said. "The man came for dinner, not lessons."

"Nu, is that why he came? He can't get brisket and potatoes at home? They don't make these things in Manhattan?"

"I don't know what they make in Manhattan," she said sharply.

He threw up his arms. "And this is my fault too?"

Magda's tiny nostrils flared. She was cradling a ceramic bowl filled with green apples and yellow pears, and she began to press it tightly against her stomach, as if to crush all things rounded and sweet, all the wayward stubborn impulses she harbored there. Aaron for his part did not back down. From the head of the table he glared at her, his expression as gray and uncompromising as the Rebbe's on the wall behind him. He was missing the third button, I noticed, on his white shirt. Now he fingered the hole absently, as if there were some connection between the two phenomena, the missing button and the infuriating wife, and he mumbled something beneath his breath.

"*Sha*," said Hava. She looked down at her plate, into a trembling mass of lime Jell-O she had already half-finished. "Let's eat dessert already."

Suddenly my sympathies were with her, the sister, this plumpish down-to-earth Hava with her manifold appetites.

"I have to go to the bathroom," announced the younger boy, Arye, who apparently had the more sensitive bladder of the two. Zev went with him. I watched them head off. Because I did not entirely understand what all the tension was about, and because I did not have to go to the bathroom and had nothing else to occupy me, my thoughts slunk guiltily back to my own domestic tensions with Donna—which were, of course, about to increase drastically. Then again, prior to the past week, things had been tense between us for some time. Were we capable of change? I looked at my host and hostess, frozen at opposite ends of the long white table. This, I thought, was where Donna and I were headed. Or had we already arrived?

Now Zev and the boy returned from the bathroom. As they walked both of them made the same diffident gesture, brushing the front of their pants with the backs of their hands, reassuring themselves that all was in place. *We become*, I thought, *only what we learn to become.*

"How about some coffee?" Zev asked with nervous cheer.

"No." Hava pushed her chair back from the table. "I'm tired. We should go."

"Go?" Zev looked disappointed. In addition to being timid he was also a little drunk. For that matter, so was I. All at once I felt a huge sorrowful identification with the man. Two nervous fellows with narrow shoulders, trying to cope with such formidable women as Hava and Donna! How were we to act in this world?

"So early?" Aaron protested. "We haven't even finished dessert yet."

"Well, I'm tired," Hava said.

"But we have a guest."

"And I have a baby."

This comeback had, I thought, a certain petulant smugness, as if the fetus in her stomach was license for all manner of rude behavior.

"She's tired," Aaron announced to the heavens, not bothering to hide his exasperation. "Our Queen Hava is tired, so that's that. Right?"

But these were old antagonisms, even I could see that, and Hava was beyond the point of acknowledging them. She turned away from Aaron altogether. Drawing her kerchief over her hair, with its adorning pattern of bright red flowers, she directed a fierce look at her sister, at once protective and accusatory. "Boys," she said, "kiss everyone good Shabbos, and we'll go."

Dutifully the pallid boys trooped around the table, bestowed a faint peck onto their aunt Magda's cheek, and then another onto Uncle Aaron's. At last they arrived in front of the strange beardless visitor from Manhattan, the one whose presence that evening had proved so entertaining and disruptive. They did not falter. One at a time, without so much as a glance at their parents, they came and leaned forward, their jaws set stoically, as if it were a vaccine and not a kiss I was administering. Moshe let me do my business and got out of there right away. The younger one, Arye, came next. His curiosity toward me took the more scientific form: he seemed to linger a moment at the end, swaying between my knees, inhaling my scent in an investigatory way. His lips were warm. I could feel on my cheek the soft weight of his side-locks, and the down of his face—the peach fuzz that might one day metamorphose into a beard as ragged as his father's, but which now seemed the very texture of innocence.

As I bent forward, I caught a glimpse of the candlelight, trapped and wavering in the chandelier crystals, and a peculiar feeling of weightlessness came over me. "Nice meeting you," I said.

When they had gone Aaron and I found ourselves alone at the table. The candles were dripping onto the white cloth.

The lower they sank, the more fitful and enormous were the shadows they threw over the walls. Aaron was rolling a hunk of wax between his fingers, molding it into a little ball. From time to time he glanced thoughtfully at Magda's chair. Its occupant had gone into the kitchen and had not come out. I heard no running water and so I assumed she wasn't doing the dishes; what she *was* doing in there I couldn't guess. Perhaps avoiding me. Or her husband. Or both of us.

"Maybe I should go, too," I said.

"Nonsense. You came all this way. Why leave so soon, just because of Hava trying to spoil things?"

"It's not that."

"What then?"

"It's pretty late. I think your wife might be a little tired."

"Tired? She's not tired. She's angry with me. That's entirely different."

"I don't mean to pry, but why is she angry with you?"

He shrugged. "She doesn't need a reason."

"Don't you?"

Another shrug. "I accept this sort of thing as part of life. Women have to put up with menstruation, we have to put up with women. At least she doesn't break dishes, like my first wife."

"Your first wife?"

He laughed. "Such a look on your face. I killed somebody?"

"No, no, it's just . . ."

"Just what? Hasids should be above such things as divorce? Don't be silly. In fact there's an entire volume of the Talmud devoted to the subject. An interesting text, very dry and complex. Unusually so. 'The very altar,' " he recited, " 'weeps for the man who divorces the wife of his youth.' "

"Think what it does for the wife."

"Yes, you're right. That's so." He held his ball of wax in front of his face, rolling it tighter between his fingers. "You know, I've got news for you, Shmuel. You and I are not so different as you think."

"Bullshit we're not."

"In lifestyle maybe. But underneath, I assure you, everything you are, I am."

To which I almost replied: *And what is that?*

"It's true," he said calmly.

"No it's not. You believe in this whole God business, for one thing."

"And you don't? Not once in your life, during a sunset maybe, or a piece of music, or the act of love, have you felt a presence other than yourself? That there are ways of knowing things other than through the senses?"

"Oh, I don't know. If you put it so broadly, maybe. I'd hardly call that a God concept."

"Semantics," he sighed. "You think it's such a hard line between these things? Doesn't every doubter have moments of belief, and every believer moments of doubt? Listen, none of us is so simple that we don't have two sides. *Yetser ha-Tov*, good inclinations, on the right; *Yetser ha-Ra*, evil ones, on the left. That's why we button our coats, you know, the opposite way from you. Right to left. To express our hope that good be ascendant over evil."

"But that makes no sense." I did not even try to keep the scorn from my voice. "For one thing, the heart is on the left side too."

"The heart," Aaron conceded, "is a complication." He brooded for a moment over the problem. "Who knows? Maybe it has no fixed place."

"I doubt you'd find many doctors who'd agree."

"*Doctors* . . ." he said bitterly. "Listen, Shmuel, don't kid yourself. I know the secular view very well. I grew up secular just like you. My parents they go to shul maybe on Yom Kippur if there's nothing else to do. They're out in Hempstead right now, wondering what they did wrong to have me turn out this way, why I'm not a nice lawyer like my brother. After all, I went to public school like everyone else. I played bass in a garage band. I ran track, screwed around with the Italian girls.

Even at college I did everything they all did. Mescaline, acid, magic mushrooms—SUNY Binghamton, it was a giant pharmacy in those days. I'd get high and read Kierkegaard, Walter Benjamin. What did I know? Maybe sometimes I'd go to a rally for Soviet Jews, that was about it for Jewish involvement."

"So what happened?"

"Mostly nothing. Nothing was what happened."

"But something must have happened, to make you want to change your life that way."

"Want? I didn't want. I *had* to." He leaned forward. "Don't you see? I had the whole package. A nice secular wife, a nice secular job in the city, a nice secular home in the suburbs where I read nice secular books and magazines and kept a nice secular kitchen. In this kitchen it so happens I smoked pot every night after my wife went to sleep. So what? A lot of people do that. But then one night the stash was empty. This was, as we used to say, a heavy thing. Suddenly I couldn't read, I couldn't sleep, I couldn't think. The world wasn't round, it was flat. Actually it was me that was flat, but I didn't know it. All I knew was I was headed for a nice secular nervous breakdown if I didn't find a way to get some meaning in my life.

"That," he sighed, "was about ten years ago. That was when I became a *Baal Tshuvah*."

"What's that?"

"It means Master of the Turning. One who has come back."

"Back to what?"

He didn't seem to hear me. He drank off a little more whiskey and sighed. His fingers were leaving a film of smudgy waxed prints over the glass.

"And don't you miss anything about it? That life?"

"Sure." He considered. "Little things, anyway. Bacon and shrimp."

"Nothing else? Your ex-wife?"

"A sweet Reform girl, my ex-wife. A teacher of second-graders. She deserved better than what I gave her." He smoothed his beard thoughtfully. "As for the rest, I still find a way to do it, when there's time. I still play guitar. I still listen to my Cream and Dylan records. I even still smoke an occasional joint," he said, "when there's time."

"I get the feeling there isn't much time."

He smiled sadly.

"But isn't it frustrating, giving so much up? Aren't there an awful lot of rules you're supposed to follow?"

"Not rules," he said. "*Mitzvot. Deeds.* The Christians, they ask for faith. We require a more active stance."

"Well, whatever. Aren't there an awful lot of them?"

"Six hundred thirteen," he said. "Is that a lot?"

"I'd say so, yes."

"On the other hand, you follow laws yourself, don't you? State laws, national laws. And you must have some ethics you follow, some precepts, codes, little personal rituals that tell you how to behave. No?"

"Oh me," I said, "I'm a lousy example. I don't know what I follow."

"You don't, do you." For a moment he looked glum.

"Besides," I said, "it makes a difference that they *are* personal; that they're instinctual and not written down."

"How do you know?"

"Know what? That they aren't written down, or that it makes a difference?"

My question for some reason pleased him inordinately. "Have another whiskey," he said.

I sipped my whiskey. Chivas Regal. A better brand than I had at home. Donna, I thought, liked Chivas too. Donna was more forthright and acquisitive than I was: she liked things of quality and demanded them as her due. Would she have liked Aaron Brenner, had I been the one to invite *him* to dinner? Would she have seen, as I did right then, an intriguing young man of keen, idiosyncratic intelligence, one who despite his prejudices was capable of losing himself, as I was not, in many rich pursuits Donna herself enjoyed, like good scotch and loud music and vigorous dancing?

"So," he said, "you've read the Torah? Mastered the Talmud?"

"No."

"Then how do you know these laws you follow by instinct aren't written down?"

"I don't," I said.

"And how do you know that, even if they aren't, it makes a difference?"

I shrugged. "It's only a guess."

He nodded quizzically and then fell silent for a moment to regroup. My willingness to give up and disavow all certainty seemed to unnerve him. I could see that he was taking this whole discussion very seriously and was not altogether sure I respected him for it. Who was he trying to convince anyway, me or himself? Why wasn't he off at synagogue? Didn't these religious guys have more important things to do on Friday nights than get drunk and shoot the shit with people like me?

Now he took up the charge again.

"The point is, Shmuel, for all the laws I have to follow, my life isn't restrictive at all. Just the opposite. What you don't understand is that I don't *have* to follow them; I *choose* to. Existence, it's like sex in a way, yes? Fail to penetrate the surface and it's meaningless. But go in there in the dark, without your shoes or rubber shields . . . submit yourself piously, *wholly*, to the natural authority behind things—then God alone knows what will result. This is how creation works."

"Well," I said, "when you put it that way, it sounds like a lot of good clean fun."

He sighed. "You're making a joke. Fine. Go ahead."

"I'm sorry," I said. "I've offended you."

"Do I look offended?" He laughed. "I'm not in the slightest. It's just that I feel bad for you. Here's the world full of beautiful lights and mysteries," he said airily, "and here you are, shielding yourself from it with one small hand."

"You know, it's funny. That's exactly what people like *me* say about people like *you*."

Now, at last, I felt that I'd gone too far. Even Hasids as

unexpected as this one, Hasids who quarreled with their wives and smoked hash and listened to Eric Clapton in their spare time, were still Hasids, I thought, and they must have their breaking point. I knew Aaron Brenner did—I'd already seen his temper in action. So I watched him furrow his brow as he processed my remark, and waited for an explosion.

But instead he merely smiled. "That *is* funny. But of course it isn't true."

"From your perspective."

"From any perspective. But enough debate. The fact is it's really no great distance from your life to mine. We see the same trees. The difference is only one of us sees the forest."

"What about Magda?"

"Ah," he said, as if he'd been expecting the question for some time now. "What about her?"

"Is she the same way? Was she also, you know . . . secular?"

"Magda?" He laughed. "Magda's a good Hasidic girl from the neighborhood. A little rose of Brooklyn. Daddy was a rebbe, grandfather, great-grandfather. A long line of blue-chip rebbes, all the way back to Novgorod. It does me honor to be married to her." He pursed his lips, perhaps considering for a moment the question of what honor it did *her*. "Nothing like us, my little Magdaleh. Never went to college. Never listened to *Music from Big Pink*. Wouldn't know Colombian from Thai Stick." Lowering his voice to a whisper, he leaned forward. "Speaking of which, I've got some upstairs."

"Some what?"

"Colombian. Very good stuff. If not for Shabbos we could do some right now."

"Thanks anyway."

He smiled. "Drugs don't tempt you?"

"Actually," I said, "I could use some more coffee, if there is any. I'm pretty beat."

"Good idea. Hey," he called out in a loud voice, "are we having more coffee, or not?"

No answer from the kitchen.

"Maybe she's gone to bed."

He sighed. "Maybe so. You must forgive her. She hasn't been feeling very well."

"I understand," I said. Though I did not understand at all.

"Her sister Hava, she wears us both out. Her and that limp vegetable she lives with. He's worth a fortune in diamonds, you know." He downed some more whiskey, and grimaced. "Of course they're in the neighborhood, we have to see them all the time. That's how it works. There's another sister, too, the oldest. A kibbutznik in Israel, crazy, promiscuous, full of socialist cant, but her I like, her I can talk to. Only her we never get to see. Hava we see all the time. Spoiled rotten. I can't tell you how many Shabbos dinners I've had to listen to that woman preen about her kids and the money they send to Israel and their vacations to London and Australia. It's a miracle I can stand her at all."

"What about Magda?"

"What about Magda, what about Magda. You keep asking that."

"Do I?"

"Relax, Shmuel." He waved his hand, as if to blow away every difficulty between us. "I'm just teasing. You've every reason to be curious. Here, another drink."

I didn't want another drink. But no one was giving me any coffee, so I took what was offered.

"I just meant, does she hate Hava too? Is she closer to the sister in Israel?"

"I know what you meant. Who she's close to . . ." He sighed, as if the whole question of his wife's allegiances was utterly mysterious to him. "Maybe, though, for such a question, you should ask her."

"I'm afraid that your wife hasn't shown much inclination to talk to me."

He narrowed his eyes shrewdly, a CPA once more. "She's inclined, all right. I wouldn't worry about that."

Worried? Hey, man, I wanted to say, I'm not *worried*. What difference did it make to me if some religious housewife in

Brooklyn, some sullen waif with protean hair and big Anne Frank eyes, ignored me or didn't? Hadn't I enough woman problems already? Didn't I have a whole life out there these people knew nothing about? Yes, somewhere over there across the river, in the *real* New York City, I had a whole life.

But what was it? At that moment, between the Chivas Regal and the long hot fruitless day, I found it difficult to get this whole life of mine in focus. Of course I knew it existed. But exactly how it operated, what fueled its motors and by what lights it steered, I was unable to recall. I sat there a moment, wondering.

Outside a police siren sailed by, making its mad music. I checked my watch. A vertical line ran down the center of its face, dividing it in half. "Jesus," I said, "it's twelve-thirty. I've got to go."

"Go?" The word had a distressing effect upon Aaron. His green eyes turned wild. He seemed awfully touchy about letting his guests go, about being left alone. But then, he wasn't alone. His wife, I reminded myself, was back in the bedroom, preparing to sleep. "Go where?"

"Home."

"Home?" He blinked at me fuzzily.

"My apartment."

"But it's Shabbos!"

"So what?"

"So you're staying here, of course. I thought you understood. You'll spend a real Shabbos and then if you want go back tomorrow after sundown."

"Look," I said, rising, "thanks for the offer, but I can't. I have work at home. Also some people who are expecting me. Nobody knows where I am."

Though this was true, I realized after I'd said it that it did not entirely bother me.

"People," he snorted. "Tell me, who are these people you care about so much all of a sudden, that you'd transgress the laws forbidding travel on Shabbos?"

"They're not my laws."

"Whose then?" he demanded.

"Yours."

"Neither mine nor yours," he said. "God's."

"Well then, I'll take my chances. I'll choose not to obey them, and take the consequences."

Now he really *was* angry. "Choose!" he said. "What do you know of choice? Look at you. No wife, no children, no community, no belief in anything. How do you choose from nothing?"

He'd begun to shout, which made it somewhat less difficult for me to walk away from him and into the front hallway. I have, at best, little appetite for conflict. By now I was ready to get the hell out of there.

"Tell me, Shmuel," he called after me, "have you ever chosen anything? Or do you only choose *not* to do things? Or do you even know?"

"Thank you for dinner," I said.

"Go." He waved his hand. "Run away."

"I enjoyed it," I said. And then I reached for the doorknob to make my escape.

But the door wouldn't open. I stood there rattling the knob, to no avail.

"Wait a minute."

Aaron got to his feet and came forward. On the way over his expression softened, as if after all was said and done he really did feel sorry for me, my inability to do these simple things for myself. "I have to let you out," he said mildly.

He turned a key I hadn't noticed was there. The sound it made was surprisingly loud; it echoed through the foyer, as if to underscore that something was opening up between us just then as well. Or was it clicking shut?

"I don't like to . . ." he was explaining, a little sheepishly, "especially on Shabbos. But the neighborhood . . ."

"I understand," I said.

"You won't find a cab. They don't come here. You'll have to walk back to the subway."

"That's okay. It's only a few blocks."

"The subway at this hour, you're sure?"

"I'm sure," I said.

But the siren was still ringing in my ears, and I wasn't so sure, it occurred to me, as all that. For a second I lingered in the doorway, preparing myself.

"Just out of curiosity, how come you stay? I mean, if it's so dangerous here, why do you stay?"

"We stay because we stay," he said.

"Oh." Serves me right, I thought. "I see."

"No you don't. Crown Heights, it's just a name in the paper to you. Did you know for example when the first Lubavitchers came there were Irish and Germans living here, Italians too? None of them wanted us here. None. Back in the sixties, the first blacks and Puerto Ricans moved in, and all the whites, even the other Hasidim, ran away. Abandoned their homes, left their yeshivahs and shuls . . . just like in Europe. But the Rebbe called everyone together and said, Enough. You can only run so much. So we stay."

"Maybe he's wrong. Maybe if they don't want you to stay, it's better to leave."

"For who? Should we live in our own little world, like they do in Williamsburg, Borough Park? Here we mix with the others. Look there—three houses down, they're from Haiti. Across the street, two sisters from Trinidad. Isn't that what you liberal seculars always talk about, integration? Well," he said, "we don't talk; we live integration every day. Maybe it will work, maybe it won't. It's not for us to worry over the future. God will take care of that. For us each day is its own. Look—" He pointed to one of the houses across the street, which was covered with scaffolding. "See? Now the wheel turns some more, and instead of too many empty houses now there aren't enough, and everyone's mad and shouting at each other and forming a hundred different interethnic councils all over again. Meanwhile we don't budge. Why should we?"

He looked at me fiercely, waiting for an answer.

I was very tired, however, and could think of no good reason

at this point why he should or should not do anything.
"Well," I said, "good luck. I have to get going."

"Whatever you want," he said.

And without further ado I descended the brick stoop to the
street, taking my leave of Aaron Brenner, and his house, and
his wife—that unhappy, reticent young woman whom I
assumed to be asleep in the bedroom.

Coming out of the building I discovered a homeless person
resting on the Brenners' front steps. Hunched over, elbows on
her knees, she was murmuring faintly to herself, incantations
of a remembered life. Though I couldn't see her face, she
seemed to me, like most homeless people, dismal and alone
beyond rescue, and the sight of her filled me with the predictable blend of shame, guilt, and impotence. The night was
warm and dry; nonetheless as I hurried past the woman gave
out a shiver. She was draped in a shawl so baggy and weathered it seemed to negate all of the available light.

Then I saw that it was not a homeless person at all. It was
Magda.

"Hey," I said, "are you okay?"

She lifted her face to me then. In the yellow glow of the streetlight it looked luminous and distant as a moon. I could hear her
breath on the quiet street. Perhaps she'd been crying. Her nose
sounded runny, and her enormous eyes had a dull veiny shine to
them, like unpolished jewels. I stepped closer to see them better.

"We thought you were sleeping."

"I was," she said hoarsely.

She parted the folds of her shawl, revealing beneath it a
long bathrobe sashed at the waist. She did not seem embarrassed to be showing it to me, so I hid my own embarrassment
by studying the robe carefully. It was made of terry cloth and
had blue stripes. Donna, I realized, had one rather similar.
Perhaps they had both been purchased at the same sale. Why
should only secular women shop at Bloomingdale's?

"Should you be out here like this?"

"This is my neighborhood," she said. "I've lived here since I was born."

"Well, it seems to be changing on you."

"Not so much." Abruptly, as if she heard her name being called from a distance, she cocked her head. "Can you smell?"

"What?"

"The Botanical Gardens, you know, are just over there. At night you can smell the flowers."

I tried, but could smell nothing save the familiar acids and grit of the pavement.

"Beautiful," she said, "no?"

"Yes."

Neither of us seemed to know where to go from there.

"Well," I said, "I really have to get going."

From her expression, this news neither pleased nor saddened her. She looked at the hand I was holding out between us as though she had never seen a hand quite like it before. I was aware of her impatience as she waited for me to put it back in my pocket where it belonged.

"I want to thank you for having me to dinner," I added. "It was sweet of you to invite a stranger to your house."

"Oh," she said, drawing her shawl more tightly around her, "we do it all the time. Aaron likes to have company."

"Well, sometime I'd like to return the favor," I said. "Have you to my place for dinner."

It was nothing I hadn't said hundreds of times before without ever meaning it particularly—just a normal bit of post-dinner chitchat, something to mumble at the door before heading off to the subway. But on Magda's face was a very grave frown, directed at her feet. I was using the wrong codes again, speaking in the wrong idiom. Somehow no matter what I did, I managed to insult her.

"I'm actually not such a bad cook," I babbled on, "I have good instincts, people tell me, and a certain talent for—"

"When?" she asked. Now she was looking at the streetlight above us.

"When what?"

"When do you want to cook this dinner?"

I would have been no less astounded had she asked me to dance a mambo on the sidewalk. "Whenever you want," I said.

"What about Tuesday? I don't do anything on Tuesdays."

"You mean *this* Tuesday?"

She nodded. "Why not?"

"Fine," I said foggily. "Tuesday."

"I don't do anything on Tuesdays," she repeated, as though even she had a hard time believing this was true. She gazed up into the yellow halo of the streetlight, where a couple of moths fluttered and zigzagged in a mad, cartoony chase.

"I live on the West Side. Do you want to write down my address?"

"You don't have a card you can give me?"

"No."

I'd never needed one, I wanted to explain. But she looked so worried and downcast that I began to fret over my cardlessness a little too.

"I can't write it down," she declared.

"Here, I have a pen."

"No, no. You don't understand." Her hands were bunched into fists. "It's *Shabbos.*"

Suddenly this tiny obstacle—my not having a card, and her not being able to write my address down—loomed very large and formidable: a deal-breaker. This Shabbos business, I thought, was getting out of hand. All it did was throw up barricades to normal human behavior. What was so restful about that?

"I'll have to call you then."

"Why?"

"To give you my address and directions. Okay?"

"Okay," she said uncertainly.

"I'll call you Sunday, okay?"

"Okay."

And with that, our business was concluded. Only after she'd turned and without a word run back into the house— and how she ran, just then, little Magda, with what freshened energies, the girlish pump of her knees, the smooth skitter of her moccasins over the brick steps—only then did it occur to me that no mention had been made of whether this dinner would or would not include her husband.

What did it mean? As I made my way over the fractured sidewalks of Kingston Avenue, past the darkened shop windows with their obscure wares, their private calligraphies, I performed a quick fact-check on our exchange. Had she avoided the question by accident or design? And what about me? Why had I avoided it? Why was I perpetuating an acquaintance I wanted nothing to do with? Why was I here right now, for that matter, and not out with Donna, my ostensible partner in life, walking under the familiar moneyed lights of upper Broadway? If I was bored and wished to sample the fruits of another culture, why not the West Side and its Korean groceries, its Indian spice shops, Japanese noodle joints, Paki news kiosks, Greek coffee shops, Tunisian chicken grills, its Italian boutiques with their plush rainbow of sweaters in the windows?

Look what happens when you take a chance, when you step away. You wind up lost in a foreign borough, inviting strange people to dinner. And never mind that; I had other problems. I was behind on my work, I had disappointed Alice on her half-birthday—whatever that was—and I had yet to face Donna's wrath. And never mind that; I had *other* problems. My apartment was a mess. How many layers of sediment in the oven? When had I last washed the floor? And never mind that, I had *other* problems. I was going to have to cook this person dinner. Aside from shellfish and pork, what sort of dietary restrictions was I up against? How was I going to pull this off? I left behind the shabby street and descended into the mordant depths of the subway. What exactly was I *trying* to pull off?

I was already deep under the river, rumbling back to Manhattan on the IRT, when I discovered I was still wearing the skullcap that the Brenners had loaned me. I took it off at once and jammed it into my pocket. Then after a while, just for the hell of it, I took it out again and put it back on my head. I looked around at the other passengers, daring them to notice. You see this? I wanted to say. This isn't me. This isn't me. This isn't me.

GLACIERS IN MOTION

Early the next morning I arrived at Donna's apartment with contrition on my face and an enormous chocolate sheetcake in my arms. Outside the sky was like shallow water: pale, wind-washed, more olive than blue. I had not slept well or long and consequently did not feel rested—the new day's travels seemed merely an extension of the night before. And yet the newspaper on the doorstep was a reminder that the same did not hold true for everyone.

Alice answered my knock, a small scrawny blonde girl in polka-dot pajamas. "Hey, pal," I said.

She rubbed her eyes, yawning.

"Can I come in?"

"Mommy's making breakfast." She pointed to the box. "What's that?"

"Cake."

Over her face came a naughty look. "Chocolate?"

"Uh huh."

"Is it for me?"

"Well," I said, "let's see. Someone said something about a half-birthday . . . but I'm not sure whose it is . . ."

"It's mine," she announced, and stuck out her tongue. "Mine mine mine."

"Who?" I brought one hand to my ear, Walter Brennan–style.

"*Mine!*" As if closing the subject once and for all, she stepped up and socked me on the hip. "That's what you get."

"For what?"

"You know."

And with that, she danced away down the corridor and vanished.

A moment later Donna appeared. She wore a man's white button-down shirt and a pair of faded blue panties, and she moved stiffly in my direction on her ample legs as if unbalanced by sleep. "Well," she said, "if it isn't the missing person."

"You'll be happy to know I just got my comeuppance from your daughter. In the form of a right hook."

"Did she punch you? Good for her."

"You both have every right to be angry, of course."

"Gee, do we? Thanks so much." She angled her head, frowning, listening for something behind her. "I've got toast burning, Sam. What is it you want?"

"I'd like to explain about last night."

"Please. It isn't necessary."

"I'm afraid for me it is."

She considered for a moment, still distracted by the goddamned toast. "Well, come explain in the kitchen then."

In the kitchen the toast was indeed burning. Also the coffee was dripping, the radio murmuring, the water running, and the whole room lay trembly and flooded with light. Alice was sitting spread-eagled on the linoleum, drawing yellow shapes on a piece of black construction paper. Donna picked up a knife and went back to doing what she'd been doing, which was slicing a tomato.

"Listen," I began. "I was on the subway, and it was really crowded and hot, and I must have spaced out because I missed the stop. I tried to call but the line was busy, okay?"

"Mmm . . ."

"So what happened was, I wound up all the way out in Crown Heights, with these people I met in Houston. At their apartment. I mean, the apartment's in Brooklyn, but I met them down in Houston, at Warren's wedding . . . Anyway these people, they're really Orthodox Jews, and I guess that's why they'd invited me for din—"

"Sam?" Donna put down her knife to look at me. "I don't know how to say this."

"Then don't. Really. Because when you start a sentence that way, it's always something awful you don't know how to say."

"Seriously," she went on, "I think I made a breakthrough last night. All of a sudden I could see my life like it was happening to someone else. All the moving parts, and all the parts that don't move but are supposed to. It was the oddest thing. I could even hear myself talking about it at some point in the future, how back in my early thirties I used to live in New York and go out with this weird, self-indulgent guy who treated me shamefully. And how it all ended one night, just like that."

She sighed. "Maybe you have to go past things in order to see them clearly. Or maybe it's just what comes when you spend two hours drinking alone on the sofa, watching a Joan Crawford movie on TV."

"Really? It's never worked for me."

"See, this is what I mean. I used to laugh at your jokes, but I don't any longer."

"I'm sorry to hear that," I said. "You have no idea."

"Go ahead, tell me a joke. Let's try this out."

"I'm out of jokes, Donna."

"Be a sport. What about these rabbis from Texas? That sounds like it should be good."

Alice looked up from her drawing. "Where's Texas?" she asked. "Is that where Grandpa lives?"

"No, honey. Grandpa's in Florida. Texas is somewhere else."

"Oh."

Under the circumstances, I decided to let the rest of my explanation drop. No one objected. No one even noticed. My presence, an old battery, had lost its charge. As if from a great distance I sat at the table and watched the females go about their work. It was very warm in the kitchen, and not having slept well I was very tired, and something—perhaps the sight of the drawings on the refrigerator, held by colored magnets in the shape of letters—made me wonder if this room was in fact where I had belonged all this time. What if this life of theirs, which was attached to my own by only a thin braid of desire— a phone, a key, a Saturday jaunt to the zoo—had made deeper inroads than I thought? What if this really *was* my life? Perhaps that was how it worked: you were treated to a glimpse of the real stuff every so often just to show you what you were missing, and all the rest was filler and diversion, the junk of a dream.

"That's a pretty drawing," I said to Alice, after a while.

She worked on without acknowledging the compliment.

"It's kind of a funny color for an airplane, though, isn't it?"

Alice frowned, studying the picture. "It's a bird," she said.

"Oh. What kind?"

She thought for a moment. "A hummingbird."

"A hummingbird! That's my favorite kind of bird."

"It is?"

"Sure. It's the way they just hang there, in the air. They're not quite flying and they're not quite standing still. They're in between."

"Between?" She looked skeptical.

"But it's hard work, you know, staying in the air like that. You've got to beat your wings very hard. You've got to have the right kind of metabolism. You've got to be very very strong."

"I'm strong!" she announced vehemently.

"I hope so."

"Are you?"

"I hope so."

She turned to her mother. "He keeps saying I hope so."

"Yes, he does," Donna said. "Honey, do me a favor. Go put your crayons away?"

"I don't want to."

"Do it anyway."

We watched her sullenly gather up the crayons and carry them off to her room.

"Listen," I said when she was gone. "I really am sorry about last night. The last thing I wanted to do was disappoint anyone."

"Don't make more of it than it is, Sam, okay? She's a sensitive kid and she's only four. Disappointment is her main form of exercise."

"I guess I don't know much about these things. Not being a father, I mean."

"You don't have to explain yourself. I know who you are." She sipped some coffee. "I'm sorry. Did that sound harsh?"

"Maybe a little," I said.

"It's just that I'm not feeling so great right now. Here it is only seven in the morning, and yesterday, oh, yesterday was a real rough day."

I nodded. "I know what you mean."

"Ah yes, back to you. Sorry. I mean, what's being sick and groggy from an abortion compared to poor you and your troubles on the subway?"

"Come again?"

"You heard me."

"Donna," I said, "that was *years* ago. Before I was even around."

"Not that one. I mean," she said in a whisper, "the one I had yesterday."

"Yesterday? You're saying you had an abortion *yesterday*?"

"Shh."

"What, you just went out for lunch and sauntered back by way of Planned Parenthood? Is that what you're telling me?"

"Look, if it makes you feel any better, I scheduled the procedure three weeks ago. After a great deal of thought and consultation." She picked up a piece of toast and stared at it. "David was very supportive. He agreed it was the best thing under the circumstances. So did you, by the way."

"Me? What are you talking about? *I don't even know what you're talking about!*"

"Lower your voice, please. Don't you remember? It was before you went away to Houston. I asked you if you could imagine getting it together to have a baby sometime soon. Do you remember what you said? Because it was truly eloquent."

"Wait, I didn't say I didn't—"

"You said, mumble mumble, sounds like something worth talking about, mumble mumble. Then you said your back was killing you."

"I don't believe this. This isn't happening."

"You're right, Sam," she said. "It isn't happening."

I went to the window. I was breathing so hard that the glass fogged up at once.

"All right, listen," I said after a moment, "what do we do now?"

Donna laughed. "Do?"

"I mean, yes, how do we go on, you know, from—"

"Do?" Her eyes were wild.

"Yes, *do*! All right? That's what I'm asking, okay? *All right? I'm asking what the fuck do you want me to* do!"

"I want you to leave," she said quietly.

And so I did.

I spent the remainder of that morning in a kind of fugue state at my living room window, watching the jets fly in and fly out as if it actually mattered to me where they were headed. I suppose I was waiting for the relief to set in. There's a relief that is said to come when one has been falling and falling and then finally hits bottom, and I was determined to stand there and wait for it as long as was necessary.

The window was not quite transparent, but I could look out through it across the borough's littered skyscape, past the constructivist jumble of laundry lines, water tanks, and antennas and right into the big wan eye of the sun. Poor game Donna, I thought: she was the real hummingbird. For years she had held all three of us aloft, hovering between loss and gain, death's zero and life's one. But ultimately even her powers weren't enough.

A cool draft swept my back, as if in addition to the window

before me there was another, unseen window open behind. I remembered what Aaron Brenner had said about choice. Had I, on some level, chosen *this*?

The relief wasn't coming, but I kept standing there anyway, because I could think of nothing better to do. Eventually my gaze drifted over to the brownstone across the street. It was a more prosperous building than mine, a co-op with fancy doors and a bright-tiled lobby, full of pink-faced young couples who had good jobs downtown and came home laughing in cabs. There had been a party on the roof the night before—a summer ritual of sorts—and apparently no one had cleaned up. The lawn chairs were still out in their lazy, haphazard clusters, and around them the tar was scattered with beer bottles and plastic cups, reminders of the world's disposable pleasures. The things you throw away.

Late, very late in the afternoon, when I could stand to be contained no longer, I went out to buy the *Times*. It was a distinct relief to get away from the apartment by that point. It would have been a distinct relief to get away from myself too, if such a thing could be managed. But how?

Anyway, I tried. At a diner on Broadway, I bought a cup of coffee and opened the newspaper, as one always does, hopefully. The coffee was thin but fresh. I could feel the caffeine squeeze my heart even as it impelled me through the trivial maddening logic of the crossword puzzle. You would never have guessed to look at me that my life was in the process of falling apart. But then that's the thing about puzzles and games: you try to work through them, but by the end they have somehow worked through you instead, bearing you up and carrying you away.

In any event, between the puzzle and my depression I was sufficiently absorbed that I did not register the presence of the fellow in the next booth until he wadded up a napkin and hit me on the cheek with it. It could not have been tossed with much force: it felt like a feather.

"Hey, Sam," he said, rather shyly. "How's it going?"

It was Ronnie Oldham from the office. Ronnie, I noticed, was doing the puzzle too. He was nursing a cup of tea, a Mont Blanc pen in his hand, wearing one of the misshapen turtle-necks he wore to cover his Adam's apple, which because of a thyroid condition, he'd once told me, was more prominent than most people's. His black hair was uncombed and hung limply over his pockmarked cheeks. His long legs were loosely crossed, revealing argyle socks and several inches of bony calf, ghost-white under the fluorescence. He looked, as he often looked, like a bespectacled praying mantis. Wisps of steam rising from his teacup had dampened his thick lenses, but he didn't seem aware of it. He had terrific powers of concentration but was lousy in social or outdoor situations. In fact, Ronnie Oldham was the sort of person, I thought, who might very well spend his Saturday afternoons doing crossword puzzles in a coffee shop.

Still, after the morning I'd just spent it cheered me a little to be out among people, spending money, running into acquaintances, taking part in things. The truth was I was glad to see him.

"Not terribly well," I said.

"Sorry to hear it."

"What are you doing here, Ronnie? I thought you lived in Hoboken."

"Moved," he said. "Ninetieth and West End. Bought a co-op."

I nodded. Late capitalism—with its co-ops and buyouts, its money markets, CDs, IRAs, and Ginny Maes—was a development that had somehow passed me by. Occasionally my mother, who kept track of such things, saw fit to update me on the various career moves and realty transactions of my old friends from grammar school, and the extent of my estrangement would sink in. But Ronnie Oldham was only twenty-nine years old, and, I thought, an even more marginal person in these respects than I was. So it was with some difficulty that I made my voice sound bright. "That's great," I said.

"My wife's money," he explained. "I could never afford it."

"I didn't know you were married, Ronnie."

"Sure. Four years now. You?"

"No."

"That woman you're always arguing with on the telephone. I thought—"

"No."

"Oh . . . so anyway, where've you been keeping yourself? I've hardly seen you lately."

"I took some time off to work at home," I said.

"Oh, right, I forgot. I heard you were trying to write some pieces. Wonderful idea. Perfect for you. How'd it go?"

"Not well."

"On the other hand, maybe your temperament isn't right for it. You may require more structure. That's often the case. I require a great deal of structure myself."

"I think my problem is with the conception. Getting focused, finding a point of view. You know."

"Interesting," he said, rubbing his chin. He seemed delighted to be in my company all of a sudden. People really are happier to be around you when you're down. Who, given the choice, wouldn't prefer to be the one offering condolence and advice over the one who receives it?

"So it's the focus that's the strenuous part, is that it? Once you're underway, presumably, there's no problem."

"Oh, there are problems there too. But they're secondary ones."

"Interesting."

I thought if he said interesting one more time I was going to leave.

"I admire you for trying, though," he continued. "I don't think I could write myself. I don't take criticism well. Plus, I'm not ambitious in that way. It's shameful to admit, but I've never really wanted to be famous. I'm a behind-the-scenes type, I guess. Strictly editorial. What I mean is," he said, taking a breath, "I'm more than comfortable with my present arrangement."

"It must be nice to know yourself so well," I said. "To have such a good grasp, I mean, on your own strengths and weaknesses."

"I don't know how nice it is. But it's probably smart."

I seemed to be a magnet for self-satisfied people that summer. Ray Spurlock, Aaron Brenner, now Ronnie Oldham. Any minute I expected the waitress and grill cook to plop down in my booth and tell me how perfectly suited they were to the work they were doing.

"I see you've finished the puzzle," I said, peering over his shoulder.

"Yes. What about you? Get Nine Across?"

I looked down at the paper, the quadratic jumble of squares. I'd filled about half of them but now that I glanced over my answers they seemed suspect, each letter an underfed inmate in some lexical lock-up, arbitrarily detained in its cell. Nine Across was blank. For a variety of reasons I was not inclined to admit this to Ronnie, whom I could now sense trying to peek over *my* shoulder. "I'm not finished," I said.

He nodded, unsurprised.

"Have you talked to Spurlock?" I asked. "He seems to be in a funk these days."

"Oh yes. The brass, you know, all came back early from the Hamptons. There've been a number of meetings. Closed doors. Jungle drums. Surly rumors."

"What kind of surly rumors?"

"For one thing, they're talking about cutting our section."

"They're always talking about cutting our section. It never means anything. It's just a polite form of harassment because we're on another floor and nobody likes us."

"Yes, but they're serious this time," he said. "These are bad days for science, you know. There's a general perception that there's just too much of it around. Even I feel it sometimes. Don't you?"

"Yes."

"We all do," he said gloomily. "Up till now, we've had it

good in this century. But lately people are beginning to resent us. Too many studies. Too much contradictory data, too many hard facts. Hard facts are hard; people are tired of them. They want science to go away and leave them alone."

"Maybe you're wrong," I said. "Maybe it's just the opposite."

"Probably both things are true. Hey, did you hear about Bill Kaplow?"

"No."

"He got a pink slip this week. This is not a rumor. Also, Jack Dow has been sent to Miami, and Sally Winner flew out to the Coast with a briefcase full of floppies. Belts are being tightened, Sam. Ad revenues at record lows. We're talking furloughs, early retirements. You hear my voice? The high pitch, the fragmented sentences? That's a sure sign of fear."

"What are you worried about? You're a star, Ronnie. They'd never let you go. *I'm* the one who should be worried."

Ronnie took off his glasses and wiped them with his napkin. It was his turn, of course, to say that *I* was a star and had nothing to worry about, but he didn't. He fell into one of his abstraction fogs instead. Thoughtfully he dipped his head for a moment to study the dried swirling film that the busboy's sponge had left on the Formica table like an enormous thumbprint. Whatever he saw there—chaos theory, particle physics—was hidden from me. But I remembered now why people at the office didn't like Ronnie Oldham. He was self-contained; he didn't care. Too busy being singularly brilliant to have any of the normal social graces—to make the allowances and offer the small meaningless lies we seem to require from our friends—in moments of expectancy he fell back upon his own resources, which were considerable, and left you to fend for yourself. But because he was only twenty-nine, and was innocent and guileless and had bad skin, you did not quite feel justified hating him for it.

"I'd better go," he said, checking his watch. "Ta Shin's got a class at five. Have to baby-sit."

"Baby-sit?"

"Yeah."

"Baby-sit who?"

He laughed and looked around uneasily. "Um, you're kidding me, right?"

"Oh God," I said.

"Sam, you knew I had a kid. I brought her to the Christmas party, remember, a few weeks after she was born? You don't remember?"

There must be something wrong with me, I thought. I seemed to be blanking out all of the important things.

"Anyway—" He leaned forward, gathering his papers, "I have to go in a sec. But do me a favor, come in early on Monday. We need to look like workaholics for a while. A united front, a busy and valuable team. Just for a few weeks," he said. "A little extra effort."

"What kind of effort?"

"You know. Politicking. Hang out in the hallways, say hello to people. They're a fickle crowd, Sam. A little banter over the coffee machine might do us some good."

"This is very strange advice, Ronnie, coming from you. I've never seen you banter over the coffee machine in all the time I've known you."

"I don't drink coffee. Too nervous making. I've taken to loitering in the men's room instead. People are nicer, I find, when their hands are wet."

"That's an interesting theory."

"I'm serious," he said. "We're talking Darwinism 101 here, adapt to survive. Because an ice age is coming, you know. Glaciers in motion. Put your ear to the ground, you'll hear the first tectonic rumbles."

"What happened to global warming?"

"I'm speaking figuratively, of course."

"Oh."

"Don't worry, global warming's doing just fine. Read the field notes I put on your desk once in a while. The ozone's in shreds. Ion bombardment from power lines. The North Sea is boiling." Ronnie was getting a little steamed himself. A line of sweat had broken out in that pinkish cleft between his nose and his top lip; it glistened like so many pearls. "Before I go," he said, "let me consult you on something that's been troubling me. It's about AIDS."

"What about it?"

"Well, where do you think it comes from?"

"I don't know. Africa?"

"Yes, but why? Immune systems are down planet-wide, this much has been documented. The question is why Africa and not somewhere else?

"I have no idea, Ronnie."

"Of course you don't," he said. "Because it's all been suppressed. But let me lay out a theory for you, okay?"

"Don't you have to go?"

"It'll just take a sec," he said. "First, consider the phenomenon of forty years-plus of bomb tests in the Pacific. Now factor in the wind patterns, the rains, the currents. See what I'm getting at? I've got the meteorological charts at the office, computer printouts, faxed from a lab in Sydney. Sam, I've talked to some of the people down there. Mavericks, brilliant fellows. They confirm everything. A consensus, you see, has begun to emerge. That consensus points to one thing." He wiped his lip with the back of his hand. "*Radiation.*"

An idea began to stir inside me.

"It's a simple matter of cause and effect. Nuclear rain over a prolonged period lowers the immune system of an entire area. Hence, systems become vulnerable to new strains of viruses. Hence, when one appears, as we now see in the monkey studies—I have the files in my office—we find an incredible rate of contagion throughout the population. Hence, borders being as porous as they are, it spreads to other areas, also weakened but maybe not as much, not yet. Massive immunological havoc ensues. Tragic," he added, not uncheerfully.

"Look, if all this is true, how come nobody knows?"

"Be realistic, Sam. It's way too bleak. Think how it would

demoralize the medical research effort—in which, let me remind you, billions of dollars are invested. Let's say you shift the focus from the virus, which maybe there's a cure for, to the irradiation of the planet, which has already *happened*. What happens then? What happens to the pharmaceutical market? What happens to the congressional committees, the government funding, the university labs? You see the problem?"

"So wait, you're saying there's some kind of a huge conspiracy to cover all this up?"

He made a face. "I don't favor the term conspiracy. Let's say an ambience—an ambience of neglect. This stuff, let's face it, it's a downer all around. Bad for research-and-development. Better to call it a crazy rumor and hope it goes away. But just wait a couple years. See what happens along the wind-path from Chernobyl, and the coast of Brittany, and a thousand other places." He gave a neutral sigh. "The bottom line is this. Nothing goes away in nature. That's a physical law. It just turns into something else. Wernher von Braun said that. And he should know. He should know."

"Your sentences are getting fragmented again."

"Fear. Naked fear. It always affects me this way."

"You're not much fun, are you, Ronnie?"

"Fun? I don't know. I guess not. Are you?"

"I don't think so, no."

"Well then. What's the problem?"

"What are you doing for dinner on Tuesday?"

"Why?"

"Because I'd like to have you over. I have some people coming. I thought I'd cook something."

He thought about it. "I'm not comfortable in dinner parties. I prefer smaller groups."

"This will be very small. I promise. We'll just eat and talk. Maybe we can dig a little deeper into this theory of yours. Maybe even talk about collaborating."

"On what?"

"I don't know. Some kind of article."

"Us?"

"Why not? If you're right about what's going on at the office, then we've got nothing to lose. And besides, isn't this what you said we need? To take the initiative, come up with some brilliant, groundbreaking piece that only we science guys could come up with—won't that show them how relevant and necessary we are?"

Already the idea was struggling to its feet in my mind, gaining a kind of shaky, teetering credibility. After all, we had untold resources to draw from. Ronnie would be happy doing the drudge work, and I would be happy doing some real writing for a change. Both of us were obviously ready to make a move. Here was a move, wasn't it? Something that mattered. Something *contemporary*. Something *important*.

Ronnie, for his part, looked dubious. "I don't know."

"We could write it together. If the magazine won't print it, we'll take it somewhere else. I know a guy at *Esquire*."

"I don't know. Ta Shin's got a class on Tuesdays. I have the baby."

"Well, bring her to dinner then. I'll whip up some creamed carrots or something. Does she eat creamed carrots?"

"No."

"Well, whatever."

"I'll have to get back to you," Ronnie said. "I appreciate the offer though. We've never socialized before, have we? I have no idea, for instance, what kind of stereo equipment you have. Tape or CD? Or DAT?"

"Records," I said.

He smiled. "I should have known."

"I keep meaning to upgrade."

"Sure," he said, checking his watch. "Have to go. See you Monday?"

"Monday."

Watching him shuffle to the door, I marveled at Ronnie. Even the pocked skin on his cheeks, with its thousands of tiny pale impressions like bird-tracks, seemed dignified and intriguing to me now. I'd had him wrong. He was no kid, no science geek lost in the pulsing lights of cyberspace, but a grown man, a homeowner, a father, with that special planetary alertness—that heightened perception of latent threat, latent promise—which parents of young children seem to acquire as naturally as the bags under their eyes.

This metamorphosis of so homely a figure as Ronnie Oldham was a little unsettling. Perhaps there were twin doors of possibility that revolved inside us all. I thought again of the morning I had spent, and the dinner of the evening before, wondering over ends and beginnings.

The coffee shop emptied, then filled again. When I glanced at the clock I found the day nearly gone.

I looked down at the crossword puzzle, still half-complete. After a certain point, you know all the clues and yet you keep going over them anyway. It's like a higher form of channel-surfing. Looking for an opening in a crowded field, searching for something that may not even be there: something unexpected, accidental. Something you don't know you know.

A Change of Position

Sunday I woke at nine, put on my sweat clothes, and rode the bus down Broadway to Central Park. It was a warm, hazy morning. The sky was just lying there, ashen and heavy-looking, as though recovering from a long debauch. But then perhaps it was my own recovery I saw there—or wished to.

The bus was nearly deserted. Two Hispanic kids in church clothes sat in the front row, speaking to each other in singsong, conspiratorial whispers. A wino was stretched across the backseat, snoring faintly through his nose. Choosing a seat halfway between them, I leaned my head against the cool window. Cathedral bells rang above us. The brakes squealed; the doors sighed; the engine made its plaintive whine. Amid all this urban music I too began to doze. As we rumbled through the Eighties, headed toward midtown, I felt myself falling into the wide, pliant net of a dream. Men with black hats and white beards were dancing around me in slow, fervid circles, swaying to music I did not hear, chanting a name I did not recognize . . . was it mine?

"'Scuse me."

One of the kids from the front row stood patiently before me. He was about ten years old with a sloping forehead and wide, bulbous eyes. His hair was cut very short. Precise lines of scalp were visible here and there, razor cuts that were like little roads leading nowhere. This divisive and aimless geometry seemed rampant of late. Despite the heat he was wearing corduroy pants and a nifty wool blazer that was a couple of sizes too big. His brown shoes gleamed.

"Hey, mister," he said. "Can I ask you a question?"

"Sure."

"You aren't Jesus Christ, by any chance?"

"Pardon?"

"You aren't by any chance Jesus Christ?"

"No."

And that seemed to settle the matter. He headed back to his seat, not so much disappointed, I thought, as relieved. Suppose I *was* Jesus Christ; what would he have said next? But then, as if having just remembered some obscure but relevant fact, he turned and clumped down the aisle again. "Hey, man," he said, "you sure?"

No one is so skeptical, apparently, as a true believer.

"I'm sure," I said.

"What's your name then?"

"Sam. Sam Karnish."

He shook his head dubiously. "You look a lot like him," he said. "'Cept for the sweats."

"I'm going to play softball," I said.

"You are?"

"Uh huh."

"What position?"

"Third."

He shook his head gravely, thinking it over. In the end it was this last bit of information that seemed to persuade him. What position, after all, would the Son of God play? Pitcher, maybe, or center field. Very unlikely he would play third base. I must be someone else.

"This is my stop," I said. "See you around."

When I got off I could see him peering out the window to check the cross-street, just in case, noting for the record that if Jesus Christ really did live in New York and really did wear sweat pants, then he could be found on Sunday mornings at the Sixty-first Street softball fields.

Honestly, I wouldn't have been surprised. With the possible exception of sex (*always*, in my experience, a possible exception), softball was the nearest I came to what the mystics among us call ecstasy—a realm of deep inner soundings, of timeless rhythms and strange, sudden elations; of grace. Not that I was such a hot ballplayer, far from it. At bat I had a hitch in my swing. It was just a little dip of the elbow, invisible to most, but it prevented me from pulling the ball with any power and consigned me to that least dramatic of categories, the single-up-the-middle specialist. There were other deficiencies. In the outfield I had what we called heavy legs. Slow to pick up the ball off the bat—heavy eyes?—I was at the same time not terribly fleet when it came to chasing it down, nor, it must be said, particularly accurate on my throws, which were launched like moonshots in a high, hopeful trajectory toward the infield before falling noiselessly to earth. Perhaps I had heavy arms, too.

Fortunately I did have talent at one position: third base. It had to do, I think, with the locale and geometry of the bag, the steep angle of vision it afforded. There was a sense of safe enclosure that came from being so close to the foul line, bounded on one side but free on all others to range as I wished, to go after balls to my left if I thought I could get them and to allow them to skip past if I didn't. I loved this dual option, this privilege of choice. The snug proximities of the infield, the meaningless patter, the eroding chalk lines, the cheery clang of the aluminum bats, the way a big swing from a right-handed hitter squeezed my heart for a moment and then released it—I loved all these things too. I loved the crumbly feel of the dirt, with its capricious, godlike dispensation of good hops and bad hops. I loved our blue polyester shirts with the gold lettering across the front announcing our concise, unpretentious name: FRANK'S TEAM. I loved our pitcher, Ernie Huddle, aloof in his territorial sanctity, moodily toeing the rubber a few yards away. I loved the presence of my friend Bando, whom I'd known even longer than Warren, behind me in left field—his stubby legs, his beer-thick waist, his diving head-first catches, his penchant for calling opposition batters "darling" and "lovebug"; and my collegial bond with Steve Burke, our gentle giant at first base, waving his big glove across the diamond, each of us devoted to the maintenance of our chosen corner. Within mine I was another person, a sharp fellow with light limbs, good hands, quick reflexes. When smashes came whistling down the line I saw them moving toward me almost magically, floating in dream-time, before I reached out my glove to snare them. I loved that. Sometimes I was so nimble and alert that I actually loved myself.

My teammates—who had expected little when I joined the squad, on Bando's recommendation, several years back—were favorably surprised by my prowess. What with my long hair and bad back and generally poor musculature, I'd been no one's idea of a natural.

"Yo, Sammy," called our captain, Frank Romano. He was lying on the grass, doing his sit-ups and leg lifts, part of a calisthenic routine so extensive he'd arrive at games an hour early to complete it. "Where were you the last couple of weeks?"

"My back's been a little stiff," I said.

"You need to loosen up more. I told you. You're sure it's okay now?"

"It's fine. Last week I had a wedding, otherwise I'd have made it."

"Weddings are nice," Frank mused amiably, upside down. "Good for business. How many rolls you think the guy shot?"

"It was a woman. And I have no idea."

Frank ran a photo lab in Yonkers, which was never far from his thoughts. Every summer he nagged us to pose for team pictures, and every summer we turned him down. "Figure ten if they were WASPs. For Greeks or Italians, at least twenty."

"They were Jews," I said.

He considered. "Twenty-five."

"What about the game? How'd you make out?"

"Very bad. One for six. A lousy single."

"I meant the team."

"Lost a doubleheader. But it was the Cards. They always kill us."

This was true, I should point out, of most of the other teams in the league as well. By and large we were a nicer group of people than they were but we had problems winning ball games, and our failures were beginning to make us all, by this point, a little less nice. Especially Frank. After all, he'd beneficently given us his name to wear on our chests and placed his photo equipment at our disposal, and what had we given him in exchange but heartache and worry?

Now he got to his feet, brushing his pants off with neat little slaps. "By the way," he drawled, an afterthought, "we put in Henry at third."

"Oh?" Henry was Steve Burke's little brother, a recent addition to the team. Tall, rangy, and silent, he was a bike messenger by profession, and he played with some of that species' manic intensity. It didn't hurt his prospects that he'd also shown terrific power in batting practice. "How'd he do?"

"Not bad. Not bad." Frank hawked some phlegm and spit it out noisily between us. "Fact I'm thinking of starting him today."

"Starting him where?"

"I dunno," Frank said. "Somewhere in the infield." He spat again and looked down the right field line, where several of my teammates, Bando and Henry among them, were lazily shagging flies.

Frank, to his credit, had never wanted to be manager. Several years ago he had been chosen by default, because he was a good guy and a good shortstop, and because he was better than the rest of us at keeping track of the money and remembering who and at what field we were supposed to play the next week. I would not say he was a bad manager, but rather that he was made uncomfortable by the responsibilities.

Short and frizzy-haired, pug nose reddened from every stray pollen, Frank had his hands full already. Three kids, a live-in mother-in-law who spoke no English, a photo lab getting killed by the chain stores—no wonder he brought so little energy to the personnel decisions that awaited him on Sunday mornings. He'd have been a lot happier left to himself for a change, I think, than he was dealing with all the phone calls, lineup cards, equipment shortages, position switches, bruised egos, and frenzied arguments with the umpires that being a manager required. When presented with more than one of these tasks at the same time, he had a habit of jiggling dirt in his hand and spitting irascibly, as if to free himself of some bad taste in his mouth. He was doing that now. I knew what it meant.

"Starting him at third, you mean," I said.

"I dunno. I haven't figured it out yet."

"Frank, you can't do this to me."

He shook his head and spit again, before falling into the next phase of his warm-up routine, deep knee-bends. "I haven't done anything," he said.

But very soon, once he'd completed his toe touches and jumping jacks and called us all together, he did. Though Frank's voice as he read out the lineup sounded unusually gruff and regretful, when he arrived at the seventh spot—*my* spot—he did not read my name. It took a moment for the import of this to sink in. Everyone on the team, even Henry, had come over during batting practice to pat me on the ass and tell me how badly I'd been missed in the debacle of the previous week; but now, gathering their gloves and retying their cleats, they all avoided my eyes. At least I assumed they did; I could not know for certain, as I was busy avoiding theirs.

"Hang in there, Sammy," called Bando over his shoulder. Trotting out to left field, he made a flecking motion of nonchalance with the tip of his glove. "We'll get you in soon." Then they all arrived at their predetermined spots, and Ernie finished his warm-up tosses, and Charles, our catcher, snapped the ball down to Jeffrey at second base, where he applied a swift tag to an imaginary runner, and the game started. I had to watch from the stands. There I sat with the wives and the gym bags and the coolers of juice and, spaced among us at odd intervals, like musical notes in some atonal opera, the park vagrants in their tattered clothes, their morning languor. Above our heads the great towers loomed. The Hitachi sign on Fifty-ninth Street kept flashing out the current weather—89 degrees, Partly Cloudy—as if it were somehow news, as if we weren't all perfectly capable of registering its hellishness ourselves.

Two lousy weeks away, and I'd lost my position. Of course compared to all the other things I had lost that weekend it was no great tragedy. But my hold on this slippery planet as it careened through space was getting more tenuous, it seemed, by the day.

"Hey, Sam." It was Bando's wife, Thea, looking up from the Arts and Leisure section a few rows away. "Why aren't you out there? Not feeling well?"

"I've been benched," I said.

"Too bad. I always enjoyed watching you, you know. You were very entertaining."

This was flattering at first, but then, when I heard what tense she was using, I grew despondent.

"Oh well. It's just a silly game." Crinkling her nose, she went back to her reading. A shopping bag from Zabar's was open between her legs. A cunning consumer, Thea drove in from Park Slope every Sunday not for the pleasure of watching our games but in order to arrive at the delicatessen when it opened, so as to avoid standing in line. Later, if the day was fair and there was nothing better to do, she might condescend to drop by and check us out.

She noticed me looking at the bag. "Bagels, croissants, rye bread. What's your pleasure?"

"I'll take a croissant."

"Here."

The croissant was springy and moist, still warm from the oven. As I chewed it I looked over the field at my teammates, who had already fallen three runs behind. Then four. Once the game began to slip out of reach, I could feel some of my internal tension go with it. Thea was right: they *did* look silly out there, flailing around in their beaky caps and polyester shirts, a bunch of overgrown boys, failed jocks, making their inane chatter, pretending it mattered. It didn't. I knew it didn't, and knowing that should have been useful in some way, only I was unsure how. Behind us the sun peeped through the scrim of clouds, spilling in pools over our shoulders and onto our laps. I was content for the moment to be eating breakfast with Thea, whom I'd always liked. Not everyone did. She was a cellist with a very minor reputation and a lot of grudges.

"You're Jewish, aren't you, Thea?"

She narrowed her eyes at me. "Why? Taking a poll?"

"Just curious. Know very much about it?"

"Well, I know enough to agree with those nice Jewish boys Marx and Freud. It's all bullshit."

"How so?"

"Come on, Sam. It's for fuzzballs. People need an escape route, a trapdoor from the hard stuff. That's it. All religion does is provide an aesthetic for intellectual surrender."

"Like music, you mean?"

She cocked an eyebrow. "Nobody kills," she said, "because of music. Nobody has a kid they don't want because of music. Music doesn't make you give your brain over and it doesn't lead you away from what's really important."

"Like what?"

"Like what? Like ourselves. Like our fucked-up political and social structures. Like oppression of other people. Lots of things."

"So you spend a lot of your time thinking about these other things? I mean, since you're not distracted?"

She narrowed her eyes. "You're trying to start a fight with me, aren't you, Sam?"

"Not at all."

"You got benched and you don't like it, so you're taking it out on me."

"No, no, I'm not taking anything. I'm just curious." I considered for a moment. "This morning on my way down here a kid asked if I was Jesus Christ."

"You know, now that you mention it, there is a weird resemblance."

"Shut up, Thea."

"I mean it. The long face, the nose, those big wet brown eyes . . ."

"Shut up, Thea."

"Oh, Jesus wasn't so terrible. He gets a bad rap, but aside from some questionable advertisements for himself he was okay. All he really wanted was for Jews to be authentic Jews. That's what the Sermon on the Mount was about, you know: not abolish the law but fulfill it. All that Christian stuff only came in later, with that asshole Paul."

"I thought you didn't know anything about religion."

She shrugged. "I never said I didn't know. I just said it's bullshit. By the way, how was the wedding?"

"It was okay. Kind of confusing."

"That crazy Warren. You actually got to meet the blushing bride?"

"Debbie, yeah. She was okay."

"She's a kid, for God's sake. I bet she didn't like you, did she?"

"She'll warm up. Anyway, it's hard to get to know someone at their own wedding."

"Uh huh," she said. "You should have brought Donna. *That* would've been interesting."

I nodded. Donna, of course, had been pregnant that weekend. While I was on the plane. While I was drinking myself into a stupor at the wedding. While I was being chauffeured to the airport by the Brenners. Donna had been pregnant the entire time.

Two pregnancies with two different women, and what did I have to show for it? O for two. How many more at-bats would I get?

"Hey," Thea asked, "you okay?"

I shrugged.

"You're having some kind of identity thing here, aren't you, Sam?"

"How can you tell?"

"You have that fuzzy look guys get. I've seen it before. Bando went through one of these episodes last year, you know, after his mother died. But you probably know all about it."

"No. No, I didn't know."

"Men," she snorted. "What would happen if you dropped all the sports shit and actually talked to each other once in a while?"

"We'd tremble with fear."

"Ha! Right!" Briskly she dusted her hands of crumbs. "Well, it wasn't pretty. He moped around the apartment for months. Every Sunday he'd talk about going to mass. He missed confession, he said. He wanted to get back to it. But he never went. I guess he was waiting for me to tell him what to do. But I'm not his mother, you know?"

"What did he want to confess?"

"Who knows? Maybe he was having an affair."

"Bando? Nah."

"You're right. Look at him out there—who'd have an affair with that?" She watched him fondly for a moment as he scratched his bearish stomach and hollered insults from the outfield, amusing himself. "Well then, maybe the masturbation. He does it a lot. I don't care, but I know he feels like he shouldn't. The problem is, he's got just enough twisted Catholicism in him to believe his jerking off a few times a week caused that seventy-two-year-old bitch to have a stroke."

"And what happened?"

"What usually happens? It passed."

I looked out at Bando in left field, jiggling one leg as he

waited for the next pitch. A few times a week? Good Lord. I
wondered, given my current rate of self-abuse, how many old
people I myself had done in.

"You know, it's funny," Thea went on. "All his mother ever
used to talk about when we got together was the Jews. Lovely
people, she'd say. So intelligent, so cultured, such a rich history. Einstein, Brandeis, Golda Meir, Barbra Streisand—she'd
tick them off on her fingers, the whole wonderful tribe. Then
the second I'd leave the house she'd start counting the silverware." She frowned. "Not that my parents were any better. My
father, you know, hasn't spoken to me since I married Bando."

"I had no idea."

"Oh, he keeps track of me through Mom and my brothers,
but that's it. Won't visit, won't call, won't send presents on
my birthday. This, mind you, from an intelligent and cultured
Jewish person. A *Democrat*. Thousands of phone calls for
Cuomo and the UJA, but not one to his daughter. Now," she
said with a bitter laugh, "any other questions you want to ask
me about religion?"

"I guess not."

"I don't like things that make us separate. That's no trick, is
it? We're separate to begin with. The problem is to come
together."

There seemed to be a growing consensus that this was
indeed the problem. However, my thoughts were no longer on
matters of the spirit, but—triggered by Thea's last words, and
the sight of her plump bare arms in the winking sunlight—the
flesh. On the graph of my consciousness there was a point where
these two lines threatened to converge, and that point, I
remembered now, was the Hasidic woman, Magda Brenner.
Who was coming over for dinner in a couple of days. Dinner and
what else? What lines on what graph were converging for *her*?

"Your father is religious, then?" I asked Thea.

"Mmm." She'd gone back to Arts and Leisure.

"Suppose I was going to cook your father dinner. What
would I be likely to make?"

"Why would you want to cook him dinner?"

"Let's just say I was going to. Hypothetically."

"Well, let's see. He loves bland, mushy things that take a real long time to cook and keep my mother in the kitchen all day in servitude. Kugel, cholent, *tsimmis*, *knedlach*—" She paused. "What's the matter?"

"Thea, I don't even know what any of that shit *is*."

"So what? It doesn't matter. He wouldn't eat it at your place anyway."

"Why not?"

"Because it has to be cooked in a kosher kitchen. Do you have one?"

"Of course I don't have one. You've seen my apartment. I hardly have a kitchen."

"Then you're out of luck."

"Wait," I said, "what about bringing food in? Suppose I found a kosher restaurant, I could just bring in the dinner, right?"

"I guess so, but it'd be pretty expensive. Kosher places tend to charge a lot. It's a narrow market, so they can get away with it."

There was a moment of silence as I considered the fallen condition of my finances. And yet what about this new article idea, this collaboration with Ronnie Oldham? If it went well—and how could it not, I thought, given the urgency and scope of the subject—it would enhance my career prospects enormously, to say nothing of the tertiary benefit of perhaps doing some good in the world. Yes, I told myself, everything was going to work out. Because that was the kind of person I was: the kind for whom everything worked out. Of course, seen another way, I was the other kind of person too.

"That's okay," I heard myself telling Thea. "I can blow a little money once in a while."

"There's a place on Columbus that's supposed to be good. My parents go there sometimes."

"Columbus. Perfect."

"So tell me, who's this hypothetical dinner for, anyway? I take it my father isn't really who you have in mind."

"Nobody you know, Thea. Just some friends."

"Uh huh."

"*New* friends," I said.

She laughed a little. "You may not believe this, Sam, but I think about other things, from time to time, than you and your sex life."

"Me too," I said, rather desperately, because I so much wanted it to be true.

By now the third inning was over. I had no idea what the score was. In front of the bench, Frank thoughtfully consulted the napkin on which he'd written the lineup. After a moment, he tucked it back into his pocket and headed out to shortstop. When he got there, he stopped, hesitated, and turned and waved in our direction.

"Look," Thea said, "they want you."

"No they don't. He's just waving hello."

"He's putting you in. What's the matter with you?" Thea demanded. "Don't you know when you're being *called*?"

It so happened Thea was right. "Come on, Sammy," Frank was hollering. "Stop gabbing and let's play ball."

Hastily I reached for my mitt. The leather was like a living thing, soft and warm from its sunbath; it slipped onto my fingers so easily it might have been my own hand the Spalding people had used for the model. Unfortunately I'd left my cap at home and had to run out on the field bareheaded. Then when I arrived at third base I found young lean Henry still there.

"Hey," I said, "what gives?"

"Don't look at me," said Henry. Uneasily he smoothed the dirt around with the toe of his cleats. "It's up to Frank."

"Frank?"

"You're out in right, Sammy," Frank called from shortstop. He was blowing bubbles with his chewing gum, a sure sign of authority-distress.

"Right?"

"Sergio pulled a muscle. We *need* you out there."

This was exactly the kind of transparent managerial lie that Frank, who was blushing as he said it, had never learned to execute properly. However, I didn't push the point. I went out to right. What choice did I have?

When I got there I really did miss my cap, because the sun was blasting directly into my eyes. Everything before me wore a tight sequined skirt of light. The field itself shimmered like a vision, albeit a distant one. Out in the long, humming grass, under that hot unblinking eye, a feeling of cool detachment stole over me, as if I were watching everything, myself included, through the wrong end of a telescope. At home plate the batters looked toylike and remote as they waved their frail sticks, and the chatter of the infielders—putterinthere, putterinthere—sounded as tinny and querulous as birdcalls. I had been playing softball on Sunday mornings for over a decade; yet the game before me did not seem quite like softball somehow, now that I was standing at the wrong position.

There was a pop fly to short. I saw it for a moment and then it was gone, lost in the yellow haze, the tease and flutter of overhead kites. Behind the backstop, couples were strolling along the cinder path, bouncing toddlers on their shoulders, headed for the children's zoo across the park. What was I doing? What was the score? How far from the lines I stood, how out in the field. How lost. The gnats swarmed, the bells bonged, the sun swam in my eyes like a river of gold, and for a moment I felt I was under water, a pearl enclosed within the crusted shell of myself. With terrible clarity I was able to see everyone I knew—my teammates, Donna, Warren Pinsky—receding from my life. Or was it my life that was receding from them? In any case, we were all headed in different directions.

A ball fell out of the sky and landed in my glove. I threw it in to Jeffrey, who seemed to want it, and resumed my brooding meditations.

I looked up at the high towers that ringed the park. Behind

the gleaming windows, people were stirring. For them it was not the hazy dream-time of a game, but the cool linear reality of Sunday morning. Coffee, newspapers. Music on the stereo, an oven heating bagels, your spouse in the shower, children wrestling on the carpet, a list of home improvement projects taped neatly to the refrigerator. Sunday morning. Oh, once or twice, as the day peeled itself like a fruit, you might catch yourself at the window, sipping a mug of coffee and observing what unfolded silently below: the weekend ballplayers on their bumpy diamonds, so immersed in their rituals and codes, their stylized choreographies, that they never thought to look up to see you looking down at them, never thought to stop and wonder, as you did, whether at a certain point when it came to games it was better to play, to watch, or to ignore them altogether.

"Hey, Sammy," I heard someone call.

I looked over to see Bando waving from the sidelines.

"Look alive, willya?"

My chest fluttered wildly. Another line drive, I thought, headed my way. But searching the sky I could find only that big yellow beachball, the sun, hovering in place, not coming down. No way to catch that. So I did not understand at first why Bando was waving at me, or why Frank was hollering at me from the coaching box, or why Thea was watching me so thoughtfully from the stands. What was *their* problem? Why place me all the way out here if they were going to change their minds again the moment I got comfortable?

Then the opposing team's right fielder jogged up to inform me that, seeing as how their half of the inning was now over, I should probably go ahead and get the fuck out of his way.

CHAPTER 8

FRESH STARTS

It so happens we came back and *won* that game with a late-inning rally, in which my own contributions—several effort-less catches in the field, and two hits in three at-bats—were, as Frank himself acknowledged later with a swift pat on my butt, "a real factor." All of which heartened me considerably. When times are bad it's important to be resilient, make adjustments, find new positions from which to operate. Walking home up steamy Broadway, Frank's words flowed through my head like a mantra. A *factor, a factor.* Look at all these people who'd only just woken up and gone out for the paper! Here it was noon and they had done nothing, while I had lived an entire life, it seemed, as a factor out on the ballfield.

Off the ballfield, of course, was another story. But perhaps I would prove resilient there too. The most important games of your life were mental ones, after all. And I was ready for a fresh start. It was time to put past failures behind me, throw off old habits and immerse in the here and now. That's what being a factor was all about, wasn't it? Turning things around, coming from behind. I could feel it happening already. The sun was hot but my nerves for a change were cool. I watched my reflection sail across the shop windows, exempt from clutter inside and out. There was nothing to hold me back.

Thus by the time Tuesday night and my ambitious little dinner party rolled around, I had good reason, I think, to believe that the very singularity of its composition, inspiration, and cuisine might combine, when factored through the factor of myself, to yield a rare and perhaps even magical evening. But I'll come to that in a minute.

First, I want to talk about how well things went at the office.

As Ronnie had advised, I arrived early on Monday. Too early. I was so restless at home and so eager to get in and start turning things around already that I arrived at seven-thirty, before everyone but the janitors and the security guard, who blinked at me sleepily over his console as though I were some wayward and perplexing apparition. The lobby floor was still damp; I could hear the squish of my soles as I walked, and see their impressions behind me, marking my progress across the glistening tiles. But it was pleasant to be there early for a change. It gave me an opportunity to study the building, take the measure of that enormous beast in its sleek repose. The bland chromatic art on the walls. The pale carpets stretching down the unlit corridors. The receding lines of closed doors, their shadows like headstones in the bleached light of morning.

In the deserted bathroom, water was running in all the sinks. Methodically I combed my hair, knotted my tie, tightened my belt. Then I gave the whole ensemble some hard scrutiny in the mirror. The person who scrutinized me back was an old acquaintance I had been ducking for weeks: a midtowner; a sober, expectant man with a cherry leather briefcase, a man who knew where and how to lunch. I gave him a cordial nod of welcome. Then I went out to my cubicle.

For several hours I whittled away at the disorder on my desk, processing clips from the bureaus, reading memos from the stringers, collating files from the library. My colleagues filtered in and out but I scarcely noticed. Outside a passion play of construction and demolition unfolded across the skyline, shirtless men wielding hammers and drills, poised like dancers on their slanting beams. But I kept my back to them. The doughnut cart as it rattled past, the gunshots that rang out on

Sixth Avenue, the brief hubbub when one of the Kelly Girls ran screaming out of Gene Unger's office—I ignored all these too. They were everyday occurrences; I would not let them distract me. I had always been too prey to distraction, and what had it yielded? A cluttered desk, a cluttered life. Time to wipe it clean and start again.

By late morning I was so immersed in this new campaign of mine that I'd almost forgotten why I'd come in so early in the first place: namely, to shore up my crumbling position in the company. So I got busy with that next.

I cruised out to the coffee machine, hungry for contact. The morning pot had boiled down, as it usually had by that hour, to a crusty, brackish residue. In the old days the secretaries would keep it replenished, but those were the old days, when ad rates were shamelessly inflated and Science was still lodged up on the fortieth floor with the other departments. Now we were on our own down here, our skeleton crew, in our corporate purgatory, where the fundamental principles of evaporation held sway and where even on those few occasions there was a visitor to receive, we had no receptionist to do so. All support details we had to take care of ourselves. So I made a new pot and stood there watching it drip for several minutes, waiting for someone to happen by whom I might impress with my rolled-up sleeves and aura of selflessness.

Nobody did. Ronnie Oldham and Allen Reid were buried in their respective cubicles, strictly do-not-disturb. Bob Sedgwick and Cynthia Dunleavy were on vacation. Only Gene Unger was around, loitering at the far end of the corridor, fingering his pipe and squinting to read, for the ten-thousandth time, every cartoon affixed to every darkened office door. Gene was a difficult case. By virtue of his connections—his uncle had been a managing editor in the fifties, his mother a much-beloved copy chief—he enjoyed a lifetime tenure at the magazine which apparently no amount of indolence, incompetence, or sheer boorishness was capable of eroding. He was notorious for his drop-by chats, which were really long metronomic soliloquies about famous people who had at one time or another hung their coats in his father's closet. It was all very sad, of course. But most of us begin to resent feeling sad after a while, and go out of our way to avoid it, which is why by this point everyone on the floor had taken to keeping their doors closed and their lights off during work hours. We were prepared to hunch and cower in the dark if it spared us a visit from that bathetic angel, Gene Unger.

But apparently even Gene had something better to do that day than stop and banter with me at the coffee machine. He veered off down the corridor. I was left standing there with an approachable look on my face, wondering how long I could possibly keep it up, when Arlen Ashby, of all people, came wandering through the corridor in one of his late-morning gin funks. I was so desperate for human contact I gave him a big warm hello.

Perhaps Arlen was a little desperate, too, because he gave me a big warm hello back. Actually he said "Hallo," in a jaunty, just-sailed-in-from-Westport accent that for all I knew might have been authentic. Arlen was from old money and had once been a power on the board but that was years ago; his time had passed. Now there was an air of deteriorating ornamentation about him. He still dressed well but his face was turning into a Jackson Pollock. Broken blood vessels dotted his nose; liver spots speckled his forehead; wild white hairs sprang uselessly from his nostrils and eyebrows. Time's siege was at work upon him. And yet he was conceding nothing.

Arlen's nod to me was abstract but cordial, almost shy. He did not appear unhappy to see me, or whomever it was he thought he was seeing when he looked at me, and I took that for encouragement.

"How you been, Arlen?"

"*Very* well," he said. "Very well indeed."

For a moment he swayed unsteadily before me, watching the coffee drip. "Making coffee?" he asked.

"Yes."

He made a tsking sound of regret through his front teeth. "Can't drink it anymore," he said. "Doctor's orders."

"Sorry to hear that, Arlen."

"Can't be helped. The inner organs are up in arms. They held a meeting in there, presented a list of demands. Now the doctor says I have to go along. But you Science fellows down here, you understand this sort of thing better than I do."

"I guess so."

"Which reminds me," he said, "I was looking for you the other day."

"Yes. Ray told me."

"I've been reading the most marvelous book by some fellow over in England. Oxford College, I believe. Fascinating stuff. He understands how it all works—physics I mean. The motion of subatomic particles, etcetera. He's particularly fine on this business of the ultimate heat death of the universe. Fascinating stuff."

"Oh?"

"It seems there is a substance called Empathy. Very destructive. I don't fully grasp it just yet, but they say it will do us all in over time."

"Wait, you mean *Entropy?*"

"Yes, yes, of course. I suppose you've heard about it, then? A fairly popular area these days, is that it?"

"I suppose so."

"Indeed. Well, it's fascinating stuff. I wonder if you'd care to explain it to me some time. I find it's increasingly important to me, in my later years, to comprehend the essence of things. The enduring principles. Nowadays I try to read only important books on large concepts. Histories, biographies, science. No more movies or novels. A waste of time, don't you think?"

"Probably so."

"Now about this Entropy business. I'd like to pick your brain about it, if you don't mind. What do you say? Willing to kick it around sometime with an old man?"

"The thing is, Arlen, I really don't know very much about

it. You might do better talking to one of the other people, someone with a better background in physics. Like Ronnie or Cynthia."

"Who?"

"Ronnie Oldham. Cynthia Dunleavy." When neither of these names appeared to register upon him, I added, "Of course, I'd be happy to try and do what I can."

"Good. Say, lunch tomorrow?"

In truth I was thinking that I did not really have time to go out for lunch, not this week, with this new article proposal to work on and this towering backlog on my desk to sort through. On the other hand, Arlen and his thirst for essentials might prove a good influence. I was still deliberating on the question when another of the white hairs from upstairs, Harry Flood, strode by on his way to Graphics and nearly knocked us both over.

Harry Flood was a perfect bastard. Not uncoincidentally, he also placed a solid third on the magazine's power chart, just above Ray Spurlock. Imported from Dallas in the late sixties, he was king of the numbers crunchers. Indeed, looking at him now, pounding down the hallway on his boot heels—black-pored, big-shouldered, his pink turkey-wattle neck and his great round belly swaying pendulously over his belt—the epithet seemed almost literal. One could only pray Harry Flood would confine his crunching to numbers and leave the rest of us alone. On his belt he wore a bright red buckle shaped like a football, and around his neck, a narrow black string tie that was almost lost in the vast white sea of his chest. His boots were yellow snakeskin. Exactly how many snakes had gone into their manufacture was a question Ronnie Oldham once ran through his computer. It estimated six. Six *mature* snakes.

Pausing, Flood glanced dispassionately at Arlen, then at me, then back at Arlen. "What are you two boys cooking up, heh? You look thick as thieves."

"Hallo, Harold," said Arlen, with an expression of forbearance.

"Plotting a takeover, eh? I know your type. Who's this?"

"Samuel Karnish," I said, extending my hand.

He ignored it. "New man?"

"Not really. I've been here six years."

"Department?"

"Science."

"Never read it," growled Harry Flood.

"Oh, Harold never reads anything," Arlen informed me. He laid a hand on my shoulder. If Flood frightened him as he did me, it was not apparent. He seemed merry, unperturbed, impervious to assault. A quart of gin in the morning can have wonderful effects. "Anything but pornography, that is."

"*Bullshit*," roared Harry Flood.

"Harold likes to look at naked girls. Vietnamese. It's rather a fetish of his."

"*Bullshit*," Flood roared again, and turned on me. "He's pulling your leg, boy. Don't pay any attention."

"That's what I figured."

"See," he drawled, winking at Arlen, "those girls are *Malaysian*."

At last I caught on. They were only kidding around. These two were *friends*. Without allowing my expression to change, I did a quick rewrite on all my intricate surmises about the dynamics of the board. I really had no idea how things worked behind the scenes.

"What's the name again?"

"Karnish."

"Karnish . . ." I watched Harry Flood carefully as he digested this information. Had he seen it before on one prospective layoff memo or another, on some list he carried of the marginal and the unproductive?

"Been with us six years, Karnish?"

"That's right."

"Six years, and yet we haven't met before. Don't you find that strange?"

It so happened we *had* met before, several times, at a number of seasonal corporate functions. I'd even met his wife, a handsome

155

and acerbic woman who deserved more from life, I thought, than the small diamond broach she was wearing and the attentions of Harry Flood. But I didn't mention this. What I said was, "Actually, I haven't been in Science the whole time. Before that I floated around a little. I worked in half a dozen different departments."

"A pinch-hitter, that it?"

"I suppose so."

Flood's eyes narrowed to slits. "You sound unhappy about that."

"Oh no."

"I'm sorry if you're dissatisfied by our operating plan. The fact is good policy requires it."

"Oh sure," I mumbled, "I didn't mean—"

"Separation of departments," he continued, "yields increased efficiency. This has been demonstrated historically. Keep the jurisdictional borders clean, and fewer blockages develop in the flow of process. Of course there are drawbacks, esprit-de-corps-wise. But then a fella can always find something to complain about, can't he? You have a better organizational plan, maybe?"

"No."

"Too bad. Because we're open to advice. There's a myth that's been propagated by parties unknown. This myth says in effect we aren't open to structural change. Not true. Our doors are open to all employee input, however feeble or stupid. In fact we welcome it. Right, Arlen?"

"Samuel here," Arlen put in, "has an exceptional mind. Did graduate work in philosophy and literature at Columbia, you know. And he was just telling me about some fascinating stuff."

"Oh yeah?" Harry Flood narrowed his eyes still further. He was not impressed, but *I* was. I was downright *moved*. Though seemingly unable to place the names Ronnie Oldham and Cynthia Dunleavy—two of the finest editors on our staff—somehow, six years after my interview in his office, Arlen still remembered those half-completed master's degrees on my résumé. "Like what?"

"Oh," Arlen breezed, "it's all very complicated, very scientific.

We haven't really gone into the details yet. But no doubt the boy could be of great help to us, should we decide to restructure."

Suddenly, from the expectant way they were both bearing down on me, I recognized the moment for what it was: an opportunity to do myself some good. "Well," I said, "I suppose I have a few rough ideas."

"Yeah?" Flood had begun to perspire. Or perhaps he had been perspiring the whole time and I had just begun to notice. The smells of his body issued through his blazer, a dark perfume, blended coarsely, an amalgam of sweat and alkaloids and pipe tobacco. "Like what?"

"Well, I've been working on some . . . there are some article ideas I think we should consider. I'd rather not go into them right here, of course," I said, looking around uneasily, in case any of my colleagues might overhear this foolishness.

At once some kind of nictitating membrane flickered warily over Harry Flood's eyes—the blink of a political predator. "Sure," he said, "understand completely. Appreciate the discretion. Come on up and see me and we'll discuss them in private. How about lunch?"

Who'd have thought it? Six years at the magazine in perfect obscurity, and now two lunch invitations from the heavy hitters within ten minutes. The office, it seemed, was a mental game too. Like pinball. My collision in the hallway with a besotted Arlen Ashby had somehow bounced me right into a lunch with the great and powerful Harry Flood. Now colored lights were going off on the scoreboard. Bells were ringing. Or were they alarms?

"Lunch when?" I asked.

"Christ, I don't know. Tomorrow."

I looked over at Arlen, who had his neck craned at an odd angle, tracing some pattern he saw, or thought he saw, among the perforations on the ceiling.

"I can't tomorrow," I said. "I've got something scheduled."

"Shit, Friday then. You like sushi? My secretary'll make us a reservation down the street."

"Friday sounds fine."

"Right. See you then. And you, Arlen, why don't you sober up for a change and do some work? Here, try some of this coffee. Looks fresh." Then he strode on down to the photo lab in his pointy yellow boots, string tie ticking back and forth like a metronome, leaving Arlen no chance to inform him of the small mutiny in his stomach, the one that had rendered it inhospitable to coffee and was somehow in his mind related to the eventual heat death of the universe—a subject we'd be exploring together, he reminded me with a farewell pat of the shoulder, the next day over lunch.

Around five o'clock, feeling more than a little pleased with myself, I got up from my now-immaculate desk and waltzed into the tiny crammed archive of reference books, computer hardware, junk food, and periodical arcana that was Ronnie Oldham's cubicle. Ronnie was on the phone, half-hidden behind a stack of manila envelopes. When he saw me he blinked and pulled his glasses down low on his nose. Then he muttered a few things into the receiver and hung up.

"Are you okay?" I asked. "You look shell-shocked."

"Never mind me. How's it going with you?"

I proceeded to fill him in on the day's triumphs. Ronnie indulged me but did not seem terribly interested in the details. When I came to the part about Harry Flood, however, he hunched forward, and his mouth closed into a glum line.

"What's the matter?"

"Haven't you heard?"

"Heard what?"

"Flood's out. As of Friday. Early retirement."

"But we just made a date for lunch on Friday."

"Well, don't count on him picking up the check."

"Who told you this, Ronnie?"

"That's the word in the bathroom. He's not alone either. It's like I thought. A general shake-up."

"But this is impossible. The man's a lion."

"He's a terrible person, you mean. It's universally acknowledged. Hard times are hard on terrible people, too."

"So who else?"

Ronnie's eyes shifted uneasily. "I'm, um, not at liberty to say."

"You're not at liberty to say? What the hell does that mean?"

"I'm sorry, Sam. It will all become clear in the next few weeks, I promise. But I'd be betraying my sources if I said any more."

"The hell with your sources. What about me?"

"All I can say is, I understand your concern. As far as I can make out, our fate, at the present juncture, is still undetermined. They're dealing solely with the senior execs at this point. It's unclear as to how it's all going to trickle down, department by department."

"What about Arlen Ashby?"

"Ashby? He's harmless—I doubt he has anything to worry about. But Harry Flood is radioactive. Even to be seen talking to him, as you probably were today, sets the meters clicking. It could hurt you."

"But it was only five minutes. And it was the first time."

"I'm aware of that. The point is there's a chance you were seen. You could be misidentified as one of his allies by someone with opposing intent. This is a very delicate period, Sam. My advice is to lie low for a few days."

"But you just advised me to lie *high* for a few days."

"I'm aware of that."

"In fact I came in early today because of you. You and your goddamn jungle drums."

"I'm aware of that, Sam. I'm just telling you what I heard. Naturally you're free to do what you want with the information. It's just that you were kind enough to invite me to dinner and so I thought I'd be your friend and try to help out if I could."

"I'm going home now."

Ronnie nodded. "I think that's a good idea."

"Well, be that as it may, I'm going to do it anyway."

"You're mad at me but it will pass, I know it will. By the way, am I still invited for dinner tomorrow?"

"Yeah, yeah. I guess so."

"I think I can make it after all. Ta Shin's at yoga so I'll have to bring the baby, of course, and I'll probably have to leave early. What time?"

"Seven-thirty."

"What are we having?"

"Kosher food. I'm not sure what kind."

"I'm a vegetarian, you know. I hope you're taking that into account."

"I think of nothing else."

"I should warn you that I usually arrive early. It's an awkward habit but I can't help myself. I'll aim for seven-thirty, but my prediction based on previous experience is that I'll see you at seven-fifteen. And I'll bring the materials we talked about, of course."

"What materials?"

"The research. You know, for the piece. Don't tell me you've forgotten?"

"Oh yeah. No. Right, the article."

"Didn't I tell you? I was on it all weekend. Faxes, E-mail, document searches. We're tearing up the Web, Sam. Circuits are buzzing. Messages pouring in. They're lining up out there to get on-line with us."

"That's great, Ronnie. Really."

"Here, let me show you the files. It's very exciting. There's enough here for *ten* articles. Maybe a whole book."

He began to hunt around his desk, shoving papers aside and knocking things over in a kind of information-panic. Watching him, I felt something very cool and formless begin to settle over my limbs. I had to get out of there.

I thought of Donna and my stomach rippled, as if a very large stone had been dropped into a very still pond.

"Show me tomorrow," I said, and went out the door.

*　　　　*　　　　*

At home that evening I lay on the sofa with a bottle of beer, listening to the loud, vacant hum of the air conditioner. It occurred to me that the way things were going, I had a great many evenings like this to look forward to. No wonder Arlen Ashby had sought me out: I was turning into a regular poster boy for Entropy.

Finally I put in a call to Warren Pinsky. Just back from his honeymoon, he sounded cheerful, and I told him so.

"Not cheerful. Relieved. There's nothing left to do but the thank-you notes. Yours, by the way, will have to wait until your present arrives."

"It hasn't gotten there? I sent it last week."

"Express?"

"I'm not sure. Maybe just regular."

"Always send express, Sammy. Life is short and the postal process is long." Warren sighed. "I just hope it's something expensive and tasteful and that it can be returned if Debbie doesn't like it, which, I should warn you, she probably won't."

"I'll win her over, Warren."

"Of course you will," he said. "Speaking of which, what's the Donna Report? You never did tell me at the wedding."

For years the Donna Report, as he called it, had been a formidable document, rich in hermeneutics, intricate with arguments, disclaimers, and footnotes. But now the whole thing amounted to hardly a memo.

"Bummer," said Pinsky when I was through. "Oh well, on to the next."

"Bravo. Spoken like a man on his third wife."

"You mean that as an insult, but you're wrong. The fact is, Sammy, you've always been too much of a brooder. The body's like the brain: it needs fresh blood. If you're smart you'll go out and *cherchez* a few *femmes*, chop-chop."

"Maybe you're right, Warren. But I haven't met a woman in years. I wouldn't even know where to start."

"What about that little Brooklyn cutie from the plane?

Don't tell me you weren't attracted. Your eyes were like dinner plates."

"Don't be ridiculous. She's a Hasid. A *married* Hasid."

"Listen, marriages end all the time, as you should know almost as well as me."

"So do affairs," I said.

"Well, just because something ends is no reason not to begin it. If people lived by your system, nobody would ever do anything."

This seemed like a worthy point to consider, but I reserved it for another time. "Even if it were possible, which it isn't, what about the Jewish question?"

"People overcome differences," Warren said breezily. "Debbie, for example, is lactose-intolerant. Does that mean we can't share a meal together?"

"We're talking about a religion, Warren, an entire way of life. It's not some allergy you shake off with a change of diet."

"You can shake off anything you want, Sammy, if you work hard enough. Look at Nixon, Teddy Kennedy. Hell, look at *me*. I got off antidepressants last week; already I've stopped apologizing all the time for things I didn't do. I'm driving a car now, a big car, made in Detroit. And that's not all. I've taken up golf."

"Oh Jesus."

"You know, the problem with us New York snobs is we dismiss things we've never tried. It so happens golf is a very enjoyable game. You get out on that green, all that open space around you, and there's this tiny point of contact which if you hit just right makes the ball fly true."

"Plus those cool spiky shoes."

"The point is, wise guy, there are these tiny points of contact everywhere you look. Everything's a lot more flexible than we like to admit."

I sighed. "I hope you're right."

"And while we're on the subject of things you're wrong about, let's move on to religion, okay? Listen, I've read everything in my time from the Gita to the Gospels, and when all is said and done, it's really just one thing. Essentially it's a psychological issue: Some people can tolerate not knowing why they're alive, and some can't. The rest is commentary."

"And which is better?" I asked. "Not knowing, or knowing?"

"Hell," he said, "whatever works."

There was a brief pause.

"You know what I can't figure out? What they were doing down in Houston in the first place. She said it was some kind of medical procedure."

"Sure," he said, "that makes sense. We're loaded with new technologies. People come here from all over. Brazil, South Africa. We're very popular."

"I wish I knew what it was."

Warren groaned. "I know what you're going to say, and the answer is no."

"I wasn't going to say anything."

"Sure you were. You were going to ask me to find out for you."

"No I wasn't. And even if I did, I'm sure you'd have plenty of good reasons to refuse."

"Sure. Want to hear them?"

"It isn't necessary . . ."

"My job, one. Medical ethics, two. Hospital protocols, three. Shall I go on?"

"Forget it."

"Chain of command, four. Difficulty of access, five. Lack of any good explicable motivation, six . . ."

"Warren, I understand. Really. Let's just forget it."

"Good. We'll just forget it."

So we left it there, and went on to speak of other matters—the honeymoon, the Yankees, the weather. But I knew that nothing would be forgotten. People do not forget, as a rule. Every slight, every grudge, every abrased firing of the nerves—they all stick around. Von Braun's dictum applies to consciousness as well: nothing goes away, it only changes form. A comforting notion from one angle but from another, claustrophobic. If things don't go away then you carry them with you all the time, the same half-formed ideas, the same stale memories, and in view of this Warren and I were naive, I thought, to believe any substantive change was possible. All we were doing was maintaining postures from our youth, which, like most postures, had not stretched with the years but stiffened and constricted us like casts. And yet here we were, with two decades of evidence to the contrary, still trying to hitch a ride on the Change Express. Warren had ridden his all the way to Texas. What about me? So many trains had already left. When would mine arrive? What was the fare? And would I even know it for what it was, should I ever stumble into the proper station?

A World
of One's Own

Okay: the dinner.

In my own defense, I really was prepared to lay out the money for an elaborate kosher meal. There was no way I could have known that the restaurant Thea put me on to would be closed for the summer, the owners at some bungalow colony upstate, playing the ponies and taking the waters. In any event, their absence was a sobering development. I mean that literally. I was still feeling the effects of my three-hour, four-martini lunch with Arlen Ashby when I arrived at the restaurant and found it dark, and I stood there clutching my credit card, my big nose pressed against that locked door—taking some momentary comfort from the cool, unblemished glass, which lay like a mother's palm upon my forehead—and thought, maybe this dinner just isn't meant to be.

Meanwhile it had begun to rain.

Apparently it was not my fate that summer to have good luck with telephones. It took ten minutes to find one that was still operational; at which point, standing in one of those paltry metal half-shells that pass for phone booths these days, I hastily flipped through the yellow pages, looking for kosher restaurants. There were several to choose from. The first two I called were closed however. The third was on Essex Street, a place called Goldberg's. The prospect of going all the way down to the Lower East Side disheartened me; I'd as soon have flown to Tel Aviv. But the fourth and fifth places were closed too. The sixth was not a restaurant per se, but a kosher pizzeria. Anyway it was closed.

That did it for Manhattan. Goldberg's or nothing.

The rain was gathering force. I went out into the streaming gutter to hail a cab. For a while I merely stood there waving my arm at the passing traffic to no effect. I might as well have been at the ocean, trying to hail a wave. Then a gypsy Plymouth came barreling down from Spanish Harlem, swerved across three lanes, and lurched to a stop before me. Gypsies are opportunists, of course; they thrive on bad weather, on this kind of lesser-of-two-evils situation. I hesitated a moment at the sight of the car—which seemed to have come directly from some tabloid disaster—until the driver honked three times to impress upon me his urgency. Then the rain began to impress upon me *its* urgency. So I got in.

The backseat smelled of smoke, doughnuts, motor oil, and ruined leather—the source of which I now discovered to be my own shoes.

The cabdriver at least was happy to see me. Because of the rain he was having a very good day, or else a very bad one, or else he was unbalanced to begin with. His skin was lustrous black; his eyes, staring out from his identification plate on the dashboard, had tiny reddened pupils which I could only hope were from the flash. Pealing out into the traffic, he chewed a granola bar for energy and addressed me in the rearview mirror. Essex Street? No problem. Unlike some of his colleagues in the transport business, he'd been here two years, knew the city backward. Originally he planned to study law at Queens College, but found it too slow. He liked driving a cab better. The money was first rate. He had a wife and two daughters back home in Nairobi and a Greek girlfriend in Flatbush. No problem there either. In three months he'd have saved enough for a medallion; then he'd bring over his family, install his girlfriend in a better apartment, hire his nephew to work nights, and buy third-tier season tickets for the Knicks. To expedite all these carefully thought-out plans he drove very fast. He shot across the park, turned south, and flew at high speed down the long, bumpy leg of the FDR—which was being surgically reconstructed, as usual—all the way to Grand Street, a rigorous trip to begin with but particularly so at rush hour in an unlicensed cab bereft of shock absorbers.

On Essex he did not so much pull over to the sidewalk as point the car imperceptibly in that direction and pause, clapping out a rhythm on the dashboard, as I got out. Then he zoomed off down the cratered street.

Goldberg's turned out not to be a restaurant, exactly, but a worn, cavernous delicatessen. It was nearly sundown and they were about to close. A heavy-set woman was squeezing water out of a mop. Plates were slamming into dishwashers. Shades had been drawn over the side windows, so it was left to the fluorescent tubes on the ceiling to highlight in yellow the scars on the wood floor. The tables were laid out cafeteria-style, with bowls of pickles as centerpieces. The pickles looked glazed and haggard in their brine; they might have been sitting there for decades. So for that matter might the half-dozen customers scattered around, finishing their meals. Impeccably outfitted in vested suits, they loitered over their sandwiches, chewing every bite with fastidious thoroughness and running their eyes just as fastidiously down the folded pages of their newspapers. What had Aaron Brenner said, back on the plane? All writers, all readers, are Jewish. In the beginning was the Word.

I took a seat and contemplated the menu. Talk about words: it went on for several pages. The air reeked of mustard, salted fish, the flesh of giant animals. The odors were dense, orgiastic. Foot-long salamis dangled from the walls. Lined like tanks along the counter were corned beefs, tongues, pastramis, briskets. Fatty food, dinosaur stuff, tickets for oblivion. Clearly the men wolfing it down were strangers to the Science page. Faces swollen and mottled, suits straining at the joints. This was what came of too many meals alone. This rage at dusk, this tearing of flesh. When dinner was over they'd all be heading directly to the hospital for bypass operations. But then that was the word for the entire Lower East Side: bypassed. Buckling in the middle, warping at the edges. Succumbing inch by inch to the moneyed call of the surrounding neighborhoods, Little Italy and Chinatown, the East Village and TriBeCa. And where would these guys take their meals then?

Something slithery and wet touched my ankles. "Close," said the woman with the mop, gesturing toward the door.

"I need takeout."

She directed me toward the counter. "Jimmy," she called. "He wants takeout."

A bald, corpulent man with hooded eyes, Jimmy was pushing a hunk of beef through an electrical slicer at the moment, filling orders. Closing or not, he seemed in no particular hurry. With great delicacy and patience he caught each piece from the spinning blade, slapped it onto a piece of wax paper, then wiped his big hand on his bloody smock and started again. Though the work looked pleasant enough, almost magical in a way, Jimmy's mood was precarious. When I cleared my throat he glared at it as if he would be attending to that choice bit of white meat next. No doubt I was holding him up too. Perhaps he could see right through me to my true self, a half-drunk half-Jew with a nonkosher kitchen, up to no good.

"What'll it be?"

"What's good?" I asked, my eyes on the spinning blade.

He scowled. "Whattaya want?"

I want you to tell me what's good, I thought. But he wouldn't. No shortcuts, no something for nothing; to find out what was good you had to make an investment of time and money. I paced the counter, pointing to whatever caught my eye, and in this fashion wound up with several pounds of cold cuts, a quart of potato salad, four knishes, a loaf of rye bread, a bottle of brown mustard, some cookies, and a six-pack of cream soda. So much for my gourmet kosher dinner. Still, it managed to total close to forty dollars. The taxi fare came to another forty-five, round-trip. That made eighty-five, not counting the exorbitant tips I bestowed upon both cabbies, and the dry cleaning bill for the damage my suit incurred on the drive uptown from the puddle of grease at the bottom of the shopping bag.

By the time I finally arrived home, it was closing in on seven-thirty, my wallet felt thin as paper, and I was about one calamity away from ditching the whole dinner idea and going to a movie.

But Ronnie Oldham was waiting for me.

Cross-legged upon the welcome mat, he was reading a paperback under the buzzing light from the stairwell. He was so absorbed in the book that he didn't notice me at first. It was his usual fare: science fiction. The world in its present form was not grotesque or unsubtle enough for him; he required epic moral fantasies, robots and superheroes, to give him a jolt. And yet Ronnie, I reminded myself, was among the brightest people I knew.

Socially he was at a loss, as always. From the way he was decked out I could see Ronnie did not quite know what to make of my dinner invitation. Instead of his usual jeans he wore brown pleated trousers, a white dress shirt, and an all but iridescent green tie. A bouquet of red roses, wrapped in tissue paper, lay across his knees. Roses! In the dim light the blooms looked, like Ronnie himself, top-heavy, ludicrous, and hopeful.

Their scent however was lovely; it swelled out to fill the hallway.

"Hey," he said. "You're here."

"Sorry, sorry. I got caught in traffic. How long have you been waiting?"

"About half an hour," he admitted sheepishly.

"Well," I said, "you warned me."

"I really tried to hold off. I walked around the block six times, but then it started to rain again. What's in the bag?"

"Dinner."

He wrinkled his nose. "Smells like pastrami."

Oh Christ. On top of everything else, I'd forgotten he was vegetarian.

"That's okay," he said with a shrug. "Beggars can't be choosers."

"Look, Ronnie, I'm sorry. But I got knishes and potato salad too. And some rye bread. You won't go hungry."

"No problem," he said agreeably.

"You're a good man, Ronnie." He was, too. I was glad I'd invited him to dinner.

"Hey, what's a knish?" he asked. "I've seen them on those hot dog carts everywhere, but I don't think I've ever tried one."

"A knish? It's like a big lump of processed potato, fried in fat."

"Oh," he said.

"They taste better than they sound."

"Sure." He got to his feet. "Well," he said, "I guess I'd better bring her in."

"Bring who in?"

Now that he had risen from the floor I could see, curled up in a stroller behind him, nothing less than a living, breathing baby, fast asleep. "Isabel," he whispered proudly.

"You know, I thought you were kidding the other day. When you said you were going to bring the baby."

"Oh no," he said.

In the dim light only her profile was visible—the rise and fall of one doughy cheek, the lower lip glistening with saliva, the tiny frothy bubbles that had, in the moisture of her dreams, taken shape at the corners of her mouth. Her face was dark and perfectly round. I remembered that Ronnie's wife was Chinese. "Cute," I said.

Ronnie nodded, but vaguely; he seemed to be expecting more from me in the way of spontaneous enthusiasm. "In fact," I went ahead and added, "she's beautiful."

He beamed. "Really? You think so?"

"Oh yes," I said.

"She's completely bald, you know. And jug-eared, like me. Most people consider her kind of funny-looking, actually. But you think she's beautiful?"

Ronnie's concern on this score, though poignant, was beginning to try my patience. "Beautiful," I repeated, almost daring him to argue with me.

Meanwhile he was trying to push the stroller into my apartment without waking the baby and without dropping either his book, his backpack, or the roses—a considerable task. I helped out to the best of my abilities. As we lifted her over the welcome mat the baby gave a little yawn, then stretched and shuddered spasmodically, and we froze for a moment, Ronnie and I, looking at each other in a kind of involuntary male pre-panic until she'd settled back into her curl. Then we resumed. We'd almost succeeded in squeezing gingerly through the door without further incident when Magda came steaming out of the elevator wrestling with an umbrella and, in her haste and nervousness, practically knocked us all down.

"Oh," she said, "I'm sorry."

With the collision her umbrella had fallen out of her hand and clattered to the floor. It lay there on its side, neither closed nor open, a lethargic, disobedient animal. Magda glared down at it resentfully for a second, then turned to the baby, who was now wide awake, of course, and letting us hear all about it. "Is she hurt? I didn't mean to—"

"She's fine," said Ronnie. To prove the point, he lifted Isabel out of the stroller, jiggling her in his arms to quiet her down. "But what about you? Are you okay? Did you hurt yourself?"

Magda made no answer. Experimentally she touched one hand to her hair—which had changed styles yet again. Now it was long, shaggy, and black. It gave her face a soulful and undernourished air, the face of a lonely sophomore in a Bennington dorm, strumming folk songs on a guitar.

"Well, anyway, hello. I'm Ronnie." He extended his right hand. "For some reason Sam's just standing here not introducing us, so I thought I might as well do it myself."

She stared at his hand, and at the baby on his shoulder, uncomprehending.

"Ronnie and I work together," I explained. "At the magazine. We're collaborating on an article. And this is his daughter . . ."

". . . Isabel," Ronnie said.

Magda cast a furtive glance in his direction and then turned away before he could stick out his hand again. Another person, one more sensitive to propriety than Ronnie Oldham, would have thought her behavior rude. Magda herself seemed to falter. Her eyes, surveying the room, betrayed a flicker of uncertainty. What magazine? What article? What daughter? What crazy world had she entered, where men bring each other roses and children?

"And you," Ronnie said, pushing on, "you must be Sam's girlfriend, right?" He was trying to be a regular guy, but regularity was not his forte; it came out like a challenge.

"Girlfriend?" she asked.

"Aren't you the one who calls him at the office all the time?"

Reluctantly, her gaze sought me out. Her eyes were filmy and smaller than I remembered. Perhaps she had an allergy, a cold. I hoped so. I did not want to think I had cost her any tears on the way over. The last thing I wanted, all of a sudden, was for any of this to matter too much to any of us.

"This is Magda," I said quickly. "Magda Brenner. She's not the person you're thinking of." As this made for a rather tepid introduction, I added, "She's a friend."

"Oh," chirped Ronnie agreeably. "Great."

Both of us turned to Magda, who was wriggling out of her coat. She too had dressed up for the occasion—but in her case dressing up was more a matter of dressing down. Gone were the shawl, the high-necked blouse, the ankle-length skirt. Gone were the thick stockings, the beauty parlor hairdo, the air of a distant past. In their place stood another person entirely: a slim, expectant, raven-haired young woman in a bright blue sleeveless dress.

Well, if I was looking for evidence of the world's elasticity, here it was. Who'd have guessed she had all that *skin*? Milky and smooth, with small constellations of freckles and moles spilling over her shoulders—even Magda seemed perplexed by how much of it there was to contend with. She stood there rubbing her palms over her forearms, as if despite the musty heat she was exposed on all sides to chilly drafts. I had a brief, hopeless impulse to put my arms around those narrow shoulders. Someone should, I thought. The sight of her in that blue dress gave me a new, grudging respect—and a new, grudging dislike—for her husband and the other Hasids. No wonder they made their women cover up. No wonder they made them sit in the balcony. Surely after thousands of years of practice they knew, when it came to distraction, what they could and couldn't deal with. You want to pray? Try and pray around *this* . . .

Oh, I won't say she was beautiful, she wasn't. Or was she? What did it matter? She wasn't real to me at that point. She was still a blur, a field of shifting energies and strange attractors.

Possibly Magda caught me staring and that was what made her face go hard. She did not care to be looked at, or else she cared about it too much. Or else she did not know what to make of me yet, either.

"Well, come on in, everybody," I said, and we all tromped down the hallway to the kitchen.

No sooner had we gotten there than Ronnie announced his need to use the bathroom.

"Listen, can you do me a favor? Maybe watch Isabel for a minute?"

"Sure," I said. "Just set her down over on that chair. I'll keep an eye on her."

Ronnie laughed uncertainly. "Um, she's only eight months old, Sam."

"So what?"

"So she doesn't sit on chairs. And she's not ready to go back in the stroller. You have to hold her."

"Oh. Okay, sure."

Isabel took advantage of the transition that followed to

examine my face closely. If that little dough-girl felt any of the same apprehension in my presence that I did in hers, she managed to conceal it. Her dark eyes as they roamed my features scrunched down at the corners, as if in response to a private joke. She touched her fingers to my lips a couple of times, assuring herself they were in the correct place, then burrowed into the soft spot beneath my shoulder bone and settled there, giving out a breathy, contented sigh. She was not quite as heavy as I expected, but then why should she be? She was only eight months old.

Magda, with nothing to hold onto, drifted awkwardly around the kitchen. The baby and I watched her closely. What would she bump into next?

"I'm glad you could make it," I said.

"I said I would come."

"I know. But people say all kinds of things."

"Do they?" There was no irony in her question. She really wanted to know.

"Sure. What they actually do, though, is another matter."

"Well," she said flatly, "I said I'd come, so here I am."

Here she was. She wore no makeup. Her legs and shoulders were bare, her feet shod only in leather sandals. The sandals were soaked and dripping on the linoleum. So was her hair. Even her eyelashes were dripping. Despite this, she projected an aura of dry resolution. Here, after all, she was. One was forced to take her presence seriously, if only because she took it so much that way herself.

"Would you like a towel to dry yourself off?"

"No, thank you."

"How about a drink? I have some wine in the fridge."

"No, thank you."

"Seltzer? Juice? Coffee? I've got plenty."

"I'm fine," she said. "With dinner I'll have something. Besides, you have your hands full with the child."

"About dinner," I said. "I'd better warn you. It's going to be sort of terrible."

"Oh no. I'm sure it will be fine."

"No, I mean it."

I proceeded to give a quick summation of my efforts to secure a good meal, none of which, from the look on her face, particularly impressed her. She listened patiently but not carefully, her eyes on the little half-Chinese girl resting on my shoulder.

When I was finished, she coughed and looked away. "Your friend seems nice," she said.

"We're not really friends. We just work together."

"Yes? Then why did you invite him for dinner?"

"I don't know. He interests me. Plus there's an article we might be working on together. Do you mind?"

"Why should I?" She gave me a direct look. Perhaps, I thought, she really is an innocent. Perhaps we all were.

"Ronnie *is* a little awkward," I said, feeling a little awkward myself. "But very bright. You should hear him on chaos theory, for instance. Or fractals."

"I'm sorry," she said. "I don't know what they are."

"Fractals? We ran a story on them last year. They're mathematical objects that don't fit into the ordinary world of lines and surfaces. They're not one-dimensional, they're not two-dimensional, they're not three-dimensional. They're in between."

"Between what?"

I thought for a moment. "I'm not sure I can explain it."

"Oh."

This enlightening dialogue was followed by another in our series of lengthy, uncomfortable silences. On my shoulder, the baby had fallen asleep again. Her mouth was open; her breath smelled sweetly of milk. Carefully, so as not to wake her, I began to open the food containers with my free hand, waiting for Magda to ask about the food and the method of its preparation. But it seemed she had already strayed beyond that border. Hands on her hips, she stood gazing through the window above the sink and out into the air shaft. Perhaps she'd never seen one before. I was no longer quite so glad she had made it, after all.

"So," I said, "how do you like the place?"

"The place?"

"The apartment."

"You've lived here a long time?"

"Fairly long, yes."

She turned and made a show of interest. Honestly, what was there to see? A toaster, a blender, a coffeemaker, cereal boxes. A couple of satirical *New Yorker* cartoons taped to the refrigerator which, reviewing them now through her eyes, I thought to be perfect illustrations of my own facile, frivolous existence. A pine-planked table, warped from steam. Two director's chairs, cheap ones, sagging at the joints. A pile of last week's newspapers next to an armada of last week's beer bottles. Some flea market cracker tins Melinda had left behind when she moved. An empty fish tank.

My place, I suddenly realized, was full of junk. So this, I imagined her thinking, was what she'd been missing? This abundance of discards? This *dreck*?

Dreck, it so happened, was one of the few Yiddish words I knew.

"What's that?"

She pointed to the print above the stove. It was a rather famous Gauguin portrait of two dark, voluptuous Tahitian women cradling melons. Melinda had bought it when we'd first moved into the apartment and lacked the money to frame it. Now, after some dozen years of exposure, it was badly faded. The edges were curling and torn; drops of grease were spattered like measles across the bottom. And yet I could not bring myself to throw it away. "Do you like that?"

"It's so colorful."

Was she being condescending? Was colorful a good thing in her eyes? "I think they have the original over at the Met," I offered. "It's much more striking. Maybe we could go see it sometime."

She stepped back from the poster and frowned. "Met?"

"The Metropolitan Museum," I said.

She looked blank. Almost serenely so.

"You know, the big one on Fifth Avenue? With the neo-classical pillars and the mimes out in front? You're trying to tell me," I said, "that you've lived in New York your whole life and you've never heard of the Metropolitan Museum?"

"This makes you so angry?" she asked. "It's such a crime?"

"I'm not angry."

"Maybe you're wondering who is this strange person standing in your kitchen, who knows nothing about the ozone at the poles or the museums in her own city. Maybe you're wondering, why have I invited this person to dinner? What does she want from me, this person? Isn't that right?"

"No."

She gave a bitter laugh.

"I know who you are," I said gamely.

"Impossible."

"It's true."

"Oh? So tell me, then. Tell me what you know."

"You're someone who wants to step away."

She turned white. Or rather, whiter. "And how do you know that?" she asked in a whisper.

"Because," I said, "why else would you be here?"

That shut her up entirely. She pivoted back in the direction of the window and, as though it were a mirror she was gazing into and not an air shaft, raised one hand to pat her hair in place. She needn't have bothered; not a wave had moved.

For my part, I examined a scratch on my finger. It occurred to me that in answering her question with another, I'd sounded less like myself and more like her husband than I'd intended. Perhaps she had realized that too.

Now footsteps became audible in the hallway. For a moment I could not conceive of whom they might belong to.

"Hey, great, she's asleep," Ronnie said, wiping his hands on his trousers. "So, are we eating soon? I'm famished."

*　　　　*　　　　*

177

Despite the rocky start, the meal itself went fairly well, in the sense that we all ate and drank what was in front of us without any screaming or violence. It was not, however, a lively event. If not for the asthmatic wheezing of my air conditioner and Ronnie's peculiar habit of smacking his lips when he chewed—they made a gay little chirp, like castanets—the room would have been funereally quiet. Magda said almost nothing. She kept both hands, the one she held her fork with and the one that bore her wedding ring, on the table, as if prepared to flee at any moment. Each time I looked up with a fresh conversational gambit in mind it was that simple, unpolished gold band—purchased no doubt on Forty-seventh Street, through her brother-in-law—I saw first, and which defeated me. There is no form so exclusive as a perfect circle, and no circle quite so perfect as a wedding ring.

Ronnie tried to draw her out as well, but he hadn't a prayer. I admired him for the attempt though. And I maintain, even now, that I wasn't crazy to think these two people might get along. In theory, their youth, their seriousness, their aversion to small talk, and their hermetic and marginal status in the contemporary biosphere should have meshed very nicely. But in practice it went another way altogether. In practice they were both too weird. Ronnie was overly earnest and insistent and Magda was overly edgy and repressed. When he'd pepper her with questions she'd recoil, and when he answered one of hers he did so at such length and with such vehement punctiliousness that by the time he was through a kind of terrible glaze had descended over us all.

Awkward he may have been, but Ronnie wasn't dumb. When it became apparent that Magda would not follow him on his conversational excursions, he gave up on her and directed his questions to me—specifically, my lunch with Arlen Ashby. I could see the results disappointed him, as they had me. The only one not disappointed by the experience was Arlen himself, who'd been drunk to begin with and had managed to remain that way the entire time.

He had taken me to a swank Italian place on Third Avenue where he was a regular, and casually ordered a huge blue-chip meal for us both. It turned out that among other difficulties Arlen was a widower, and childless. He seemed to have a lot of free-floating paternal energy that was going unused and which he brought to bear on lunches like these. Once we were seated, he broke a roll neatly in half and signaled for a cocktail. In his gray double-breasted suit and salmon tie, fastened with a neat gold stickpin, he looked, from the head down anyway, very crisp and elegant: a man of stature imparting generational wisdom in a dark bistro. But his eyes were already glassy as they locked onto mine. "Like this place?" he asked.

"Sure."

"Good."

So much for chitchat. Now he let me have it. Apparently Arlen had been reading up on thermodynamics all morning and could wait no longer to share it with me: Gibbs, Clausius, St. Augustine—the whole picture. It was some session. He did not so much pick my brain as turn his own inside out, and I'll admit that what I saw there humbled me. Arlen Ashby seemed to have discovered in Entropy—the idea that systems, over time, tend to run down and become increasingly disordered—a paradigm of his own career, a harmonic convergence between his personal fate and that of the universe. The discovery appeared to elate him. Perhaps in mastering the second law of thermodynamics Arlen thought he could negate it, and perhaps he was right—he did in fact appear to gain force, not lose it, as the hours rolled by. His back grew straighter, his cheeks flooded with color, and at times from sheer enthusiasm he would bounce up and down on his seat, as if our conversation were proceeding on horseback. Of course, it might have been only the gin. But by the time our pasta arrived he'd already left me and my rudimentary, floater's knowledge far behind. He swung his fork and swilled his drinks, and his voice—a marvelous reed instrument in its own right— soared over the Muzak, and it seemed to me right then that Arlen Ashby was capable of negating anything he pleased.

I did not say much. Always happy to be instructed, I ate that heavy food and drank that chilly liquor and otherwise kept my mouth shut. So dazzled was I by Arlen's performance, in fact, that I lost sight of my real purpose in coming to lunch—self-advancement. Later I'd curse myself: Here I had one of the big boys right in front of me for two hours, exuberant and full of gin, and never once did I turn the discussion to this new article Ronnie and I were planning, or my hopes of moving to the front of the book; never once did I refer to that fallen sphere of profit and loss that awaited us when we returned from lunch—the one in which I for one was currently in danger of losing my job.

By the time our coffee arrived, Arlen's eyelids were beginning to droop and his sentences had taken on a pleasant, singsong rhythm. It was three-thirty. "Well then, young man," he said, laying his gold card upon the silver tray, "we must do this again sometime." After which the two of us returned wobbly-legged to the building, riding the elevator in silence to our respective floors, and then proceeded into our respective offices to fall heavily into our respective naps.

"Oh well," Ronnie said, playing with his fork. "Ashby was a long shot to begin with. He was never really a serious option."

"Option for what?"

"To stand up for us, Sam. We need a stronger, more reliable presence. If Flood's out that leaves Spurlock or Teagle, maybe, or Rasmussen. They all know my work. I'll try to sound them out tomorrow in the men's room."

"Did you tell them about the article yet?"

"Of course not."

"Why not?"

"Because we don't have an article. All we have is the idea. We haven't written anything yet."

"But, Ronnie, don't you get it? The writing is the least important part of this. The guys upstairs don't care about the subtleties. They want sexy, high-concept stuff to put on the cover, so they can sell ads."

He considered this. "You're right, Sam. Absolutely. I should have thought of it myself." His mouth turned down at the corners. "Ta Shin's always telling me I'm not savvy enough about these things."

"Well, for what it's worth, I'm not savvy either."

"That's what worries me," he said. "It seems like one of us should be."

He proceeded to fill me in on some of his researches, devouring half the bread and all four of the knishes in the process. Magda listened, or didn't, it was impossible to tell. Dutifully she finished her cold cuts but refused another portion. I too had little appetite. Collectively we'd eaten, I found myself thinking, less than ten bucks' worth of my hard-won meal. So what? What was money for, if not to blow it on awkward dinner parties for people one barely knew?

As the evening progressed, I watched the sunset register against Magda's bare, pallid, tomboyish arms, turning them first rosy and pink, then a watery imperfect blue, veined like marble. So the world impresses itself upon us: fickly, changeably, transiently. At one point she lifted her head and caught me staring and I expected her to harden again or blush, but she didn't. She stared right back.

Even with the sun down, the room was too warm for overhead lights, so I went off to get some candles from the pantry. When I returned, however, and saw my guests silent over their plates, I was revisited by the image of the Brenners and their guests that Friday night: the long table aglow in candlelight, the children big-eyed and yawning, the adults in their black robes and white dresses. I changed my mind and left the candles unlit. Ours, I thought, was not that sort of occasion. We were no family, the three of us. And this was no Sabbath.

So we drank our coffee in the encroaching darkness, listening to the rain drum at the windows. Then Ronnie hunted through my records and found some old piano jazz he liked, and we listened to that.

*　　　　*　　　　*

ROBERT COHEN

At some point the baby woke up. She was lying in the stroller by the sofa when we heard her quiet, spasmodic coughs. At first it was only her eyes that blinked open, regarding us dispassionately for a moment; then she appeared to catch on to how disconcerting it really was to find oneself awake and ungrounded in a strange apartment, and her mouth opened too. She began to wail.

"Uh oh," said Ronnie. With an air of hopeful but tentative authority, he lifted her out of the stroller-jiggling her for a while on his shoulder. The method, which had been successful earlier in the evening, this time only seemed to incense her.

"Maybe she's hungry," I offered.

Ronnie consulted his watch. "She shouldn't be. I fed her right before we came. I don't think she needs to be changed, either."

"Well, what is it then?"

"I don't know. Usually she just sleeps, wherever she is. This is kind of unprecedented, to tell the truth."

"Maybe she's hot. She looks flushed."

"I think you're right. Can we turn the air conditioner on?"

"It *is* on. It's been on for hours. This is the best it gets."

By this point the baby's face was scarlet—her crying, as we stood over her, had only intensified—and we were beginning to yell across her like two people in a hurricane. The only one not busy overreacting was Magda, who was not reacting at all. At first she simply ignored the three of us, picking at the food on her plate as if the entire commotion were taking place in another apartment, or on a radio she had not been listening to anyway. In time, however, something—guilt, irritation, or plain curiosity—got the better of her. Frowning, she put down her napkin and came over to the sofa, where Ronnie and I were taking turns bouncing Isabel on our shoulders to no effect. At last she pushed us aside and took the shrieking child into her arms.

Though she was an aunt at least two times over, she did not

182

seem very experienced at this sort of thing; there was a stiffness and deliberation in her movements I was unaccustomed to seeing in women with children. Apparently Isabel was, too, because during the transfer her crying, which I did not think could possibly get any louder, did. Still, Magda held her own. It was impressive how she hung in there, what resources of obstinacy she was able to summon. Cradling the baby very close, she swayed back and forth, bending at the knees and murmuring nonsense syllables in time to the music. Her voice was low, pleasant, unyielding. At first it had no visible effect, and one was left merely to admire the effort. But soon the crying began to diminish. I suppose even a baby gets bored with crying eventually. After a while her eyes went droopy, her limbs lost their tension, and she subsided into soft, chastened sobs.

Ronnie, hovering nearby, nodded and whispered encouragingly, "Good girl, good girl, good girl."

"Well," I said. "That's a relief."

Magda said nothing. She was still stroking the baby's fine fuzzy scalp, dreamily, with the back of her hand. I was already half in love with her. And Magda? For the first time since we'd met she seemed to be relaxing and having a good time. Then again my perspective was limited. She may have been perfectly expert at relaxing and having a good time, and it was only that for a change she was not having to deal with *me*.

Soon the sobs could no longer be heard, and only the music and Magda's soft breathy voice remained. The baby was asleep.

Things picked up a little after that. Our difficulty with the baby had, as crises will, drawn us together. We all held our breaths while Magda laid her—with some reluctance, I thought—on the sofa. Then we set up a retaining wall of throw pillows, and an additional safety net of blankets on the floor, until that whole side of the room resembled an enormous crib. Then I cleared the table and brought out the cookies from Goldberg's. Somehow the way they occupied the plate did not seem quite festive enough for the occasion, so I went and grabbed a bottle of brandy I had been saving, poured out three glasses, and we all toasted our victory over chaos.

Magda, the star of the moment, was quietly glowing. Some personal triumph had been registered, some score evened in a contest that preceded our acquaintance. She paced around the living room, nibbling a cookie, spilling crumbs on her blue dress which she disdained to brush off. Ronnie went back to leafing through my records again, tsking at their condition. Pulling an album from its jacket, he blew some dust away and frowned as he contemplated the antiquarian mechanics of my stereo. The LP, once he set the needle to it, proceeded to crackle and hiss alarmingly, confirming his worst suspicions and making him, in the process, very happy.

But the baby, we were all proud to notice, slept on.

"Such a sweet girl," Magda said to Ronnie. "A beauty."

"Thank you."

"You know," she said, "there are three things to be learned from children. They're often happy for no particular reason, they're never idle, and when they want something they demand it vigorously."

I was so startled by this sudden foray into the world of human discourse that I could hardly follow. I had to ask her to repeat it.

Ronnie's head was bobbing agreement. "You have children yourself then?"

"Oh no. It comes from something I read."

"Really? Where?"

She shrugged. "It doesn't matter."

The admission seemed to puncture her.

"What's so bad about idleness?" I asked, trying to rescue us with levity. "I'm idle most of the time."

Magda stared at me thoughtfully. Then she turned to Ronnie. "You're not, are you?"

"Not really," he admitted. "Ta Shin thinks I could use some

work in that area. She says I keep myself busy so I never have to just, you know, *sit*. She says in a mind-body sense I'm kind of a disaster."

"But she stays. So she must love you very much."

He blushed. "I love her too, of course."

"And she listens when you talk about your work? She shares your interests?"

"Ta Shin?" He giggled. "She's an architect. She wouldn't know a black hole from a quark."

"But you're happy with her?"

"Oh yes."

"I know nothing about architecture," she complained. "And I've never even heard of a black hole. I don't even know what a black hole *is*." She stared at her fingers, as if these were only the first two of a long list of deficiencies she had on her hands.

Ronnie gave her a sympathetic look. "But you must have studied physics in college?"

"Who went to college?"

"High school then."

"Oh, high school . . ." She heaved a sigh to convey how much she had retained from that particular venue.

"Well, if you like I can explain it. Would you like that?"

She gave a cautious nod.

"Well, a black hole is simply what's left behind when a star collapses. What happens is that the field becomes very dense, so dense its gravity vacuums up everything near it. Nothing, not even light, escapes." He frowned. "Actually that's not quite true. Something does escape. The draw is so strong, you see, that it breaks up the surrounding subatomic particles, so one part gets sucked into the hole, and the other part, its twin you might say, goes floating off into space in the form of radiation. It's kind of useless, and it lacks a target, but it measurably exists. The discovery of this phenomenon has been an enormous help to us. I mean, the scientific community," he said. "There were some photographs taken by the Hubble telescope. You may have seen these in the magazines a couple of months ago. No? Or maybe in the *Times*?"

She shook her head in a way that foreclosed any additional inquiry as to the nature of her reading habits.

"Well," he went on, "these pictures show a disk in the Virgo Cluster. It's a good size too—more than three hundred light-years in diameter. This disk, it appears to be a black hole. No one's ever seen one before so it's hard to be sure. We can't really see *this* one either, of course. Not the hole itself. But we can see the maelstrom of energy that surrounds what should, if the theory's right, be one."

"And why is it important to see it?" she asked.

"Why? Because black holes provide our best model for what could be the end of the universe. And for the beginning, of course. The Big Bang."

"The creation, you mean?"

"Yes," he said. "The creation. Exactly."

"Then they must tell you about God too. Who we also can't see, but can see what surrounds Him."

"Well," he said, rubbing his chin, "that's an interesting analogy."

"But it's true," she asserted.

I was afraid he would laugh at her then, or perhaps even blow her off. But I needn't have worried. "What these things tell you," he said, "depends on who you ask."

"*Nu*? So I'm asking you."

"I'm not the right person. The right people are out on the campuses, in the labs. But some of them would say that what we've learned to this point proves that *some*thing's going on in the universe, other than the random fact that it just happens to be here. They'd say the whole thing's too marvelously complex to just have plopped itself down for no reason. God may be subtle, Einstein said, but He isn't mean."

She nodded vaguely.

"And some, of course, would say just the opposite."

This last remark was my own contribution. It was rewarded

with two frozen smiles from my guests, as if I had intruded on a delicate matter that couldn't possibly concern me.

"Sam's right," Ronnie conceded. "In some quarters, both Einstein *and* God have been taking a beating. And the entire Big Bang model could be wrong—there's plenty of evidence for that, too. It could be the universe is simply a self-enclosed entity that's neither expanding nor contracting. If that's the case, then the whole idea of a larger meaning or a creating moment is impossible."

"Impossible?" A look of unease crossed her face.

"Sure. Because nothing would have preceded what the universe is now. It would all just . . . be."

She seemed to shiver.

"I think you must be wrong," she said.

"Possibly so. It could be we just haven't decoded it yet. We're still operating in the dark in some ways, and that's always dangerous. Without a map it's difficult even for the best minds to grasp what's there. Take Aristotle—he thought the heart was the seat of the intellect. I mean, talk about way off, right?"

She nodded, though vaguely; I don't think she was following him any longer.

"All of which is why the whole field of cartography has become so exciting. Charting, tracking, patterning—that's where the really interesting technology is right now. That and virtual reality, of course. Creating a world of one's own, according to one's own specifications." Even more than black holes, virtual reality was a subject dear to that young man's heart, one he'd already dropped into the conversation several times that evening—and, I suspect, most evenings—without success, and the fact that Magda had begun to look a bit weary and distracted at this point did not deter him from commencing a short tutorial on the subject. We followed along as best we could, half-interested.

"But what's the use of it?" asked Magda when he was finished.

"The use?" Ronnie looked blank.

"Yes. Why would anyone go to so much trouble?"

"It's the perfect escape," I said. "Like the Bahamas, only cheaper."

Ronnie frowned to let me know that this was precisely the sort of shallow interpretation he expected from me.

"The point," he told Magda, "is not what for. At a certain stage of development the technology becomes workable, thus it is made to exist. We do these things because we *can*. You see that, don't you?"

She couldn't, of course. But she did not appear to mind letting Ronnie hold forth on the subject a bit longer. What would we have done without him? What would we have talked about? I looked at the roses he'd brought—they were beginning to wilt from the heat, but their scent was undiminished. Ronnie was undiminished as well. Suddenly I felt glad and hopeful about our collaboration, our shared corporate fate. I poured us each another brandy. Magda went on to ask a number of polite questions about the ozone layer, black holes, and the cost and availability of child care in the neighborhood, and between her questions and Ronnie's marathon responses and my occasional unsolicited interjections we passed the better part of an hour involved in what even I had to concede was, looking back on it, a relatively normal conversation.

Then Ronnie and the baby left, and all turned strange again.

For one thing, Magda did not avail herself of the opportunity to leave. Nor did she offer any excuse for not leaving—having to use the bathroom, for instance, or make a phone call, or drink some water, or any of the usual ways one might contrive to remain behind if one was up to some sort of contrivance.

"Very nice person," she commented, when I returned from letting Ronnie and Isabel out the front door.

"Did you like him? I couldn't tell."

"He's a bit of a *nudnik*, but I liked him. But I was uncomfortable sitting here with him. It was very strange."

"Why?"

"I'm not used to meeting people."

She said this matter-of-factly, without self-pity or surprise. Nonetheless it moved me deeply.

"What's the matter?" she asked. "Why are you looking at me that way?"

"It's just that I thought you told me you had a lot of visitors."

"Oh, that's different. They're from the neighborhood, they come over on Shabbos, or sometimes just to kibitz. Also I meet them with Aaron. It's strange to meet someone by myself is what I meant. And speaking English."

"But you were born here."

"In my house we spoke Yiddish. We still do. And anyway," she said, "what am I supposed to talk about? All this asking about what people do, about work and jobs. What could I possibly say about what I do that would interest anybody?"

"Speaking of which: what *do* you do?"

She laughed. "Not very much."

"No, really, I want to know."

"Well . . ." she glanced up at me uncertainly, as if trying to determine whether I and my interest were to be pitied or feared. "I cook. I shop, I talk on the phone. I clean the house. I try to knit sweaters for all the new babies. I try to read Talmud sometimes, or Rashi, so we'll have things to talk about on Shabbos. Usually after a while I give up and sneak over to Hava's to watch television with the boys. Aaron hates it," she said, "when he catches me. He thinks it makes me passive."

"What do you watch?"

"Oh, soap operas, comedies, it doesn't matter. The boys like 'Star Trek' the most." She gave a flat smile.

"Star Trek"? She should have said something before. It was Ronnie Oldham's favorite show.

"So. That's it. I try this, I try that. Sometimes I paint a watercolor. I have a set of paints. It's very old, it belonged to my mother. But I'm no good."

"How do you know what's good? You don't go to museums. Have you ever studied?"

"I don't need a teacher to tell me. I just know. Besides, there's no time to learn." This line of reasoning must have sounded feeble even to her, for she shook her head crossly. "Oh, that's not it either. It's just I waste so much time for no reason. I think Aaron must be right: I *am* passive. I don't seem to have interests anymore. Or friends. I'm too high strung, I think. Or not high strung enough. It has something to do, I think," and her eyes now were brimming with tears, "with the way I'm strung."

She wiped her nose with a napkin. "Listen to me go on. It's shameful."

"No it isn't."

"They say, you know, the proud are reborn as bees. They're too stubborn to submit to God, so after they die they have to be born again. Always buzzing: I am, I am, I am."

"Is that such a terrible fate?"

"Of course it is. All this ego, this self. What's the point?"

"The point is, maybe this buzzing self is all you've got."

"Don't be silly," she said. "There's God."

"Is there?"

"Of course," she said.

"Well, let's say you're right. Why would God go to all the trouble to give you an ego if not for you to use it?"

"Now you sound like Hava," she said. "Hava's answer to everything is I should just be myself and stop worrying. She's perfectly comfortable being selfish. She wants what she wants and she gets it. I'm a feminist's nightmare, she says. She drags me along to women's groups at the shul, trying to change me. But I get so bored there."

"Why?"

"Oh, it's just gossip. Tiresome women getting together to eat cookies and complain about their husbands. I don't see the point of so much complaining."

This last sentiment alarmed me. Complaining for me was like third base—a position from which I knew how to operate. I took the activity very seriously and did not like to see people run around disparaging it.

"So you can see," she continued, "why I doubt anything I do would interest your friend."

"What about me?"

"Yes. Or you. But you're different."

"I am?"

"You can see right away that your friend has his things he's decided are important. Maybe they are, maybe they're not. But he's all wrapped up in these things and he hardly pays attention to anything else. That's what I meant before when I said he reminds me of people I know."

"Like Aaron?"

At the sound of the name her limbs went stiff with tension. Or was it my own tension she felt? Between the two of us, there was no shortage of tension to go around. "Not just him," she said. "Everyone. Zev, Yossi . . ."

"Yossi?"

"Oh, he lives next door. You passed his house when you came to dinner. Yossi I used to flirt with when I was twelve. Now he's married too. A nice girl, much nicer than me. The Rebbe, bless his name, knew what he was doing when he chose her. She's nice and good and so what if she weighs a hundred and sixty pounds? She's given him four children already." She drew a breath, rubbing her bare arms with her hands; no doubt she was unaccustomed to *having* bare arms and found them hard to get used to. "What I'm trying to tell you is your friend is familiar to me. Everyone I grew up with is like that. The only difference is they're surrounded by others just like them, and your friend has only his work and his family. So he's lonely."

"And you?"

She frowned. For a moment she appeared ready to answer the question, but then the moment passed, and we fell back into silence, the mode of communication that in the end seemed to suit us best. It did not help matters that Magda showed so little curiosity about *my* life. Nothing about this mysterious girlfriend of mine, or my job, or my past. Perhaps she knew what she needed to know already. Cradling her elbows in her palms she stared into the folds of the tablecloth, her face grown sullen and pouchy. The rain had stopped. I turned to the window, but with the overhead light on I could see only the reflection of its too-bright halo and beneath it, two people and a bottle of brandy, superimposed upon a black sky.

A couple of plaintive guitar licks came floating through the walls. My neighbor, the public defender, was playing the blues again. His wife had left him at Christmas and moved to Seattle to open a coffeehouse. Wasn't that a terrible thing?

Magda stifled a yawn.

"You're tired," I said.

"It's the brandy. It happens with schnapps, too. Aaron says I'm a cheap date. That means," she added quickly, "that it doesn't take much alcohol to knock me out."

"I know what it means."

"Oh," she said. "Of course you do." She scratched at the back of her hand. "What time is it?"

"Ten-twenty."

"So late?"

"Yes." I hesitated. "I should get you home."

"Yes."

Having agreed on this point, however, seemed to release us for the moment from any obligation to enact it. We leaned back in our chairs. Magda, cheap date or not, finished the rest of her second brandy, and I finished the rest of mine. Then, as if out of habit, both of us looked over to the sofa where baby Isabel had lain; the outline of her impression was still visible on the cushions.

Magda yawned again. She was beginning to exasperate me.

"Does Aaron know where you are?" I asked suddenly.

She nodded.

"And he approves?"

She nodded again. "He likes you," she said.

"For Christ's sake, why?"

"I think," she said carefully, "that he sees part of himself in you."

"Oh? Which part?"

"I don't know," she said.

"Well, what did he say about me?"

"You'll think it strange what he said. You won't understand."

"Try me."

She smiled nervously. "At the airport in Texas, after we dropped you off. He said, 'You never know in advance how an angel will look.' "

"An angel! That's great. That's fucking marvelous."

"This is what he said," she maintained.

"Well, do I look like an angel to you?"

"No." She spoke quietly but firmly. Her eyes were getting smaller and redder by the second.

"Let's face it, the man's crazy as a bedbug. He's out of his mind."

His wife, by the merest movement of her shoulders, allowed as to how perhaps this was so.

"I mean, what does he think we're doing?"

"Having dinner," she said hoarsely.

"And what about after dinner? What does he think we're doing now? Does he even care?"

"Of course he cares. If you knew him at all—if you could see him with those boys at the detention center . . . he's out there once a week, you know, just to give guitar lessons, but for them he's a father. They tell him everything. It's practically all he thinks about, cares about, how to be a good Jew, how to help other people, how to make them—" She broke off in order to gnaw at the fingernail on her pinky, as if she'd only just noticed how long it was getting. "He cares a lot," she concluded, wrapping up the subject for good.

"Okay, so he cares a lot. So why don't you go home then?"

I believe it was at this point that she began to cry in earnest. I had no idea why. She looked worn out. The tears did not dissolve her but instead brought out a dignity and composure that were both extraordinary and, I thought, altogether false. Now of all times her posture improved. Head high, neck straight, shoulders back, she stared directly into the bookshelves that lined the opposite wall and read or pretended to read the spines, as if the real business of the moment was literary inventory and this other thing—this hot water trailing down her cheeks—was not even worth mentioning.

"Walt Whitman," she noted hoarsely to herself. "Aaron has this one too."

For some reason that only made the tears come harder. Still she refused to acknowledge them. Whatever they were they did not, she seemed to think, originate inside her, but had been imposed upon her, or conveyed through her, by some unseen and capricious higher power. She was just *here*; the tears were not her responsibility. And yet they kept coming and coming.

She looked so courageous in that moment, so fierce and willful and so hopelessly screwed up, that my heart went out to her. My heart, it should be noted, had not gone out in some time. I was amazed it even remembered how.

Something she'd said earlier occurred to me.

"Your marriage. It was some kind of arrangement, wasn't it? That's how you people do it."

She glanced absently in my direction; she had all but forgotten I was there. "You wouldn't understand," she said.

"Forget about my understanding. Just tell me yes or no."

"If you like, yes, it was a *shiddich*. I was chosen for him."

"And he for you?"

"It's not so simple as you think."

She grew quiet, withdrawing into herself again. The hands and knees folding into each other, the face shutting down. Her eyelashes, my God, were about an inch and a half long.

Just to make the stillness complete, there was no longer any music playing anywhere. My neighbor had gone to bed.

About what follows, I offer no excuse. Surely it is obvious

by now that I am not a man of action. But I was operating on the day's third brandy and second hangover, and I was very tired, and the prospect of yet another pregnant silence between us was almost as intolerable as that of the hot, sleepless night that awaited me when she left. I really only wanted to get her attention, I think, to seize and anchor it for a moment. And I was so nervous that when I leaned across the table I nearly poked out my eye on one of the unlit candles. Of course I had every reason to be nervous, given what I was about to do.

Magda's eyes, when she saw my face floating toward her, got very wide, stretching out to horror-movie proportions; the pupils trembled in their shimmering pools. Was she still crying? Had she stopped? Was she about to start again now?

I could hear that internal engine of mine coughing out its old refrain: bad idea, bad idea, bad idea . . .

Oh hell. I'd always been a sucker for bad ideas.

I kissed her. Because of the table between us, our only point of contact was at the mouth. Hers was parted the merest sliver of an inch, a narrow chasm that seemed to open involuntarily and against her better judgment but through which I could taste all the moist troubled weight of her breath. Make no mistake, I told myself: this is the end of the fantasy, the point of departure. Or was it return? All I knew was that at last I was going *some*where, boat slipping its moorings, ropes and tethers falling away limp on all sides. Perhaps it was the brandy, only that. But there were warm winds in my chest and warm tides in my veins, and they all converged at that hopeful point where my lips met hers in a duality of twos . . .

But it turned out I was traveling alone.

My emotions were sufficiently transcendental that I nearly lost Magda in them altogether. What *she* was feeling, what kind of nerve-static buzzed below the surface, I had no idea. Her lips, it grieved me to discover, were cool. When I left them they did not pull away, but neither did they push forward. In the end, I realized later, having had more than ample time to reflect on the matter, they had not so much joined as they had fleetingly resigned themselves to mine.

Then they disappeared altogether. And they took Magda with them.

CHAPTER 10

FAVORS AND REWARDS

I saw nothing of Magda for several weeks. This did not surprise me, or even, on a certain level, disturb me very much. Magda and the challenges she presented were clearly more than I could handle at the moment. My own life was more than I could handle too, as I seemed determined to demonstrate. But there was no choice: Donna and I were quits, and no one else was willing to handle it for me.

It turned out to be somewhat hotter in New York that August than even the most hard-core global-warming alarmists had anticipated. The sun was a kind of comic book version of its usual self, orange and bloated beyond recognition; even after it quit for the night the heat did not diminish, the haze refused to lift. It was thunderstorm weather without the thunderstorms. People hunted avidly through the cable channels, looking for a new and better forecast, some rogue front swooping down from the Great Lakes to wash the sky clean. But nothing changed. The air held and clung; the streets turned soft, miasmic. In the morning I trudged to the subway on gelatinous legs, and in the evening I trudged back, and everyone I passed had the same look of weary, half-ironical disbelief that people in New York come to know so well—that hey-come-on,.you-must-be-kidding,.we-can't-really-be-expected-to-live-this-way look.

The hours between I passed in my cubicle at the magazine,

which had become a very chilly place indeed. Every week it seemed a new manager flew in on the Concorde—young men with solemn accents and quiet shoes—to oil the gears of transition. Harry Flood was gone: the merger artists had eased him out with their golden hands. Now he was said to be holed up at his summer house in Montauk, licking his wounds or cooling his heels or doing whatever huge intemperate people like Harry Flood do when they have nothing else to occupy them. A few other big guns were on the ropes, too. The rest of us kept our heads down, trying to stay out of trouble and quietly polishing our résumés. But there were times when my neutrality faltered, when my back went stiff or my will to work went slack, and I'd leave my desk and go lie on the carpeted floor of my cubicle and think about Harry Flood, marooned out on the far end of Long Island—proud, lustful, petulant, ringed by phones and lawyers, smashing tennis balls on his private court. Did he miss the place? Did the place miss him? Did it matter?

Ray Spurlock at least seemed untouchable, though it was difficult to be certain as he was not around for much of August. He was on a vision quest down in Mexico with the Tarahumara Indians. Vision quests were the latest craze among upper management. *Forbes* had run a piece in their January issue called "Alternative Forms of Corporate Rejuvenation" and this had had a good deal of influence. The Japanese claimed impressive results with ritual dancing and chants; the Germans were keeping pace with sweat lodges and peyote. The consultants had put their heads together and decided that the least we could do, in the interest of competitiveness, was send a few lousy executives into the highlands.

"You mustn't take any of this restructuring too seriously," Arlen Ashby told me. "Every few decades the great wheels turn. There's nothing to be done but get out of the way."

Out of the way we were. The two of us were still taking long lunches together once or twice a week. Apparently the Entropy session had been only a starter course; Arlen was hungry for more. I suppose, being as bereft of fathers as he was of sons, I wanted more of him too. Having polished off thermodynamics with dispatch, we were now proceeding down some private list of arcane curiosities he had been amassing over the years. El Dorado. Atlantis. The last campaigns of De Soto. Lost cities, doomed expeditions. It was as if Arlen was preparing for a voyage of some kind himself, rummaging through history's attics, throwing old chests open, looking for a map or compass, something, anything, that would help get him there intact.

And so it came as no surprise when, the week before Labor Day, we took up the matter of Amundsen and Scott and their race to the Pole. Naturally Arlen's sympathies were with the loser, Scott. Failure has its own poetry, its own artistic glow, and Arlen, I was beginning to realize, was a connoisseur of such things. Things that ran down, fell short, depleted themselves on the brink of achievement—these were his obsessions, the grand equations he pondered in the dark hours, trying to isolate the variables. Over lunch he read to me excerpts from Scott's journals, which were found beside his frozen corpse:

" 'I seem to hold in reserve something that makes for success, and yet to see no worthy field for it,' " he recited, in his low and sonorous voice, " 'and so there is this consciousness of a truly deep unrest.' "

For some reason—the cool fire of the gin, the lingering tang of the piccata, all this soft heat and abundance that lay beyond the dead man's reach—Arlen Ashby was moved in the course of this recitation to shed a couple of tears. I watched them descend, tracing perfect lines down his cheeks, each one pointing like an arrow to the oversized organ that pumped in his chest.

"Hey, Arlen, are you okay?"

"What? Oh fine, fine."

"That's very beautiful," I said. "What he wrote. I feel I know just what he means."

"Indeed." He blew his nose. "Well, you're welcome to borrow it if you like."

I did, too. We both turned out to be full of emotion that day. For poor Scott; for the brutal, heroic Amundsen; for all the nameless idealists consigned to frozen graves because of them—but most of all, I think, for Arlen Ashby himself. Because I understood now, watching him fold up his silk handkerchief and tuck it neatly into his pocket, what had happened to the man, what had brought his career to ruin and waste. Arlen, like Scott, was another dabbler, a failed Renaissance man—the kind who, finding no suitable vehicle for his ambitions, was doomed to a life of quixotic quests, false starts, late arrivals, and bad luck. There are those who in seeking everything wind up with nothing. Who cannot or will not settle in, settle down, seize a niche and call it their own; who spend their lives straining, with increasing desperation, to forge a design for themselves from the discarded designs of others. I knew what that unrest was like. Oh, I knew. And Arlen knew I knew. At his age, Arlen Ashby was shrewd enough to discern just who was a factor in this world and who was not.

"Well then," he said, examining the check, "I suppose we must get back."

And so we did. Back and forth, from the office to lunch, from there to destinations obscure or unknown, and then back to the office—an amiable and circular journey, up and down a river of gin. I was to learn a great deal from Arlen Ashby in those weeks, but nothing with a value that was quantifiable, nothing that was useful in the here and now. The goings on at the office, its Machiavellian alignments and divisions, its warning signs and portents—these were left unremarked. On the one occasion I screwed up my courage to ask about Harry Flood, Arlen darkened severely, his mouth tight as if from soured wine. "Harry Flood," he snapped, "is on his own. And so are we all."

Anyway, I didn't mind. In a fit of common sense, I'd given up trying to ingratiate myself at the office through any means other than hard work.

Toward this end, I was now showing up every day promptly at nine and staying until well past seven—by far the longest, most regular hours I had ever worked in my life. While I would like to report that the experience was a positive one, it wasn't. At first the days were a blur, the week a dreary, featureless landscape I staggered across like a sleepwalker. Just rolling out of bed in the morning to the clarion call of the alarm clock was a formidable project, a slow, halting exercise in urban renewal. Frequently in the past I used to wonder why I did not have a more normal life. Now I knew. I wasn't good at it.

Ronnie Oldham, who'd put himself through college as a lab technician and had never had a vacation in his life, was not sympathetic. "Sure it's enervating," he said. "But you're looking at it the wrong way around. You need to be patient. Go far enough into the room and you no longer notice the walls. Then you know you've arrived."

He had ample time to coach me on these matters. The two of us were now meeting regularly in Ronnie's office after hours, trying to hammer our AIDS piece into shape. It was like trying to hammer mercury into shape. It didn't help that the reports from Sydney, upon inspection, were somewhat spottier and less convincing than Ronnie had been led to believe. We had to roam around a bit on what people at the magazine never tired of calling the information highway, looking for alternate data. Fortunately, this is a good epoch for data: there was plenty to choose from. Our arrival on the Net had sent rippling waves of transmission across the seven continents; now, as the waves began to ripple back, I discovered what Ronnie Oldham had known for some time—that there was an entire underground community out there of cerebral misfits just like him, a cabal of brilliant hackers who did nothing but E-mail back and forth in their cranky numerical codes. It was like joining the Shriners, the Masons. Tapping into our computer mailbox at the end of the workday, we'd be greeted by dozens of memos, salutations, catcalls. Paris and Bombay weighing in with support; Capetown and La Jolla making threats. Behind his glasses, Ronnie's eyes, as they ran across the monitor, were giddy with reflected light. Many of the names were familiar to him. These were his friends, his club, his virtual family. He was having, I realized, a wonderful time.

"Look what just came through," he called out very late one evening. "Turin. Immunological suppression reports. Somebody must have cracked the security code of the public health service."

"Great," I said. "Let's go home."

"Home?"

"It's nearly ten."

"Which means it's nearly 4 A.M. in Italy. And *they* haven't gone home."

"The coffee's stronger over there," I said. "Come on, Ronnie. Haven't we got more than enough raw data already?"

"Sam." Ronnie pushed his glasses back up his nose, frowning, as if it was only the gravity of my recalcitrance that was driving them down. "I don't think you quite appreciate what's going on here. There's a *process* underway. We conceived this process, we brought it into this world, and now we have a responsibility to care for it. It's bigger than us now; it's an independent thing."

"Well, if it's an independent thing, let it write itself for a while."

"Stop being clever," he said. "There isn't time."

"What's the rush? Forty years of nuclear testing isn't going to go away in one night."

"Yes, but now everyone knows what we're doing. This is how the information age works. Every little byte triggers a chain reaction. Even as we speak, grinds are at work in every stack of the electronic library. Thousands of documents out there. Enough to support any number of big, splashy articles."

"Or to contradict ours."

"True. Which is why we have to be thorough. We're talking about governments here. Big energy companies, important figures. Thin-skinned and litigious people."

So we stayed. Late nights, stiff backs, take-out food with unpronounceable names. But slowly, almost imperceptibly, the piece took shape. Rather, we began to *give* it shape. The work was slow and difficult and there were times our own high intentions became obscured by fog, and I would find myself wondering if there was indeed any connection between two such disparate things as nuclear fallout and immunological disease, or had we only contrived it from wisps and suspicions. But I stayed. I stayed because Ronnie did, though it was more than that. I stayed because making connections between disparate things had become the project of my life. And, even if it wasn't, I think I would have stayed anyway. Because I had to. Because I had tried everything else and nothing had worked, and now there was only this. Always in the past I had spread myself too thin, hedged too many bets; it was time to go ahead and put up the whole stake.

Ronnie was right: this was how to get things done. Enter the room and forget the walls. Immerse in content. Submit to it. Try to see things through, as opposed to seeing through things.

And that was how August went: working, immersing, submitting. I had no contact with Donna, or Magda, or Aaron Brenner. In fact I had no social life at all. I rid myself of superfluities, made my days as regular and strenuous as a massage. Every morning I did fifty sit-ups and push-ups and walked to midtown. Every evening I came home, read for an hour, and went to bed. I cut back on television. I cut back on movies. I cut back on sugar, beer, red meat, coffee. I cleaned my apartment, putting the junk in boxes, hauling them out to the garbage shaft. It was eight in the evening when I started and six in the morning, the sun peeping over the rooftops, when I lugged the last box out to the incinerator.

"What are you doing out here?" asked Mrs. Pearl across the hall, who had opened her door to get a look at me. "Throwing out the garbage?"

"That's right," I said.

"But so early?"

"It's not early, Mrs. Pearl. Not early at all."

"You should be ashamed of yourself."

But in fact I felt very hard and resolute, standing out there in my bathrobe, amid the empty cans and bottles and the tied-up stacks of newspaper, listening to some old cassettes bump and tumble down the chute. After all they were only tapes—easily snapped, easily burned—why let them bind me any longer?

"Such a racket," said Mrs. Pearl, and closed the door firmly behind her.

The weekend of Labor Day, as part of my new campaign of good works, I flew up to Rochester to see my mother.

My mother, at sixty-three, had been a widow for a quarter of a century now and was rather accomplished at it. Her health, save for some intermittent arthritis, was pretty good; her job kept her busy and engaged in the community; and as people do who have lived a long time alone, she had many intimate friends, a number of whom had become, in the past decade or so, widows themselves. Once a month they gathered in my mother's dining room to nibble pâté and smoked cheese, drink Chardonnay, and discuss the book they had chosen the previous month—by dint of its urgent social message or front-page review in the *Times*—to read. There is no need to make fun of them. They were bright, accomplished women with the time and resources to be conscientious about culture, and if it was rare for Alvin Ailey or Yo-Yo Ma or an exhibit of early or mid or for that matter late Impressionists to come through town and not have my mother and her widowed friends in attendance, so be it. Occasionally there were dates with men, often older men, divorced men. No doubt from time to time there was even some kind of sex involved, though to be honest I did not like to ponder the specifics of it.

Somewhere along the line my mother had lost her waistline, and with it some of her high ex-debutante airs; she was just another suburban matron now, with a gray shag haircut and baggy cotton shorts, and a house that loomed too large around her.

The house too had lost some of its form around the edges, succumbing to the pull of the surrounding woods. Even from the far end of the driveway I could see the lawn needed mowing, the hedges trimming, the garden weeding, and the driveway itself, which was buckling at both ends, replaning. And that was just the outside of the place. Inside there were flaws in the ceiling plaster, and small leaks and blockages in the ventilation system, and porous foundation walls that let in too much of the ambient moisture. And there was my mother, with her creaky arthritic joints, trying to go on as she always had, with her Jackie Kennedy stoicism, her wry, lap-swimming poise. But the pool was longer now. Her doctor had advised her to move to a smaller place in one of the cheerfully named condo developments outside of town. She was not so sure. The doctor was twice divorced and wore a hair transplant; at sixty-three, she would not be taken in by the romance of shucking burdens and fresh starts. Besides, the house was paid for, her office only a few minutes away, she had friends on the block, and a kitchen window that overlooked a yard full of rhododendrons and wisterias, bluejays and cardinals . . . why give these up if she didn't have to?

Meanwhile, until she decided on the right course, she'd play it smart, seed the ground for both possibilities. Which was what she used to tell me smart people did.

Toward this end I had been recruited to go through the stuff in storage and help prepare the house should she decide to sell it. The basement was cluttered with rusty tools hanging on rusty hooks, tools neither of us knew how to use. They were to be hauled off. The top shelf of the garage had been impenetrable for years; about its contents, material and animal, she wouldn't even hazard a guess. Also the upstairs closets were stuffed with cartons, each neatly sealed with duct tape, and these, my father's clothes, were to be gone through right away.

"I should have taken them to Goodwill years ago," she said. "Somehow I never quite made it."

"Okay, Ma. I understand."

"Do you?" She looked me over worriedly. She did not want to read me wrong. She was sitting at the kitchen table, sipping tea and listening to Chopin. The telephone lay within reach. Her case files were spread before her like a fan. There was a strain between us I couldn't identify, a tension that crept into our silences. A restraint. The truth is we held certain things against each other, my mother and I. On her side I suppose there was a question of fairness. Here she'd worked hard all her life, her losses and struggles had been significantly more taxing than mine, and yet somehow I was the one to emerge intractably depressive, while she'd been left to play out forever the role of chipper, can-do parent. It must have seemed a raw deal.

It seemed that way to me too. So I spent the next two days trying to make up for it. I emptied the basement, cleared out the garage. I pruned the shrubs, fixed some broken storm windows, changed the oil in the old Pontiac. I did all the chores I never did as a child until my father died and there was no choice. As I went back and forth to the hardware store in a fury of penance—undertaking small repairs, delegating the big jobs to professionals—I wondered what it said about the man, and about myself, that he had never asked me to help.

The business of his clothes I saved for last. It was not sentiment that held me off, I don't think, but dread—of their odors and textures, their specific realities. I preferred my memories formless, open-ended. So it came as a minor surprise when I rummaged through the faded cartons, separating the clothes to be thrown away from those to be donated to Goodwill and the Salvation Army, to find that I wasn't bothered in the slightest. They had no power over me. They were just cool, nameless things I was sifting into piles: darks and whites, salvageable and unsalvageable. Then, too, goodwill and salvation were concepts that appealed to me these days; I was eager to support them any way I could.

Sunday night I came down from the attic exhausted and found my mother at the table again with her tea and her files. "I need to show you something," I said.

She lifted her head, eyes big and weary behind her bifocals. "Are you all right, honey? You look so strange."

"It's just this old picture, that's all."

"Mmm." She squinted at the photograph for a moment. "What about it?"

"Well, where did it come from?"

"Why, it used to hang in the hallway, next to the staircase. Don't you remember? It was there for years."

"It did? Why?"

"Honey, don't you know?" From the judgmental way she looked up at me over her glasses, we might have been discussing one of my disappointing report cards from junior high school, not this weathered old photograph of a tall, bearded, hawk-nosed man in his sixties or seventies. Who was he? The expression on his huge narrow head was severe. He wore an embroidered caftan and a long black coat over a collarless shirt, with fringes that stuck carelessly out of the trousers. There was something raw and aggrieved in his gaze. Despite the inevitable fading over time, his eyes, as they suspiciously regarded the camera, burned like sullen torches through the woods of his beard, as if he had been pulled away from some matter of infinite importance, and for what? Only *this*? This clicking toy with its flare of light?

"Honey," my mother said, "you don't know your own great-grandfather?"

"Good Lord," I said. "Mine?"

"Who else's?"

"But he looks like a fucking *Hasid*!" I cried.

"Does he?" My mother reviewed the picture again. "He was quite religious I think, yes. But of course I never met him. Why, does it matter?"

"I'm not sure," I said. "I'm not sure if it matters."

"Well, you were named for him, you know. Samuel came from Shmuel. Come now, we must have told you *that*."

"Ma," I said, "you guys never told me *any*thing."

"Oh that's not true. That's just you feeling sorry for yourself. There were plenty of things we told you but you were too dreamy to hear. Of course your father—" she conceded, "was not big on talking about his family. Whatever happened was over *there*, was his attitude. We were another thing altogether."

Thoughtful now, she blew on her tea. "He was relieved when he got sick, you know. I've never told anyone. But he was. Because he didn't have to feel guilty any longer."

"Guilty about what?"

"Leaving." Her voice was muffled.

"For a second there I thought you said living."

She looked at me soberly. "I did."

A veil fell over her face. I watched her struggle with it for a moment as if it were something to be shaken off, cleared away. She had always been the sturdy, focused one, the one equipped to go on. Even that Summer of Love, my father jaundiced and dying beside her, she had kept her poise, her sense of present motion. There had always been her work to brace her, her files, thick and messy, evidence of larger tragedies. Here they still were, her Brotherhood of Man—immigrants from Russia and Cambodia, welfare mothers, mental patients, Vietnam vets, retirees, the disabled—each one a voice in the chorus of need, imploring her to transcend her personal worries and resume the good fight, tear down the walls that separate black from white, rich from poor, native from alien, us from them. If she had in her universalist fervor torn down one wall too many, was that such a crime? Watching her tight, veiny hand scribble notes in the margins, I thought: *But she has always acted out of love*. And so might my father have acted. Trying to fill the American mold, letting go of the past, not simply out of guilt, nor simply for the sake of convenience or freedom (whatever *that* is), but for love: love for this woman—this handsome, driven woman—and for this handsome, driven new country as well. And for me. I had thought him in retreat from the world but perhaps I was wrong. Not the movement away that is despair, but the movement toward that is love. And yet even love turns out to be divisive in the end. Even love, for all its creative force, has its own destructive powers, its own solutions and dissolutions. Even love in its erasure of lines can't help but inscribe a set of new lines, within.

On Labor Day we went out with some of my mother's friends for a picnic in Highland Park, where the lilacs bloom in such profusion they are awarded their own annual festival. It was a bright clear afternoon, with cool winds whisking down from the lake and a huge cerulean sky revolving overhead. I lay drowsily in the long grass. In a few hours I had to pack for my flight to New York, but New York seemed far away now. My attachment to the place seemed only vague, habitual, a noisy and demanding game I'd played for years but was not necessarily good at, like softball.

Driving home, we swept past the mammoth Kodak plant, which loomed on its slope above the thickets of trees, humming away even on a holiday afternoon.

"You want to know something terrible?" I asked. "I don't even know what he did up there."

"Oh, it had something to do with contrast, I think. Light and shadow, getting the right proportions to come out in development. They were always fooling around with the process." She looked at me. "Poor Sam. I'm not much help to you, am I?"

"It doesn't matter. I was only asking."

She thought for a moment. "You know, your father had problems with his back too."

"No, I didn't."

"He had to go to the hospital for two weeks once. You must have been about four. We had us quite a party, you and me. Hot dogs, banana splits, doughnuts, all that junky stuff he disapproved of. I let you stay up late watching TV. You even slept in my bed. That may have been a mistake, I think."

"Why?"

"Because you got spoiled, honey. You ran away crying when he came back. It took me forever to find you."

"He must have loved that."

"Oh, he laughed. He said he expected it. He always expected the worst, your father." She giggled to herself like a naughty, headstrong girl. "Now I'll tell *you* something awful."

"Go ahead."

"I cried too."

"That's not awful."

"Oh yes it was," she said. "Because I was happier living alone, just with you. I knew it then. I loved your father, of course, but he was so . . . so *heavy* all the time. Somehow I just felt freer when he was gone."

I was silent a moment. Finally I said, "I think for me it was just the opposite."

"Was it?"

"Some things loom larger when they're not there."

"Well," she said after a while. "I suppose you're right."

Later, at home, we made iced coffee and carried it out on a tray to the backyard. I lay down in the hammock for an hour or so, drowsily rocking in the late afternoon shade. My mother sat at the picnic table, nibbling a cookie and reviewing the front page of the newspaper for the second time that day. Perhaps she thought the news would improve if she read it again.

Groaning, she rubbed her feet; the world's injustices were pebbles in her shoes.

"Are you okay, Ma? Can I get you anything?"

"I'm fine," she said. "Don't get up."

"More coffee?"

"Fine," she repeated sharply. She rubbed her long fingers, wincing as she reached the joints. Like most people, pain made her irritable. Or perhaps she was merely irritated with me: me and my questions, my thickening waist, my broken marriage, my lusterless record of underachievement. It could not have escaped her notice how little of the world I had won for myself as I lay there swinging back and forth, suspended between the birch trees. "So," she said, "your plane leaves at six?"

"Right."

"I should drive you. I wish I—"

"That's okay. I'll take a cab."

"Well, don't forget to call the airline. They have delays, you know."

"I know."

Suddenly, as if I had not agreed with her but insulted her instead, she looked furious. "This job of yours. It doesn't seem to be *going* anywhere."

"I'm working on it, Ma."

"And Donna. What about her? You never even talk about her anymore."

"I don't think I really want to get into it right now, if you don't mind."

She put down the paper. "You were always a gloomy boy. Right from the start. You used to cry when I held you and cry when I didn't. And so skinny back then. Your father used to say it was like your skin felt too tight."

"That's funny. It often felt that way to me too."

"Well," she said bitterly, "it wasn't."

But then our eyes met, and as quickly as the anger had risen between us, it fell away. What was the point of pulling out the old dull knives when we were made of the same materials, stitched with the same thread? Alone in this house together all those years, we had always been just a little too close, my mother and I; we lacked the buffer of mystery between us. Mystery, it seems, is just another casualty of survival.

"You better go get ready," she said with a sigh.

"I will."

"Come give me a hug first. I never get to hug you anymore."

Despite if not because of the fact that I had several years of intensive psychotherapy behind me, I had to restrain myself, as we embraced, from climbing all the way into her lap, so good did it feel to let my mother's hands enfold me this way.

No shadows, no ghosts. Just me. For I am what remains. The end of the line.

"I'm sorry to be such an old crab," she says. "I don't know what's wrong with me. And here you were such a love, coming all this way to help. But sometimes I really want to . . ." She shakes her head, unwilling to finish.

"What?"

"Punch you right in the nose." Suddenly she laughs; she has surprised herself and me both. "No kidding, honey! Just to wake you up!"

"Well, I'm up now," I say, "so there's no need to punch me. But you can if you want."

"No, thanks. Too busy." Her nose crinkles up. "Now you better go shower, or you'll miss your plane."

"Here I go."

"Call the airline first," she says, picking up the paper and folding it in half the long way, as they do on the bus, as she has done her whole life.

Back in New York, a remarkable thing happened: this new philosophy of mine began to pay off.

After an entire month of good works, it dawned on me that I was no longer quite so stiff when I woke up, or quite so tired when I went to sleep, or quite so frantic and remorseful during the hours between. Even the black hand of loneliness had lost some of its power. I was coming through.

And then, as if to confirm this progress, Ronnie swung by my cubicle to deliver unto me a piece of astonishing news.

I was lying on the floor at the time—hugging my knees to my chest as part of my lower-back regimen—but he did not appear to notice. "Hey," he said, "I just wanted you to know. I showed a rough draft of our piece to Spurlock."

"And?"

"And he's got a lot on his plate right now. But he expressed interest."

At this, some light object turned heavy inside me.

"What's the matter?" he asked.

"Is this a joke, Ronnie?"

"Not at all. He said it's an intriguing idea and we should take a few weeks to work it into shape. Then he wants to sit down in a group and meet."

"Probably he says that to everybody."

"Why are you being so skeptical? I'm telling you, Sam, he's *interested*. We're actually making this happen. Does that scare you?"

"Why should it scare me?"

"I don't know. You look kind of pale all of a sudden. What are you doing on the floor anyway?"

"It's for my lower back. Don't worry. I'm fine."

"Good. Because I hope you're prepared to get serious about this. We're on the brink, you know. There's no turning back now."

After he left, I got up from the floor and paced my office. Suddenly I was ravenous. Though it was not yet twelve, I went out for lunch and ordered a steak, with coffee and cheesecake for dessert. Afterward, in a swoon of enzymes and blood sugars, I walked down to Barneys, where I bought three linen shirts I didn't need. They cost me a hundred and twenty dollars and would need to be expensively maintained, but when I put one on in the changing room it felt so crisp and cool, so nicely aligned to the bumps and hollows of my cartography, that I decided to leave it on for the rest of the day.

Then I decided not to go back to the office, but walk the forty blocks home instead. In the heat of the past weeks, this distance had seemed huge; now I felt I could traverse it in a single stride.

On the way, I worked up a tremendous thirst and stopped to reward myself with a soda. Then, passing an appliance store on Broadway, I went in and rewarded myself further by putting a down payment on a new air conditioner, which I brought home in a taxi. Normally in a taxi I really did immerse in the here and now, devoting all my attention to the meter, but this time I ignored the clicking numbers and looked out the window instead. Tenderly I patted the massive box that rested on the seat beside me—this expensive machine I had bought to deliver me comfort. I knew how it felt. I was in a box too. But I was headed out. Pretty soon we'd both be plugged in, channeling currents that were all around us, running through us, wiring us to everything—the air, the sun, the walls, the floors, the webbed geometry of the power lines overhead and the sunken deposits of the earth below . . . Yes, we were going to be plugged in pretty soon. Once we were out of the box, that is. Once we were out of the box.

When Aaron Brenner called one evening in mid-September, it seemed to have nothing to do with this new pared-down life of mine. He caught me, however, at an off moment. I was sitting on the couch watching a ballgame and enjoying my dinner, feeling every inch the hardworking bachelor at midweek. Outside the sky was a big gray plate smeared with runny violet leftovers from sunset. The days were growing shorter now. And cooler. I looked at my new air conditioner, immaculate and silent in its wedged window. Canadian breezes were sweeping in. To receive them I'd thrown the other windows open and pulled back the curtains, so that as I ate I could see one of my neighbors across the street watching television in his living room, and he could, if he so chose, see me doing the same in mine. I wondered if my silhouette, in that gathering darkness, looked as forlorn and austere to him as his did to me.

When the phone rang I gave a start. There is a certain quotient of shame involved in living alone. You feel it every time the curtains swing open and there you are again, exposed in your solitary postures, your private indulgences. I felt it now.

"So long without a word?" Aaron said, in lieu of a hello. "We thought you might have left town."

Immediately I was on the defensive. Who would leave town? A fugitive. A criminal on the lam. *He knows*, I thought. *He knows.*

But knows what?

"I was visiting my mother for a few days. Why, did you call?"

"Six or seven times I called."

"Sorry," I said. "The damn machine must be broken again."

"No no, it answers fine. I didn't leave a message. Those machines, they unnerve me. Such a waste, these devices we buy to help us remember every last thing. You think God wants us to remember everything?"

"Sure He does. Why not?"

"Because, as Reb Baruch tells us, if there were no forgetting, a man would dwell incessantly upon his own death. He would never embark on anything."

"Hold on," I said. "As an accountant, you don't use a calculator?"

"Of course I use."

"Well, isn't that the same principle? Isn't a calculator a memory device too? What does this Reb Baruch have to say about them?"

My engagement with the question seemed to please him; his voice grew peppy and sharp. "First of all, the Rebbe, may his name be praised, has been dead two hundred years. Secondly, what can I tell you? You have a point, but so what? We don't shy away from such contradictions." He cleared his throat. "In the Kabbala there's a word, *Tsimtsum*. It refers to the fact that during the creation, to provide room for man and his freedom, God and His law *retracted*. Left a little space. Like a father who teaches his son to walk. You leave a little space behind the boy, a little ambiguity. Maybe the boy falls down in that space, maybe not. It allows for a number of possibilities."

By this point I had lost track of what fall and what possibilities—or whose—we were talking about. As Aaron went on, I wiped my fingers on the Metro section of the newspaper, smearing the print. A wing bone slipped out of my lap and fell under the sofa. Too tired to chase it, I looked out the window at my neighbor across the street, who was, I saw now, talking on *his* phone. Was he discussing the Kabbala too?

"...anyway," Aaron was saying, "that's not why I'm calling. I'm calling to ask a favor. It's about Magda..."

Immediately, with the mention of her name, the distance between us vanished. *He knows*, I thought. *He knows*.

"... helpless, in some ways. And I realize we hardly know each other, Shmuel, and it's not appropriate to impose this way. But sometimes you get a feeling about people. There are people you know all your life who you wouldn't ask favors of, and others you meet once or twice and you would. You see," he said, "Hava had her baby."

I suppose I really do need machines to help me remember things. It took a few seconds to recall that Hava was the name of this man's sister-in-law, whom he didn't like, and who had been pregnant the evening I met her. Though he did not sound altogether pleased, I went ahead and offered congratulations.

"Sure," he said, "another boy. The *bris* is Friday morning. Which is why I've been trying to call you. Because I can't make it."

As I was still unable to see what any of this had to do with me, my next question was motivated by simple curiosity. "Why not?"

"I have to go to Hershey, Pennsylvania. Fridays I teach guitar out there at the Juvenile Detention Center."

"Couldn't you cancel? Or get someone to cover for you?"

"I could, sure. But I won't."

"I don't understand. I thought circumcision was a big deal for you people. Especially, I should think, when it's your own nephew."

"Sure it is. But these kids at the JDC, they're a big deal too. What've they got? Only television and comic books. Nothing else. No future, no structure—no adults they can depend on to do what they say. So when I started the class, I promised myself and I promised them: whatever happened, I'd come every week. So when I had the flu, I came. When the car broke a piston and I had to take the bus, I came. Friday I'll come, too. So there we are." He sighed a wan little sigh, as if he were repeating an argument he'd already run through several times with someone else. "The reason I called is to ask if there's any chance you could drive Magda to the *bris*. I realize it's asking a lot. But Magda," he explained, "doesn't drive."

"Why would she have to? I thought Hava lived in the neighborhood."

"They do. But the *bris* is up at her in-laws', in Rockland County. I realize it's complicated. Zev's parents, how do I say this? It doesn't take a psychologist to see they're a lot like Hava. Very controlling. They have most of their family up there. Also Hava likes to be pampered—she likes their big fancy house a lot better than her small one, especially with the holidays coming. The whole thing gives me a headache, to tell you the truth."

It was beginning to give me a headache, too. "But there must be plenty of friends from the neighborhood who will be driving up there. Can't Magda get a ride from one of them?"

Aaron sighed again. "I'm afraid you don't know Magda very well."

I waited for him to elaborate upon this point, but he seemed to think it wasn't necessary. Anyway, he was right: I didn't know her very well. And I intended to keep it that way. If only he'd stop trying to throw us together.

"Listen, I'd like to help you," I said, "but I have a big meeting that night and I'm going to have to prepare for it."

I did, too: Ronnie had scheduled our powwow with Ray Spurlock and Jack Teagle for dinner that Friday. Dinner meetings were the rage of late. No one wanted to get caught away from their desks during the workday. Too much was happening. And the meal itself offered a measure of protective warmth. No one to this point had been fired over dinner. Though there had been plenty of firings over lunch and breakfast.

"I thought you said you were working for yourself now," Aaron said coolly.

"I was. But, you know, money . . ."

"Yes, money. I see."

"I'm not completely free to—"

"Look, I understand. If you can't, you can't."

"Still . . . maybe . . ."

"Maybe? Maybe what?"

"Maybe I can. I don't know." I tried to think for a second. "I have to figure out whether I can or not."

"This is such a big decision, Shmuel? You need to agonize so much? You're a very lucky man, you know, if this is what constitutes for you a big decision."

"I know," I said.

There was a pause, during which I had the opportunity to make my mind up and then change it again, several times.

"So," Aaron said, "what'll it be? I'm sorry to put you on the spot like this, but I need to know yes or no. Whatever you want is fine with me. Just do what you want to do."

I had wanted to kiss her. There was no denying that at least once in my life, I had done exactly what I wanted to do. Still, as I had come in my fuzzy way to understand the challenges of maturity, it seemed to me that primary among them was that mature people did not always do just what they wanted to do, but for some reason, the opposite.

"I'm sorry," I said. "I'd like to help you, but I don't think I can."

"Okay, fine, I understand."

"Do you?"

"Don't worry about it, Shmuel. After all, you can only do so many things at one time."

"Right, I know, it's only—"

But he had already hung up. The dead tone on the line seemed only to certify that our brief involvement in each other's lives was at an end. A good thing, no doubt. He was stimulating company, but it was time to get on with my life. Enough clutter. Enough confusion. I was a new man now.

I looked out the window at my neighbor across the street to see how his phone call was going, but the shades were drawn.

Not ten minutes later, the phone rang again. I assumed it was Aaron calling back. At least I half-hoped it was. No sooner had this new man returned to his droning ballgame and room-temperature chicken than the old man inside him began regretting having turned Aaron down. At the same time I knew that had I *not* turned him down, I'd have regretted that too. The mind, they say, is essentially dual, like the organs by which it is exercised.

Anyway, it wasn't Aaron calling back after all. It was my friend Warren Pinsky.

Had it gone out over the Internet that I was lonely and available for service? Was Warren in the same boat? Because I began to suspect, as he ran through the usual inventory of his booming prospects, that he was leading up to something strenuous.

It took several minutes of chitchat before he sprang his surprise. "By the way, that information you wanted?"

"Information?"

"That business regarding your Hasidic friend. You know, his health problem?"

I must have been very tired that evening, because even though I had just spoken to this Hasidic friend, I did not at first understand Warren's reference. This despite the fact I *had* no other Hasidic friends—and let's face it, not many secular ones by that point either.

"Oh, yeah. Right."

"Oh yeah right? That's it?"

"Listen, Warren, let's just forget it, okay? It doesn't matter."

Warren made a peevish sound through his teeth. "What do you mean it doesn't matter? I exhausted three different favors to find out what was wrong with the guy."

"I guess you wasted your time then."

"No, Sammy, *you* wasted my time."

"You're right. I'm sorry."

"Okay, apology accepted. But it's too late. I did all this work already, and now I'm going to tell you whether you care or not." He cleared his throat to heighten the suspense. He was feeling exceedingly good about himself, Warren was, for having done me such a favor. "Low sperm count," he said.

"That's it?"

"That's it."

"Warren, are you kidding? Who flies all the way to Texas to get diagnosed for a lousy sperm count?"

"Wake up, Sammy. Fertility is a booming field; there's a whole smorgasbord of sophisticated treatments available. Little fancy tricks they do to make the sperm frisky. I'd tell you about them if we weren't both so squeamish. Anyway," he went on, "your friend had the whole work-up, soup to nuts. He did this, by the way, after having already received the same work-up from three different clinics in New York. Reputable and expensive ones. This is a very determined person, in my opinion. A person who leaves very little to chance. A nut, in other words."

The station wagons in the driveways. The squabbling. Resentment of the fertile sister. The way she looked at Ronnie's little girl. *There are three things to learn from children . . .*

"Still there, Sammy?"

"So wait, what were the results of this work-up? What's the prognosis?"

"I don't know. That would be favor number four, and I only have three friends in the whole place. Luckily, it doesn't matter to you either way."

"Find out, Warren."

"Why, for Christ's sake? What do you care?"

"Listen," I said, "that little ghetto they have out there, it *runs* on kids. Nobody has less than five or six of them. Now, suppose you were a young Hasidic couple and you were having fertility troubles, what would you do?"

"What am I, Dr. Ruth? How would I know?"

"You'd go to every clinic you could find. You'd check out every doctor, have every procedure. The pressure would be enormous. And if those didn't work, you might even—"

"Might even what?"

"I don't know. Something. Something . . . you know, desperate . . ."

As happens when I fall under the sway of emotion, a kind of stammering vagueness had come into my voice. Hearing it, Warren groaned. "Oh boy, Sammy. You're getting worse and worse."

"I'll talk to you later, Warren."

"Worse and worse," he said.

"You'll do it?" he asked. "It's no trouble?"

"A pleasure to be of service," I said.

"Wonderful. This is really wonderful, Shmuel. And to pay you back, I'll do your taxes if you want next year."

"For free?"

"Of course for free. And I'm very good."

"It's a deal," I said.

"And in a few weeks you'll come to the house for the holidays maybe?"

Apparently nothing short of my packing up and moving to Crown Heights was going to be enough for this man. "The holidays?" I asked. "Which ones?"

"Everything's a joke for you?" he said. "Even the Days of Awe?"

"Look, Aaron, you have to understand. For people like me, the only awe we feel on Jewish holidays is that alternate-side-of-the-street parking is suspended. That's it. Should I pretend to be what I'm not?"

"You don't have to pretend anything. And as for what you're not, Shmuel, that doesn't concern me. What concerns me is what you are."

"And what am I?"

"You don't know?"

I waited, with some trepidation, for him to tell me.

"A *mensch*," he said. He sounded grave, as though in identifying me this way he had ensured a melancholy fate for us all.

Brother, I thought, after we'd made our arrangements. First an angel, now a *mensch*. What next, the messiah himself? Suddenly I was full of regrets again. I picked up a wing of chicken and stripped away as much as I could of the yellowed skin, but when that was gone nothing but bone remained.

HIDDEN SAINTLY PERSONS

As we drove onto the George Washington Bridge the spires were like silver threads, taut and dewy and glittering in the sunlight. You could almost feel the strain, the dynamic tension that results from stitching disparate things—earth, water, sky—together. At least I could. Magda Brenner, peering over the dashboard at the high brown cliffs of the Palisades, seemed unaccountably tension-free. Perhaps this was old hat to her; perhaps she took fifty-mile trips with strange men every Friday morning. The city and its familiar weight behind us, she leaned back, stifled a yawn, and without preamble or transition asked me how old I was.

"I'll be thirty-six in a couple of weeks."

"Thirty-six," she said. "That's a very good number."

"Not really."

"Oh yes. Thirty-six. It's twice eighteen, which is the number for *chai*, life."

"No kidding."

"And the Baal Shem, he was thirty-six when he first acquired his name."

"No kidding."

"Oh yes. Also there are thirty-six saints, you know."

"Saints? I thought only Catholics believed in saints."

At this her face became clouded with doubt, as though she were momentarily uncertain about just what Jews did or did not believe. "Oh," she said, "not those saints, no. But the Mishnah says there are thirty-six hidden saintly persons in every generation, and it's their righteousness that sustains the world."

"What does it mean, hidden? Hidden from who?"

"From everyone," she said. The sleek blue dress was not in evidence today. This one was tailored more along her usual lines: a dull green, high-necked blouse, a black shawl with a spray of flowers, and a beige cotton skirt that fell most of the way down her calves, exposing, as though reluctantly, a chalk-white sliver of ankle. She had chosen the outfit to make a point, I thought, but to whom? Carefully she smoothed the skirt over her lap and, gazing down into the river at a solitary tugboat passing beneath us, she added, so softly I had to strain to catch it, "Themselves too."

"No kidding."

"Why do you keep asking if I'm kidding? Do I seem like such a kidder to you?"

"Look," I said, "be honest with me for a minute, okay? Do you really believe all this shit?"

"What do you mean?"

"I mean, these saints and angels and good numbers and bad numbers—do you actually take it seriously?"

"Why not?" she said, unruffled.

"Because it's patently absurd. It has nothing to do with reality."

"Oh yes? And what do you take seriously?"

Rumbling down the exit ramp, I turned to review her profile—one hard brown eye, one fierce bump on the nose, one steep and uncompromising chin—and wondered why I should find it so difficult to articulate something that seemed so obvious, namely, what I took seriously and why. Then I wondered if my companion might not be wondering the same thing. Then I proceeded to wonder about a number of other, completely unrelated things, as is my habit when driving long distance.

A couple of minutes passed. We listened to a golden oldies station on the radio. They were playing "Runaround Sue."

"There's a story," Magda said at last. "I don't know, maybe it would help you understand why we live the way we do. Do you want to hear?"

I shrugged. In truth I was in no mood for stories, and would have been content with the scenery and the radio and the low vacant thrum of the tires on the road. But I preferred to have Magda talking than to have her silent and watchful beside me, swallowed up in her long clothes.

"It's said that when the Baal Shem faced a difficult task, he'd go off to a certain spot in the woods, light a fire, and meditate in prayer. And what he'd set out to do was done. So, some years later, the Maggid of Meseritz was faced with the same task. He went off to that spot in the woods and said, I can no longer light the fire, but I can still say the prayers. And what he wanted was done." She paused to scratch an itchy spot on her wrist. "So. More years pass. One day Reb Leib of Sassov is faced with the same task. He also goes to the woods. He says, I can no longer light the fire, I don't know the secret words of the prayer, but I know the spot in the woods to which it all belongs. Well, that also turns out to be sufficient."

People let me put you wise, sang Dion on the radio, *Sue goes out with other guys . . .*

"And on and on, through the generations. Finally, Reb Israel of—" she hesitated, "of . . . oh, *some*where . . . anyway, he too is called upon to perform the task. But he doesn't even get out of his chair. He says, I can't light the fire, I can't say the prayer, I don't know the place. But I can tell the story of how it was done. And that had the same effect as the actions of the other three."

I waited, but apparently that was it for the story. Magda, looking straight ahead, had begun to hum along to the music.

"What was the task?"

"The task?" She blinked.

"Yes. What were they supposed to do?"

"I don't know. That's not the point. The point is," she said, "some things you do because other people did them before you. The point is to keep things going. That's the point," she repeated, and resumed her study of the passing landscape.

Fortunately, in preparation for this excursion of ours, I'd spent some time in the magazine library, researching Jewish history, so at least I had a vague idea of who this Baal Shem fellow was. The *Besht*, as he was also known, was a famous teacher and wonder worker in the Ukraine two centuries ago. His brand of Judaism was a raucous and populist affair, emphasizing fervor, joy, piety, and miracles. Baal Shem translated to "Master of the Word." Or "Master of the Name." Apparently it translated both ways. This sort of maddening textual ambiguity was endemic in Judaism. Words within words within words. It took a genius to decode it all, which was exactly what the *Besht* was said to be—inordinately gifted in wisdom, blazingly charismatic, endowed with a vast array of mystical healing powers. There were a number of other things said about him too, of course, and the dynastic succession of holy men that followed him, but heading north in the center lane of the Palisades Parkway on a crisp autumn morning, the radio blaring doo-wop and my stomach rumbling from zero breakfast, I could not for the life of me remember what they were.

"It's all so unlikely," Magda said, seemingly reading my thoughts.

"What is?"

"Oh, I don't know. Driving up here like this. I feel like I haven't been out of the city in years."

"Me too," I said.

"But you can drive. Can't you go whenever you want?"

"Yes and no."

In one of those trivial acts of economy that seemed to rule my life, I'd let the insurance payments lapse on my car and was reluctant to use it. I should not have been using it, for example, right now. Legal questions aside, it was fourteen years old and in terrible shape. The acceleration was sluggish, the shocks threadbare, and a mysterious abrasive warble had developed under the hood on our way out of Brooklyn and had remained with us since, making a sound like a large dog pulling frenziedly on a short leash.

"I love it, you know," Magda said.

"What?"

"Brooklyn. The neighborhood. I know it isn't the way it was for my parents, who never even locked their front door, but still, it's very nice. But sometimes I wonder if maybe I'd be happier somewhere else."

"New York is a difficult place. I think most people would be happier somewhere else."

"Would you?"

"No. I don't think so."

"Why not?"

"Because I'm a depressive," I said.

"*Sha.*" Her nostrils flared. "What is that? Just a word."

"Maybe so."

"Well, you're so depressed, then why don't you see a psychiatrist?"

"I have," I said. "Believe me."

"So?"

"It was valuable in some ways. But in the end there wasn't very much he could do about it."

It felt odd to speak of David this way, in the past tense, with this air of mordant fatalism. And yet it was true. Or so I realized only now, in retrospect. Perhaps Donna was right and one had to be past things in order to see them clearly. All I knew was that with summer's end something had ended in me, too, some swollen notion of myself had parched and died. Time to sweep out the cage, I thought.

Magda was regarding me skeptically. "I don't like all this psychology," she said. "It's selfish."

"Oh?"

"Of course when you don't belong to a community you're going to feel crazy and alone in the world. Why pay someone to tell you what's obvious?"

"That's not what you pay them for. You pay them to help you find a solution."

"Just for yourself? Is such a thing possible?"

"Probably not."

"Definitely not," she said.

I remembered what Warren had said down in Houston: it was all about systems now. Nonetheless Magda's certainty in this matter—in most matters—was beginning to wear on me. "For some people," I said, "the search for a solution is a big step itself. It challenges them to be more active, more focused. Would you deny them that option?"

"Most people have too many options. What good does it do them?"

"Better they should have too few?"

She shook her head. "All I know is, you can't always help things by talking."

"Well, maybe you're right. The new thinking says it's really all a question of drugs and genetic predisposition anyway. Of personal brain chemistry, if you like."

But she didn't like, or else she didn't care, or else, and this seemed most plausible, she had no idea what I was talking about. She peered thoughtfully through the windshield and off into the distance, nodding her head in time to some obscure rhythm of the motor. It was a lovely drive. The light was crisp, the wind cool and sinuous. Maples were dropping their twinned, helicopter-like seeds onto the tall grass, thousands of them, greens and yellows and browns, twirling slowly down, hushed and dreamy as fallout.

I rolled down the window. There were exit signs here and there along the road, pointing to Sparkill, Nyack, Spring Valley. We succeeded in passing by each of these fine cities without any additional conversation. I kept my hands tight on the wheel, and Magda busied herself with the scenery. Meanwhile the oldies station played hit after hit, running through its memory banks in its tyrannical fashion. No interludes for the mediocre, the unsuccessful, the unmemorable. Just hits. What would become of us?

Farther north the wind began to gather strength; it zithered through the windows and drummed inside my head. Magda drew her flowered shawl tighter around her shoulders. "I think this is our exit," she said.

She consulted a wrinkled slip of notepaper in her lap upon which she, or her husband, had written the directions. "It says we're supposed to head west at Stony Point."

"Stony Point? You're sure?"

"Yes."

"We passed Stony Point two exits ago."

"I'm sorry," she said at once, "it's my fault." Her voice was matter-of-fact, even resigned, as if she'd been half-expecting to screw up at this sort of thing. "Can't you turn around?"

"Not right now I can't. We'll have to wait for the next exit."

"Oh," she said.

"It looks like you're going to be a little late."

She checked her watch. "Yes."

"We should have been paying better attention."

"We're going to be very late," she mused, more to herself than to me. "We might miss the whole thing."

"I don't think so. Just a few minutes, probably."

She considered for a moment.

"No," she said firmly. "We're going to miss the whole thing."

"How can you be so sure?"

"Because," she said, and her pale cheeks were mottled with blood, "I want to."

But we did not miss the whole thing. Magda's resolve proved, under the merest duress, to be no less tenuous and shaky than most of her other resolves. All I had to do was ask, "Where else, then?" and she folded her cards at once. Personally, I was relieved she changed her mind. Where would we have gone, out there on the open road, set free from our errand? What would we have done?

I pulled up to the house and turned off the ignition. For a

moment we merely sat there listening to the engine tick as it cooled and letting our breath out slowly, as if an explosive device under the hood had just failed to go off. Two oak leaves, veined and yellow, dropped soundlessly against the windshield, then eased to the ground. Crows shrieked in the trees. The lawn next door had just been mowed, and the car was filling up with the sweet mossy smell of mowed grass. That, and the sight of the painted A-frame houses set back from the road with their fences and gardens and backyard pools, and the leaves falling in quiet luxury around us, later to be raked into neat little mounds and burnt in the gutters—it spun a path through my chest and right into my suburban heart. After twelve years on Ninety-fourth Street, even prosaic Rockland County seemed to my eyes as lush and exotic as Maui. At the same time, I knew deeply where I was. Contemplating the Oldsmobiles and Buicks in the driveways, and the big houses resting behind the sloping lawns, I felt an odd, knowing sense of entitlement. *My keys*, I thought, *would fit those locks*.

"Would you like to share this before we go in?" Magda asked.

She was holding a cigarette in the palm of her hand.

"No, thanks. I don't smoke."

"I don't either," she said. "But I need something today."

I pointed to my watch. "We're already half an hour late."

"I know."

This knowledge did not deter her from lighting the cigarette. She engineered for herself a hesitant puff. Only when she lifted her head and I saw the jagged red flare at the tip and smelled the sweet, reedy smoke that emerged in loops and wisps, did I realize it was not a cigarette at all.

"Good Lord," I said. "Where the hell did you get *that*?"

But she'd closed her eyes and set her jaw, and I had to wait a second for her to blow out the smoke. "I stole it," she said, smothering a cough. "From Aaron."

"Great." Feverishly I started rolling up my window, so the

good people of Rockland County would be spared that portion anyway of our exhaust. "What next? Want to go knock over a liquor store?"

"What are you so upset about? I thought I'd need it this morning, I told you. It has nothing to do with you."

"Uh huh."

"Anyway, it says in the Talmud: a person shouldn't flee from life's pleasures."

"What is it with that Talmud of yours? It seems to give the okay for all kinds of crazy shit."

"If you read it you'd understand."

Stubbornly, she brought the joint to her mouth, puffed at it, and choked off another cough.

"Tell me something, just between us. Have you ever done this before?"

"Of course," she said.

"I don't believe you. Look, you're getting it all wet. Here." I took it from her. "See? Like this."

True, I had only limited acquaintance with the Talmud, but when it came to the casual use of controlled substances I was on somewhat firmer ground. Tutor and pupil, we sat there passing the joint back and forth. It was nice to be the one doing the instructing for a change. It was nice to be smoking grass, too. In fact it was better than nice. Soon I had all but forgotten what we were doing on that shady street, in front of the big house with blue shutters that loomed at the far end of the tilting driveway. I'd all but forgotten Magda, too, silent beside me. What other accommodations she was planning to make with life's pleasures—and which ones—lay, for the moment anyway, outside the range of my thoughts.

By now the car's cramped interior felt rosy and grand as a cathedral. I leaned my head back against the vinyl and closed my eyes. Lights flared. Bells bonged. Water trickled in ivory fountains . . .

"Hey, you," Magda said. "You're not falling asleep, are you?"

"Not asleep, no."

"Well . . . so . . ." Her hand was poised on the door handle; her eyes, puffy and red from the grass, drifted lazily toward the steering wheel. "Are you coming in?"

I hadn't even considered what I would do when we arrived. What I'd be *asked* to do. "Should I? I mean, is it a good idea, do you think?"

"Good?" She pronounced the word slowly, as if its meaning were somehow obscure to her. "Why not? You'll be bored out here. And there will be food."

"What kind?"

"The usual. Bagels, fish, cheeses, cakes . . ."

At this, my stomach, that fickle and greedy maw, issued a low rumbling vote of its own.

"I don't know," I said. "I'm pretty squeamish. I'm not sure I can watch this kid get hacked up."

"Oh, you don't have to watch. Lots of people don't."

"What about my clothes?" I was wearing blue chinos, a white Oxford shirt, and a pair of black sneakers. That morning, dressing before the mirror, it had seemed a snappy and flexible outfit, appropriate for all occasions. But it did not seem very flexible to me now. "You don't think I'm underdressed?"

"Psh," she said. "You're fine."

"And what do we say to people? I mean, when they ask who the hell I am?"

"You're Aaron's friend," she declared simply. "You're Aaron's friend, and you're doing us a favor. Okay? Everyone knows how helpless I am when it comes to going somewhere in a car."

She pushed at the door with her shoulder. As if to simultaneously confirm both her helplessness around motor vehicles and the general insufficiency of my resources, the door was stuck. She had to sit there waiting as I went around to let her out. Then we strode side by side across the humming lawn.

On the slate steps Magda took my hand and gave it a brief, dry squeeze. "Ready?" she asked.

We rang the bell and waited at the door.

Over our heads there rose a great rustling: a flock of geese on their way south. They formed a wondrously symmetrical V, like the head of an arrow. As they passed above us, every dog in the neighborhood began barking at once. But that was the way of things out here in the suburbs. Animals came and went, following the inborn clocks and maps of the species. Dogs gnawed at their tethers; squirrels chased their own tails; moths bumped loopily against the checkered screens. White people drove to other white people's houses for a variety of ceremonial engagements, and then drove back home again. There was a system of aspirations at work, a methodical and particularized apportionment of tasks, and standing there on the top step, waiting to be ushered into the house, I felt a cool placidity that came from knowing my place, my role in things. I was Aaron's friend and I was doing everybody a favor. The people inside would understand that, I thought, even if I myself did not.

The first point to make about the *bris*, then, is that we arrived forty minutes late and high as clouds.

The second point to make is that of the thirty or so adults present (there were at least that many young children), only about half were, strictly speaking, Hasids. Apparently Zev's parents were Orthodox but not Hasidic—a distinction that meant nothing to me but everything to Magda. Some of their friends, she informed me in a harsh whisper, were not Orthodox, but Conservative, and a few were not even that but Reform—the most perilously thin and crooked branch of the faith. All the same these labels were, in Magda's view, unnecessarily complicated: for her the many complexities of human experience were reducible to a single operation, Hasid or Other. Half of these people were Other. I was Other too, of course, but for the moment we were letting that ride.

Because the ceremony had yet to begin—apparently we weren't the only ones to arrive late—we had to stand around for a while first. It was only mildly awkward. True we received our share of curious looks, but no one came forward to challenge or denounce us, no one sounded an alarm. The children were running around, noisy and demanding of attention, and so for the most part we were left alone. This suited me fine. I was aware of Magda, however, growing increasingly restless beside me. Absently she picked at her dress, scratched at her wrist, fussed with her hair. Someone came around with a tray of little honey cakes and paper cups full of orange juice and whiskey. She took three of the cakes and ate them at once. Then she drank some orange juice. Then she began to nibble the rim of the cup.

"What's the matter?" I asked. "Are you just nervous, or are you stoned?"

"I don't know. What does stoned feel like?"

"You'd know."

She groaned. "Why don't they start already?"

"Relax. I'm the one who doesn't belong here, not you. Where's your sister, anyway?"

"I don't know."

"But you must have lots of friends here, no?"

"Oh, friends," she muttered under her breath, looking around, apparently unable to find anyone in the room who fit that category.

We stayed put, then, in the corner we had occupied since entering the house, wedged between two upholstered chairs on one side and an enormous teak bookcase on the other. To pass the time I looked over the shelves: Moshe Dayan, Golda Meir, Sholom Aleichem, Herman Wouk, Abba Eban . . . Zev's parents, it seemed, only read books by Jewish people. I wondered what they'd do if I ever wrote a book; would they only read half?

After a while one of the older couples, assuming we must be hanging back out of shyness, came over and introduced themselves. Their names were Hal and Barbara Korman, or Korngold, or Kornblatt. The marijuana had blocked my ears and it was a struggle to hear them. "Come in from the city?" Hal asked me.

I nodded.

"Whereabouts?"

"Upper West Side." I looked over at Magda and Barbara, wondering what they were talking about so intently.

"What kind of time you make?"

"What?"

"The drive," Hal said. "How long. Hour? Hour and a half?" He frowned, as if this were a matter of terrific importance to him. All he wanted was a pleasant little chat with another non-Hasidic man like himself; why wasn't I coming across?

"More like two," I said. "We got a little lost."

"Ah." He nodded, relieved for some reason, and straightened his yarmulke. Rosy and perspiring in sport coat and slacks, he either had high blood pressure or else had come straight from the golf course. Beside him his wife looked cool in a handsome pantsuit. From the attentive way she kept looking at her watch, I guessed that Barbara was running on a different, faster schedule—more gainfully employed, more business-savvy—than her husband. I thought of my mother's friends. Stuck at home with the kids in the fifties and sixties, gone back for a master's in the seventies, endured their first lousy jobs in the eighties. And now, just as their husbands had begun to wilt and soften like old fruit, it was their time. The cold actuarial facts had set in. The men were burning out, receding. Men, let's face it, don't have what it takes: they aren't built to endure. Hal and his friends, for instance, did not from the look of things have good teeth, good cholesterol, good blood pressure, good hair. They were not computer-friendly, not modem-linked. They did not fax or network. They were aging white males with failing prostates and big American cars, and they'd had a good run for a while, but now it was time to pull over and let those nifty Hondas and Toyotas blow past on the left. Even they seemed to know it. They huddled together in the corners of the room, chatting about sports, wine, and traffic. Keeping out of the way.

At first glance I felt sorry for them but upon reflection my sympathy faded. After all, they'd worked hard and been loved for a long time. Who was I to feel sorry for *them*?

"A nice couple," I heard Hal say to his wife as they walked away. "Reserved, but nice."

I glanced over at Magda to see what effect this judgment might have had on her. None: it had sailed right past. She was still scanning the room for someone she knew and trying not to be too obvious about her discomfort. If she had been paying the slightest bit of attention to me I'd have told her what I now knew for certain: that everything was going to be fine. It was a beautiful morning and this was a friendly crowd, full of the good will that accrues on landmark occasions. Here I'd been expecting to stand out, but me and my chinos were fitting right in so far.

I was fitting in so well, in fact, that when we finally met up with Hava and Zev they did not remember who I was. "Simon, is it?" Zev asked, quizzically pumping my hand.

"Sam. Sam Karnish."

"Oh?"

"Congratulations," I said. "On the baby."

"Yes . . . and you're a friend of whose?"

Granted, they were tired, the home they were in was not their own, things were running late, the place was crawling with well-wishers, the bagel person hadn't shown up yet, and their infant son, sleeping soundlessly for the moment in his blue-domed bassinet, was about to have the foreskin of his penis mutilated by that alarmingly wrinkled old gentleman sunk into a love seat across the room. They had every reason to be distracted. Nonetheless it was humbling to be forgotten so quickly. After all, I'd taken the entire morning off from work to drive Magda up here—putting her, me, my career, my automobile, and now my sobriety through a good deal of unnecessary stress—just to attend their son's circumcision. The least they could have done was recognize me.

Not that they seemed any better disposed toward Magda. Some bad blood was in the air. A long table draped in white linen dissected the room; it stood like a wall between the two of us and the two of them. On it were bowls of apples, dates, pears, figs, oranges. Above the gleaming fruit, Zev and I shook hands and made our halting exchange, while Magda tittered quietly beside me. When it came time for her to say hello, she delivered a formal nod in the direction of her sister and brother-in-law, and they delivered a formal nod back. Aaron's absence was not remarked. My presence was not remarked. The new baby and his impending fate were not remarked.

Suddenly I felt something hairy on my shoulder. A bearded wide-body of a man had draped himself over me and Magda, pulling us toward him in a vigorous bear hug. "*Mazel tov*," he crooned warmly. "*Mazel tov* to all you kids."

"*Abba*," Zev said, in a tone of forbearance.

"Almost ready to start. Any minute."

"Good." Zev sighed. "You remember Magda, of course."

"Remember? Of course I remember." He gave us both another squeeze. "How are you, sweetheart?"

Magda blinked at him. Obviously this man who looked nothing like Zev was in fact his father, with whom on family occasions she had enjoyed similar small talk in the past. And yet she did not appear happy to see him. Her shoulders were quaking, and she was biting her lower lip. Was she about to cry?

"Fine, Herb," she mumbled. "Why not?"

"Where's Aaron? Don't tell me he's working, today of all days. He's working?"

"Oh well," she said, "I'm afraid—"

"He takes it too far. I don't like to criticize. I work hard myself; you have to in the jewelry business. But the problem with Aaron is he takes it too far. Work or no work, there's such a thing as occasions you don't miss."

"Oh yes . . ."

"There are choices involved. Priorities. I realize it sounds old-fashioned in this day and age. But this is what separates us from the *goyim*. Priorities. You know what I'm saying? Priorities."

It was this last repetition of the word that burst the bubble of Magda's composure. She let out a shriek. No, she wasn't crying, I saw now: she was *laughing*. And what a laugh she had! What lusty and bestial sounds this young woman gave out!

"Hey," Herb said uncertainly, his smile fading, "what's so funny?"

"I'm sure she'll be fine in a minute," I said.

"What about now?"

"Now I'm not sure."

"Why? What's the matter with her? Honey," he said, leaning down to get a better look at her, "what's the matter with you?"

By this point it would no longer be accurate to say she was laughing; it was more like squealing. Her voice, strangulated to a high breathless pitch, was nearly lost to us—though I imagined that somewhere outside those dogs were perking up their ears—and in her eyes was a helpless, naked appeal, as if the bottoms of her legs were on fire. People had begun to stare. Magda, unable to stop, unable to hide, resorted to the old kids' trick of bending down and pretending to fiddle with the laces of her shoes. This too failed to work. The giggling did not subside; now, by way of a finale, she looked like she was going to pass out as well.

"Honey, what's the *matter*?" Herb asked. "Not feeling good?"

In his bewilderment, he had addressed himself to me. He looked into my eyes—his beard so close I could feel the static electricity popping against my cheek—rather trustingly, I thought, expecting to find there an ally, someone to confirm he'd been right about this priority business. Only after a moment did he appear to realize that he had no idea who I was.

"I'm sorry," he said, "but do you look familiar?"

Well, that did it for Magda: if there had been any doubt before, she was now officially hysterical. Her chest was heaving, her lips trembled, her cheeks were flaming red; her mascara had begun to trail in broad muddy streaks down her face. Her nose was bright red as well. The result was that she bore a marked but unfortunate resemblance to a clown. It didn't help matters that she kept losing her balance. In fact if Zev's father hadn't had his arm around her, she'd have been literally rolling on the floor, I think.

People were staring. Determined to rescue her if I could, I stuck my hand out, right into big Herb's face. "My name's Sam," I said.

"Who?" He was still looking worriedly at Magda.

"Sam—that is, Shmuel Karnish. I'm a friend of Aaron's."

"A friend?" Herb seemed skeptical. I'd spoken too loudly, or not loudly enough. Or else he reasoned that as a friend of the family I should be held responsible for the husband's working habits, the wife's hysteria. Anyway, he was beginning to make me very nervous. I looked down at his arm, which had not as yet released me. There was a bruise of some kind on the inside of the forearm. Had he been in a fight recently? The world of men, they say, is divided into two types: those who fight, and those who don't. This one looked like he belonged in the former group—perhaps even a high official in it, a vice president or district supervisor of belligerence.

Now I waited for Magda to come to *my* rescue. But of course she was in no shape to rescue anybody. So I had to do it the hard way.

"By the way," I said, patting Herb on the shoulder, "congratulations. Your grandson over there is absolutely beautiful."

Herb's expression changed. "You've seen him? My little *bubeleh*? My angel?"

"Oh yes. Incredible kid. Great forehead, perfect nose. All the tools, really."

"Well . . ." Herb said, warming.

"Isn't it funny," I gushed on, "how you can tell right away with some babies. Makes you wonder about nature and nurture, doesn't it? Some babies, it's right there on their faces the second they pop out. Like, Oh, *hello*, world. Where does it come from? Is there some kind of gene or chromosome, do you think, that accounts for why some are so dull and shape-less-looking and others so alert, so responsive, so . . ." I gave up, waving my hand in the air to indicate the great range of ineffable things that some babies' faces are.

Herb regarded me uncertainly, as if the very length and unctuousness of my speech had mesmerized him. The pause gave me an opportunity to consider the bruise on his forearm. Only it wasn't, I saw now, a bruise . . .

"What about you," he said. "Boys or girls?"

"Sorry?"

"Your kids. Are they boys or girls?"

For a moment I stood there blinking at his round cheerful face, horrified. I had the next lie ready on the tip of my tongue, but it was stuck there. I couldn't get it off. I could only stand frozen and tremulous as Herb withdrew his big hand from my shoulder, placed it in his pocket, and took a little half-step away.

Now that it was too late, Magda finally recovered her voice and began to stammer out an explanation. "We met Sam . . . down in Houston . . . on the same *plane* . . ."

But our host had already gone off to greet someone else—the bagel person, at last. Zev and Hava were also gone, attending to some last-minute details of their own. Which left no one to hear how clumsy and tentative Magda's explanation sounded, or to see how much blood had flowed into and drained out of her face in the process. No one except me. "Are you okay?" I asked.

"Why? Is something wrong? I mean do you think I'm having a reaction? To . . . I mean, to what we—"

"I think we both are."

"*Gevalt*," she moaned. "What do we do now?"

"Go to the bathroom," I said. "Wash your face with some cold water."

"I'm so hungry."

"Do this first."

"Okay. But will it help?"

"Yes."

She took a step away, then turned to look over her shoulder at me. "You'll stay here?" she asked.

"Yes."

"You promise?"

"Yes."

Watching her weave through the crowd, I tried to grasp, through the fog in my head, exactly what it was I had just promised to do. Extracting promises from men seemed to come naturally to her—more naturally, at any rate, than giving them came to me—and, registering this, I began to wonder if it was me and not Magda who was being transformed by our culture clash. But transformed how?

At least I'd finally heard her laugh out loud. It was some laugh too—high, manic, and horsey. In truth it sounded less like laughter than like someone choking.

"Sshh," Hal Korman whispered behind me. "It's starting."

"*That's* the *mohel*?" his wife whispered back.

"Who do you think, the caterer? They all look like that."

"A guy that old. I'd never trust him with *my* kid."

"Don't be ridiculous. He knows what he's doing. He's experienced. Take my word, better too much than not enough."

"I'm just saying—"

"Sshh. Here he goes."

The whispers of the Kormans, the warmth of the morning, the rustle and static of this room full of strangers, the dry leafy residue of the drug on my tongue, the benign gurgle of percolating coffee in the next room—all were having their effect upon me. The room blurred and smeared. At the same time I thought I could feel some stalk of my perception ripening into a flower.

"Can you see?"

"Nothing. And I'm on tiptoe."

"Can *you* see?" Hal asked, tapping me firmly on the shoulder.

"Not too well," I whispered back.

"Ach. I never see anything."

An empty chair had been set conspicuously to the side ("for the prophet Elijah" Hal whispered in my ear); beside it stood a table laid with a white cloth. On the cloth sat a bottle of purple Manischewitz wine and a naked baby. The baby, his nap interrupted, looked a bit stupefied. Was this a dream? According to the Talmud (Hal continued), each of us is taught the entire Torah in utero, but in our journey down the birth canal an angel taps us on the lips—an impression we retain forever—and makes us forget it all. Thus we begin life already betrayed by education, with only a blank slate upon which to record our blunders in the world.

Not that this was the baby's only predicament. Here, leaning over him, was an old man with a knife. And here at his feet was another old man, his alleged grandfather, prying apart his ankles. What kind of vengeful conspiracy was this?

Big Herb's expression was fierce; you could see that for him this was a matter of first principles. No force of man or nature, not even the prophet Elijah himself, if he ever deigned to show up, would close the legs of his grandson before the business of the day was concluded. Family jewels were at stake. Linkages. Witnesses were lined along the mantel, watching from their frames—children, grandchildren, nephews, nieces, dressed in caps and gowns, wedding suits, birthday clothes. Yes, this was family business, all right. I was just a crasher, a disinterested observer, but for everyone else this was the real thing. Covenants were being written, bonds forged, lineages carried over. Priorities . . .

The point, Magda had said, *is to keep things going*. Where was she anyway? Still in the bathroom?

Over Herb's shoulder the old *mohel*, draped in his yellowed tallis, rocked back and forth on his heels, grumpily chanting his way through the Hebrew prayers as if daring the rest of us to keep up. No one tried. Zev and two other bespectacled, shoulderless Hasidic men—his brothers, I assumed—looked on gamely, but as the event unfolded the brothers began to glaze a little around the eyes, receding, an inch at a time, in the direction of the nearest wall. Dutiful Zev remained. His hands clenched and unclenched; a vein, twinned and forking, pulsed at his temple. Otherwise he was still. The rest of us watched with varying degrees of discomfort as the baby, pink and squirming against the immaculate whiteness of the sheet, began to cry.

Now the old *mohel* reached for his knife. Like a carpenter reaching for a tool. As if something was about to be built, not severed.

Leaning forward, he resumed his chant. A pale rainbow of urine rose from the baby, splashed soundlessly against the tallis, then fell away. The *mohel* did not so much as blink. His tallis was already yellow; no doubt he'd been pissed on before. No doubt in his line of work he'd been scratched, kicked, screamed at, shit on, and spattered with vomit—to say nothing of the indignities he'd had to endure from the *parents*. What did it matter? In his hands he bore the brand of the people; their covenant was his to confer.

Now he raises the knife.

All at once the room seems to rear up and draw itself together. Behind me one Korman groans, the other issues a sigh. The baby whimpers. The *mohel* grunts. Zev's brother blows his nose. Outside a thousand geese are screaming, a thousand dogs are barking, a thousand cars are roaring toward the Thruway. . . .

Down comes the blade. As it descends, it's caught by a stray mote of sunlight through the window, so that for a moment it brightens and glows like fire.

Now the baby, registering the tension, begins to kick. I cannot see his face but I can see the pumping of his feet, tiny and blood-red, as he struggles to pedal free of his grandfather's grip. How hard it is to get free when the world has you by the legs! How hard to be let loose!

Big Herb grimaces, sets his big jaw. Broken lines deepen like graves upon his brow. A kind of code. *Learn this first*, the lines say. This first must be endured. This first is who you are. Today the flesh is cut; tomorrow maybe a number is tattooed upon your arm. The brand of the people . . .

This is the way of things. Fathers and sons. This is how it's been set up, laid out, in that fat scroll of instructions, the Torah. Fathers and sons: a covenant of blood. Fathers and sons, all the way back to Abraham and Isaac . . .

This pain first, and then the other ones.

This first—

The next thing I knew I was watching the play of lights upon a shallow pool of water. The odd thing about this pool was its location, high above my head on the ceiling. Then I saw that the pool *was* the ceiling—which, like the other walls of the house, was painted a pale, aquatic blue. Anyway, I lay there. A peculiar audial traffic of whispers and hums washed back and forth just beyond my angle of vision. They were vaguely familiar. It seemed to me that I'd been hearing these sounds and staring up at the ceiling like this for a long time. It seemed to me that in fact I'd spent a good deal of my life in this position, on the floor, staring into other people's ceilings.

"Hey, hey, easy," a man's voice was saying. "Take it easy now."

Whoever it was, he was sitting behind me, lightly stroking my hair. I could smell the wine on his breath, the deodorant under his arms. My mouth tingled. I was conscious of some distress in the room, an air of diluted commotion, and I wondered if it had anything to do with me. "What happened?"

"You fainted," the man explained.

"Oh Christ."

"Don't worry about it." He continued to stroke my head, his palm moist on my brow. Or possibly it was my brow that was moist—somewhere along the line I had broken into a cold sweat. "Happens all the time at these things."

"It does?"

"Sure. There's no shame involved. The body goes its own way sometimes."

What he was saying sounded true, I thought. But why was my body's way always the same?

"Now, I don't want to rush you, but if you're up to it, maybe you should sit up. Think you can sit up, maybe?"

"I think I can sit up."

Lifting my head, however, I encountered some resistance, and had to set it down again.

"Okay, take it easy," he said. "Don't rush it. The thing is to get the blood flowing the way it should. That's the problem right there. The blood has to find its proper level."

I nodded.

"What are *you* looking at?" he barked at someone. "He's fine, he's fine. Go and eat already."

"He looks like a ghost," I heard a man say.

"Leave him alone. He's just catching his breath."

If only out of loyalty, to prove my new friend right, I tried to sit up again. This time I pulled it off, more or less. My rewards for the effort were a dull throbbing at the base of my skull and a cascade of sighs from the remaining onlookers. Everyone seemed happy and relieved. Nothing terrible had happened; the knife had come down and yet all remained intact. Later perhaps they'd recall that the baby cried harshly for a while until the *mohel* wrapped him in a blanket and rubbed a drop of wine into his gums, after which he fell asleep. And, oh yeah, someone fainted. Right in the middle of everything. Who was that young man anyway? Some friend of the family's. Some friend of Aaron's from the city . . .

"Better now?"

Finally I was able to turn around, to put the solicitous voice together with the solicitous face. My benefactor was a tall, thin, high-shouldered man with glasses. He looked about forty. His beard was short and dark and neatly trimmed around a wide, generous mouth. He wore no hat, only a mauve skullcap, which was safety-pinned to the dry frizzy bird's nest that was his hair. And yet there was about him an air of youthful intensity that made me certain he was a Hasid.

"Yeah, I feel better. I think I do."

"Happens all the time," he said again. His expression, though kind, was a little fatigued, as if he had spent a lifetime propping up all the strangers who fainted at these things. His white shirt was open at the neck, revealing a prominent Adam's apple and a tiny scar, about an inch long, at the base of the throat—remnant of an old operation. "It's just the blood," he said, "moving around in the body."

Finally I was on my feet. People were drifting back toward the food. A group of Hasidic men were chatting animatedly in one corner of the room. No sign of Magda. Where was she? Had she ever returned from the bathroom? Had she hitched a ride home with someone else?

"You're looking for someone? I can maybe help?"

"Just a friend," I said. "I'm sure she's around here somewhere."

"Ah, a woman." He gave a knowing nod. Men of the world.

"Yes."

"You think maybe you lost her?"

"Knowing her, it's definitely possible."

"I've got a sister at home you know. A *sheinkeit*, a plum. Twenty years old, very bright, keeps a kosher kitchen like most people have to pay for."

"She sounds very nice. But I'm afraid—"

"I'm not trying to sell you, understand. I just thought maybe seeing as how you lost the first one . . ."

"I didn't say I lost her. I just said I can't find her."

"Sure," he said. "But it's important to know when to give up, you know. When to press forward, and when to look somewhere else."

It seemed to me in that moment that I had given over far too much of my life to other people's philosophies. "Look, could you excuse me for a second? I'm going to try and find the one I came with first."

"Sure, sure." He raised both palms to show me how little there was in them to hold me. "My name's Yossi, by the way. Yossi Klein. And you are?"

"Sam. Sam Karnish."

"A pleasure."

"Look, I really—"

"I'm a friend of Hava and Zev. I live next door to her sister. And your connection to all this is what?"

I could think of no good answer to this question. "I'm sorry," I said, "but I really have to go." And I ran up the stairs to the bathroom.

Magda wasn't there. As if to remind me of the fluid state of her loyalties, the hot-water tap was running, a steady flow that she, or someone, had forgotten to shut off. The mirror was clouded with steam.

She wasn't in any of the bedrooms either. Nor was she in any of the rooms downstairs. I looked in the kitchen and the den and even peeked into a couple of closets. Nope. Hal Korman hadn't seen her. Zev hadn't seen her. Herb hadn't seen her. The president of the synagogue hadn't seen her.

Circling in vain through the living room, I bumped against someone's knee, and turned to find it belonged to the *mohel*. The old man, his job complete, had taken off his tallis and settled back into the love seat. There he sat alone with a glass of schnapps, legs crossed, mouth a thin line in his beard, eyes wandering over the proceedings without interest. Finally they had settled upon me.

"*Nu*," he said. "Come, come."

He grabbed me by the hand and pulled me close. I could smell the liqueur on his breath, the musks of his clothing. He'd extracted a piece of paper from his coat and closed my fingers around it. His hands were long and delicate—a violinist would covet such hands. Then he commenced a feverish monologue, which, because it was entirely in Yiddish, I was unable to decode.

"I'm sorry," I said. "I don't understand."

This prompted another speech, also in Yiddish but, in concession to my difficulties, louder. I passed the time examining the slip of paper he had put into my hands. Another business card! The recession was certainly taking its toll; everyone I met these days was eager to do business with me.

Now he pointed over my shoulder to the table where the cutting had taken place. Elijah's chair was gone, appropriated for other purposes; all that remained from the ceremony was the bottle of plum-colored Manischewitz wine, half full, and the spattered tablecloth upon which it rested. The *mohel* tapped me on the forearm and made an inquisitive slicing gesture with his hand. "*Nu?* he demanded. "You want?"

"I'm sorry," I said. "I'm not even married."

"Not?" He looked confused.

"Listen, thank you, really, but I have to go. I came here with someone, you see. I have to go find her."

"Ach." He waved me away with his long hand. "Find, find."

But Magda was not to be found. I performed one more brief reconnaissance of the house and then, starved and defeated, went over to try and salvage some breakfast out of the event The fruit bowls were seriously depleted. So were the bagels and lox, the noodle pudding, the sponge cake. A few lumps of herring lay broken and twisted in their white oniony juice. I grabbed a fork and looked around for a paper plate.

Time to get going, someone said.

I recognized the voice: it belonged to Yossi, the man who'd helped me when I fainted. I wasn't sure if I'd properly thanked him before, and intended to do so now—and while I was at it, ask if he'd seen Magda anywhere—but when I swung around it turned out he was gone, too.

At last, when I had given up all hope, I found her. She was out in the car.

For all its problems, that gimpy little vehicle of mine seemed to suit her perfectly. She sat in the driver's seat, moodily punching the buttons on the radio. No music was coming out; the ignition was off and I had the keys. Not that this appeared to make any difference to her. Up and down, FM and AM, she jabbed at the buttons with her index finger, and kept jabbing even after I fell into the passenger's seat.

"Well," I said, "I guess I owe you an apology."

She greeted this statement with the blankest look imaginable.

"I mean, I knew I was squeamish, but I didn't think I was *that* . . . Anyway, I'm sorry if it embarrassed you. If it's any consolation, it embarrassed me too."

"What?" she asked.

Her eyes were rheumy. Either she'd been sitting out here smoking her husband's grass, or else she'd been crying. Neither struck me as promising news.

"You didn't see what happened?"

"No."

"How could you not see? Everyone saw. Where were you, anyway?"

"I was in the bathroom."

"The *whole time?*"

"My stomach hurt," she complained. "I had cramps, can I help that?"

"I suppose not."

"So, what did you do already?"

I shrugged. "Nothing. It's just that I sort of lost consciousness there for a minute. No big deal."

"You fainted?"

"Not exactly. Well, sort of. Luckily this guy who claims to be your neighbor helped me out."

"Neighbor?"

"Yossi something."

"Yossi *Klein?*"

"I think so, yes."

"This is perfect," she said. "Yossi and you together."

"He wasn't so bad. He was actually very nice."

"Oh, he's very helpful, that Yossi. Always stopping by, offering to move things around with his big bony shoulders. I could do with a little less of Yossi's help, to tell the truth." She paused, and the corners of her mouth wavered tentatively upward. "You *fainted*?"

I shrugged. "Happens all the time at these things."

"Oh? And how do you know that?"

"Yossi told me."

"Yossi again! You had such a good long talk, the two of you?"

"Listen, I needed to talk to someone, didn't I? Because frankly I found the whole thing barbaric."

"Ah," she said.

"We ran a piece on circumcision, you know. The research shows it's medically unnecessary, if not harmful. I mean, talk about your ridiculous rituals."

"Yes of course," she said mildly. "Ridiculous."

In truth I was thinking that the *bris*, or what I'd seen of it, had not really been so barbaric as all that.

"It's much smarter," she said, her voice tightening a notch, "not to do anything. A child is born but so what? Better to just let the occasion pass without comment."

"I didn't say that. I just don't see the point of a ritual so painful. Why not some other kind?"

"*Nu*? And how do you decide which one?"

"You figure it out. You gather all the information, you factor in the medical circumstances, and—"

"And by now the boy is ten years old. It all comes to the same. People like you, after you factor all the factors what you come up with is always the same. Nothing."

"It's just that I'd rather not—"

"You'd rather look down and make your smug comments about how ridiculous and barbaric these people are. The smart ones, oh sure, the really sophisticated ones, they do nothing. Right? Well if you were really so smart, you know, you'd never have come along today in the first place."

"I never claimed to be smart," I said.

I hadn't intended the remark to be funny. But Magda gave a short, reluctant laugh and then turned her attention to the side window to hide it. People were streaming out of the house and heading for their cars—carrying food, calling out reminders, hugging and kissing each other good-bye. The party was over.

"Well," I said, "where to now?"

She put her hands on the steering wheel and considered for a moment as the engines revved around us. "What are we close to?"

"You're kidding, right?"

"I'm a kidder again?"

"I don't know what we're close to. I have to look at the map."

"So go ahead."

She watched dispassionately as I pulled the map of New York State out of the glove compartment and unfolded it so it lay over our laps like a blanket. Somewhere around Poughkeepsie our knees touched glancingly, then pulled away, then touched again. I was reluctant to look at her; I had no idea what she might say next. To distract us both, I began to point things out on the map. In my nervousness I made an unnecessarily elaborate production out of it. First I showed her our location, pedantically noting its distance from our starting point, and then went on to identify by name and/or number each of the many towns, highways, and bridges that zigzagged out in all directions like a vast, rainbow-colored web. Magda said nothing. Her eyes roamed hungrily over the map. For all I know she might even have been listening. At one point, as Sammy's Michelin guide rolled merrily north up the Hudson, through Bear Mountain and New Paltz and into the lower Catskills, she interrupted to ask, "Woodstock?"

"Yes. It's right there. Above Kingston."

"But why is that name so familiar?"

"Well, they had a big concert there, you know." I ran the

numbers through my head—in 1969, she'd have been a baby. "Forget it. It was a long time ago."

"Oh yes that's right." She clapped her hands together. "Aaron played me the record. He was there."

"He was?"

"I think it was his older brother that took him. They had a band together in the garage. He said he saw that Jimi Hendrix there!"

"Well, that's the place."

"Is it far?"

"About an hour and a half, I think."

"Well, that's close, yes?"

"Compared to what?" I asked. "Albany? Because taking into account it's the opposite direction from the city, and there isn't anything to see, and coming back we'll hit all kinds of weekend traffic, and my car is completely untrustworthy, it's kind of a long haul."

"Okay," she said. "Compared to Albany then."

I laughed. She did too.

Well, there it was. Skipping work. Smoking dope. Passing out. Flirting with young women. Driving to Woodstock, of all places, in an unreliable, uninsured car. It was all very regressive, of course, very stupid and irresponsible, but I'd tried out smart and careful lately and had found them wanting. They hadn't fit. Too tight. Time to try something else.

I folded the map and returned it to the glove compartment. Then without a word Magda got out on her side, I got out on mine, and we did a kind of awkward and apprehensive do-si-do in front of the headlights before settling back into our former roles of driver and passenger. It was still only 11 A.M. Once my key was safely in the ignition, Magda reached forward to click on the radio. Ella Fitzgerald was singing "How High the Moon."

How high indeed? Releasing the hand brake, the years seemed to flake off me in layers, like old skin. My head felt light. It occurred to me that having passed out so recently might be responsible for this light-headedness of mine. But I wondered: might I, in losing consciousness, yet gain some new kind as well?

Magda picked up the remains of the joint from the ashtray, examined it curiously for a moment, and then passed it to me. "You want more?" she asked.

I shook my head. I didn't need it. Which did not prevent me from helping myself to the rest of it, anyway. After twenty-odd years of smoking grass, I was able to predict with some certainty that I would have a sore throat and a headache tomorrow. But the hell with tomorrow. The parkway beckoned with its long finger, its directional arrows, its on-ramps and access roads and vessels of delivery. Tomorrow was an abstraction. The hell with it. And while I was at it, the hell with yesterday too. The reedy smoke was skating big, slow circles in my head. I remembered this feeling from past joints, past women, past lives. They were all still with me. Time, they say, is only one thing, one state without borders. No set past, no set future, but one eternally unfolding moment that ripples around us when we fall into it. Or jump—

The last point I want to make about the *bris* is this: even though I had not been invited, knew no one present, and fainted dead away at the first sign of blood—I left there feeling that somehow it had all been meant for me. *I* was the one who had gone through something powerful. *I* was the one who had been initiated into some new, unfathomable reality. I know it makes no sense, but goddamn it, driving away I felt like *I* was the one who had just been born.

A GLASS HOUSE

All day I had a premonition that my car was going to break down. I could not say why. Even the Science people will concede that there are forms of knowledge which elude our understanding. Extra sense organs within the body, shadow synapses of no tangible weight or mass which occupy a portion of one's inner space, and which come into play in the form of dreams, whims, intuitions, déjà vu, and other not terribly respectable phenomena associated with mysticism, the unconscious, and pure chance.

As for my car, one basis for my premonition lay in the fact that it had broken down frequently in the past. Statistically speaking, however, there was a better than even chance that it would hold up. But I knew it would not hold up. I knew it would break down, somewhere on the New York Thruway between Woodstock and Yonkers, and as a result Magda and I would be thrown together for the evening in foreign territory, without a vehicle, and with all kinds of troublesome consequences.

As it turned out, I was wrong. It was Aaron's car that broke down. Which meant we were still in for consequences, of a different but no less troublesome kind.

There we were, driving through the Catskills. Just to the east, running beside us like a commentary, the Hudson made its leisurely way up toward Canada, or down *from* Canada, I was unable to remember which. Anyway, it was in view the whole time. The sun was creamy and cool, and the breeze came off the water in silky, serpentine waves, as if the air too were a fluid thing, subject to currents and tides, mysterious migrations. I could feel autumn's chill in it, bearing its message of permanent revolution—divest yourself, pare yourself down, soon enough it will be time to move on.

Indeed, as we worked our way north, the trees began to shed weight, get spindly and tough. Discarded leaves stuffed the sewer grates and massed in blood-red piles by the sides of the road. Apples tumbled into the tall grass. Ahead of us the mossy pastures and deciduous slopes rose and loomed over the windshield only to, at the last moment, lose their hold and slip away behind us, the hiss of their passing foliage like the noise the radio makes between stations—distant and imminent and meaningful and useless, all at the same time.

Magda had taken off her shoes. One bare foot was nestled like a conch into the space between her thighs and the vinyl seat. I could see her pale toes with their tiny erratic nails—the most sexual glimpse I'd had of her. The other foot she tapped at intervals on the floor in front of her; not so much in time to the music but as if she were manipulating an invisible brake or gas or clutch pedal of her own.

As we progressed toward Kingston, a pattern began to emerge. Every time I slowed down she seemed to press against her accelerator; when I sped up, I could sense her foot poised over her imaginary brake.

"Zev's father," I said, breaking the silence. "What do you think of him?"

"Herb? Why?"

"I was just wondering."

"He tries to control everything. He always has a comment, a judgmental remark. He's boorish and obnoxious and he cheats his customers and brags about it behind their backs. If I had my way, I'd never see the man again in my life."

I digested this slowly. Then I asked, "He was in a concentration camp, wasn't he?"

She shrugged.

"Well, I'd imagine such an experience would harden a man."

"Oh yes? You would?"

"To endure something like that—think of the resources you'd have to summon. You'd have to become rather brutal yourself, I'd think. There'd be all kinds of control issues."

"Control issues," she repeated wonderingly.

"I just mean—"

"You're a funny man," she said. "Here you don't know the first thing about Judaism, not even the basic prayers. But put a number on a man's arm and suddenly you know all about them. You're their best friend."

"I wouldn't say that."

"Thousands of years of history mean nothing to you, but five years of gas chambers, that means everything. It's perverse, no? The side that suffers and chokes and is defeated, that's the side that feels like a Jew. The healthy part is out playing with the *goyim*."

"I never claimed to be something I'm not," I said. "I'm only half-Jewish, remember?"

"What half? You're not Jewish at all."

Her opinions on this subject had a clarity and force I had not heard from her before, and I was inclined at first to believe her. But then I remembered my father's face in the window of our cabin that summer: puffy and yellow, already indistinct, a prisoner of the glass and its frames. Was he thinking of Rose, his absent sister? Was he hearing her violin?

"You've no right," I said quietly. "You don't know."

"I know what I see."

"Oh? And what's that?"

"People like you are sentimentalists. You want to feel part of something and yet you don't want to get too close. That's why you indulge yourself with this half business. It gives you an excuse to be the way you are."

"Hey," I said, gunning the gas a little, "I was just talking."

"This also bothers me. When someone disagrees with you, you run away. Why can't you face what you are? Why does it make you so uncomfortable?"

To which I said nothing. I was tempted to remind her that I was not the only one running away at the moment. I was further tempted to remind her that I was not out playing with the *goyim*, as she put it, but out with *her*, on what was intended to be a joyful, impulsive adventure. But what was the point? Besides, there was something to what Magda had said about me. It hadn't really sunk in when she'd said it but perhaps it would later, when I thought about it more, when I was alone. Later there'd be plenty of time to dwell on such things. Because if there was one thing I could predict with any certainty, it was that at the end of the day I was going to find myself alone.

As most people on this planet now know, the famous concert at Woodstock was not held at Woodstock at all but some sixty miles down the road in the placid, sloping hamlet of Bethel. Magda of course had no idea. This was fortunate in a way. She was very anxious—or claimed to be—to see the fabled place her husband was so taken with, the one where that Jimi Hendrix had done his thing, and while I did not wish to disappoint her, neither did I wish to drive so many miles out of the way. So I cut a corner, and lied a little about the actual location of the event. I pushed it back to where it made more sense: that is, Woodstock proper, the town we happened to be approaching at the moment. In fact, to hear me describe it, the concert had actually taken place right there in the center of town. Yes, Virginia, once upon a time half a million young people— hungry, unwashed, and stoned out of their minds—shoehorned their way into the triangular green at the corner of Tinker Street and Mill Hill Road, between the Dutch Reformed Church and the Laughing Bear Batik and Woodstock Pizza, to witness the dawn of the new era.

Magda merely nodded. The ludicrous claims I made for the

concert did not appear to surprise her. On the other hand, perhaps she wasn't listening.

We parked the car in front of a bakery, and got out. There was no meter. The sweet yeasty fragrance of new bread combined with the free parking to lift my spirits: a benediction upon our visit from the local gods. Side by side we traveled the sidewalk. Magda, one shoe dangling from each hand, walked very lightly and deliberately on the balls of her feet, like a ballet dancer. It was a warm afternoon and a number of people were out; some of them were walking barefoot too. And Magda's flowered shawl and high-necked blouse seemed, in that winking sunlight, no more exotic or otherworldly a costume than the tie-dyed shirts and madras blouses worn by the tanned, loose-limbed women around us. In fact of the two of us, it was me who stood out—me and my corporate shoes, my mail-order chinos. I was the one who looked like a foreigner, a refugee from that fallen island at the end of the Hudson. Magda fit in just fine.

In truth she looked oddly serene as we rambled through town, past the boutiques, the metaphysical bookstores, the craft shops and art galleries and sidewalk bridge-table tarot readings. I talked the entire way. She wanted Woodstock? I'd give her Woodstock. Melinda and I had rented a cottage in Phoenicia one summer, so I was familiar with the area, and I passed on what I could recall in the way of local lore. When that ran out, I launched into an exuberant commentary on the Age of Aquarius, supplying along the way capsule biographies of Janis Joplin, Richie Havens, Sly Stone, Pete Townshend, and every other performer I could remember from the movie and the album—which comprised, it so happened, all I knew of the event. Unlike Aaron I had not been present. But so what? Not having been present but feeling you have is the fundamental experience of late-century life. Not living, but knowing. The triumph of the secondhand is almost a cliché by now, as inevitable and soporific as the "Tonight Show." Everything is disposable but nothing disappears. It all gets recycled.

Still, as we meandered through the streets, I felt rather like a blind man leading a blind woman up a blind alley.

As we passed the general store, Magda gazed longingly at the fudge in the window. "Should we get some?" she asked.

"If you want."

"Maybe just a little," she said doubtfully, and added, "I didn't eat this morning."

I went along. I did not care for fudge, but it was worth it just to watch her stand at the counter, eyes huge and greedy, palms pressed like a supplicant's to the glass display case. When she wheeled around to face me, her hands coming together in a soundless clap of pleasure, she was, I thought, *literally* a kid in a candy store, and it seemed possible to forget in that moment the whole issue of keeping kosher. "What kind should I get?" she asked. "White chocolate or dark?"

"I don't care."

"Well, what do you like? We'll share. My treat."

"I don't want any," I said. "Get whichever appeals to you."

My apathy in the matter did not deflate her. She turned to the girl behind the counter, a buxom teenager in a yellow Bob Marley tee-shirt. "What kind is better?"

"Oh," the girl mused dreamily, "I like them all."

Magda frowned. Here she had put herself in our hands and neither of us had been at all helpful. Was this to be the free life?

Finally, she chose a particularly gooey dark chocolate, and paid for it with some crumpled bills fished from the pocket of her dress. I reached for my wallet but she waved me off. "No," she said, "I want to pay."

Examining the lump of sugar in her hand, she hesitated. Then she ate the whole thing herself, huge bites, before we were even out the door.

Licking her fingers, she smiled. "Very good."

Out on the sidewalk her avidity, fueled by sugar and transgression, increased. She kept running ahead, dropping behind, pausing before windows and doorways, cupping her hands over her eyes to peer inside, as if expecting to find something important hidden from view, some brilliant object that would redeem this strange pilgrimage of ours. It was all quite touching. Her eagerness, her receptivity to the town and its pleasures, her mouth with its smear of fudge in one corner, her own modest version of a shopping spree—in the end, she was not so complicated as she seemed. Having spent her life with her back to this world, naturally she expected a great deal from it once she turned around. But she had not yet decided, I thought, what to expect from herself.

Among the other things I blamed her husband for, I blamed him for this. Aaron had played that Woodstock album a few too many times, made it sound too good. He'd hit that sixties nostalgia button for all it was worth. And who was I to talk? What had I been doing for the past hour? It occurred to me that this was how divorced men of a certain age went about charming young women: you embroidered the past, fashioned colorful and seductive stories from that worn, fading material, and in so doing you underscored the sacrifices you'd made in renouncing it for their sake. But there were consequences to such stories. I could see them now, as Magda prowled through the clutter and kitsch of the flea market, puzzling over every slogan on every tee-shirt, fingering every pastel scarf, every hand-dipped candle, every stick of incense, every neo-Hopi bracelet and earring. She bought a pair of dangling silver hoops with blue bird feathers and put them on at once, tossing the gold studs she'd been wearing into her pocket. She studied every lousy piece of ceramic pottery as if it had been dug by Schliemann out of Troy. Yes, through the funhouse of borrowed and improvisory flashbacks that was Woodstock, Magda Brenner, the rebbe's daughter, was searching for something. What was it? News of its existence had trickled down to her over the years, but she'd never had the time—or *taken* the time—to investigate. Until now. Now she bent to examine the wares closely, all the while cocking her head at a birdlike, inquisitive angle as if straining to hear, in the casual hubbub of the afternoon crowd, the voice of another God, one more popular and persuasive than her own.

In the end, however, all she could find to buy were the one pair of earrings and an old mirror. About three feet high, in a battered sandalwood frame, the mirror looked like something that had been forcibly detached from the top of a bureau, and a rather cheap bureau at that.

"What do you think?" she asked, studying herself with her usual gravity in the streaky, spotted glass. "Do you like it?"

"Do you?"

She frowned. "Well, it's sturdy. And I like the shape. I think maybe it would go in the bedroom."

The woman behind the table glanced in my direction, waiting for me to confirm that this was so. Her smile was provisional. Stocky and hale, gray hair piled up like a helmet, she had a shrewd, military air—a grunt in some volunteer legion of bric-a-brac salespeople, waging the daily battle. Was I ally or foe?

But I was in no position, of course, to confirm anything.

"How much do they want?" I asked.

"That's twenty dollars," the woman said.

I knew three things at once: that she had snatched the figure right out of the air; that the mirror, at any price, was a piece of junk; and that I would call neither of these first two things to the attention of Magda, who was already fumbling in her pocket for a twenty.

The bill she emerged with, however, was a ten. "Okay?" she said to the saleswoman. "I can't go any higher."

"Fifteen."

"No. I don't have any more."

The two women glared at each other for a moment—without anger, without curiosity, taking each other's measure. I said nothing. Some current of female information was passing between them, and I knew not to interfere. It occurred to me that I had business of my own that awaited me back in New York: our big meeting with Ray Spurlock was scheduled for seven-thirty. Or was it eight? In any event, a great deal of preparation had gone into arranging it, and I did not want to arrive at the last minute, breathless and distracted. Still it was early yet. No reason to cut things short, not just now, when Magda was finally hitting her stride.

And indeed, when we left the flea market we had the mirror with us, purchased for ten dollars.

"You see?" Magda said happily, lugging her prize. "I'm not such a rube. I know how to bargain when I have to."

"Very impressive. I was about ready to give in."

She nodded. "I know."

We proceeded on our walk. The sun was so high we cast no shadows, and no shadows were cast upon us. Magda stopped every so often to inform me how pretty things were. Nothing escaped her notice. The trees with their transfigured leaves, the shops and their hand-painted signs, the tie-dyed shirts dangling like flags in the windows—all were lovely to her and worth remarking. Even the skinheads loitering in the record store, who paused to take turns flexing their tattoos in our mirror, seemed to engage her interest. Watching them head off down the sidewalk in their matching jeans and motorcycle jackets, she sighed meditatively, and I wondered if she was thinking, as I was, that those boys were not far from her own age. Not half so far as I.

"I'm hungry," she declared. "I think I need a proper meal."

"Okay."

"And then you know what I want to do?"

I shook my head. I really had no idea, by that point.

"A movie," she said.

"Is that allowed? I thought you guys stayed away from that kind of thing."

"Actually," she said, blushing, "we're not supposed to. But once in a while I sneak off. I took my nephews to the last *Star Trek* movie. It was very good."

"Well," I said, not terribly enthused by her taste, "if you want to, we should go."

"That's right," she said. "If I want to, we should, right?"

"Right."

Big talkers, I thought, as we walked on in silence. This whole thing was getting out of hand. Suddenly I felt like a divorced father squiring a moody teenage daughter around town. Beam me up, Scotty!

"Look." She pointed to a tiny restaurant on the corner. It was a health food place that featured vegetable and fruit drinks and expensive, tasteless-sounding salads. Perhaps she reasoned such a menu would atone for the fudge. "This looks good," she said.

"I was hoping for a pizza."

"My mouth is so dry. I feel like I haven't eaten in days."

"That's from the marijuana."

"Oh, I know." She said this rather saucily, pirouetting on the balls of her feet. "Come on, let's go in. I've never had health food before."

"All right. If you want to—"

"—we should," she said, suddenly delighted with us both. Our first shared joke.

Inside the restaurant we were greeted by a sign: PLEASE WAIT TO BE SEATED. But Magda did not wait. Apparently Magda had done enough waiting in her life and was ready to try something else. Marching directly to a booth in the back, she plunked herself down and, humming the reggae tune she'd picked up at the record store and been humming ever since, sat there tapping her fingers on the table. Like Donna, I thought. All at once I was certain I'd made a huge mistake. But which one? Donna? Magda? Or this me who was turning one into the other?

Our seating ourselves did not exactly endear us to our waitress, a crew-cut mesomorph in a one-piece jumpsuit, her nose and ears riddled with rings. When we came in she'd been comfortably ensconced in a chair by the kitchen, drinking carrot juice and reading a book—a book she now dog-eared with obvious reluctance. She rose and padded over to her station to collect her order pad. When that shapeless and formidable woman came over, threw two menus at us, and slapped down the silverware, Magda's sauciness began to falter; by the time she cleared her throat and peremptorily challenged us to order, it was gone altogether. Despite the fine bright afternoon it was dark in the restaurant. A candle flickered deep in its mesh-covered globe. In its light I could see my companion's dark eyes glide over the menu without catching hold, and for a moment I found her almost unbearably poignant.

"Hey," I said.

"What?"

"Don't let her get to you. She's just bored."

"Maybe you were right. Maybe we should go somewhere else."

"No, we're already here. Let's stay."

Because we were both very hungry we wound up ordering plates of yogurt, bean dip, hummus, baba ganoush, and about three or four other things that did not quite come together to make a coherent meal. It didn't matter. The moment it was laid out before us we both seemed to lose our appetites.

"Well," Magda sighed, turning to the window, fingering her shawl, "this is a pretty town."

"Yes."

Melinda, after that summer in Phoenicia, had wanted to move up here full-time. We used to talk about how we'd do it. Open a bookstore, get active in local politics. Neighbors in flannel shirts who did not lock their doors. Wind chimes that tinkled in the breeze like heavenly toys. Wood stove in the living room, herb bread in the kitchen. Where did such dreams go when they left? How did *they* get recycled?

"But not too healthy a place to live, I don't think."

"Why do you say that?" she asked.

"Well, it's a diorama, isn't it? You can feel how hard everyone's working to hold back time."

Magda shook her head. "The Rebbe says it's like a glass house. You walk past a glass house. Inside people are dancing. You see them dancing, but you can't hear any music, and so the dancing to you appears strange and irrational. But does that mean there's really no music?"

"I don't know. You tell me."

"Sometimes," she said, frowning at her plate, "there's music."

For a minute or so we sat there in silence, each of us trying, I think, in our respective ways to hear it. A joke came to mind about people living in glass houses, but I managed to smother it on the way out. Enough jokes. Jokes were killing me. Enough jokes.

The waitress cruised by, noted our progress, and went back to her book. *Journey to the East*, by Hermann Hesse. I'd read it myself once, or started it, years ago. Warren Pinsky used to blow most of the money he made dealing hash on used books of a spiritual nature—William Blake, Alan Watts, *Tao te Ching*, assorted Gnostics, Kabbalists, and Indian ecstatics—books which he was forever pressing upon me in a rush of enthusiasm and which I was forever picking up and putting down and ultimately forgetting to return. I wondered what it would be like to read one of those books now. Would I hear the music?

Magda was staring into the untouched food on her plate. "I thought you were hungry," I said.

She shrugged.

"Maybe it matters to you more than you think."

"What?"

"Staying kosher."

"I wasn't thinking of that."

"No?"

"No." But now that I'd brought it up, the idea seemed to deplete her spirits a little further. She dipped her head and touched a palm to her hair, patting it down on top lest it get away from her. And what else?

The candle began to sputter in its waxen pool.

"Hey," I said, "tell me something."

"What?"

"What are you doing here, exactly? I mean with me. Here, now. It's all wrong."

"Why?"

"What do you mean why? Because of who you are. *What* you are. And what I am."

"Oh, you're not so bad," she said. Perhaps fearing this compliment was not strong enough, she added, "You're funny."

"Well, I don't seem to make you laugh very much."

"No, not that kind of funny. I mean . . . sweet." She frowned at the inadequacy of this word, too. "Part of you tries to be practical and normal about things, and part of you is just this *luftmensh* who can't decide anything and doesn't really want to. I think that must be why you're attracted to me."

This last statement came out matter-of-fact and a bit weary, as if my being attracted to her was a question the two of us had long ago resolved. I suppose we were ready for a little directness. I waited for her to tell me some more unflattering things about myself. I'd been out of therapy for some years now and I rather missed having my character analyzed for me.

"You see me as someone who's had everything decided for her," she said. "Isn't that so?"

"I'm not sure. Maybe."

"You envy me for that, I think. Maybe you resent it a little too. Because you're stuck, and you'd like to be told what to do also."

"No I wouldn't."

"No," she said, "that's true too. I think you prefer not to know. To want but not have."

She sighed. All she had said was self-evident to her, and in a way only vaguely to the point; there was, it seemed, a deeper agenda at stake. Now she leaned back from the table and crossed her legs. The rustle of her stockings, the noisy friction of them, unnerved me. I could feel her coiled proximity under the table. I wanted to touch her but did not know how. My hands felt fat and clumsy. All I had were words.

"And you?" I said. "Do you envy me?"

"Of course."

She smiled unhappily.

"So what are you afraid of?"

"I'm not afraid of being told what to do. It's all I know. Maybe I'm afraid of the other."

"So you're stuck too?"

"Maybe so."

"And are we going to go ahead and sleep together now?"

"Why would we do that?" She asked this coolly, flecking at a bread crumb with her nubby fingernail.

"Because that's what stuck people do, in my experience, when they want to get unstuck."

"Really? Or are you being funny with me?"

"I assure you, I'm serious."

"And does it work?"

"At times, yes."

This did not appear to hearten her very much.

"There's no way to know in advance. It's like what Aaron said about angels. It requires," I said, "a leap of faith."

She gave this some thought. "In God?"

"No."

"In you?"

"No."

"In what then?"

I shrugged. I knew what it wasn't but could not say what it was. If any one thing defined me, I thought, it was this uncertainty, this small vacant space between no and yes.

Meanwhile Magda had finished arranging the bread crumbs into a circle. Now, still restless, she began to toy conjecturally with the colored splotches and food puddles on her plate, running them together with her index finger as in some kindergarten art project. When she was satisfied with the design she had wrought, she brought the finger to her lips and licked it clean. "Excuse me," she said. "I have to go to the bathroom."

"Again?" She had been marching off to the bathroom, it seemed, ever since I'd met her.

She smiled weakly. "I have a small bladder. I can't help it."

She clopped down the narrow aisle in her high black shoes,

bumping her hips off three different tables along the way. She was gone several minutes. What was she doing in there? All these years of erotic hide and seek—a marriage, several long relationships, and innumerable false starts—and here I was back at square one, waiting, clueless, for my date to return from the bathroom. The marijuana had worn off by now, and I was left feeling a little cranky about the day I had spent. Besides there was business to take care of down in the city. I had that meeting tonight at seven-thirty. Or was it eight?

Hoping to confirm the time, I went to the phone and put in a call to Ronnie Oldham at the office. The line was busy. What else was new?

My own bladder was beginning to make itself felt. I went off to the men's room, where, because of the size and location of the facilities, I was forced as I emptied myself to take a good look in the mirror. The sight was not rewarding. Over the past weeks—all those hours stationary at the desk, all those lunches with Arlen Ashby—I'd put on some weight; not even the most elastic definition of thin would stretch to cover me any longer. Also my hair was a mess, my eyes were lidded and puffy, and my beard—in my haste that morning I'd forgotten to shave—was coming in a patchy, angry red. No wonder she was reluctant to sleep with me. *I* was reluctant to sleep with me, and I'd been sleeping with me for years.

When I came back to the table Magda was still absent. *She's gone,* I thought without surprise.

But she wasn't gone. Now she was at the phone. Receiver against her ear, she swayed back and forth, listening to what appeared to be a long, intricate message. I remembered the swaying of the *mohel* that morning, chanting prayers over her nephew. I do not think she was praying, however. Not to the same God, and not for the same things.

"Are you all right?" I asked when she returned.

She nodded quickly. Her mood had shifted too. She did not sit down so much as temporarily perch on the edge of the bench, poised for flight. "What time is it?"

"Three-thirty."

"So late? We better get back."

"That's it? Just call it a day?"

She nodded, avoiding my eyes.

"What about this movie you were dying to see?"

She shook her head. "It's not so important."

"And what about the other things? What about the Talmud? What about not fleeing from life's pleasures?"

"Oh," she said, and there appeared on her face a mischievous little sideways smile I hadn't seen before, one that did not bode well, I thought, for my prospects, "that's only part of the quotation."

"What's the other part?"

"One should not run *toward* life's pleasures, either."

"You're kidding, right?"

She shrugged helplessly. We had already established that among our many differences she was not a kidder.

"You're dangerous, you know that? You and that goddamn book. What else is in there I should know?"

"Please," she said. "It's very late."

"It's three-thirty."

"Yes, but it gets dark around six. We need to be back before then."

"How come?"

"It's Friday . . . Shabbos . . ."

"Oh for Christ's sake."

"Please," she said, watching me toss five-dollar bills on the table. "Please don't be angry. I've had a nice time with you. It's just that some things aren't possible right now. You understand that, don't you?"

"Sure," I said under my breath. "But which things?"

Following which we left the restaurant—no healthier, to my way of thinking, than when we'd come in—and crossed the street, only to find when we returned to the car that it had been ticketed for being parked in a yellow zone.

At first I did not react at all. I merely looked at that bright yellow stripe on the curb, and thought of all the stripes and lines just like it that had been laid out around me like a running fence. Then the sheer stupidity of it hit home. Then home, not to be outdone, hit right back. This took the form of a brief but histrionic display of violence against my car's front end, and some high-volume curses directed at that witless fellow Samuel Karnish, currently on display in the middle of quaint old Woodstock, viciously beating up his own car.

Magda, sitting on the curb, clutched her mirror, waiting for me to finish. I wasn't scaring her a bit. Of course I wasn't exactly charming her either. But she held her tongue.

She must have gotten a very good grip on it, too, because she did not let it go for the next two and a half hours. The whole ride back to the city she kept her eyes closed and her head leaned back against the seat, her face a blank screen across which passing shadows played. She wasn't sleeping. I knew she wasn't, because even with her eyes closed one foot still moved to her private rhythm—up and down at the ankle, working that invisible pedal.

Which one, though? Gas, clutch, or brake?

Suffused by nameless irritations, by the time we passed the sign for the western turn-off that would have taken us to Bethel, I did not even bother to point it out to Magda, let alone confess, as I'd been meaning to from the moment I watched her buy that fudge, that I had misled her. Why bother? Clearly she was not the sort of person who had to see something to believe in it.

"He's not home."

We were in front of the house, idling in neutral. The sun was in neutral too; bloated and wan, it dangled indolently over the rooftops like some afternoon drunk. My watch read six-fifteen. We'd made it all the way to Brooklyn before dark, right through rush hour. Because I now felt like a madman, it seemed to me I was entitled to drive like one: eighty miles an hour down the Thruway, wind pounding my face, the engine roaring in my ears like applause. We'd had our adventure and emerged guiltless and intact. We deserved applause, I thought.

Now, having crossed three or four bridges and paid what seemed an infinity of tolls, here we were back in Crown Heights. The fissured streets lay quiet under shadow. The traffic lights blinked a sleepy yellow; the stores on Kingston Avenue were shuttered tight. Through the anticrime bars I could see all the portraits of the Rebbe that graced the shop windows. The old man's eyes, blue and piercing, freighted with bags, squinted at us from Benny's Tailor Shop and Raskin's Fish Store and Katz's Glatt Kosher Cafeteria, as though ticking off as we passed every commandment we had broken in our lifetimes, and every one we were planning to break as well.

Was anything we did likely to surprise him? The Rebbe too, I'd learned, had once been something of a Renaissance man—attended the Sorbonne, trained in philosophy and science, read Hegel, Proust. But then he had married, and through the agency of his father-in-law the Lubavitcher succession had fallen to him. Now, in his nineties, he was a holy man, autocratic sovereign over a prosperous farflung empire. No doubt he'd witnessed all manner of foolishness in his time. Perhaps even lived some of it himself.

The light was failing fast now. Bearded men in fedoras and black suits hurried home along the broken sidewalks. Wind-blown pages from the morning tabloids snapped like dogs at their ankles. The Prince of Wales was in town; the Yankees had dropped a doubleheader. So what? The men of Crown Heights were preoccupied with princes and standings of their own. I could hear them from the car, muttering contentiously among themselves in Yiddish. Yiddish: a dying language, a tongue of ghosts. It was fitting. They dressed like ghosts, they talked like ghosts, and in the pale halos cast by the streetlights they looked like ghosts—yet they fancied themselves to be more alive than the rest of us.

Bullshit, I thought. Bullshit and nostalgia. Get real.

A young black man crossed the street and ambled toward us. Casually, as if the block belonged not to the borough of Brooklyn but to him alone, he stepped over the curb and crossed to where my car sat in its noisy, bumptious idle. He wore a loose basketball shirt, white gym shorts, and white high-top sneakers that made his legs look even darker and skinnier than they were, and he moved with the shambling, diffident humor of a junkie. By his side he brandished a long stick.

"Oh shit," I said.

"What?" Magda asked sleepily.

"Look at this guy. He's on crack."

"No he's not."

"Look at his eyes. Look what he's carrying."

"So?"

"So he's going to hurt us."

Magda laughed. "What's the matter with you? He's only going to clean the windshield."

She was right. The man, upon closer inspection, was a kid of fourteen, the stick was a squeegee, and the only crime perpetrated upon us was the familiar urban indignity of having our windshield washed against our will. I was in no mood for it, however. I honked the horn and gunned the engine to warn him away. The kid with the squeegee took no notice. Painstakingly he went about his business, scratching some birdshit off the glass with his thumbnail and wiping it clean, never once looking up, as if sent by some higher authority to obliterate all traces of the day's excursion.

When he was finished, he sauntered over to my window, palm open, seeking his reward. "Fifty cent," he said.

"I'll give you a quarter."

"Hey, man. That's fifty cent. I did a good job."

"I didn't ask you to."

"Give him fifty cents," said Magda. "Please."

"No."

273

"Here." Magda reached across the seat to hand him a dollar, taking great care not to touch me. "Thank you, Edwin."

Edwin sniffed suspiciously, unsure whether to take the bill or not. I could see that having settled on fifty cents, anything else seemed like a compromise. Nonetheless he overcame this recalcitrant voice in his head and took the dollar. Then he dug in his pocket for two quarters change. "Okay," he said, handing them to Magda. "Take care now."

After he'd gone, I had a distinct sense that the encounter had put me in the wrong somehow, hardened some wall between us. "You know that kid?" I asked.

"Edwin does jobs for people around the holidays. Sometimes things are slow. Then he's out at the corner, washing windshields."

"And do you always give him money?"

"Why not? I was dropping coins in the *pushke* box, you know, when I was two years old. We're commanded to give. Sure some only give to Jews and ignore the blacks; I used to be that way too. But Aaron helped me see it different."

I nodded. Aaron, I thought.

Cirrus clouds had begun to drift in from the west, long-fingered, pale as X-rays against the slate sky. Music floated through the open windows. Sweet onions were in the breeze, cooking meat, peppery soups. Children were calling to each other in upstairs rooms. Another Friday night. Another Friday night in the glass houses . . .

The Brenners' house was made not of glass, however, but brick. And the windows were dark.

The car was still in neutral. In the spirit of neutrality, I had not even set the handbrake. Drop her off, I thought, and go. Enough was enough.

But apparently enough wasn't enough. Not quite.

"His car's gone," Magda said. For some reason, she did not sound particularly surprised.

"Gone?"

"He's not home."

"Where could he be?"

"I don't know. It's Shabbos. There's no other place."

"Maybe he's at the synagogue."

"He'd be home by now. And he wouldn't drive to the shul."

"All right, well, calm down. We'll figure it out. Let's just calm down and think, okay?"

"I *am* calm," she said.

This was true. I was the one who was getting excited. Magda stared reflectively out the side window, serene as a buddha.

I did pull up the handbrake, then, and we sat there for a while, reviewing our options in the privacy of our minds. The sun was fading behind the rooftops. As it went the numbers on the dashboard grew more and more legible, so I was able to observe that we were presently going zero miles per hour, that the gas tank was half empty, and that the odometer was roughly midway through its second hundred thousand miles. With all this math to distract me I found it difficult to concentrate on the problem of Aaron's whereabouts, or to remember what time I'd told Ronnie I would meet him. Was it seven-thirty or eight?

In one of the houses, a phone began to ring. No one picked it up. We could hear it distinctly from the car: the street was that quiet. The sound, against the fabric of the evening, was like something tearing.

"That could be him," I said.

She nodded.

"It's practically sundown. Is there some kind of restriction on him calling after sundown?"

"Yes of course."

"So maybe you should run and answer it?"

She nodded again but failed to move. It seemed her agreement was strictly a theoretical one. The phone continued to ring. I counted five, six, seven. Then I stopped counting, though it did not stop ringing.

"Okay," she sighed at last. "Let's go in."

"I think I'll pass."

"But why?"

"You know why."

We had spent the entire day, it seemed, debating whether or not it was a good idea for me to accompany her into other people's houses. Here we were at the end and still no progress had been made. The phone was still ringing. "Please," she said. "It's Shabbos."

"So what?"

"One should never be alone on Shabbos. They say special prayers in shul, you know, just to delay the service so the stragglers can finish. That way no one will be left to walk home by himself."

"That's nice," I said. "But I think I'll pass."

Angry now, she put her hand on the door handle and strained against the seatbelt, unable to find the button to release her. After a second, she stopped trying. Her shoulders slumped, and her expression softened; she was no longer pushing against the door, I realized, but pulling it toward her instead, using it as a shield against that relentless hidden phone.

"Do you know what I did last Tuesday?" she asked.

"What?"

"I went to that museum. The Metropolitan. Do you want to know why?"

"Why?"

"I wanted to see that painting. The one in your kitchen."

My God, I thought: *I'm her only friend*.

"Only it wasn't there. You were wrong about that; they don't have it. So I spent the afternoon wandering around. I went and saw the Tiffany windows, and the room by Frank Lloyd Wright, and the tombs from Egypt. And the Italian paintings, I saw them too. Then I ate lunch in the cafeteria. Yogurt, cookies. I had a cappuccino—it was so good! I went and bought some cards in the gift shop to send my sister Miri. I even kept that little button they give you. I have it in my bag right now."

She patted the bag in question with the flat of her hand. "And?"

"And what?"

"How did you like it? How did it make you feel?"

"Oh," she said helplessly, mournfully, "there aren't words."

I did not want to stay but neither did I want to leave her like that, alone and full of inexpressible emotion. In truth I did not want to leave myself alone either. Not with this gnawing hollowness, this irresolute echo in my chest. And then before I knew what was happening her face was very close, so close I could see the tiny brooking veins in her eyes and the black dewpoints at the end of her lashes, and a chalky, powdery scent rose from her wig and filled my head and I understood at last that she was offering herself to be kissed. *Here! Now!* Right in my car, with the phone still ringing and the engine still running and the handbrake jutting up like the lever for a trapdoor between us, Magda Brenner had finally chosen to get romantic. We hadn't even taken off our seatbelts yet.

"Your cheek," she said. "It's scratchy."

"Sorry. I forgot to shave this morning."

"*Nu?* Come closer."

Stiffly, I put my arms around her and, pretending to nuzzle her shoulder, sneaked a quick look over it instead. In the neighbors' windows, *more* pictures of the Rebbe. Also candle shadows that wavered in the breeze like spirits. We were completely exposed; anyone who wanted to could see us. The Rebbe, the people next door, possibly even Aaron himself. How did we know he was really on the phone, and not lying in wait behind the front door?

"What's the matter?" she whispered.

"Maybe this isn't such a hot idea."

"Why not?"

"Maybe we should see if that's him on the phone, first. And if we're going to do any necking, let's do it inside."

The phone, however, had stopped ringing. All was stillness, but for the dull rattle of the engine. Then I turned that off too.

Magda drew a breath, let it out. "You worry too much," she said, "about what people think."

"It's what *I* think I'm worried about."

"Oh yes? And that means what?"

"It means," I said, "that I won't be made a display of. I'm not going to be a prop for some theatrical act of rebellion. Or if I am, then it'll be *my* rebellion, not yours."

"You?" she sniffed. "What do you have to rebel against?"

"Nothing," I said. "Everything."

Naturally she had no idea what I was talking about. She'd led a sheltered, unhappy life, and her capacities for empathy were limited. And I seemed to demand a lot of empathy, particularly from women. Between the way she was and the way I was, what chance did we have?

Finally she succeeded in wrestling out of the seatbelt. "I'm going in," she said, and reaching behind her to the backseat, reclaimed her ten-dollar mirror.

Aaron, of course, was not lying in wait on the other side of the door. And yet he might just as well have been; I was aware of him everywhere in the apartment. I had not seen the man since that Friday night dinner in July—only in the most general terms could I even remember what he looked like—but his reality for me that evening was not diminished by his corporeal absence. Like the Rebbe, his image loomed over the place like a billboard, dreamlike and enormous.

Still, he wasn't there. Once I'd determined this to my satisfaction, Magda and I got on with our business. She put out a platter of cold chicken and some rye bread and we sat on the chrome chairs in the darkening kitchen, eating it with our hands. It was in truth a rather somber, stripped-down version of the Shabbos meal. No prayers accompanied it; no lit candles, no white linen, no challah, no sweet wine, no songs. Somehow in the course of events we'd abandoned all claim to these things. The chicken had been boiled and so was tasteless, glazed with a skin of gelatinous grease which we wiped off our hands with cheap paper napkins from the supermarket. There were some cucumbers and cherry tomatoes for a salad. To drink we had seltzer shot from a bottle. The fizz of the carbonation sounded loud in the dark, ominous, as if something important was escaping. But what was it really? Just gassy little bubbles, I thought. Just air.

As we ate, we took turns staring at the wall phone. From the way it drew our attention, it too might have been emblazoned with Aaron's face. And yet the sun was down, which meant it wouldn't ring. I did not know whether to be glad or sorry, but I allowed myself to ruminate for a while on the man to whom the house in which I sat, the food on my plate, the plate itself, and the two refrigerators and two freezers and two different sets of dishes for dairy and meat in their two different cabinets, each labeled neatly with masking tape, all belonged. As did by formal contract, I reminded myself, the woman on the other side of the table. She was leafing without interest through the day's mail, all of which had been addressed to this same man, this Aaron Brenner. Where was he? I could not help but feel that his absence that evening—and my presence—was less the product of accident than design. But whose design? His? Hers? The Rebbe's? The only one I could rule out with any confidence, I thought, was myself.

I checked my watch. Seven-thirty. The number impressed me as significant, for some reason.

Magda cast the mail aside and picked up her fork again. The cherry tomatoes were overripe; when she punctured the membranes they spit huge globs of seeds out into the space between us. They lay there, teeming and formless as a galaxy, waiting to be wiped up.

A cool wind blew through the open window. Magda shivered; on her arms the flesh rose in bumps. She looked like a woman who caught cold easily. Germs of a certain type were attracted to neurotics of a certain type, and vice versa. Lab research had shown this. We had run a piece in the magazine about it once—

"Oh God."

"What?"

"I have to make a call."

"The phone?" she asked. "Now?"

"Look, I realize that it's against the rules, but this is very important. I have to get in touch with some people. It has to do with my work."

"Your work?" She seemed to encounter some difficulty connecting these two words up.

"At the magazine. Look, it's hard to explain, but we had an important meeting scheduled for tonight. I have to make a call."

She thought for a moment. "Will someone be harmed if you don't call?"

"Christ yes. Me."

"I mean, really harmed. Not just financially."

"No," I admitted. "No one will be harmed."

"Not you either?"

"Me? I don't know. It's hard to say."

She looked into her lap. Her white neck was held at a stiff peculiar angle, a pigeon inspecting a sidewalk for crumbs. "Well," she said, "it's up to you."

"Uh uh. No way. It's your house, so it's your decision. You're the one who keeps all these absurd commandments."

"So if they're so absurd, why not go ahead and break them if you want to?"

"Look," I said, "just tell me, yes or no, if it's okay for me to use the phone. If not, I'll run down to the corner and find a pay phone. I don't have time to argue."

"But you're the one arguing," she said mildly. "I told you it's up to you."

"Fine. It's up to me. I'm going to make my call."

"Fine."

At which point she left the room, unable or unwilling to watch. Good.

As soon as she was gone, however, some crucial portion of my focus deserted me. It was comfortable in the kitchen, and the streets outside were uncommonly hushed, and it gave me an odd slow feeling, a kind of plenitude of being, just to be alone with my thoughts, such as they were, in the gathering dark. I knew it was an urgent matter to call Ronnie at the restaurant, but at the same time it did not quite *feel* urgent; it felt remote and almost altruistic, as though to call him would require a sacrifice of my interests and not a pursuit of them. In my confusion I thought of my mother, who was something of an expert on altruism, and was rewarded with a hot flash of shame. My mother would have given that kid with the squeegee his fifty cents at once. Then she'd have invited him home, fed him a meal, struck up a friendship with his family, and formed a task force. That was how my mother operated: outreach across the races, the classes, the generations. And what about me? How far did my reach extend?

The operator came on and I asked for the number of the restaurant. There was a little pad next to the phone which I used to copy it down. I was trying to be very cool and resolved about all this, but my hands were damp, hot, and fumbly. I dropped the pencil. The mechanical voice, as if anticipating such difficulties, began to repeat the number. I reached down for the pencil. To retrieve it without letting go of the receiver called for a sort of twister maneuver, an awkward bend and thrust at the waist which, I realized half a second too late, was the last thing one should attempt with a lower-back problem.

There was a short, sickly pop.

I felt some pain, yes. A good deal of pain. But it was only a muscle, I was certain, not a disk. Which meant that I'd be okay if I took care of myself. If I lay down for a minute, if I was careful not to move until I was ready, I would be okay.

This, then, was how I wound up on the floor of the Brenners' kitchen, staring into yet another ceiling. Incidentally, it was now seven-forty. The sun was long gone. Wind was raving in the trees; branches scratched and shuddered at the windows. Beneath the linoleum I thought I could feel the earth itself as it boiled and tossed, crusty with impatience.

Well, I thought, what now?

The receiver was still in my hand. A better future, perhaps, lay on the other end of the wire. It occurred to me that a city—a *life*—was held together by just such wires as this. One wire strung to other wires, spanning the miles of brownstones and tenements and then vaulting the dark river, over the steep canyons of midtown, into the heart of the crackling web. All I had to do was call and tell them to go ahead without me, I'd meet them later. Ronnie Oldham could never handle the suits alone. He'd become goosey and flustered; he'd scare them with his intensity and bore them with technical jargon. I was the generalist, the synthesist; it was my place to mediate between Ronnie's genius and the idle curiosity of everyone else. Yes, they'd wait. They had to. Then, once I arrived, we'd lay out our proposal to Spurlock and the other big guns, and they in turn would lay out the fat checks and tall drinks, the winking waiters with their flaming carts, the low murmur and hum of power as it generated and regenerated itself—the whole shimmering Manhattan fantasy. I felt it out there. Success was waiting; I could smell its heady perfume, hear its deep, luxurious breath in the darkness. All I had to do to claim it was get up off the floor, untangle this cord, press the right buttons on this phone, say the right things with this mouth. The right things . . .

Magda came back in the room. She had changed out of her green blouse and into a white one that fit her somewhat more tightly and did not cover quite so much of her neck and arms. "Are you finished?" she asked, pulling open the refrigerator.

"It would appear so."

"What's the matter? Why are you on the floor like that?" It had taken her a moment to notice. "Are you hurt?"

"Just my back," I said. "It'll be okay in a minute."

"How did your call go?"

"Not very well. I didn't make it."

This news had no visible effect on her. She stood before one of the humming refrigerators, examining its contents. She began to hum a little herself.

"Don't you want to know why not?" I asked.

She shrugged. "It doesn't matter."

"Maybe I *am* sentimental. Maybe that's my weakness."

"If it doesn't feel right," Magda offered, closing the refrigerator door, "there could be other explanations."

"Sure. Sure there could."

I got up off the floor at last and went to hang the receiver back in its cradle. The tightness in my back was gone. Or had it moved somewhere else?

There was an extra second of pause before I let go of the phone, and Magda registered it. "Why so sad?" she asked. "Is it the end of the world?"

"In a way," I said, "that's exactly what it is."

She frowned. "Don't be silly. There are other worlds, you know, inside this one."

"Oh please. Spare me."

"It's true," she insisted. "If you turn your back on one, another will open to you. And if not that one, then maybe another."

This new cosmic wisdom of hers did not improve my spirits. I waved one hand like a wand as if to dispel everything— her calm voice, my panicked lower back, and the encroaching gloom of the kitchen around us. "Oh well," I said. "It won't be the first time I've fucked myself out of a career."

"Does it have to do with that article you and your friend were writing?"

"I'm afraid so."

"And if you don't make this call, you can't write the article?"

"Oh we can still write it. It's just that there might not be anyone to write it for."

"Too bad," she said. "But I thought writers went about their work differently. I thought they wrote for themselves."

"Not if they want to eat, they don't."

"Too bad," she said again. "So what now? Do you want to leave?"

"I don't know."

"You wanted to before. Why not now?"

I waved my wrist again. I didn't know that either.

"It's your back?"

"No, not that."

"Aaron?"

"Partly."

"Your girlfriend?"

"I don't know," I said. "Maybe partly her too."

She frowned again. "With you, everything is parts."

I nodded. There was no use trying to deny it.

"Well," she said, "if it puts your mind at rest about Aaron, he won't be here tonight. His car broke down out in Hershey. I was just over by the Kleins."

"And who the hell are the Kleins?"

"Yossi and Sara. They live next door. You met Yossi this morning, you said."

"Oh. Right, right. Yossi."

"When I wasn't home, he called Yossi. Something about the points, or the pistons. He's not sure. One second he's driving out of the parking lot, the next he's at the mechanic's. I know they're going to ask for a lot of money, too. They always do. He doesn't know the first thing about cars."

This from a woman who did not even own a driver's license! My allegiances tipped and swayed again. Aligning myself for the moment with all the worried, weary men out there fidgeting on hard plastic chairs in dirty garages, hostage to the whims of ruthless mechanics, I reminded her that I didn't know the first thing about cars either.

"Anyway," she said, shrugging me off, "he's staying out in Hershey tonight with a couple from the Orthodox shul. Tomorrow the car should be ready. He'll drive back after Shabbos."

"Well that's a relief," I said. "Knowing where he is."

She nodded, stretching. I could still let her go, I thought. It was not beyond me. I could still disappear.

"*Nu?* It's been a long week and it's Shabbos and I'm tired. What do you say, Sam? Stay or go?"

It was the first time she'd ever called me by name; the word in her mouth sounded utterly foreign. Or perhaps it was not her mouth but my ears that made the word so strange, made this Sam fellow she was addressing seem so mysterious and remote. Stalling, I looked out the window. Next door, on the other side of the fence, the Kleins were sitting down to a Shabbos dinner. The whole idea of the Shabbos, as I understood it, was separation: to make it different from everything else. But if we slept together, the two of us, would that be different from everything else, or would it be the same?

Magda cleared her throat. "There are two parts to the Torah, the Rebbe says. A part that forbids and a part that allows."

"And which do you suppose is relevant for us?"

"Both." She gave me a pitying, exasperated look. "You still don't understand, do you? The whole beauty is that nothing is determined. It's all in process. The Rebbe says there are holy sparks hidden everywhere—even in sins. Even sins have a place in the order of things. They're like the lees they use to make wine. They help ferment the good. They give it even higher value."

"Well," I said, "that's certainly a convenient way of looking at it."

"It's the only way that makes sense. Like the Rebbe says— how should we account for the presence of evil in the world but as part of a unity that can't be divided? Just because we can't see it doesn't mean it isn't there." She observed me with some sadness. "Don't you believe in such a thing?"

"No. I believe there are good acts and bad acts, and I try not to confuse the two."

"And you're able to do this?"

"No," I admitted. "I confuse them all the time."

"So if it's so confusing for you, why should it be less so for God?" she asked. "The Rebbe says we should not make such separations. We should learn to say yes, not just no. To find the holy sparks in things."

"And how do you do that?"

"How?" I did not expect her to have an answer to the question, and perhaps she didn't either; the quickness and vehemence of her response seemed to surprise us both.

"By making them," she declared.

She had already turned to walk down the narrow hallway toward the back of the house. And I turned, oh yes I did, and followed her.

These Jews, I thought. They exalt a God who flings out the universe from a fiery hand and then retracts into the shadows, leaving us to discover and perfect it ourselves. But with what tools? The thick tomes of commentary that lined the Brenners' shelves—if it took that many volumes to explicate His meaning, how could a man like me ever hope to grasp it?

As we filed down the hallway, Magda's long skirt whispered against the walls—admonitions or encouragements, I wasn't sure. At the door of the bedroom, she paused, and I was convinced she'd changed her mind. In that dim hallway, with the guilt rising in my throat and my back in spasms and my career folding up like a stage flat behind me, I thought I might have changed mine, too. But then I saw what had arrested her.

The room was a mess. Stockings and shoes, sweaters and skirts and trousers, combs and brushes and hairpins—all lay strewn about the floorboards like the wreckage of a lost, one-sided war. A stick of deodorant, capless and crusted, teetered on the top of the radiator. Tubes of lipstick rested on the dresser like so many spent bullets. Books and magazines were everywhere: fading, broken-spined, stacked like corpses. Among the foreign periodicals were a very few in English: *Jewish Press, Jerusalem Post.* I looked for incriminating materials but could find in those piles of magazines not even one sneaky, tucked-away *Cosmopolitan.*

A tiny bulb had been left on by the bed; it gave off a hesitant, sepia light that fluttered over the disorder like a strobe.

"I'm sorry," Magda said hopelessly. "I had no time to clean."

"Don't worry. The place looks fine."

There are people one should never tell not to worry because it will only make them worry more, and Magda, as I should have known by now, was one of them. Flustered, she sank to her knees, hastily swept up an armful of stray socks, shirts, and stockings, and looked around for a place to put them. First she tried to balance them on the radiator. Then she tried to cram them in the bottom drawer of her bureau. Then she went over and peeked into the closet. I do not know what new calamities were lurking in there, but whatever she found discouraged her from entry. Finally she gave up, and let the clothes in her arms fall back to the floor with a groan.

"Well." She blew some air out of her mouth in surrender. "That's that."

"Don't worry," I said again. "Everything's fine."

"Fine?"

"Yes."

"So everything's fine, so why are you still standing in the doorway?"

Why was I? The back window was open; through it a greasy moon floated half-formed and colorless over the ocean. Meanwhile here was Magda and here was I. The chill of the evening was on our faces, the bed laid out between us like a prize. I could hear the air going in and out of her lungs, ragged but controlled, a fighter in the middle rounds. At the sound, some hard nut of lust cracked open inside me. I saw, propped in a corner of the room, the ten-dollar mirror. Even under the pale flutter of that dinky bulb our moods could be read plainly in the glass—direct, unamused, and a little apprehensive, as if we had traveled a long way over dangerous ground only to find that the truly difficult terrain still lay before us.

"Okay," I said. "I'm coming in."

Making It

I don't know why they say the flesh is weak, when it's actually rather strong. Walk by any health club and you'll see it working out, pumping iron, throwing its weight around. No, the flesh is in terrific shape these days. It's lean and mean. Also rude, capricious, passive-aggressive, wired with sociopathic tendencies.

I was feeling a little pathological myself. A little out-of-step. Even as I put my lips to Magda's breast I was at a remove, not quite able to taste the salts and powders of her skin, or feel the damp heat that rose through her pores to greet me; not quite able to immerse in her tender, troubled realities. There were too many obstacles between us. It did not help matters, I suppose, that I was preoccupied with guilt, fear, and lower-back pain. Or that I was keenly aware of what I was missing even now, the scene transpiring across the river at "21"—Ronnie Oldham and Ray Spurlock, and the empty chair between them. All of which may have contributed to the general performance anxiety.

About performance anxiety: I was not a stranger to its promiscuous and melancholy attentions. Perhaps its visits are more frequent to those of us with a higher than average load of common, nameless, workaday anxieties—I don't profess to know. But as any honest male or any vexed female of a certain age will tell you, it exists. Boy, does it exist.

Magda, however, claimed never to have heard of it. Indeed,

how could she? No Masters and Johnson for the rebbe's daughter. No Mary McCarthy, no Dr. Ruth, no Donahue, no Oprah. No sweaty fumbling with guys from the hockey team, no quickie liaisons with the boss in midtown hotels, no calorific rap sessions with embittered, battle-scarred women friends. All these windows into male dysfunctionality had been closed to her. No, apparently nothing in her twenty-four years on the planet had prepared her for the shock of my limp penis.

I was a little shocked, too. Listlessly I stared at the ceiling, thinking, *Nothing has changed.* In the ongoing war between my appetites and my ability to provide for them, I kept losing and losing. And what had I lost now?

The sex itself was touch and go, with an emphasis, I'm afraid, on the latter. Magda, as she had been all evening—as I had *made* her be—was the aggressor. It was she who pulled off her clothes first and climbed gamely onto the mattress. It was she who sat there perched on her knees, naked, unsmiling, unshy, as I fumbled out of my pants. Her breasts were smallish and pale, though not so small nor so pale as I'd thought. Had she been ashamed of her body, or of herself, she might have folded her arms and hidden behind them. But she didn't. She parted them instead, with the same perfect casualness with which she'd opened her shawl out on the front steps that Friday night two months before, and revealed to me her bathrobe. Our ends, I thought, are present in our beginnings. But which was this? Every part of Magda seemed ready to engage. Even her taut areolas were like another pair of eyes, deep brown and unblinking. Bedroom eyes.

Under pressure of this second sight, I moved forward. It's possible I was trembling. When my mouth closed over her nipple, Magda gave a brief shuddering gasp—part protest, part welcome—and slid back on the mattress until her head touched the pillow. I was already half-erect. It seemed impossible, given this warm, ardent, slender-waisted young woman beneath me, that I would remain so. But then I slid up her torso and saw how tightly her jaw was set, and the grimness of purpose in her eyes, and I realized how hard she was working, and how privately. I had to pry her lips open for a kiss; though it must be said that once I did, it was me and not her who broke it.

I paused, hovering above her, avoiding her eyes. A thread of saliva dangled between our mouths for a moment, then fell unclaimed on the pillow.

"I'm sorry," I said.

"It's me?"

"No. Not you. You're beautiful."

"Am I?"

"Yes. Yes you are."

She nodded, satisfied for the moment, though not very. For a while we merely lay there, trailing our hands over each other's bodies, registering the somehow too-smooth feel of each other's skin—which even as it rewards our instinct to explore can defeat our need to catch hold and rest—and experiencing in the silence that Wild West condition that arises between new lovers, of there being so much open frontier and so few laws governing the territory. The whole time my manhood hung like a comma, benignly suspended between us. Magda did not go very far out of her way to conceal her disappointment with it. And in case I missed the point, she went ahead and told me. "It's just that this has never happened to me before."

"Well, consider yourself lucky. It's happened to me."

"Aaron," she reflected after a moment, "never has this problem."

"No?"

"No."

"Well," I said, "fuck *him*."

"Do you have to be so nasty about it?"

"I'm sorry. It's just . . ." I found that among the other things I could not do at the moment, I could not complete my own thought. Just what? Just nothing.

"*Nu?*" she said petulantly. "What now?"

"Well, there are other ways to enjoy each other, you know. Other parts of ourselves we can, you know, use . . . I mean, to, well, stimulate each—"

"Oh," she said. "You mean oral sex."

I nodded.

"You don't need to be so delicate. Aaron used to do that all the time when we were first married. We did everything then—even sixty-nine." She smiled privately, even a little smugly, and went on to explain, "Most Hasidic men, they're completely in the dark on such things. They know only the basics, if that."

"So what happened?"

"What do you mean?"

"I mean why did he stop?"

Her smile faded. "You don't understand," she said. "It wasn't him, it was me. I *wanted* the basics."

Okay, I thought, *time to go*. I looked down at our clothes, which in discarding we'd abandoned to the abstract expressionist chaos on the floor. My pants were by the side of the bed, within easy reach. Put them on and go home. I had always wanted to be an artist but it seemed the only thing I had a talent for was the art of escape. Why not do what I was good at? What came naturally? Why not escape right now?

And yet despite all the good reasons to do it, or else because of them, I was unable to leave. "Maybe we could just talk a little," I suggested. "That might help relax us both."

"*Nu*, if you need to relax so much, maybe you should smoke more marijuana."

"Good idea."

She heaved out of bed with a sigh and went over to the desk, rummaging in the top drawer. Her back was sinewy and wide-shouldered but so thin around the waist that the sudden flare of her hips was a surprise. Then the hard tight plum of her bottom, like a boy's; the swell of her fullish thighs, the down just visible in the half-light; and the precipitous narrowing of the calves, their tiny incurving muscles flexing as she leaned forward. Perhaps it was not a beautiful body but it was a desirable one, and I was nothing if not filled with desire. How to coax it out?

"There's only these little seeds." She held up a small film canister and gave it a shake. "Can you smoke these?"

"Nothing else?"

"No. All gone," she declared, looking into the drawer.

"That's okay. Bring the seeds over. I'll eat them."

She watched skeptically as I took a handful and threw them into my mouth. They were dry and acrid and tough to penetrate and I seriously doubted they would have the slightest effect on me other than to cause stomach problems later. Still, desperate times called for desperate measures.

I held up my hand. "Want some?"

She shook her head. There were things she was willing to do to her body and things she was not willing to do; clearly this fell into the latter category. But she continued to watch me with interest, wondering what fool thing I was going to suggest next.

"Okay," I said. "Now let's talk."

"What about?"

"I don't know. How about telling me some more of those Hasidic stories."

"Ach," she said. "That will excite you?"

"It might."

Unconvinced, she climbed back onto the bed. I opened my arms but she did not return to them. Instead she lay on her back, not under the blankets but over them, and from this unhindered position addressed herself to the ceiling. "Okay, so," she said, flexing the bones of her feet, "I'll tell you. I don't think you'll like it so much, but it's very good. It's one of Nachman's."

"Never heard of him."

This nearly derailed her right away. "Nachman of Bratzlav? But you *must* have." First my limp penis, now this. Was there no end to the disappointments I would inflict on her that evening?

"Well," she said, "there are two boys, friends from the same village. One leaves home to seek his fortune in the outside world. The other remains in his father's house. This one becomes a simple shoemaker. He has very little money and trouble with his wife, who nags him. But all the time he insists on being happy. At supper he tells his wife, pass me the aperitif, and she hands him a glass of water. Wonderful, he says when he takes a drink. Now the golden soup. Again she gives him water. Wonderful, he says. Now the sweet meats and potatoes. This time she gives him a piece of black bread. And so on, through the vegetables, the wine, the dessert. Just bread and water, she gives him, but he tastes all the flavors he dreams of tasting.

"Meanwhile his friend who went off to the city has studied philosophy, science. He's become so smart he can't talk to anybody. No one satisfies him. Knowing so much, he's always comparing his situation to others, and so he's never content."

After a moment, I said, "That's it?"

"Oh, there's more. I don't remember the whole thing. It goes on and on. Somehow in the end the second friend is rescued by the first. In Yiddish we say, 'brought to dry land.' "

"You were right," I said. "I don't like it."

"Maybe I didn't tell it right. I have no head for stories. Aaron's the one you sh—" She stopped and looked at me. "Anyway, what do you care? Now you're so relaxed, you're falling asleep. You have your eyes closed."

"Oh, I always do that when I'm in bed. It helps me relax."

"Even when a woman's there you close your eyes this way?"

"Yes."

"An idealist," she groaned. "No wonder your thing won't stand up."

"Hey, I assure you, my thing would stand up perfectly fine if you'd stop talking about it."

Having said this, however, I did not feel quite so confident it was true. I opened my eyes to look at her. Her face was like a distant planet, white and round and blurry around the edges where the hair fell upon it; even the blinking, shuddering lines of her features seemed impelled by the tides and gases of space. And then I had an inspiration.

"Take it off," I said.

"What?"

"You know what."

"Don't be silly. How will that help anything?"

"I don't know. Let's try it and see."

"No."

"Why not?"

"Because," she said, "it's immodest."

But this explanation must have sounded, even to her, rather lame under the circumstances. "Oh," she sighed. "Very well."

She tilted her head back, fixing her eyes disdainfully on some point on the ceiling. Then, with one quick sweep of her hand, she pulled off the black wig.

Underneath she was not, as I'd anticipated, completely bald. A short layer of silky, colorless hair covered the slopes and hollows of her scalp like a growth of new grass. I reached out and ran my hand over it. So smooth and, in its way, lush. For a moment it was as if I had never touched human hair before, never experienced what, in its particulate fineness, human hair could be. Mindlessly I ran my palm over it a second time, then a third. Magda arched her neck, perhaps involuntarily, to accommodate me. Her eyes were open wide and still fixed on the ceiling; her breaths were fleet and shallow. I had no idea what she was experiencing. I had no idea what *I* was experiencing—only Magda, experiencing Magda. Like a blind man in love, I ran my palm back and forth over her rounded, fuzzy scalp, reading it like a cartographer, the plush plains, the scrubby hills, the tapered coasts of her temples running down to the high smooth sea of her brow. Somehow it all seemed dimly familiar, a place I may have been once, or flown over in dreams, a long time ago. In a sense I was flying now. And Magda was flying alongside me. I thought of how skin looks when a scab is peeled away—already there, already sealed and complete, already serving a purpose to which no one is privy. Her hair was like that. And as I moved my hand around within it, what had been previously soft and formless in me began to stir.

"So?" she said, almost haughtily, shaking my hand off. "You're satisfied now?"

"Not quite," I said.

"What else?"

"I'm going to cut mine off too." I hopped out of bed and began looking around the cluttered room for a scissors. But all I could find were some nail clippers. Could those work?

"Crazy person!"

"Will you do it for me? I don't think I can do it myself."

"No. Who's being theatrical now? I thought you wanted to talk."

"I do," I said. I looked at the nail clippers with some amazement. Had I really been about to use them on my hair?

I turned to face her. "I want to know why you don't have children."

"That," she said, "is not your business."

"It's him, isn't it?"

"It's not your business, I tell you."

"It's him," I persisted. "Which is why you flew to Houston. Also why he threw us together, and why he's not here tonight, and why you came on to me before, and why—"

"I told you, his car broke down. And that's not why I came on to you, as you put it."

"Tell me the truth. I'm the sperm donor, aren't I? I'm the designated hitter. I'm the guy who's supposed to give the poor Brenners their baby. Isn't that the plan?"

"You don't know what you're talking about."

"Then tell me, damn it. Tell me what I'm talking about."

She didn't tell me anything, however, for a minute or two. She busied herself gnawing at a thumbnail, yanking on an earring, scratching at a wrist. Finally she seemed to tire of hurting herself in these familiar ways. She looked around, picked her wig up from where it had landed on her nightstand, and placed it in her lap, where she proceeded to pick at it awhile, her hands meandering dreamily through its tresses, like someone stroking a house cat. "Aaron and I," she said, "are an unusual marriage."

"No shit."

"*Baal Tshuvahs* generally marry other *Baal Tshuvahs*. It puts less strain on both partners, the adjustment and so on. But Aaron was different. He'd come late to Hasidism and he was in a big hurry. He didn't mind strain, he said. He wanted total involvement. As soon as we met I could see it. We had a long talk one night. Then another talk. In both cases the talks were on general subjects only, but we were hearing more than we were saying, I think. Then he asked me if I wanted to marry him, and I said yes."

"And that was it?"

"For me it was enough. I know it sounds funny. But you know what a good talker Aaron is, how much he throws himself into things. I was a lazy girl, the youngest, still living with my father, may he rest in peace. He pampered me my father, maybe more than he should have. Six weeks I worked as a secretary for a very nice lawyer in Cobble Hill. Then what did I do? Quit. I was above such work—that's the sort of person I was. Proud, spoiled, superior. I needed someone strong and fresh like Aaron to challenge me." She bunched the wig in her fists. "Oh, I trusted the Rebbe's wisdom, sure. But that by itself wasn't what made me decide. If I hadn't admired Aaron I would have said no."

"Well," I said, "there's nothing like admiration."

"You don't understand," she said. "How could you? You go to the movies and see how people love each other and then you think every other way is wrong. For you it has to be all one person. This one person has to provide all the meaning in your life, fill every gap. If they don't you divorce them. For you it's simple."

"Not so simple," I said. "It's never that simple."

"Well, we don't ask so much of a person. There are other sources of meaning—prayer, study, charity work, family . . . This I think is why our marriages last longer than yours. We don't disappoint each other so much. When you have fewer options, maybe you work harder and don't resent so much. Unless . . ."

"Unless what?"

"Unless something goes wrong," she said. "I mean, for no reason. Like my father dying. Like . . . Aaron's family, they don't understand what he's doing, so we were isolated right away. Then it's harder, maybe. Then maybe it matters that we didn't know each other first. When there's only the two of you at the table on Shabbos, then . . ."

She lifted her thumbnail to inspect it again. Before she could do it any more damage, I reached out, took her small hand, and placed it between mine. "Listen," I said, "no offense. But what does any of this have to do with me being here in your bed?"

"Here?" She looked startled. "Oh, it was just an idea I had today, when we were in the car. Do you remember? You had the map out, and you were going on about all those places you knew, how much there was to see. I thought, *How hungry he looks. How much he wants.* For the first time I saw why Aaron liked you. You have no idea what it feels like, to be wanted by someone who wants so much. You can't help wondering, what would it change?" She lifted her bare head defiantly, as if challenging me, or anyone, to argue with her logic.

"And Aaron?" I was conscious of using the name this time, though my throat thickened around it. "Did he want this change too?"

"I told you, he had nothing to do with it. He never asked me to do anything. He doesn't think that way. In the beginning, after we met you on the plane, he just thought maybe we could, you know, help each other. I think he just felt you were a confused person he could help, as he'd been helped at a confused time in his life. And then after Houston, things seemed so hopeless, and we were getting along so badly the two of us, and all those medical procedures were so awful for him, the things they made him do . . . maybe it was that. Or maybe being a *Baal Tshuvah* and never completely giving up that other life. Not *wanting* to. Maybe a lot of things. Maybe he lost faith in waiting. Maybe in himself, and in me too I think. And maybe he looked around at all the people he knew and—"

"He chose me."

"I think," she said, "it's more complicated than that. I think we all chose each other."

"Did he think if I got you pregnant that would solve everything?"

"I don't know what he thought. We hardly speak anymore."

"What about what you thought?"

"I didn't think anything."

"I find that hard to believe."

"Of course you do," she said. She picked up her wig and fit it back over her scalp. "I think you should please leave now."

"No," I said.

I might have slapped her; she looked that stunned.

"Listen: for months people have been telling me to just do what I want to do. Well, I want to stay here tonight. That's what I want."

"But you can't do anything, so what's the point?"

"The point is we've already started. We're halfway there."

Thoughtfully she examined her toenails. The color in her cheeks went through a number of changes, as if the very capillaries were colliding in her head. I sensed an opening, and made for it.

"I want to do it differently, though. I want to try and do what you said, play by the rules, make it a holy thing. I want to know how. Say we were a normal Hasidic couple, just for argument's sake, spending a normal Friday night. What would we do?"

"Ach—" She made a gesture of futility with the flat of her hand. "We're not normal."

"But suppose we were. What would we do?"

"No, no. We've already done it all wrong. First you'd have gone to the *mikvah* . . ."

"What's that?"

"The ritual bath. For purity."

"What about you? Don't you go?"

"Yes. But it's for the man to go at sundown before Shabbos. Women go a week after their period. To cleanse themselves."

"Let's go, then. Right now."

"Ridiculous. They're all closed now. They won't open again until Sunday."

"Well, let's make our own then. You have a bathtub?"

"Of course we have a bathtub."

"We'll do it there."

Before she could successfully discourage me I was already hopping out of bed again and padding barefoot down the dark hallway toward the bathroom.

Hygiene-wise, the bathroom was not much of an improvement over the bedroom. The hamper could not accommodate its load of dirty laundry. The cap was off the toothpaste, the towels smelled of mold, and bottles of shampoo that looked old enough to vote lay toppled like tenpins against the windowsill. As in the bedroom, a tiny bulb was plugged into the wall socket, just above the sink, bathing the porcelain and the tiles in its anemic, sepia glow. It occurred to me that the Brenners had installed them to circumvent the commandment against turning lights on and off on the Sabbath. Sneaky. But I had met enough attorneys in my time to know that people who study the law are a good deal better than the rest of us at getting around it.

Magda, reluctantly pulling on her bathrobe, trailed after me down the hallway.

"You don't understand," she said, leaning sleepily against the door frame as I filled the tub. It was one of those huge bear claw bathtubs from the forties, the surface deeply veined, the drain area crusty and calcified with rust. Still, compared to the rest of the place it was pretty clean. No hair, no mold, no rings. "There are *laws* concerning the *mikvah*. The women go in one, the men in another. The water, the size of the space, the steps you take beforehand—it all has to be done right. Otherwise it doesn't count."

"If we make it count, it counts. I'm quoting you now. Am I wrong?"

She frowned and drew the bathrobe a little tighter around her. She was no logician, I could see that. Aaron was the debater, the one with the ready answers; she had only her life, which for all its limitations must have seemed relatively tidy and coherent until she met me. Or had it always been in this state? There were so many areas in which I had yet to penetrate her.

"There are laws," she asserted faintly.

"So what are they? Tell me some of them."

"Well, first you'd have to take everything off."

"I already have," I said.

"Not just clothes. Band-Aids, splinters, contact lenses, everything. You have to floss your teeth. You have to cut your nails. You have to clean the wax out of your ears. You have to blow your nose. Every part of you has to be exposed to the water; otherwise the *tevilah* is invalid."

"What's *tevilah*? What's that mean? And where's the floss?"

"Immersion," she said. "The floss is right there. In the medicine chest."

"Here. You take some too."

Her eyes took on a dull, recessive glaze as I raced around her bathroom. I might have been peddling some kind of insurance which she had already bought a long time ago from another agent, and which in any case she had no present use for. But she was too tired to resist. Numbly, abandoning all pretense of will in the matter, she too enacted the preparations. She flossed her teeth, cleaned her ears, cut her nails. She wiped away her mascara with a washcloth. Then she reached into the cabinet and pulled out, from the depths of its clutter, a slender blue case.

"Contacts?" I asked.

"It's so unusual?"

"No, of course not. I just . . ."

"I'm blind without them. Legally blind. Even with them I have trouble. I bump into things all the time."

"I wear them too," I said.

"Well you better take them out. The bath is almost ready."

I did, and left them on the side of the sink—two perfect ovals, tinted the palest blue. The moment they were out the room thickened and went fuzzy at the edges.

"You go first," she said. Shutting the medicine cabinet, she took one farewell look in the mirror, then turned away.

"Why not together?"

"Because we don't do that. And even if we did there isn't room. I told you. The water has to touch you everywhere."

"Okay, okay."

I put one foot in the bathtub. The water was warm, about body temperature; the porcelain beneath it cool and smooth as butter. Slipping in I had a brief sensation of dread. I ran my hands along the walls, measuring their height and solidity, their slickness. The tub was bigger than it looked from the outside. Once in, would I ever be able to climb out again?

At the same time I knew that was silly: it was only a bath, and I'd taken countless baths in my time. "Now what?"

"Now," said Magda, "you go under."

"All the way, you mean? Head too?"

"All the way. Keep your eyes and lips closed. But not too tight. Don't clench your fists. And remember to open your arms and legs so the water can reach you everywhere. When you're immersed, the Rebbe says, you're like an unborn child in the womb."

"That's it?"

She nodded. That wasn't it, I could see in her face, but it was enough for now. For me.

"Okay. Here goes."

The tub was not really big enough to allow me to spread my arms and legs more than a couple of inches; thus constricted, I leaned my head back and experienced for a moment a sudden spasm of nausea, which I took to be the sheer electrical tension of my resistance. There was a great deal of it to contend with. I slid down to the bottom, falling and then rising again to hang, suspended, an inch or two above it. I felt as if I were being lowered on ropes into the cavern of myself. Vaguely—it might have been happening far away—I could hear the trickle of displaced water spilling in tiny increments over the lip of the tub and onto the tiled floor, and that too seemed to be some part of me, trickling away. Instinctively I reached out a hand to contain it, but it seeped through my fingers. Then I gave up, and leaned back a little farther, and the water did its work, and some of the tension in my shoulders and spine began to dissolve, and I saw sea lights blinking and sea horses wheeling and my nausea was gone and there came floating through my head, as in a dream, Magda's instructions not to clutch my hands upon immersion but to keep them open. *Very well*, I thought. *Let it all through.*

A pale moon hovered above me, absorbing or reflecting the light. After a while, I willed myself up toward it.

"Are you crazy? I thought you'd never come up. Are you out of your mind?"

"I'm fine," I said. "I was only down for a second."

"A second?" Magda looked frantic. "I thought you were going to kill yourself. Crazy person!"

"Not crazy. Purified. Can't you tell the difference?"

She regarded me levelly for a moment. "Can't *you*?"

It so happened I couldn't. I felt giddy and elated, ready to try anything. "What happens next?"

"You want the rest?"

"Everything," I said.

"And no more craziness?"

"I promise."

"Okay," she sighed. "Next we say a blessing. Then two more dunks in the *mikvah*."

"Okay, good. Let's do it."

"*Baruch ataw adonai elohanu melech ha'olam asher kidshanu b'mitzvotav vitzivanu al ha'tevilaw*." She nodded. "Now you repeat."

I repeated the words. The unfamiliar consonants rolled in my mouth, heavy as jawbreakers, pushing my tongue in awkward directions. I did not know their meaning, of course, but it seemed less of a betrayal of the agnostic spirit to pray in a language one did not understand. Another shortcut. But I was willing, I thought: I was *doing*. And there had to be something in that.

Happily, the second immersion brought no feelings of dread whatsoever. In fact this time it seemed perfectly natural, given how much of the human body is water, that I found myself within it and at rest, that it felt so much like home. Nonetheless I had it in mind not to scare Magda any further by staying down too long, so I made it a short trip.

"Okay," she said, wiping the water out of my eyes with a towel. "Last time."

"Don't we say the blessing again?"

"No. Only once."

Grabbing her by the wrist, I urged, "Come with me. Let's do it together."

The suggestion seemed to amuse her. "But we can't."

"Sure we can. Look." I pointed to my penis, which was no longer shyly hiding its head, but now bobbed cheerfully in and out of the water. "Check it out. Hard as a redwood."

But her contacts were out, and her gaze skated over me in a slow, distracted way that suggested she could not see what I wanted her to see, even if she wanted to see it. "No," she said emphatically. "It's impossible."

"Come on. Just for the adventure."

"Impossible," she repeated. She put a hand to my cheek, running it against the stubble. Her palm was warm and dry, and as it lingered, cupping my face, it managed to convey—more than our kiss in the car, more even than our foreplay in the bedroom—the first real tenderness to pass between us.

Nothing I had done was enough. Both of us understood that now. Even with her wig off, her scalp bare and pulsing under my hand, I had failed to locate her. Or she had failed to let me. In the end it came to the same thing.

She looked at me dolefully, her features a blur. "You wanted to do this right, no? So you must go down alone."

"Okay, okay. If I have to, I will."

"*Nu?* Go then."

There was something bittersweet about this one, a kind of early nostalgia that comes with final passage, and I was aware of it even as I broke the plane of the water's surface and felt it rising, miraculously unbroken, around me. That the world's impurities were my own, and that some portion of these were dissoluble in time and water, no longer moved me to surprise. I accepted this the way one accepts all new facts—calmly and with one's whole being, the newness not so much invention as discovery. Everything now seemed perfectly obvious. Of course Jewish people immersed in the *mikvah* once a week to cleanse themselves. Of course they removed all signs of the world's clutter and paste. Of course they said a blessing. Of course there were spirits that made contact under the surface, that took shape on the backs of one's lids, floating in circles, patient, tireless, the light glinting off in rainbow shards, like angelfish, like angels. Of course those things we have bruised, loved, ignored, and feared all come back to us unbidden through the waters, to remind us that nothing disappears, everyone and everything is still around, capable of birth and rebirth, new life. Here, floating by, was my father. Here was my mother. Here was Melinda, my once-wife. Here was the child we did not have. Here was Donna, and Alice, and the child *we* did not have. Here they all were, the real and the unrealized, the dead and the living, in their mute, teeming particularity—laid out like a frieze across time's sloping window, a family of sorts, with generations that stretched forward and backward, messy and clotted and infinite as the stars . . .

High above me, Magda was humming another prayer.

And now I felt something, or someone, very close. A small mass, a cold density in the current, a phantom presence that lurked down at the bottom of things, drifting blindly and soundlessly as if by sonar . . . I could not see his face but I knew him. I knew him. And what's more, I knew he'd been here all this time. I had only been kidding myself over the years, thinking there was distance between us, that I could operate freely and alone. He was here, he was here, he'd been here the whole time.

My brother.

My dead twin, my stillborn other half. My fellow traveler. Yes, if God is a presence we feel but cannot see, then here was my God all right. Here was the silent voice, the undelineated shadow that had stalked me through life—or had it been the other way around?—and whose eternal nothingness was in fact a kind of prophesy, a dark mirror of what I with all my large, unwieldy potential had turned out to be.

Halves, say the Hasids, are not granted in heaven.

This time when I surfaced there was no moon, no towel, no Magda waiting to greet me. I sat there dripping onto myself in the quiet disorder of the bathroom, wondering where it had all gone.

The Brenners' lot, like many in Brooklyn, was long but narrow: only about ten feet separated their house from the Kleins' next door. I could see them now through the window, the Kleins and their children and houseguests, of whom there seemed dozens—without my contacts I could not tell—sitting around a dinner table illumined by candles, the deep black of their clothes and the white light of their faces like a moon in whose orbit I was locked. And yet to me they were only apparitions, no more or less real than those I'd seen underwater; or for that matter, than the pale impression of my own face, which, backlit by the tiny bulb, had superimposed itself upon the glass.

Then from deep in the house I heard the click of a lock, and the squeal of a door on its hinges.

Summoning as much dignity as a naked man in a bathtub, I suppose, is capable of summoning, I stood up. Immediately the room began to swim around me. Even out of the bath, even out here, everything was made of water.

There was a man's voice, and a woman's. Through the closed door it was difficult to tell if they were speaking English or Yiddish. Anyway, it didn't matter. I was pretty certain I knew whom they belonged to.

I reached for my contacts on the sink but could not find them. Had they fallen onto the floor? Hastily I groped for my clothes, which Magda had been thoughtful enough to drape over the hamper. When I put them on they felt warm and roomy, as if my exertions in the bath had caused me to drop a great deal of weight, but there was no time to puzzle over this or to look for my contacts or my shoes or the button I now discovered to be missing from the chest of my shirt. Footsteps were pounding in the hallway. It sounded like a great many of them, a whole posse of vengeful husbands, armed to the teeth.

The hell with dignity. I went straight for the window, heaved it open, and pulled myself through. A steel cyclone fence ran along that side of the house, separating neighbor from neighbor, but there was room to maneuver on either side. I was only about eight or so feet above the ground; it was my intention to jump clear of the whole mess. Eight feet was nothing. Or was it? Actually, eight feet, now that I looked it over, was a considerable amount of empty space.

For a minute I hesitated on the windowsill, belly scraping the frame, deliberating. Next door the Kleins and their friends were ushering in the Sabbath with songs and slivovitz. Did they see me out there, waving like a tree limb in the darkness?

But then, would they even have recognized how banal the whole thing was? A lover fleeing through the bathroom window. How dreary! And yet here it was happening. Though the day had had more than its share of disappointments already, it was this last blow—this familiar bit of bedroom farce—that was in its way the lowest of all.

Another was this: below me I saw a thick stand of rose shrubbery growing against the house. The roses were gone now, but in the moonlight I could make out the lean, aspiring silhouettes of their stems, and smell the dank mulch of their beds, layered with growth and decay, a warning of nature's tangled dualities. The thorns would tear me to pieces if I fell. On the other hand, from the growing intensity of the footsteps behind me, I'd be torn to pieces if I remained where I was.

Make a move. Make a move. Make a move.

A few feet away, the moonlight raked and glittered on the cyclone fence. Hitching up my pants, I fixed it in my sights, and jumped.

THREE VISITATIONS

"So," a voice was saying, "you're finally with us."

I opened my eyes. A television was beaming down at me with its square, open, cheerfully moronic face. Tom was chasing Jerry across some cluttered cartoon landscape, knocking things over, trailing whirling clouds of dust. The soundtrack for this mad pursuit was loud and frenetic. Horns tooted, flutes fluttered, a hundred violins whined and screeched. Cymbals crashed.

"Yo. Down here," said my visitor, standing at the foot of the bed, irritably jiggling a pineapple.

"Warren?"

"Don't even try to talk, Sammy. It's depressing. You sound even worse than you look. And it's my job to tell you, you look pretty bad."

"Mmph. What time is it?"

"Six-fifteen."

"Saturday?"

"Saturday. Saturday night." Warren began to croon to himself, sotto voce, "Saturday night is the lone-liest night of the week."

"Ugh." I felt sluggish and dazed. The lights on the ceiling were harsh, inquisitory; they buzzed over my head like cicadas. The back of my skull ached. So did the front and the sides. It seemed to me I had been meandering along the border between consciousness and unconsciousness for several hours now. Or was it days? The border itself seemed the most meager and transparent of threads. Indeed, when I closed my eyes, the room disappeared at once, and I was still floating in Magda's bathtub, buoyant and immune, and Warren's voice was just a harmless little trickle over the side.

"Christ, look at you. They're saying two weeks in bed at least. That's not even taking into account the concussion, the multiple lacerations. You were lucky, you know; it could have been a lot worse. You practically impaled yourself on that goddamn fence."

"Did I?"

He scowled. "What are you, Spiderman, Mary Poppins, jumping out of windows? I've got news for you, Harry Houdini. We're not kids anymore. We're middle-aged, halfway there. The days are gone when we can stay up all night and do whatever we want to our bodies. After the feast comes the bill. Speaking of which," he said, "how's your coverage these days? Is this going to break you?"

"I don't know. The plan at work is pretty good. I really haven't thought about it."

"Probably better not to. But you'll let me know if you need help?"

"I'll let you know."

"Good." Abruptly, now that the day's business had been transacted, he softened. "How do you feel, by the way?"

How did I feel? In the haze and stupor of the past hours, it was the first time the question had arisen. This by itself seemed a good sign. "Believe it or not," I said, "pretty good under the circumstances."

"Of course you do. So would I, if they doped me up with as much Demerol as they've been giving you all week."

"All day, you mean."

"No, Sammy." He cracked a nut with his front teeth. "I mean all week."

Warren went over to the window. There, framed by moody dusk, he nibbled some pistachio nuts he carried in his pocket, collecting the husks in his palm and then tossing them by the handful down onto the street. "You know, for its age, I've always thought Mount Sinai's a pretty nice hospital. The parking is scandalous but the cafeteria's way superior to ours. The nurses are better-looking. Even some of the doctors seem okay. I wonder what kind of a benefits package they offer."

I tried to shift my weight a little, and groaned with the effort.

Warren turned. "Ah, Sammy, forgive me. I'm just upset. I love you like a brother, you know. Even if you are a total fuckup."

"What're you doing up here, anyway? Is there some conference?"

"What conference? I came to see my good friend Sam Karnish who's lying half-dead in the hospital."

"But I don't understand. How did you know I was in the hospital?"

"I got a call."

"A call? From whom?"

"I don't know. There was a message with my service. It said you'd had an accident and were laid up in the hospital and needed looking after. So I got on the first plane."

Some of the skepticism must have shown in my face, because he quickly added, "Okay, fine, it took a day or two to make arrangements. And I had to square things with Debbie of course. Not that she objected; in fact she was all for it."

"Yeah," I said. "Right."

"I'm serious. My impression is that Debbie has adopted you as her next cause. Now that she's straightened me out, I mean. She says you're unhappy and need people in your life who you can't alienate even if you try to. She has a lot of faith in people, Debbie does. It's very refreshing. Anyway, the point is I got here as fast as I could."

"Well, thanks. It's sweet of you. Of both of you."

"Don't mention it. You'd do the same for me." He narrowed his eyes. "Wouldn't you?"

"Yes, of course I would."

"Don't say of course like it goes without saying. Some things need to be said. Otherwise how do we know?"

"I suppose we could have faith in people, like your wife does."

"Give her a few years," he said. "The world hasn't gotten at her yet. But it will. It will."

Perhaps it was only the Demerol, but Warren, as he stood there nodding knowingly, seemed to have an odd glowing nimbus around him as if illumined from behind. His eyes were bright with secrets and his bald spot gleamed like a sallow halo under the long bars of light.

"What is it?" I asked. "What aren't you telling me?"

"Forget it. Some other time, when you're feeling better."

"Come on."

"Well, it's just . . . how do I say this?" He blew out a long breath. "It seems there's a little bitty Pinsky on the way."

Suddenly I was very tired. I could hardly keep my eyes open.

"Frankly, I'm not sure how it happened. I'm thinking seriously of suing that diaphragm company—they're putting out an inferior product. But anyway, there you have it. This is how the world keeps going, I guess: with a bang *and* a whimper." He frowned. "It's bad timing, of course, what with Debbie in school and all, but she says she can handle it."

"Can you?"

"I doubt it. But who knows? It's possible I've been ready for something like this for a long time, and never knew it." He looked at me closely. "What's the matter? You don't look so hot."

"I'm happy for you, that's all."

"Thanks," he said warily.

I was getting impatient for him to leave. It took a great effort on my part not to say so.

"By the way," I said, "thanks for the pineapple."

"Don't mention it. It was Bando's idea. I'm crashing with him."

"You can stay at my place if you want."

"Thanks but no. You've got enough problems without a houseguest. Besides, Bando needs me. Thea's out on tour so he's lonely. What're these?" He lifted two books that had been lying face-down on the bedside table and inspected their covers. "Hey, William James. Great book. Is this my copy?"

"It might be. It's certainly not mine." Warren was giving me a headache. Why didn't he go already?

"This other one can't be mine. Look . . . it's in Hebrew. What, you taking some kind of course at the New School?"

"Let me see."

Both of the books were used, *heavily* used: yellowed, broken-spined, dog-eared, intricately creased and battered, the pages redolent of coffee and perspiration and some kind of vinegary substance that might once have been wine. The first was *The Varieties of Religious Experience* by William James. The second was not quite a book, only a pamphlet that had been unevenly glued between cardboard covers. The words on the spine and title page were in Hebrew, but when I turned it over, I found that the reverse side was in English. The title was *The Beginning of Words*. The author was a man named Ezra Hook.

"They're not mine," I said. "They must belong to the guy in the other bed."

"What guy?"

I looked over to the other bed. It was empty.

"Buck up, Sammy," Warren said. "You'll be fine. This is a great city, you know. Maybe after Deb finishes her residency we'll move back. Think of all the fun Pinsky Junior could have here. The tabloids, the crowds, those shitty Sabrett hot dogs, the NO RADIO signs in every car, the bums who sell used records and magazines on the sidewalk—God, how I miss them. Those secretaries in midtown with their business suits and running shoes and their heartbreakingly sensible cartons of yogurt . . . wonderful to see them again. I don't know why I ever left."

"You were miserable and lonely and your car had just been stolen for the third time. That's why you left."

He waved me off. "This morning, you know what I did? I went several blocks out of my way to buy a paper from the Indian guy on Broadway I always used to buy from. Every day for ten years I said hello to this man, and every day for ten years he did not say hello back. He'd sit there behind piles of coins, some of them mine, but not once when I needed change of a dollar for the bus did he give it to me. Not once. So now I've moved away and I'm feeling frankly sentimental. This morning I go up to him and hand him a dollar for the *Times*. How are you, Vikram, I say. Haven't seen you for a while, been out of town, got married, a new life. And you know what he said to me?" Warren gave a contemplative snort. "He said, no change today."

Some nurses rustled by in their white suits. I closed my eyes.

"And I'll tell you another thing," Warren said, inspecting the mezuzah that had been nailed to the door frame. "I never thought I'd say this, but I actually miss *Jews*."

I nodded dreamily.

"Oh sure, we've got them in the sunbelt, but down there it's like . . . well, you've seen it. Even the rabbis wear sweat suits. It's the America thing. Wide-open spaces, do whatever you want, cork's out of the bottle, etcetera. It's not like here, where everyone scurries around like a bug."

"And that's what being Jewish is for you?" I murmured. "Feeling like a bug?"

"Hey, Sammy, don't knock it. It may not be shooting Uzis in the desert, but it's better than nothing."

I settled deeper into the false down of the pillows. Through the window I could hear the evening traffic swishing down Fifth Avenue like a rainfall.

"You get some rest," Warren was saying from across the room. "I'll come by tomorrow, and you can tell me the whole sordid story of how you got here. Okay?"

"Okay."

"Good. First, though, I have to pee."

He went into the bathroom and closed the door. Through the wall I could hear his urine splashing merrily in the bowl. Now that I was falling asleep and now that he was preparing to leave I discovered a great deal I still wanted to say to Warren. I was prepared to apologize to him for the trouble I'd caused him; at the same time I wanted *him* to apologize, too, for having left New York and the conspiracy of bachelorhood and failure that had kept us together.

Darkness was coating the window like a glaze. Emerging from the bathroom, Warren brushed a hand across his fly—reassuring himself, as we all do, that we are not too exposed on our travels. My chest went tight: I loved this man. Suddenly all I wanted was to wish him luck down there in America, his new country, with his new wife and new child-to-be. Yes, I wanted to say, you've been ready all this time, babied yourself far too long, as your friend I should have told you. But I was too tired to ask for forgiveness now. At least I should see him out, I thought, I should see him to the door. Then the fog in my head cleared for a moment and I remembered I was in traction. A terrible thing to be in traction, of course. But Warren would understand. He could see for himself that now, for the first time in my life, there was a very good reason why I was unable to move.

Ronnie Oldham arrived at ten o'clock on a Sunday morning, as I was having my bedpan changed. The procedure seemed to engage him. Standing wide-eyed at the foot of the bed, he nodded from time to time in a clinical, approving, and proprietary manner, a visiting hospital administrator on an extended field trip. He was dressed in one of his MIT tee-shirts and a pair of faded ill-fitting blue jeans, on one leg of which three stray Cheerios from that or some other morning's breakfast had attached themselves, apparently without his knowledge. What are Cheerios made of anyway? Even as he settled into the bright blue visitor's chair and crossed his legs, they clung to the denim in a triangular constellation, a tiny hollow planet and its tiny hollow moons.

"I'm sorry," he said. "I was going to bring flowers, but the gift shop was closed."

"Forget it. You've already brought me flowers once."

He regarded me quizzically.

"That dinner at my apartment a couple of months ago. You brought roses, remember?"

"Right. That Jewish girl was there. What was her name? Martha?"

"Magda."

"Right, Magda." From the way he sighed, the name might have held for him some of the same associations it held for me. But he was merely catching his breath from his walk down the corridor. "Well, how are you feeling, Sam?"

"I'll be on my feet in another week. Or so they tell me."

"Good." He nodded, taking me at my word, distractedly folding and unfolding his long wrists. "That's very good."

He looked unsure what to say next. His gaze flickered up to the television, then down again. I'd been watching one of those Sunday morning political roundtables. Ronnie, of course, was never one for politics. His reading consisted of science fiction and technical journals. The universe, bucking and shuddering from explosions, was in the process of expansion; that was plenty enough event for him.

"So, Ronnie," I said, "what's going on?"

"You mean at the office?" he asked with alarm.

"Of course I mean at the office."

"Do you really want to hear about the office now? Or should it maybe wait until you're out of the hospital?"

"I don't know, Ronnie. You tell me."

"Well," he said, "that depends on your mood. How generous you're feeling. How inclined to see the other guy's point of view."

I laughed.

"That's what I was afraid of," he said.

"Oh, go ahead. I'm numbed out on painkillers anyway. You may as well tell me."

"Sam," he said, and took a breath, "you have to understand my position. There I was at the restaurant in my brand new tie, which Ta Shin bought me for the occasion, waiting for you. I thought it'd just be Spurlock and maybe Teagle. But they also brought along Al Moorehead. Also some guy from *Sports* who I didn't even know. They weren't in very good moods either. Teagle kept tapping his pen on the table and glowering at us like why were we wasting his time already, and we hadn't even ordered *drinks* yet. Meanwhile I kept heading off every five minutes to call my machine, to see if you left me a message about coming late. I told them I had an upset stomach. They weren't too impressed by *that*, let me tell you."

I waved my hand. "Go on."

"Sam, I wonder if I'm managing to convey to you how awful it was. These guys are a very intimidating group, Teagle especially. Big arms, thick necks. Expensive clothes. I don't do well around such people. Then they start in with the vodka martinis. I don't drink, as you know, but finally I got so nervous I went ahead and had one. Actually it may have been two. Have you ever had a vodka martini? They're wonderful, aren't they? I think I must have had three or four of them just waiting for you to show up.

"So. By now it's already half-past eight, and they're arguing about some movie I haven't seen, and still no word from you. I thought a fight was going to break out any minute. So, just to break the ice, to distract them, I mean, from how mean they all were and how drunk I was getting and how late you were . . . I started to tell them, in these very general, very tentative terms, understand, about what we'd done so far, and what the data was showing."

"And they hated it."

"Yes."

I sneezed from the air conditioning. Ronnie waited patiently for me to regain my composure.

"Maybe not hated, exactly," he went on, "but they were sort of bored by it, I could tell. There was some yawning, some fidgeting, looking at watches. And I wasn't doing a very good job either, let me tell you. I was nervous and talking too fast. Whenever I started to get into the really good stuff, I could see I was losing them. The whole thing would've been a complete debacle, in fact, if not for Arlen."

"Arlen? Wait—you mean Arlen Ashby?"

"Yes."

"What was he doing there?"

"I don't know. I had the impression it was sort of an accident, like he'd had nothing else to do that night and just came along for the free dinner. But you were right, Sam. Underneath all the booze Arlen's quite a shrewd and interesting character. And he's really excited by stuff like this. In fact it turned out later he'd taken the clip-files on both AIDS and radiation home with him the night before. He actually did *homework*. Can you believe that?"

"I can believe that."

"Well, he started asking me these questions, and some of them, I must say, were really provocative. Pretty soon we were having a discussion, and I made reference to some of the E-mail that's been coming in from Sydney the past week, and the others got curious, and, I don't know, all those martinis . . . things started to move along. Before I knew it Al Moorehead was asking me for advice about his hard drive, and the guy from Sports was showing me Polaroids of his sailboat, and Jack Teagle was smoking his cigar and yelling at me from across the table, which it turns out is what he does not only when he's angry but when he's excited, too."

"What about Spurlock? What did he say?"

"Ray played it very cool. Didn't say a word until later, on the way out. Then he said, and I quote, "This thing has possibilities. Don't fuck it up.""

"That's great."

"Uh huh. He also said to have it in by Tuesday so the fact-checkers and graphics people could get on it. So help me, Sam, unless I heard them wrong, they were talking about the cover.""

"The cover? Wait, you mean the *front* cover?"

"Uh huh." He smiled uncomfortably. "Unless the Pope dies or something like that."

"The front cover? And a byline too?"

"That was my impression."

"Ronnie, that's amazing. I can't believe it."

"I know." He was frowning.

"So wait, you said Tuesday? But so soon?"

"Yes, you see—"

"But do you really think we can get it together so soon? I mean, with me stuck here like this?"

"Well, that's a good question, I . . ."

"I think it's too soon. Definitely too soon. Let's try and put them off a couple weeks. They'll go along. I mean, it's not so topical an issue that they can't push it back a little."

Flushed, Ronnie looked down at his high-top sneakers, and addressed himself to them—the flapping soles, the elaborate ink doodles on the toes, and the hopeless tangle of laces that kept them on his feet. "I knew this would happen," he mumbled. "I'm always telling stories the wrong way around."

It took me a few seconds to figure it out. In that time, all the chemicals that had in the past week been shot or dripped or leeched or otherwise finagled into my body through every available orifice for the express purpose of dulling pain—all kicked in at once. There was a terrific *whoosh*. When it passed, my head felt light and round and full of air, a toy globe. The rest of me felt no pain at all. So little pain did I feel that it seemed to preclude the very possibility of pain. At that moment I was certain I had never felt any pain in the past, and would never feel any pain in the future, even if I wanted to, which I didn't of course. I wanted to feel nothing. Which was what I felt. Nothing.

"Oh," I said. "I get it."

"I'm really sorry, Sam. I'm really, really sorry."

"Don't worry about it."

"I tried to tell them, of course, that there was no way I'd go ahead without you. But you were right: they don't work that way."

"I understand, Ronnie. Really."

"Do you? Well," he sighed, "I suppose it's just the way of things nowadays. The age of the individual is over. The big labs, the think tanks, the team concept—that's where the money's going. Nobody supports the solitary creative talent anymore, working out on the margins."

"Just out of curiosity, how'd it turn out?"

"The piece? Um, okay. They're still fiddling with it up there. They gave it to some of the rewrite people. The idea is to make it scary, but not too scary."

"I see."

"They want to lay out the broad picture. But not *too* broad. They're cutting back on the politics and the question of blame and focusing instead on the opportunities for future global cooperation in this area, given the right leadership and legislation. That sort of thing. Probably it'll wind up so darn upbeat that neither of us will recognize it."

"Don't sell yourself short, Ronnie. You've got a lot of energy and a great head. I think you're headed for the front of the book."

"Well," he said, blushing, "so are you."

"We'll see."

"No really," he said. "Because if this turns out well, all sorts of stuff becomes possible. Remember Scotty Chavez? He had that one cover two years ago and after that he had his pick of people to work with. It could go that way with us, too." By now Ronnie, working hard at enthusiasm, was leaning forward and gripping my forearm in his long hands. "This could be a new beginning, you know, for both of us."

"Let's take it one day at a time for a while, okay? I've got to get out of this bed first."

"Right, right. Of course. That's the first thing." He folded his hands back into his lap. "Ta Shin, you know, has back trouble too."

"Oh?"

"She's on a strenuous regimen of Iyengar Yoga. It seems to really work. You should give her a call when you get out. She'd be happy to recommend a teacher."

Now that there was no pain any longer, I realized it was only the pain that had been keeping me awake. Without that surface tension, I felt myself growing loose and dopey again. "Maybe I will. I could use a teacher."

He nodded, pleased. "Anything else I can do? Anything from the office?"

"The office?"

"Sure. I'm running down there later. Want something from there?"

Yes, I thought. Six years. I want six years back.

"Just give my regards to Arlen. If you remember."

"Sure I'll remember. He thinks very highly of you, you know. He told me so at lunch the other day."

"Arlen," I said, "has a weakness for losers."

"You're not a loser," Ronnie said quickly. "You're just having a rough patch."

"Yes, right. I'm just having a rough patch."

"The first thing is to get out of the hospital. That's the first thing."

"First things first."

"Right."

"First one goes out. Then one returns."

"Um, sure, Sam. That's how it works.

"There's an inward science too. It's in Reb Hook. The light of hearts, the radiance of souls . . ."

"Reb who?"

". . . it's all written down. There are two kinds of people. There are masters of proportion, and there are chaotic souls. The world for them is a chamber of yearnings . . ."

Ronnie's look of alarm intensified. "Reb *who*?"

". . . all written down . . ."

"Sam, hey, are you in pain?"

"Yes," I said, "and no."

"Good Lord. I'm getting a nurse."

"Good Lord."

Then Nurse Díaz was leaning over me, her tiny cross dangling herkily-jerkily from its silver chain, just above my nose. As if we were lovers, I thought. Lovers at the far end of a kiss, with one frail bridge of saliva between us . . .

"Okay, hon," she whispered, administering a fresh needle, a fresh puncture, "just relax, now, just relax . . ."

I did as instructed. The last thing I saw before I went under was her wide, overburdened face and the deep black windows of her eyes—the veined webs in the corners, the taut pupils and their surrounding aureoles, flecked and stippled with gold.

"I have unreal hands. The things I see are not real things . . . Persons move like shadows, and sounds seem to come from a distant world."

This passage—I came across it in the James book—pretty well sums up my days and nights in the hospital, the stillness and quiet of their duration, the weatherlessness. I had fallen deep into a net, and there was nothing to to but lie there until I was released. Down on Fifth Avenue, the buses shuddered and roared and the drumbeats of construction pounded, but the din could not climb high enough to reach me. I was exempt from New York, out of the loop. My watch had been put away somewhere and I had no idea what time it was: in a sense it was all one day.

In bed, staring at the ceiling, I thought of all the other beds and all the other ceilings, all my previous spells of immobility— on my office carpet, and at the *bris*, and out in right field, and standing at my living room window—and it began to seem credible that these periods of inertia had been more than plain inertia. Perhaps they had been stops on a journey of sorts, or perhaps they were themselves the journey. But a journey to where? I did not know the Bible, I did not know how to meditate, I had nothing like a coherent creed and nothing like a coherent desire for one. And yet I knew how to lie down. I'd always *needed*, for some reason, to lie down. Was it possible that for people like me, lying down was a form of transcendence?

To puzzle this out, I turned to the books that had been left on my bedstand.

James I devoured all at once, in a kind of ecstatic trance. Reb Hook went down a good deal slower. The book was a meditation upon *Gematria*, a form of Jewish numerology in which each letter of the Hebrew alphabet was assigned a number, and each number could be interpreted to reveal hidden esoteric codes and meanings. For example, the fact that the Bible begins with the second letter of the alphabet, *Bet*, could be interpreted to mean that God created everything on two levels: the heavenly and the earthly. But this divisiveness was so great that afterward, unlike all the other days of creation, God did not say "It was good." However on the third day, the Torah states, not once but twice, that "it was good." Which meant there was a *third* dimension to creation, one that successfully healed the divisiveness of the first two days.

This struck me as good news. I was searching for a third dimension myself, a synthesis of inner divisions. I hadn't been kidding with Ronnie: I really was eager for a teacher. Skimming the pages, phrases would lodge in my head for a while and then pass back out again, as if the book were somehow skimming *me*. *Zohar* and Kabbala . . . Strange fires, chaotic souls . . . The end of days, the remaking of the world—and always, everywhere, these fractions and dualities. Even the dimensions of the holy ark, which wandered with the Jews in the desert, were marked by halves. Why? "To teach," the reb wrote, "that the incomplete is more attractive and acceptable to God than the whole."

Another thing I learned about the ark that day was what was actually inside it—*Nothing*. The ark was empty. A wind-box, a hollow vessel, a barren womb. Apparently there is nothing that compels one forward like an absence.

Absence, wandering, incompleteness. Well, I thought,

marking my place in the book, if these were the traits that the Jewish God valued, wait until He got a load of me.

In the end, however, I suppose I am really a material being, with a limited capacity for otherworldly travel. After a while the inaction and silence began to wear me down. The hum and flow of the hospital—the doctors cruising by on their rounds, the stop-and-go traffic of visitors on their hushed, fearful errands, the ghostly echoing hollowness that swallowed the place after hours, like a deserted underground parking lot—had not seemed quite real to me at first, but as the first week turned into the second, it came to seem almost *too* real. That Italian lady with brain cancer in the room across the hall, where did she go? Home to Bensonhurst? Or to that other home, the one that waited, sun-shot and silent, at both ends of life's circular driveway? What about the girl without kidneys in Room 313? What about that architect in the AIDS ward? They were around the week before but they were not around now. And that pineapple Warren brought me, why did Nurse Díaz put it in the refrigerator at the nurses' station? Because natural things perish. This was the lesson the hospital could teach and that books could not. Consciousness might hang around forever, but matter did not. Matter *mattered*. And time was precious.

This, it seemed, was the real inward science: not the going out, but the return.

And so all at once I became very busy. The phone, which had been my nemesis for months, I now put to use. First I called my insurance company, and was told they would cover eighty percent of my expenses. To cover the remainder, I called my broker and arranged to sell the last of my father's stocks. It was not the way anyone had ever imagined the money would be spent. But it was necessary, and I wasn't going to sit around feeling regretful about it.

Then I put in a call to Ray Spurlock. "I hear you've taken my advice," he said. "I told you to try staying in one place. Little did I know. How are you, bucko?"

"Not so bad."

"Famous last words."

"No, really. I'll be out of here in a few days. I'm just calling to confirm I still have a desk to come back to."

Spurlock took a moment to answer. "Well," he said, "yes and no. Yes, there's a desk to come back to. No, it isn't yours."

"Whose is it?"

"Gene Unger's."

"Gene? But I thought he had life tenure, like the Supreme Court."

"So did he," said Spurlock. "But he handled it well, let's give the man credit. He made a nice little speech at lunch, quite moving in its way. Turns out the man is not without charm. Who knows, he might have been waiting for a shove like this for years. Some people need to be shoved, don't they? Or else they'd never move."

"People need to get past things," I said, "in order to see them clearly."

"Are you all right, bucko? You sound different somehow. You're not sore about that AIDS piece, are you?"

"No."

"Because I had no choice. There was an empty space that had to be filled. You realize that, don't you?"

"Sure, Ray."

"If it's any consolation, I recognized your hand in there in a couple of places. A bit sloppy, but some artful flourishes. You continue to show signs of development."

"Thanks."

"See you next week then?"

"I think so, yes."

"Next week," he said.

As it happened, I no longer had the same car to go back to, either. Left too long in one spot on West End Avenue, that rough beast had died a slow, noiseless death and been towed to the purgatory of the impoundment lot. All this was reported to me shamefacedly by Bando, who had taken the thing over from Warren Pinsky, who had fetched it back from Brooklyn for me. Somewhere along this circular chain of responsibility the car itself got lost. Still, I didn't mind. Letting it go would save me a number of delinquent insurance and registration fees. And I was happy to be consigned to public transport for a while—part of the collective urban fate, subject to the whims of a larger engine, steered by a larger hand. No, the loss of my car was not a loss at all, in my view, but a gain. I was cutting down again, freeing myself of unnecessary burdens.

Of course nobody ever frees himself for long. Soon enough it's time to get back in the game and start acquiring a whole set of new ones.

This was a process my mother, for one, seemed to know a good deal about. When I finally called she sounded frazzled and distant. Hearing that I was in the hospital and hadn't told her, and was about to exhaust the last of my father's legacy to boot, did not exactly lift her spirits. "And I was hoping you'd help me *move*," she said.

"Move? Move where?"

"I found a condo, honey, across town. It's only one bedroom, but there's a foldout sofa in the living room. And it's not too expensive or tacky. In fact it's quite nice. Nice and new."

"Are you sure that's a good idea, Ma? I mean, one bedroom? Is that even big enough?"

"How many beds do you think I need?"

"But what if your circumstances change? What if you meet some old stud at the library and want to shack up?"

"Samuel," she said. "For God's sake."

"I'm just saying, you don't have to do this. You can stay where you are. I can fix up the house for you."

"Oh really? Since when?"

"What I mean is, I can try."

"You fix yourself, honey," she said. "That's what I want. You in one piece. By the way, did you like the present?"

"What are you talking about?"

"I thought you might like to have that picture. I had it reframed for your birthday. Probably you'll find it waiting for you back at the apartment."

There was a pause. I was aware that it was my turn to say something.

"I thought you'd be pleased," my mother said.

"I am, Mom. It's just that I really have to go now."

"Go where? Aren't you still in bed?"

"Let's talk tomorrow," I said. "I'll call you in the morning."

"You'd better," she said, and hung up.

There was one last call to make.

Dialing the number, fragments of the day's news washed through my head. Losses and gains, random shoves of fate. Motion ceaseless and eternal. And here came another birthday: Thirty-six. Past the halfway mark now. And yet this was a very good number, someone had told me. Then I remembered who that someone was.

"Hello?"

"Alice, it's me."

"*Daddy!*"

"No, pal," I said. "It's Sam. Remember Sam?"

"Oh," she said, recovering. "Hi."

"Listen, is your mom there? Can I talk to her a minute?"

"Mommy's taking a nap. On the couch."

"She is?"

"Uh huh. She has her shoes off and everything."

"All right, well, do me a favor, okay? Can you take down a message?"

"I don't know how," she complained.

"Well, if I tell you, will you remember? Can you keep a message in your head, do you think? Just until your mommy wakes up?"

She thought about it a moment. "Is it long?"

"No way. Very short. Very short and simple."

"Okay," she said tentatively.

"All you have to tell her is, I'm sorry. I'm so sorry."

She giggled. "That's all?"

"That's all."

"I can remember *that*."

"Can you? I hope so."

She laughed. "You always say that. You always say I hope so."

"Do I? Well, I suppose you're right."

There was a pause.

"Know what?" she whispered.

"What?"

And her next words, this four-year-old girl who could not as yet write her own name, let alone take down a message, conveyed a degree of empathy for adults and their affairs that some might call precocious and others, tragic: "I say it a lot too."

"Take care of yourself, Alice. I love you a ton."

"Bye-bye," she said.

Outside the sky was low and dark, the rain pouring in sheets. I lay there with my hand on the phone, watching it fall.

"What's the matter?"

My physical therapist, a perky young rock 'n' roller named Amy Linck, had come in for our session, and was giving me a frank look over her personalized coffee mug. "Convalescent blues?"

"I suppose so."

"Cheer up. You're making great progress. You know, at first I thought you'd be a lot of trouble. But you're actually very easy."

"Thank you. You're actually very pretty."

When Amy grimaced, a hard light bounced off her teeth and the freckle at the center of her forehead disappeared. She fingered the ID tab pinned to her blouse and shook her big head of spiky hennaed hair. "What is this? That's my fourth pass today."

"You have to understand about us invalids. We have a rich fantasy life. It's nothing personal."

"Yeah yeah," she said. "Tell me about it."

"Forget I even mentioned it."

"It's just I like guys a little younger. It's a more serious generation. They keep themselves up better."

" 'Keeping up is hard to do,' " I crooned sadly.

"Anyway, no biggie. You'll be out in a few days, tops. Then you can get back to your life."

Right, I thought. *My life.*

There was a knock at the door. Both of us turned to see who it was.

"I'm interrupting?" asked the visitor. "Maybe I should come back another time?"

I'd been waiting for him, of course. Waiting a long time. But now that he was here, I found it hard to remember why. Aaron too seemed to be suffering a confusion of purpose. He took three cautious steps inside the door, then hesitated, then took one small step back. From his left hand dangled a shopping bag; in the right he held an umbrella, the point of which he'd been tapping halfheartedly against the door. Both the bag and the umbrella were soaking wet. So were his fedora, his ankles, and his shoes. A puddle was widening on the floor where he was standing, like oil from a leaking engine. He looked around the room, breathing heavily through his mouth, trying to decide where to put down his things.

Amy, having turned to stare at him, now swiveled her neck to stare at me. "You know this guy?"

"Yes."

"Well," she said coolly. "That explains it."

"Explains what?"

"I've seen him before. Out in the hallway, just sitting for, like, hours. I wondered what he was doing."

Aaron Brenner blushed and looked at the floor. "I stopped by once or twice," he said. "Just to say hello. But you were always asleep."

"Shit," Amy said. "It wasn't once or twice."

"And who is the young lady?" Aaron asked me.

"This is Amy, my physical therapist. Amy, this is Aaron. My accountant." It cheered me up a little, I'll admit, laying claim to all these busy professionals.

"Well, if he's an accountant," Amy said haughtily, "he should be better at counting."

"Yes," Aaron conceded. "Maybe so."

By now he had laid out a course to the windowsill, upon which he proceeded with some delicacy to place his umbrella and shopping bag. He waited, with an air of polite apology, for Amy and me to conclude our therapy. I glanced over at him a few times, wondering who it was he vaguely reminded me of. Then I realized that someone was myself. He'd entered in the same halting manner I'd entered his house that first time—not the second time, though; I'd entered differently the second time—and this more than anything alerted me right away to how much he had lost since then.

Silent by the window, he stroked his beard and contemplated the rain. The trees of Central Park were ablaze with color, so perhaps he was contemplating them too.

Meanwhile Amy moved officiously between us, gathering her equipment together, making a few notes in my file. "All right," she said, rushing a bit. "We'll have a longer session tomorrow."

"See you then."

"Righto." She gave Aaron a last look of distrust before she left, but he failed to notice.

"So," he said, turning to me, "how are you?"

"Look, if you mean what is the state of my spiritual life, I don't really think I can say at the moment. It's much too—"

"No," he said, trying to smile, "I meant only, how are you feeling?"

"Oh. Better. Much better, thanks."

"You got the books?"

"I wondered if they were from you."

He shrugged. "I thought you might find them useful. They

helped me at one time. But it's hard to predict. Everyone is different. Everyone has their own . . . their individual needs, and so forth . . ." His voice trailed off into a thicket of private preoccupations.

"They help," I said.

"Good." This time he did manage a smile; it crossed his face quickly, then slipped off the other side. "Terrible out there, isn't it?"

He meant the rain, which was coming down in torrents. The windows were runny and trembling as egg whites; the room was drenched in grays. Nonetheless I could see the changes wrought in Aaron since our last meeting. They weren't subtle. He had put on additional weight around the middle, so his pants, wrinkled and creased, now bulged precipitously under his belt. His face was drawn. There were leaden bags under his eyes that had not been there before; they spoke of long nights' residence in darkened rooms. His forehead was deeply creased. His jacket was creased too; also stained, spattered, and multiply discolored, as if among other indignities he had recently been trod upon by some huge and careless animal. He looked in truth even worse than I did. In his expanding girth another button had popped off the torso of another shirt, and no one had as yet undertaken to repair it.

He cleared his throat. "You know the one about the dog and the weddings?" he asked.

"Is this a joke?"

"A joke, yes, that's right," he said.

I shook my head.

"A dog is invited to two weddings. One is held very near, the other far away. The dog thinks, okay, there's plenty of time to get to the near one. So he runs first to the farther one—and misses it. Now he's out of breath. He turns around and runs back to the nearer one, only the meal is over already and they won't let him in. So he misses both."

"There's a point to this, of course."

"You can't have all the pleasures of this world and the next one both. You can't have the individual appetite and the communal one both. It's impossible," he declared. "You have to make a choice."

"Who is it we're talking about, exactly?"

"You know who we're talking about."

"I'm afraid I—"

But now there was another knock on the door: The orderly rattling in with his dinner trays. At first his haste was such that he did not even notice Aaron. "Karnish?"

"That's right."

"It says here kosher meal. This is you?"

"This is me."

After he had moved on to the next room, Aaron looked at me thoughtfully. "You ordered kosher on the plane to Texas, too," he said. "That's why I first noticed you."

"Oh, that. It's just a trick I learned from a friend of mine. You get served first, and the food is better."

"I see," he said mildly.

"You disapprove?"

"The right action for the wrong reason. But it's not for me to judge." He pointed to the dinner tray. "Maybe you need help with that?"

"I can manage."

"Here." He came to the bed and took the tray from my hands, gently but insistently. Clearly it relieved him to be in motion, to be of use. Frowning, he sniffed at the food. It did not appear to meet his standards. We were sitting close enough at this point that I could feel the pressure of his bones, hear the breath whistling through his nose, smell the oils in his clothing—from rain, from perspiration, from long hours of study on old wooden benches—and count, or so it seemed, every one of the pores that spread like a blackened galaxy across the inner lobes and hollows of his ear. This was what happened, I thought, when you spent time in another man's bed. It gave you too much entry. It opened all the doors and windows between you.

Now here we were on *my* bed. Aaron methodically unfolded

the napkin over my lap, then eased the silverware through the plastic package, peeled the top off the margarine, and, mumbling to himself some prayer or other, spread it over the chewy, tasteless poppy seed roll that was apparently a Mount Sinai specialty. Finally he dug the fork into the wan, gelatinous mass that was supposed to be my kosher chicken Kiev, and directed a piece of it into my mouth.

Patiently he waited for me to finish chewing. "Good?"

"Not bad," I said. "Want some?"

"Thank you but no. I'm eating too much as it is."

He fed me another bite. When I'd swallowed it down, he nodded toward the bag on the windowsill. "I brought you your clothes." He began preparing another forkful. "I thought you'd want them back."

"There must be a mistake. I came here in my clothes. They're in the closet."

"You came here," he said, "in *my* clothes." He cut me another piece of chicken, then turned his attention to the peas. "They were lying over the hamper in the bathroom. My pants, my shirt, from the day before. You must have put them on inadvertently. You were I believe in a great hurry." His mouth gave a rueful twist. "By the way, it might interest you to know. When they brought you here, everyone in the Emergency Room of course assumed you were one of us."

"One of who?"

"A Hasid. A Hasid brought by other Hasids. What did they know from half-and-halfs? You had the clothes, the big nose, even a scratchy little beard." His smile was less mocking than bemused. "So you see, even before you chose the kosher meals, they were prepared to give them to you anyway."

He paused to scrape the last of the peas from the plate, but they rolled off his fork. Suddenly the light of amusement left his face. He looked utterly desolate.

"Where is she?" I asked.

He waved his hand in the air.

"Gone?"

"You didn't know? Flew out the door like a bird."

"No," I said. "I didn't know."

He nodded, digesting this. It did not appear to brighten him any. "Yossi from next door, he came over that night. It was him, you know, who called the ambulance for you."

"Yossi? Not you?"

"I wasn't there. I was out in Hershey dealing with the carburetor. A small job, not expensive, but it kept me there all of Shabbos." He sighed. "I called Magda to tell her. She wasn't home. So I called Yossi. I figured he'd invite her for Shabbos, maybe, everything would be fine. Anyway, he didn't get around to it. They had company, dinner ran long, maybe too much schnapps, they got carried away, who knows? So later he comes with friends to invite her for dessert. She says no. Then she goes past them in a big hurry and disappears out the door. She was in her bathrobe, he says."

"Then what?"

"Then you fell out of the sky and started screaming. Here, you want the Jell-O?"

"No."

"I'll have it then." He wolfed it down in three bites. Crumpling the napkin, he placed it along with the fork and spoon onto the empty tray, and swung the whole mess away from us. "Yossi called the ambulance and rode up with you. It makes no sense, of course: there are a dozen good hospitals in Brooklyn. The Rebbe himself when he had his last stroke went to Maimonides. But for Yossi, Mount Sinai is the one he trusts. Why? Because this is where he had his thyroid operation."

"He rode in a car on Shabbos?"

"Sure he rode. What are we, Christian Scientists? If it's an emergency . . ." Distracted, apparently, by the residue of Jell-O on his hands, he rubbed them against each other, trying to get them clean. "I bought her that bathrobe, you know, on her last birthday. From Bloomingdale's. Sixty-eight dollars it cost."

"I'm sorry," I said.

"Pff. Don't be."

It was not clear to me quite how generally I'd intended the apology, or he'd intended its dismissal. But neither of us seemed eager to push the blame issue any further.

"Where is she now?"

He waved his hand again.

"Well, how do you even know she's okay? I mean, if she was walking around Crown Heights in her bathrobe at one in the morning—"

"She's okay, she's okay. We know a few things." He ticked them off on his fingers. "She used her key to Hava's and spent the night there. Hava and Zev and the boys were still up in Stony Point, so she had the place to herself. She had cereal for breakfast, Raisin Bran. She forgot to put the milk back in the refrigerator as usual. Then she left."

"In her bathrobe?"

"Maybe she took some clothes from Hava's. Don't worry, she knew what she was doing. She stopped at the bank and withdrew half our savings. Also her passport from the safe deposit, which gives me a good idea where she might be."

"Where?"

"Israel. Her sister Miri's over there. Miri she gets along with pretty well. So I left a message on her machine to call if she heard. That was a few days ago." A muscle twitched in his jaw. "Those machines, they're everywhere now. Miri's got one, Hava and Zev have one, Yossi has one. Finally this morning I went to Forty-seventh Street and bought one myself," he told me. "In case she calls."

"What does Hava say?"

"What does Hava ever say? I'm a terrible person. Overbearing, stingy, selfish. Even my sperm are selfish. They don't swim together the way they're supposed to." Now he rose from the bed and went to the window. The rain had slowed and the lights of the city were now visible in their careless clusters, their harsh and transient arrangements. "I drove her to it, that's what Hava says."

"And what do you say?"

"I say the same thing."

"But you don't know that. What would have happened if your car hadn't broken down? There are other factors, you know. Accidental ones."

Aaron shook his head. "The *Besht* says there are no accidents."

"The *Besht* has been dead for centuries. And when he did say things, they were about a simpler world."

"And so?"

"So maybe you drove her a little. Maybe she also did some driving herself."

He nodded wearily, skeptically. He did not go on to say what both of us were thinking: that I had done my share of driving as well.

He stood there in his wrinkled black suit, pondering the evening skyline as if it posed a geometrical riddle he alone could solve. He *was* selfish, I thought. The pious are the most selfish of all. They take ultimate positions, think in absolute terms about things they can't possibly know, and in so doing blind themselves to the true processes of the world, which are often accidental ones, disorderly ones. What was his word? *Inadvertent.* Well that was me, for better and for worse. But Aaron could have used, I thought, a little more inadvertency himself.

He blew out a breath. "It's been," he said quietly, "a lousy year."

I nodded. This was true. It had been a lousy year.

"All this week in shul I kept thinking, praise God it's over. Praise God the year comes and then goes and then there's another one so everything starts again. It may be that's how Magda feels too."

He was silent for a moment. When he spoke next, it was the window he addressed, not me. "Did I ever tell you, Shmuel, how I became a *Baal Tshuvah*?"

"I seem to recall something about the flatness of the world."

He smiled. "Yes, true. But it wasn't so strictly philosophical as that. You see before I left my other life for good, I dabbled a little bit myself. I came into Brooklyn on the weekends. Checking it out, you might say. There was a rebbe I used to study with, very vigorous and learned, generous with his time. And he had this daughter who used to bring us tea."

"Aha."

"Yes. She was only eighteen, this girl. Skinny, moody, lots of black hair. All day she used to sit in the back room drawing pictures—gorgeous, angry pictures. One day I was on my way to the living room and I peeked in. Guess what I saw? A picture of *me*. It was what you'd call I guess abstract, but still, it was me. I knew it was me." Weakly, he coughed into his hand. "So you see, Shmuel, I was right all along. You and I, we aren't so different, not—"

And then he lifted his head and turned, and I could see the red rims around his eyes, and a terrible weight descended. It bore down hard upon my weak spots—the rifts and fissures, the double joints—and squeezed. For a moment I thought I too would cry, but I didn't. Even regret, even grief and loss, I could not give into wholly. The fractions went on forever. Never to feel just one thing, never to be just one thing. I thought of that baby boy crying at the *bris*. Even for the chosen there were two sides to the coin: the joy of election and the pain of entrapment. Even being chosen had its dualities. Because one thing it means to be chosen is this: *being chosen means you have no choice.*

Aaron wiped his eyes and blew his nose into a white handkerchief he'd fished from his jacket. Then he folded the cloth neatly and put it back. "Well," he sighed, "as it says in the Kabbala: judgment at dusk, mercy at dawn."

"So what now? Will you go after her?"

"I don't know," he said. "Will you?"

"I don't think I'm in shape right now to go after anybody."

He nodded slowly. "Neither am I."

"But you're her husband."

"So?"

"So maybe you have a responsibility to try."

He gave this idea his consideration for a moment, as if it were a new wrinkle he had not thought of before. "I may," he said. "It depends on a number of things. I've already presented a petition to the Rebbe to discuss it."

"That old coot? What the hell for?"

Aaron looked at me sharply. "Don't underestimate the Rebbe. He has a superior mind. I value his advice."

"And you'll do what he says?"

"I'll listen to what he says, yes."

"And if he says let her go, you'll let her go without a fight?"

"Enough fights. There've been plenty of fights already. As it says in the Torah, HaShem will fight for you and you shall remain silent."

"But to just hand yourself over like that to a third party," I said. "It's crazy."

"Oh but third parties have their uses, don't you think? Don't forget it was the Rebbe, may his light shine, who gave his blessing to our marriage in the first place. So yes, I'll listen to him. I'll reflect on what he says. I'll pray to God for a miracle and reflect some more. Then I'll decide."

"You understand, of course, that by the time you've done all this listening and reflecting, it may be too late."

"What choice do I have?"

"Get on a plane. Track her down. Tell her you love her. Promise a lifetime of devotion. Better yet," I said, "tell her you'll go into counseling. Women love that."

"They do?"

"Sure. There are plenty of things you can still try, you know. New drugs. In vitro. If that doesn't work, you could get a proper sperm donor. Or adopt. That is, if you really *want* her back. You do want her back, don't you?"

He shrugged. "Everything we want we can't have."

"You can have some things, though. Or would you rather just sit around waiting forever, like you do for that fucking messiah of yours?"

"I wait," he said, "for that fucking messiah of *ours*."

"Well, I've got bad news. He's not coming. What if Magda's as close as you'll get? I say go after her right now."

Aaron frowned. "Listen to the forceful one, flat on his back."

He was right, of course. On the issue of taking an active stance in the world, I was no one to talk. Because even now a possibility shuddered in my chest—perhaps Magda was as close as *I* would get, too.

"Well, Shmuel," he said, rising to his feet. "I have to go. There's a lot I need to attend to."

"Are you coming back?"

"If you want me to come, I'll come."

"Good. What are you doing, say, day after tomorrow?"

"Day after tomorrow?" He was so surprised he almost laughed. "But that's Yom Kippur."

"Oh. I guess you have all that atonement stuff to do."

He nodded.

"That stuff we do, you might say a different way. You might say, At-one-ment."

"Well, whatever. I suppose it's going to keep you in synagogue all day?"

"Probably so." He fiddled with the damp brim of his hat, trying to straighten it out. "And you, I think they intend to send you home pretty soon, no?"

Home. The word echoed trancily in my ears. Home.

"Maybe after the holidays," he said, "we could get together for a meal some night. There's a new restaurant I heard about up near you, on Columbus Avenue. A kosher establishment. We could try it."

"I'd like that."

"We could talk about books. Or music. We could even get high and talk about God. You'd be surprised how much fun that can be."

He said this so gently and with such open good will that I suddenly wondered if I was being patronized, as I had once—

it seemed a very long time ago—patronized him. "I'm sure it would be a blast. But I doubt we'd get too far."

"Where should we get?" he asked. "Is God an answer, or a question?"

And with that he moved toward the door on his soggy shoes. I watched him go with reluctance. In truth I did not believe I would see him again.

"Hey," I called out after him, "you know what I'd really like to talk about? I mean if we ever did get together?"

He half-turned in the doorway. "What?"

"Your system. The one you told me about on the plane. Number two."

"Ah, at the track you mean."

"Yes. Whatever happened? Did you give up on it?"

"Of course not. But I'm making modifications. Soon I'll try out number three." His eyes burned into me. "Every lock has its key. But God loves the thief who breaks the lock open."

"That's good to hear. If things don't pick up, I may be resorting to burglary pretty soon."

Nodding, he glanced around the room one last time. He seemed to be trying to remember something. "I have to go," he said finally.

"I'll call you."

"Call, yes. And if I'm not there—"

"I'll leave a message."

"Yes. Do."

And on that final note of instruction, he disappeared.

Too late, I saw the umbrella lying on the windowsill. It was, I observed upon inspection, the same umbrella Magda had brought to my apartment that night—the one with which she'd been wrestling so unsuccessfully—and after all the wear and tear it looked, I thought, pretty shot. The nylon was frayed at the edges, and several of the spokes were bent. I wondered if Aaron would miss it. Probably not. Umbrellas, after all, were ordinary disposable things, like viruses and sorrows—people were always leaving them behind inadvertently and

then picking up new ones. Who knew where this one had orig-
inated? Or where it would end up? For the moment it lay on
its side at the window, and the movement of the air through
the vents made soft ripples in the fabric, so that it appeared to
be breathing rapid, shallow breaths, and its black folds were
like the wings of some grounded angel, decorative but useless,
protective of no one.

THE HERE AND NOW

"But then he returned to his work as if nothing had happened." That is a saying which sounds familiar to us from an indefinite number of old tales, though in fact it perhaps occurs in none.

KAFKA, "Reflections on Sin, Pain,
Hope, and the True Way"

I suppose that if life does have any geometry, it's a circular one, a curving plane that meets itself coming and going—as, Ronnie Oldham tells me, Time itself does. Such is my thinking, at any rate, as I ride the elevator down to the ground floor, watching the numbers flare on the overhead console, their backward countdown to Zero. And then I am sailing through the lobby, which smells of coffee and flowers, and my foot is triggering the mechanism that governs the glass doors, and as they fly open my reflection splits neatly in half and disappears with a sigh.

The next thing I know I am out on Fifth Avenue in the startling daylight, and everything, even the passing cars, even the dying leaves, looks polished to a shine. And it seems as if the earth in all its clarity has been created for me anew—though of course I know that if anything, it is the other way around.

I stretch, my back unfurling like a flag. Immediately a taxi pulls up as if under a command.

"Where to?" calls the driver.

"What?"

"Where you want to go?"

"Never mind," I say. "I'll walk."

Hefting my bag, I cross the street to Central Park. Birds wheel and cry. The trees are a canopy of fire. A young woman in Capezios races by, long hair flying, then shrinks into a spot in the distance. Forty blocks to my office but I'm in no hurry. I have the park to my right, the street to my left, the towers of midtown laid out before me like a vision. If only the whole thing could go on forever—this sidewalk, this hour, this narrow miracle between rivers; If only I could travel this border through every one of the world's profligate oppositions and come out whole on the other side.

But of course the sidewalk does not go on forever. It ends at Fifty-ninth Street, across from the Plaza. And from there I proceed to my office, to begin picking up the pieces of my life.

There's an article I'd like to write for the magazine some day. The subject: astronauts. What has become of them, now that we have given up on outer space? Is there a halfway house for former astronauts? A twelve-step program for reentry? The adjustments must be considerable. Because it does not seem possible that having had a taste of how it feels to be up there, sprung free of gravity, swimming in starlight, one will easily resume one's place on earth.

I pick up the pieces of my life all right.

Then, once I have it back together, I fly off to Israel.

This time the plane is full of Hasids. Noisily they roam the aisles, fussing with their seatbelts and coats, their shopping bags full of gifts from a prosperous exile. Only during takeoff do they settle down; then once we're in the air they spring back up again, conducting their own business, obeying their own laws. Meanwhile I try to attend to the techo-chat of the pilot and the elaborate pantomime of the stewardess as she instructs us all in the art of survival. And as the great wide-body jet rises, banking steeply over the cemeteries of Queens.

I sit there staring down into the sea of headstones. How urban the dead are. How densely configured. Plant all the trees and flowers you want, but there the stones lie in their stark, labyrinthine formations, like some sprawling and unprosperous outer borough.

"First trip?" asks the man next to me. To my great relief, he is not a Hasid.

"Yes."

"Business?"

"Not exactly."

And with that, his curiosity is exhausted. He folds his *Wall Street Journal*, puts away his reading glasses, and closes his eyes. He wears a double-breasted suit and Italian shoes. His hair is fine silver, his face pouchy but vigorous. The face of someone whose season tickets are honored, whose handicap is low, who has investments that accrue around the clock, around the world. A frequent flier. But when he falls asleep his mouth slides open and there is a whiff of decay in his breath, sour and industrial like an eastern wind. Suddenly his head seems doll-like and frail, and the imprint of capillaries that speckle his cheeks is like some private language—a coded message of dashes and dots—as if the very pressure of his blood is revealing itself to me through the pale, crinkly paper of his skin.

I recall something I read in the hospital: *any action can be the one on which all depends.* Well, I think. We'll see.

We are out over the ocean now, and I absorb myself in that for a while. Then I reach into my carry-on bag for the Hebrew-English dictionary I bought at Barnes and Noble, to prepare myself for arrival.

A card falls into my hand.

Aaron Brenner, CPA, Brooklyn, New York.

I fold it in half and use it for a bookmark.

*   *   *

"You're too late," Magda's sister informs me brusquely. "She left last week."

"I see."

"Aaron sent you? That's why you're here?"

"No."

She narrows her eyes. "Then why?"

"I'm here for myself," I say.

"Too bad. She wasn't expecting you. You're the last person on earth she'd expect."

"You know who I am then?"

She nods. Grudgingly, when I do not retreat, she invites me in for coffee. The small apartment is bright but spare, the walls mere painted cinder blocks. Through the window however there's a bountiful view: cotton fields, orange groves, banana trees, and the scrubby sloping hills that lie beyond them to the west. I've been warned to stay away from those hills; they lie on the other side of the green line. Which is neither green nor a line, of course, except on the map. Anyway, I'm not supposed to cross it.

Miri stands at the sink, filling a pot with water. "I only have instant. You want?"

"Fine."

"You should have called," she says. "You could have saved yourself a lot of trouble."

"When do you expect her back?"

"Who knows? She might not come back at all. It's up to her."

Miri scratches her elbow, waiting for the water to boil. She wears a denim workshirt, shorts, sandals; her hair is an anemone of black curls. Compared to her sisters, Miri is larger and heavier, attractive in a blockish, big-boned way, and if her manner is gruff it is untainted by Hava's self-satisfaction or Magda's shyness. Of the three, it is this one, the oldest, who is the most formidable. This is the one who got away from men altogether—found her own place, grew her own hair, set her own terms. I wonder briefly what it would be like, were Miri the one I came for.

Taped to the refrigerator is a child's drawing, done in red and purple crayon, of a basketball player. Michael Jordan. Fortunately for us men, one can get only so clear of us. There are limits.

"I take it," I say, "that you two didn't get along so well."

Miri looks at me hard. "You're wrong. We got along fine. It was the kibbutz she didn't like."

"Why not?"

"Who knows? Too many people maybe. Too many rules. She wanted to see the desert, she said. She wanted to try to paint it."

"I see."

"She's a fool. Do you see that? A kid. All those years in Crown Heights with my father and sister and that husband of hers—they've stunted her growth. Now she's an artist all of a sudden? A bohemian?"

"Maybe," I offer, "she was that all along."

"There's no all along. There's just what is, what you do. But she's my little sister, so there you are." She puts down her coffee and scratches at her elbow again. "And you, you're a bigger fool than she is. Chasing after her this way. Why don't you go home where you belong?"

"Why don't you?" I reply hotly.

"Listen, you. This *is* my home. I vote here, pay taxes here. High ones. My children go to school here. Two weeks a year I go to some shithole in the Negev for reserve duty and come back with a rash. You think it's so easy? Who are you to tell me I don't belong?"

"You're right." I stand up, my coffee untouched. "I won't bother you anymore."

"Tourists," she spits. "You come for a week and think you know what's what. For you this place is a symbol. That's why you're here, isn't it? To have a nice symbolic experience? Climb Masada, buy a few trinkets in the Old City, then go home a real Jew?"

"I'm here for Magda," I say.

"Then go find her. Idiots. The truth is you deserve each other."

And so I have come to the desert. To the foot of the *real* Mount Sinai. Not that I truly expect to find Magda out here; though such a thing, I'd like to think, is not impossible. No, in the end I came to the desert for the oldest and simplest of reasons—to bake in the sun's own kiln, to cleanse and harden myself, and to try to discover, in the annihilating vacancy of the Absolute, something that grows.

Then too, I could think of nowhere else to go.

There are about a dozen of us staying here at the hostel: two pensioners from Australia, a gay couple from South Africa, a Dutch anthropologist, six born-again Christians from San Bernardino, and me. In the evenings we come together for communal suppers, then read, write letters, play backgammon or chess. On the whole we get along well. The born-agains, with their guitars and high seriousness, have proven to be unexpectedly pleasant company. Even the gays think so.

The anthropologist is a big, lean, freckled young woman named Aneka. She is as plain and direct as noon. It so happens Aneka is half-Jewish too. Half her family died in the ovens; the other half (she all but jokes) helped send them there.

The two of us go out hiking every morning, before the sun gets too strong. The hothouse intimacy that arises between travelers bonds Aneka and me together in a strong but impersonal way. There is nothing romantic at issue. Aneka is in flight from a marriage, and in a way I am too—from the *Brenners'* marriage. So we confine our talk to what lies immediately before us: lunch, snakes, visa problems. And of course, destinations. For travelers there is always another destination ahead.

Meanwhile here we are, wandering the desert. The days are full of maps and guides. Small pleasures, manageable tasks, observable sights. In the cloistered gardens of St. Catherine's monastery, Aneka and I eat bread and figs under the almond trees. Then she goes wandering off and I lie in the shade, listening to the drone of the bees and the monks and the gonging bells from the Chapel of Transfiguration nearby.

"You're sad?" she asks when she returns.

"No."

"Maybe you will find her soon."

"It wouldn't change anything. The damage is done. Besides, I'm not sad."

"The damage is good?"

"I hope so," I say, and a moment later add, "Yes."

Our last day we have reserved for the mountain itself. It is one hell of a trek. There is a long circuitous path traveled by camels, and a short but steeper route called the Steps of Repentance—three thousand of them, built, it is said, by a single monk. Our group decides to avoid the camel dung and take the steps. That monk must have been in terrific shape; the steps go all the way up the rugged slope.

Of course we realize as we climb that it's impossible to say for certain whether this is the real Mount Sinai, provided there *was* a real Mount Sinai, historically speaking, in the first place. But the ascent is exhausting, and we stop worrying the question well before we reach the top.

The Egyptians, Aneka says, call this place *Gebel Iti*: the Mount of Losing Yourself.

Along the way she tells me of her postdoctoral research, about which she is very passionate, and which has taken her to three different continents in the past three months. Man, she claims, is nomadic by nature. She cites the Gebeliya bedouins who populate the valley below us. The songlines of Australia. Kalahari Bushmen who follow the lightning to find water, greenery, and game. Tirelessly she marches up the steps, yelling these things over her shoulder. We were born in the desert, she says. Surrounded by predators. Thirst and fear our twin engines, exodus not the exception but the rule. Then along come the Hebrews and Greeks to do what they do best: turn necessity into a virtue. They take two concepts, Wind and Spirit, and conflate them into a single word—*pneuma*, or *ruach*. Thus motion is transformed into divinity. Instinct becomes practice, physics metaphysics. This, says Aneka, is how civilization does its thing.

Finally we attain the summit in the wild dying light.

The air is thin and cold; the silence yaws open like a gate. Now that we have arrived we are not certain what to do with ourselves exactly. How to respond. For a few minutes we stand around, awkward, breathing hard, slipping out of our backpacks, taking in the view. The sun is half-gone. Africa, Arabia, the Red Sea, the Gulf of Aqaba—all lie spread out below like some flushed and quivering dream. What is there to say? And yet to capture the moment somehow seems important. A few of us take out cameras, wide-angle lenses. A couple embraces. A man bursts into song. I look over at Aneka. She has spread out her sleeping bag and unlaced her boots, checking for stones.

Meanwhile I stand here waiting.

Now the sun dips below the horizon. The sky is left vacant, the deep craggy bowl of the landscape is glazed with roseate light. I spread my arms. *Okay*, I think, *here I am. Are you satisfied now?* This bloody and shimmering blur in the distance—isn't this the place? Isn't this ground zero, the cradle of us all? Isn't this the place to start?

But no: there is only the sputtering wind, the howl of a jackal, the entry and exit of my own breath. Nothing is revealed. No voice rumbles in the silence, no presence lurks in the shadows. It may be that Magda was right, and I merely lack the tools, or the will, to find them. But in the end I do not believe they are there. I do not believe in such things. And yet there's no comfort in not believing. And yet there's no comfort in dangling between.

The sky a great net, its stitches failing.

Nu? What now? Tomorrow I must come down off this mountain. My visa will expire and I'll have to move on. Aneka says Cyprus is worth a look. Another small, divided country with everything at stake. But then so is New York. Honestly, I don't know if I have the stamina to keep traveling much longer.

Now Aneka leans forward to lace up her boots. Supper is ready. The pilgrims are gathering by the fire. For a moment I hang back, alone and unseen at the top of the world. Then from out of the darkness, I hear them calling my name.